International Harvester

**By
Matt Erickson**

Damnation Books, LLC.
P.O. Box 3931
Santa Rosa, CA 95402-9998
www.damnationbooks.com

International Harvester
by Matt Erickson

Digital ISBN: 978-1-61572-756-8
Print ISBN: 978-1-61572-757-5

Cover art by: Ash Arceneaux
Edited by: Pam Slade

Copyright 2012 Matt Erickson

Printed in the United States of America
Worldwide Electronic & Digital Rights
1st North American, Australian and UK Print Rights

All rights reserved. No part of this book may be reproduced, scanned or distributed in any form, including digital and electronic or mechanical, including photocopying, recording, or by any information storage and retrieval system, without the prior written consent of the Publisher, except for brief quotes for use in reviews.

This book is a work of fiction. Characters, names, places and incidents either are the product of the author's imagination or are used fictitiously, and any resemblance to any actual persons, living or dead, events, or locales is entirely coincidental.

*For my wife Pam.
Thanks for keeping me.*

Chapter One

Patricia Stadtler regained consciousness slowly, dully aware of a metallic hum somewhere in the darkness to her left. The ache in her head exploded with each shallow breath she took. She struggled to open her eyes, as it felt as if they were pasted shut. With an extreme effort her eyelids fluttered open, she winced at the dazzling light falling upon her. Spots danced before her eyes, as a swirling universe of microscopic stars shone throughout her field of vision.

Am I dead? she asked herself. Grimacing, she closed her eyes and took a deep breath as her head screamed in protest. It would be easier to keep her eyes closed she thought. *But, what happened to me? Where am I*, she wondered. *I remember running. Yes, I was jogging in the park and then...*her memory failed her. She opened her eyes again, this time gradually, allowing her pupils time to adjust to the light. The light was bright, but not as blinding as before.

As her pupils contracted and her vision cleared she gazed up at an unfamiliar ceiling. The light came from a single bulb mounted onto a beam, its pull string fluttered in the random wisps of air pervading the drafty space. Unfinished, with exposed water and heat pipes as well as air conditioning ducts, the ceiling was low, no more than four feet from her face.

The damp, musty smell immediately told her she was in a basement. *Bad things happen in basements*, her inner voice warned. Naked beneath a thin white linen sheet, she felt faint breaths of air tickling her body as drafts seeped in beneath the steel door next to the foot of the stairs. The buzzing sound ceased and then there was silence. She dared not breathe for fear of making any noise. Her arms and legs were numb—she needed to stretch them out as silently as possible.

She tried to raise her right arm but was unable to move it. *Oh, my God! I'm paralyzed*. A flush of fear filled her. *No, I have feeling, but I can't move. What happened? What happened to me?* It was only then she noticed her extremities extended out from her body, she was spread-eagled. Her arms and legs were filled with pins and needles, she'd been in this position for some time. Sweat sprang from her pores slicking her body in rivulets of fear, her nostrils flared at her own stench. *This is one bad dream*, she told herself knowing it was no dream. Everything was too vivid to be a dream, the sights, the smells, the sounds, and now the silence, it was all too real for dreamland.

She attempted to prop herself up on an elbow to get a better look at her surroundings and found her wrist was shackled to the side of the bed. *Bed? This is no bed! It's a metal table!* She almost correctly thought, looking down at the glistening, stainless steel table beneath her. *An operating table! Holy shit! What did I get myself into?* She flexed her long, muscular legs and pulled them toward her with all her might and succeeded only at farting, a tiny squeak escaped into the cool, damp basement air. She relaxed her legs and lay helpless to contemplate what, if any options, she had.

She turned her head toward the right and saw the walls were cinderblock, there were four small windows, one in the center of each wall. The windows were draped with blackout paper, so she had no idea what time it was, whether it was day or night. She hadn't the faintest idea of how long she'd been down here, but it must have been for some time because despite her terror her belly rumbled for sustenance. The shiny table beneath her glimmered with a cold, dead light. The table was frigid to the touch, her skin was pimpled with goose bumps, her erect nipples stood clearly visible jutting up into the linen sheet, yet she was sweating profusely. Stadtler began to sob, a soundless, diminutive bawl.

"There now, don't cry," came a soft, soothing voice from behind her. It was a man's voice for sure, but not overly deep.

Stadtler tried to arch her back and crane her neck backward toward the voice, but was unable to. After a moment's silence the owner of the voice came into her field of vision. He was a man all right, a rather handsome one holding a tall metal stool in one hand and a book in the other, he had been reading while he waited for her to wake up. He placed the stool down on its legs a few feet from the table and took a seat. He brushed a lock of medium length blonde hair away from his face and stared at her. She immediately noticed his left pupil was dilated while his right seemed to be normal. He seemed to pick up on her discovery and smiled. She looked away, down to his hands which were wrapped around a paperback he'd apparently been reading. *The Girl Who Kicked the Hornet's Nest*, she had read it herself.

"Do you like to read?" he asked in a cool soothing voice.

She trembled, so was unable to answer and stared at him.

"Okay, I understand you're scared and you should be. I won't lie to you though, you won't feel a thing," he said in nearly perfect unaccented English.

What's this freak gonna do to me? she asked herself.

"You've got gorgeous eyes, don't you? Do you mind if I have a closer look at them?"

"N...n...no, go ahead," she stammered.

The man slid off of the stool and reached into the back pocket of his jeans and retrieved a pair of rubber surgical gloves. He pulled the gloves over his hands and then took a pen light from the pocket of the oxford button down he was wearing.

Oh, God here we go, he's gonna screw me with a light to get himself going.

He flipped the light on and hovered over the table.

"Please don't hurt me, my family's got money."

"It won't hurt a bit, I promise," he said caressing the side of her face with one gloved hand.

As he peered into her light blue eyes she stared directly into his. Upon closer inspection not only was one of his pupils dilated much more so than the other, it was also a different color. The normal eye was a deep, cobalt blue while the eye with the dilated pupil was also bluish, but streaked with green.

After inspecting her eyes he said, "I'm not really interested in money, I've got plenty. Well, in all honesty money is a secondary concern of mine."

Christ! He's gonna cut out my eyes!

"I've got a few questions for you and then we'll get on with our business?" He disappeared from her view and when he came back the novel he'd been carrying had been replaced by a clipboard.

"Business, wha..."

"Please be patient, questions first. Answer truthfully and we'll be on our way," he advised bringing a pen up to the clipboard. He was clinical, cold, without emotion.

She nodded.

Name?"

"Patty Stadtler," she whimpered. *Never go running alone at night Patty!* She'd heard her father warn her, how many times, a thousand maybe.

"Age?"

"Twenty-three, twenty-four next week."

"Place of birth?"

"Highlands, New Jersey."

"Nice town, a fine beach. How long have you been here?"

"Two years."

This isn't too bad, maybe he'll let me go after all. No freakin way idiot! You've seen his face. There's no going back, this is it.

"Any college?"

"Fordham."

"Job?"

"I...I...I'm a legal secretary.

"Hefty tuition to become a secretary. You must be going to law school I hope."

"Yes," she lied.

"Where?"

"Hofst" she began to say and caught herself.

"Long commute to Hofstra from here, wouldn't you say?"

"Well, I got in, it's just..."

"Boyfriend from up here? Not many from up here go to school in the city."

Here we go, he's gonna rape me. My legs are already spread, what's to stop him? Bite him if he gets close enough, is all I can do.

"Yes, no, well, there was. It's over now."

"It's a shame, you're a beautiful girl. I'm sure you hear it all the time."

He looks familiar, like a celebrity. Rock star? Actor? Model?

She said nothing.

"All right then, what's your favorite color?"

She paused before replying, "Purple."

"Hhhm, very romantic. Also the color of royalty. Did you know?"

She shook her head back and forth.

"Well we've got a few hours before we're due to leave. Why don't you get some rest and I'll take care of everything."

Leave? He kidnapped me. My parents will pay the ransom. I'm gonna live, at least there's hope now!

"Please let me go, my parents will pay whatever you want, I promise."

"I've told you already money is very secondary to me. I need something else from you."

Those weird fucking eyes! That's what he wants! He wants my eyes!

"Do you want my eyes? I see you..."

He began laughing, not loudly or cruelly, more to himself than anything else.

"My whacked out eyes, yes? I could see how you might think I was after your eyes, they are quite stunning. But no, I like mine just the way they are. Born different colors which I think is cool. The dilation was caused from fisticuffs in the school yard when I was young. I'll keep mine just the way they are, thank you."

Heart pounding and sweat dripping, she asked, "What about mine then?"

"I told you I wouldn't lie to you and I haven't. You're eyes are part of it, but a rather minor one. Get some rest, I'll be back when it's time."

He left her field of vision. She heard his footsteps, catlike ascending the stairs to the first floor.

* * * *

Two and a half hours dragged by, it seemed like an eternity to Stadtler. Her body screamed in revolt as she twisted and turned in vain attempts at gaining an advantage on the handcuffs which stole her freedom. *Will he kill me? Where is he taking me? Am I dreaming?* Exhausted by her efforts she began to cry, a low sobbing at first which quickly transformed into the hysterical shrieks, characteristic of terror and impending madness. After she'd screamed herself hoarse she lay upon the cold table awaiting the return of her captor. It was a short wait as she heard his light footsteps descending the stairway.

"I'm sorry," the blonde man said to her. "I should have stayed with you, to comfort you in your time of need," he added. "You see, I had some business to attend to and I needed some quiet. I also didn't want to bother you with any details."

"What are you going to do with me?"

"You will make many people very happy."

Oh, God! He's a sex trafficker! He's gonna take me to some strange country, probably in the Middle East, where I'll be a sex slave to sweaty, smelly ragheads. They love white women. Love to make them subservient.

"What are you going to do with me?" she asked again.

"You'll be accompanying me on a trip," he responded.

"Where are we going?" she asked hopefully as snot ran out of her left nostril and onto her upper lip.

"Canada."

Canada? Why in God's name would he take me to Canada? It made no sense. There were plenty of white women in Canada. Jesus, prostitution is legal up there I think!

"Why?"

"Like I said before, you'll make seven maybe even eight people very happy."

"What do you mean?"

"You'll give many people, many sick and dying people, new leases on life," he replied without any hint of emotion. He was more and more detached in his speech and mannerisms as the exchange went on. He pulled on another pair of latex gloves and using a gauze pad he wiped the tears from her eyes as well as the snot from her lips and nose. His tone never wavered, "You'll provide life for those in need of it and in return you will gain many lives."

What is he talking about? I've got to get him close, close enough to bite. Maybe I can talk him into uncuffing me and then, maybe I could kick him in the balls and make a run for it. Offer a blowjob and bite his cock off, that would be best. Yes. That's it. What else is there?

She summoned what little courage and imagination was left and said, "All right, I'll go with you."

"There is really no choice in the matter."

"One thing though. If I'm travelling with you I'd like to get to know you better," she rasped rolling her pale blue eyes down toward what lay beneath the thin white sheet covering her naked body.

The blonde man smiled a thin, humorless grin. "I've no interest in you. I've already seen you bare and although you are attractive, I'm already spoken for. My bride to be wouldn't approve of such behavior on my part. I've never known any of my business partners in that way, it's bad policy."

"My parents have..."

"I know," he said holding up a gloved hand, "lots of money. I don't need it. I'm self-sufficient."

His eyes went dark, she knew there was no bargaining, and then her bladder let go. Urine streamed out of her, the dampened sheet clung to her thighs as it dripped down below her buttocks and onto the table. It meandered its way down through the vented slits in the top of the autopsy table and settled in the reservoir made expressly for fluid containment. Not bothered in the least the blonde man turned his back on her.

He disappeared into the back room of the basement and when he returned, he was wearing surgical scrubs, and wheeling in a large portable lamp, a Medline surgical lamp. The lamp was rectangular with what looked like an antenna growing from its center. She'd been to the dentist and gynecologist enough to recognize the examination light as soon as he set it beside the table. He plugged the lamp into a socket at the foot of a support column and switched it on. The basement was bathed in the other worldly iridescent glow operating rooms feature. He disappeared once more and came back pushing a cart of sterilized surgical instruments. It was then she knew.

As she began to shriek in recognition and horror, the blonde man uncapped a bottle of chloroform and held a wadded cloth over the mouth of the bottle. He gave the cloth a generous soaking and then cupped it over her nose and when she'd calmed down a bit, over her mouth as well. Within seconds she was out.

Time was of the essence in the blonde man's profession. He had prepared his instruments while his "patient" had been under the first time. He looked at his watch, a $25,000.00 Piaget, and sighed.

At least she didn't ask why he was asking all the personal questions like the last one did, he thought with relief. He briefly pondered what his mother had told him when he'd first graduated from the Naval Academy. '*You should always know the people you work with, dear,*' she'd said to him. '*It goes double if you're murdering them,*' he added with no emotion.

Running right on schedule he flipped on the sound system, a state of the art Pioneer accompanied by surround sound Bose speakers, and hit the play button. Beethoven's *Symphony Number Nine in D Minor* floated down from the ceiling and reverberated from the walls. The blonde man preferred the first stereo recording of the *Ninth Symphony* as performed by the Berlin Philharmonic under the direction of Ferenc Fricsay in 1958. The orchestra tuning sound of the first movement, snaked around the support columns as the blonde man went back to his business associate atop the cold, gleaming table.

Stadtler's breathing was deep and steady, she was a very healthy specimen. Having promised she wouldn't feel a thing, he made it a point not to go back on his pledge. He donned his safety goggles and then reached down below the main tray of the instrument table to where there was another, smaller shelf. From it he brought up the Paslode CF325 cordless framing gun he used for his procedures. Much quieter than a gun, even a low caliber variety such as a twenty-two, the nail gun's report was less offensive than a youngster's bb or pellet gun.

There would be much less mess to clean up also as there would be no exit wound. After years of experience the blonde man knew at what precise level to calibrate the nail gun for optimal performance. The gun was used by house framers throughout the world, and was able to sink a three and a quarter inch nail flush into the toughest of lumber. Relatively light and battery operated it served him as a field weapon on occasions, as well as in his operating theatre.

I dare not damage the face, oh no, no, no, not this beautiful face, he thought. With the thumb and index finger of his left hand he gently opened her mouth. With his right hand he wedged the nail gun into her mouth. Not wanting to tear the flesh of her mouth he wiggled the gun in as gently as possible, he needed a contact point to engage the firing mechanism. As luck would have it, she had a slightly larger than normal size mouth. *Looks a bit like Carly Simon*, the blonde man thought without a trace of humor or remorse. Aiming the gun up at a seventy-five degree angle, the blonde man made contact with the roof of Stadtler's mouth, the gun's battery whirred to life. Checking the angle one last time to be sure the shot was true he pulled the trigger. *Whoosh!* The nail discharged, shot up through the roof of the woman's mouth and pierced her temporal and parietal lobes before lodging securely in the top of her skull. *Like a partial birth abortion*, he thought. Stadtler's body convulsed straight and then lay limp. A gush of blood pulsed from her nose while a torrent filled her gaping mouth and overflowed down her neck and over her shoulders. *There's no pain at all.* He adjusted the autopsy table to a seven degree angle thereby allowing him to work on an almost level plane while the blood and other fluids drained into the blood gutters and pooled within the reservoirs.

Without pause the blonde man selected a scalpel from the instrument tray. He gently retracted her left eyelid and slipped the blade in beneath her eyeball. With one graceful circular incision he extracted her eyeball. Delicately squeezing the slate blue eye between his thumb and index finger he took a cursory glance at it before dropping it into a vial of saline solution. He repeated the procedure with her right eye and then sealed the vial and placed it into the refrigerator in the back room.

The first movement of Beethoven's *Ninth* was winding down when he selected a second, larger scalpel and opened her up with a neat Y-incision exposing her sternum and ribcage. He filleted the skin away from the bone completely exposing the ribcage. He then picked up the IonFusion bone saw and placed its blade directly upon the first rib beneath the clavicle on the woman's left side. With each descending rib he cut under the arm and toward the back, as far away from the vital organs as possible. For the next ten minutes Beethoven was intermittently drowned out as the whining saw's teeth bit through the ribs of the newly deceased jogger.

Tiny shards of bone, bits of flesh and flecks of blood jumped from the blade sprinkling her face in a grotesque mist of gore. By the time the saw had chewed through the last rib the Ninth's second movement was underway. With the woman's ribcage severed on the left side he took a short break during which he changed the saw's blade. With the fresh blade he commenced sawing the right side of the rib cage. Most surgeons would use rib spreaders to gain access to the vital organs, but without the aid of another surgeon as well as nurses, the blonde man preferred the saw.

When the whining died down he placed the saw on the instrument cart and listened as the second movement gave way to the third, the lyrical slow movement. The blonde man was lean, but exceedingly strong. With the ribcage severed as he wanted he reached down and seized the sternum in his right hand and pulled it free from the body, sinews and cartilage snapping, in a single piece. He placed it at her lifeless feet.

The vital organs unprotected, he selected a finer scalpel and went straight for the lungs. Pink and soft they appeared nearly perfect. Humming along to the trombones he removed the lungs and placed them in a steel bowl of saline solution. He then proceeded on to the heart, liver, kidneys, and lastly the pancreas. As he extricated the pancreas and placed it in a bowl for safekeeping, the choral finale of the fourth movement swirled throughout the basement operating room.

Selecting a final scalpel the blond man carefully cut into the tender flesh of the woman's throat. With painstaking precision he guided the scalpel to the right, below the jaw line and over to the jaw hinge. Slowly he brought the blade up and then behind the right ear. He did likewise to the left side of the woman's face. With the lower half of her face slit cleanly open he carefully worked the scalpel inside the incision separating the flesh from the bone. With short, precise strokes he sliced upward toward her hairline. When he reached her eyes he was able to flip her face up and tuck it back over her hair and pin it there with his left hand. The cutting became easier as his view improved and when he reached her hairline he was able to lengthen his strokes and increase his speed. Reaching the crown of her head, he pulled down on her hair working the scalpel quickly back and forth between her skull and the retreating skin. Slicing all the way down to the nape of her neck he peeled her face and hair off and then made one backhand stroke to free the bloody mask from its host. He held her face nose to nose with his own and admired his work briefly and then carefully placed it in an extra large, circular Tupperware container. He poured saline solution over Patricia Stadtler's scalped face and hair until it was submerged. The blonde man affixed the container's lid and pressed down sealing it airtight. He carried the container to the back room where he stowed it in the refrigerator.

He transferred each organ to a heavy duty freezer bag of its own, making sure each one was well appropriated with a sufficient amount of saline. The eyes would, of course, remain a pair in their own cozy vial. He sealed the bags shut and placed them and the vial in the rear room refrigerator.

The blonde man sat down on his stool to take a short break. Glancing at his watch, he took note that it took him sixty three minutes to dispatch and harvest his patient. He was happy with the time, the *Ninth* still had over a minute until it played out. He wiped sweat from his brow and took a deep breath of self-satisfaction.

After a few minutes he rolled the instrument cart into the back room and settled it before a foot controlled slop sink next to the refrigerator. He set his instruments into the sink, stepped onto the hot water pedal and added bleach and disinfectant. He placed the bone saw atop the drain board and left the tools to soak. He stripped off his surgical scrubs, pivoted to the combination washer and dryer beside the slop sink, and dropped them into the washer. He added detergent, set the cycle for hot and pushed start.

Naked, the blonde man undid the cuffs on the wrists and shins of the corpse, and stared at the faceless, scalped head. *A shame, but necessary*, he thought. He fastened a heavy duty garbage bag to the foot end of the table with clamps on either side and pulled the lever which held the table level. Carefully he angled the table down toward the waiting garbage bag. Slowly, the remains slid down the table and into the bag. When her legs and reaped trunk slipped into the bag he leveled the table to stop its progress. Then he grabbed her under the armpits and folded her torso forward so her faceless head was nearly touching her knees. *It's amazing how limber they are if you take care of them early*, he thought.

He shoved her head down between her legs and pushed her down into the bag. She wasn't very big—the bag enveloped her and swallowed her up. The bottom of the bag hit the cement floor with a wet thud, but the clamps held. He unhinged the clamps and wrapped the bag clockwise tying it shut with a twist tie. He double bagged the corpse for safe measure and then hoisted it over his shoulder and carried it toward the refrigerator. An oversized commercial Viking, he had removed all of its interior shelves with the exception of the topmost where the dead woman's organs now rested. On the side of the refrigerator was the slop sink and next to it was an enormous freezer. Into the spacious freezer he laid her remains beside the denuded skeleton of a previous donor. The skeleton had belonged to a man about his own size. Never knowing when such an object would come in handy, he decided to keep it.

Afterward he scrubbed down the autopsy table clearing it of tissue and bone before stepping into the shower in the rear room. It was a cursory cleaning at best. He sought to avoid any odors and congealing of fluids. Nonetheless, his casual cleaning was much superior to most people's efforts, as he was fastidiously clean by the highest standards. Once he had finished his business transaction and returned home again he would scour the instruments, table, the whole room, in fact, with bleach. There was plenty of time for finishing later. Now his time was precious, he was on a schedule.

* * * *

The shower was hot and comparatively long, at twenty minutes. Emerging from the fog of the steamy shower stall he breathed the cool air of the basement in, noticing the thin aroma of blood within its cinderblock walls. Most would never have noticed with the bleach fumes fresh, but his senses were particularly attuned to blood, much like a shark. He couldn't help but smile, he'd had a productive morning he noted with pride. With a deep sense of accomplishment he sprung upstairs and then to his bedroom on the second floor.

Ten minutes later he was back in the basement packing Patricia Stadtler's organs into an Igloo Playmate cooler he'd had since the early 1980's. He had, in fact, found the cooler while scouring the dunes on a Moonless summer night during the summer of his seventeenth year. Roaming the beach with his friends he'd charged up into the dunes while his friends walked along the shoreline smoking a joint. Like iron to a magnet he ran to the top of the dune and after stumbling around in the darkness for more than a minute, he ran into what had pulled him up onto the dune. A smile spread across his face as he recognized the red and white box for what it was.

He reached down toward it, depressed the button at its side and slid the cover back. Within it lay over two sixes of Budweiser tallboys. The ice was mostly melted, but still, what a find. *Whoever had left this treasure was in quite a hurry,* he decided. He slid the cover closed and hoisted the cooler up into his right hand and ran for the shoreline. The young blonde man had made it back to his friends, in time to take one last draw off of the smoldering roach. He exhaled and then opened his treasure chest for all to see. He was the hero of the night, he would never forget it. He would always cherish his lucky cooler.

Now, with gloved hands, he packed dry ice into the bottom of the cooler. He placed a cardboard cutout which he used over and over atop the dry ice. He retrieved his patient's organs from the refrigerator and gently laid them on top the cardboard. He peered back into the refrigerator for reassurance. Stadtler's skinned face stared eyeless up at him seemingly accusatory in the silver bowl, its subcutaneous tissue floating outward in the solution. *I'll be back for you dear.* Twin lobsters, still alive, went atop the organs for good measure. He closed the refrigerator door and covered his precious meat, with another piece of cardboard and then with more dry ice. He slid the cover shut and blessed himself with the sign of the cross. Each time he used the cooler he flashed back to the first time he ever saw it. He considered it a partner of sorts.

Five minutes later the house was locked and the blonde man and the cooler were on the road. The Volvo was not flashy, but very reliable. As were many cars of its make it was black. *No need to attract unwanted attention and it worked out just perfect for its purpose,* he thought. *A fuel injected hearse.*

* * * *

Within fifteen minutes he was at the airport. He pulled into his reserved parking spot and killed the engine. Trotting across the near empty small carrier parking lot he made his way toward the hangar with the cooler clutched in his right hand. Approaching the guard gate which neatly divided the security fence he slowed to a walk. As the guard looked up from the *Buffalo News* the blonde man flashed a cheery smile his way.

"What's for ma this time, Lenny?" the guard, a rail thin man with a greasy handle bar mustache, asked not really interested whatsoever. Mick worked the gate at the small carrier port for the better part of twenty years. He took his job seriously, running strangers and their baggage through the detectors as well as checking their identification. Regulars though, he routinely waved through without so much as a second glance. The blonde man was his most regular, they had been on a first name basis for over ten years.

"Couple of lobsters, Mick. Hard for her to get out and get them herself," the blonde man, Leonard Schenk to the guard, replied.

"Oh my, nice to have a good son."

"Wouldn't be here without her. She deserves the best."

"Nothin' for me?" the guard asked.

"Not this trip. How'd you like the peppers?"

"Best stuffed peppers I ever had."

"Getcha on the return."

"Aha, good trip to ya, then."

"Have a great day, Mick."

The guard tipped his cap not caring if Schenk was carrying TNT in his igloo cooler. He went back to the sports section, it was mid-summer, the Bills were in training camp and he hoped for a better season than it had been in quite some time. By the time he had come to the bottom of the second paragraph about a quarterback controversy he had all but forgotten about seeing Lenny Schenk.

Schenk routinely kept three sets of identification on him at all times. On this day he had a New York State driver's licenses and passports in the names of Leonard Schenk, Phillip Gant, and Carl Heydrich. According to Heydrich's passport, the blonde man enjoyed dual citizenship as it identified him as an American and a Canadian.

Schenk walked briskly by the commercial carriers to where his Cessna 340 waited for him. The ground crew for the little twin engine prop plane consisted of a single man, Kurt Bly. Bly received the call from Schenk to ready the plane two hours prior as was the norm. As usual Bly had the plane gassed up and ready for take off an hour later. He had already loaded the cargo for the trip, five boxes of airplane parts.

The blonde man's father had been a pilot during the Korean War and then an aeronautical engineer working freelance for McDonnell Douglas in the late 1950's and early 1960's. His father, whose name was Arthur Gant, had developed a certain screw the United States Navy, Marine Corps, and Air Force depended upon for the production of the F-4 Phantom. Holding the patent to the screw, Gant made a mint as the Phantom was a mainstay during the Vietnam War. Having made his fortune by 1971, Gant released the rights to the screw as an act of sheer patriotism, in his mind.

The Phantom II which depended upon the same screw, did in fact, see action right through the 1990-1991 Gulf War. The aircraft was finally put out to pasture in 1996. Arthur Gant had long since retired and spent most of his time touring the eastern seaboard's finest golf courses by the time the second Phantom was laid to rest. Despite his retirement Gant kept in close contact with his friends in the industry. He founded *Generations Air Supply* in 1975 as a lark hoping to entice his son, Phillip, into the aeronautical field. He'd suffered a debilitating stroke at the hands of a surgeon and spent the final nine years of his life a vegetable. His passing was a bitter sweet time for the Gant family.

Young Phillip Gant took to flying like a hawk among sparrows. Graduating from the prestigious Salzberg School in southern Connecticut in 1982, the boy was recruited by the U.S. Navy for flight school. The combination of the prep school's superior reputation, his perfect vision, and strong math and science skills got him noticed early in his junior year. In the fall of 1982 he entered the Naval Academy and then flight school and by the outbreak of the Gulf War he was hitting Iraqi bunkers with smart bombs from an F-14A Tomcat. After the war had ended he remained in the Navy to complete his initial service requirements, and then took over his father's business which both men considered to be a hobby more than anything else.

In the shadow cast by the fuselage, Bly sat in a folding chair as Gant a.k.a. Schenk, Heydrich, and Previt walked across the tarmac toward the plane. The sky was powder blue, the Sun high up, the day perfect for all except Patricia Stadtler.

Bly was texting his buddy Earl about meeting at the Buffalo Brew Pub after work for some beers when Gant stepped up beside him.

"Hey Kurt, we all set?" Gant asked with the cooler at his side.

"You bet boss," Bly replied, tipping his sweat-stained Blue Jays cap from his head, wiping his brow and then pulling it back tight.

"How are you today, my friend?"

"Good, no complaints. Except for the old fart of an inspector who's here to high water all the time. Pain in the ass, that guy is."

"It's his job, you know the deal."

"Yeah, after all these years you'd think I would've gotten used to the inspections."

"Us more than anyone else?" Gant asked somewhat curious.

"Nah, the usual. A random inspection. But no worries boss! We're clean as a choir girl."

"As always, thank you," Gant replied. "Everything all right at home?" He couldn't help but pry a bit to make sure his mechanic was on good terms with his wife.

"Never better, we've got another one on the way. Sherry got the sonogram yesterday. May be a boy. Good God, I'd kill for a boy. After three girls a boy would be nice. To pass on the family name, you know."

"Well then, we've got to discuss a raise for you. A dependable worker with a fast growing family, you could use some more money, right?"

"Sure, everyone could."

"When I get back we'll talk money."

"Sounds good, safe flying."

Gant nodded and wordlessly climbed up the fold out stairs leading into the body of the plane. Bly rolled up the stairs and gave his captain the thumbs up. The interior of the Cessna was left intact, there was seating for six including the pilot and copilot if there was one. There were no passengers on this flight save the one in the cooler. The aisle between the foursome of passenger seats was occupied by the five boxes of airplane parts.

Gant fired the engines and waited patiently as they thrummed harmoniously to life. After five minutes of the engine's drone Gant gave the thumbs up to Bly who then removed the chocks from beneath the aircraft's wheels. Gant placed his left foot on the left pedal and lightly stepped down on it moving the airplane forward. He gave the bird a little gas and teetered down the runway to await direction from the man in the tower. Using the yoke Gant navigated the Cessna toward the center of the runway. It was a Tuesday morning, business was slow, Gant waited less than four minutes for radio approval for take off. He firmly gripped the big, black throttle and pushed it slowly forward and then with more force until the aircraft was accelerating toward takeoff speed. Achieving the desired momentum of 56 knots, he grabbed the yoke in both hands and pulled it slowly toward his chest. A man of many talents, Phillip Gant soared off into the mid-summer day with nary a care in the world.

Chapter Two

Detective Dan Wilder slurped from a cup of coffee while he examined the photo of the latest woman to go missing. In his mid forties, Wilder had bloated considerably around the waist as most of his counterparts had. He wheezed out a breath, it was hard giving up the smokes, but had done so after his brother died of lung cancer five years prior. He put the photo down on his desk and picked up the thin sheaf of paper which had accompanied it in the file folder. He leaned back in his chair to read the particulars about one Patricia Stadtler, now missing for a day and a half.

Wilder read the information regarding Stadtler aloud to Marguerite Hamilton, the other detective assigned to the case. "Born in 1989, Stadtler is twenty-three years old, five feet seven inches tall and approximately one hundred and ten pounds. She has blue eyes, shoulder length blondish/brownish hair, and was last known to be jogging. According to her roommate she preferred to run in Woodlawn Beach State Park."

"Roommate male or female?" Hamilton asked.

"A girl, name's Carly Abrams."

"Age?"

"Twenty-five."

"What'd she say?"

"Said Patricia went running as usual at nine o'clock the night before last."

"Abrams a runner too?"

"Didn't look that way to me. Looked a lot like me."

Hamilton shot him a glance of disapproval.

"Late to go alone for anyone, especially a woman."

"Abrams said the same thing. Said it was a point of contention between Stadtler and her dad. According to Abrams the father said something about Robert Chalmers."

"Meaning Chambers, of course."

"Girl had probably never heard of the Central Park Strangler."

"No doubt, because he was news two years before she was even born."

Detective Hamilton was slight in stature but was a tae kwon do instructor as well as an excellent shot. With chestnut hair neatly pulled back into a bun and piercing olive eyes she commanded attention from those who knew her. In her late thirties she had toyed with the idea of becoming a singer during and after college, and then found her voice fell short. She had been with the Buffalo Police Department for over thirteen years, two shy of her pudgy counterpart. She saw her fair share of missing person's cases during her eight years as a detective, most of them runaway children. All but five were resolved quite quickly and of those five that played out only four went unresolved and most probably poorly.

"Boyfriend?" she inquired.

"Nope, not that Abrams knows of."

"What about Abrams, she have one?"

"Yep, guy named Dave Fuller. Bartender. Was working at one of the local dives at the time of the disappearance. He's got a bar full of drunks who will attest to his whereabouts."

"Any relationship with Stadtler?"

"The roomie says they rarely crossed paths. I thought I saw a little bit of jealousy in her eye as she said it," Wilder replied.

"How old is he?"

"Older, late thirties, let's see," Wilder said, looking over his own notes he'd written down. "Thirty-eight."

"Robbing the cradle a bit."

"Yep, everybody sleeps with everybody nowadays."

"We should have another look at him."

"Agreed."

"What was she wearing?"

"A green reflective vest for sure. Probably a red T-shirt as best as the roommate can speculate. Probably had blue running shorts over black spandex leggings, nothing out of the ordinary. The roommate went through her dresser to see what was missing and that's what she came up with."

"She didn't see her leave?"

"Wasn't there. She got in at eleven fifteen. She's a waitress at McSwane's in the First Ward."

"The roommate says she left the apartment at nine o'clock, right?"

"That's the story. Said she's a creature of habit, everything's on a schedule. She jogs late because she works as a secretary during the day and then goes to night school."

"I get up early, get it out of the way," Hamilton said.

"Me too," Wilder smiled rubbing his belly.

Frowning at Wilder's attempt at humor Hamilton went on, "Let's say the roommate and her boyfriend have nothing to do with this, and they most probably don't, do we have any other people of interest?"

"Nobody jumps out."

"All right, what else?"

"She's from down state, Long Island. Parents are very worried as expected."

"Went to school up here and decided she liked it over the rat-race?"

"Oddly no. Graduate of Fordham in the Bronx, major in economics, minor in communications."

"So where does that leave us?"

"Pretty much no man's land. The dogs are out in the park right now."

"Let's go," Hamilton said reaching for her keys.

* * * *

It was little more than four miles from the Franklin Street police headquarters, to Woodlawn Beach State Park. After turning south onto the Buffalo Skyway it took the detectives less than five minutes to get to the park. It was midmorning on a Saturday, joggers and cyclists were out in droves enjoying the picturesque view of Lake Erie as they fought their own personal battles of the bulge. Many of them were on their way to the park and were soon to be disappointed.

The vehicle entrances to the park at Gateway Boulevard and off of Lake Shore

Road were cordoned off, with barricades put in place by the park police. At each entryway a white and green New York State Park Police cruiser kept watch, red lights flashing. All other entrances to the park via foot or bike traffic were manned with officers from one of the three responding departments.

The detective's unmarked Crown Victoria pulled up to the barricade in front of the park's main entrance off of Lake Shore Road. When the park officer opened his door and approached the car Hamilton flashed her detective's shield his way. Seeing the shield and then recognizing the woman behind the wheel the officer continued toward the barricade a little faster. He lifted the barricade up with both hands and shimmied it over to the side of the entryway to allow the Crown Vic passage.

"Just like an Easy Pass," Wilder noted.

"Wish it worked on the bridges and tunnels downstate," Hamilton said.

"It does, most of the time. For me at least."

Hamilton drove through the entrance and then wove through a sea of police vehicles. Navy blue with yellow lettering and horizontal striping, five New York State Police cruisers were neatly parked side by side, their red flashers blinking rapidly. A solitary trooper had stayed with the vehicles while the others had joined the discussion taking place two hundred and fifty or so feet beyond a park bench covered with bird droppings. Recognizing Hamilton and Wilder the trooper tipped his purple banded cavalry-style Stetson to them.

Hamilton pulled up close to him and greeted the trooper, "Hey Timmy! What've you heard?"

"Not much so far," the trooper replied adjusting his purple necktie. "I just got here a few minutes ago. I'm checking in with the barracks before I head into the fray."

Wilder leaned over from the passenger seat a bit toward Hamilton's side and said, "Everyone's at the party today, huh Tim?"

Smoothing out the creases in his neatly pressed grey wool uniform pants the trooper nodded in agreement and then just a touch of a smile crept across his face. Although good-natured, the smile was bitter as well. "Don't worry, don't worry," said the trooper. "I've got no problem with you taking over. You've got the jurisdiction over us. I'm not so sure the park boys will want to give it up so easily though."

"We'll see what happens," Hamilton replied. "See you out there," she added before coasting forward.

Randomly parked to the north of the trooper contingent, were three white cruisers with blue horizontal stripes belonging to the Buffalo Police Department. Choosing to stay neutral, or as close to it as possible, Hamilton rolled up to the barricade set up by the park police and killed the engine. She was quickly out of the car and walking toward the crowd of uniforms before Wilder had pulled himself out from the passenger seat. A hundred or so yards beyond the ongoing pow-wow were the K-9 units, three of them. One was a white Suburban with green lettering which identified it as a New York State Park Police vehicle. The other two trucks were from the city department.

Wilder chased down Hamilton and fell in step beside her. Easily she picked out and identified the city cops she worked with routinely as their navy blue, almost black uniforms sharply contrasted with those of the other two departments. Still well over a hundred feet away from the cluster of cops it was difficult to distinguish the troopers from the park police as their uniforms were so similar. Closing to within fifty feet she was able to make out the purple-tied troopers standing to one side, the black-tied park police to the other and the city cops mulling about in between.

"Morning gentlemen," Hamilton said with as much enthusiasm as she could muster, which was pretty fair considering the circumstances.

"Morning," a few of the men and one of the two female officers replied distractedly. Wilder and Hamilton thought nothing of the weak reception and knew not to take it personally. These cop's minds were occupied with things much more important than etiquette.

"Have the dogs had any luck," Wilder asked, a bit out of breath.

"Not yet, but they haven't been at it for all that long," replied a big, burly women wearing a park department uniform.

"Who's in charge here?" Wilder asked.

"I am...or was, up until now," an older man with a burnt orange mustache going gray replied from the center of the assembled officers.

"What do you mean, 'was'?" Hamilton asked.

The oak leaf on the man's lapel identified him as a colonel with the park police. His nameplate read Sheridan. The likelihood that the case would be theirs was strong, but she did not expect to be handed it on a silver platter without even an argument. Wilder was astonished at the ease with which the man surrendered his authority.

"DA called as you pulled up. She says it's you two who get the case. Said you had experience and success with this sort of thing in the past, and I'm inclined to agree. The city also has more resources at its disposal for this sort of thing. And honestly, these types of cases rarely end well and I'm not sure I even want to lead this thing. Also, I know the DA doesn't."

Sheridan stared at Hamilton and Wilder as if expecting their direction.

"Thanks for your frankness and your assistance," Wilder offered. "Plus your professionalism."

"At the end of the day we're all really on the same team, right? Catching bad guys is the job description. I just hope the Feds don't have to get involved. I'd like New Yorkers to take care of their own problems," Sheridan said.

"You did an excellent job on containment. As far as I can see there are no civilians in the park," Hamilton added.

"Pretty simple," Sheridan took no compliments.

"Coordinating three different departments can be touchy, I know and I think you did wonderfully with..." Hamilton was saying when the colonel held up one rough, weather-beaten hand for her to stop.

"I know what you're saying. Trying to save face a little for the old colonel, right? Don't worry about it young miss detective, find this girl. You tell us what you need and I speak for all the park police when I tell you we're here to help. That's a promise," the colonel finished with a tear in the corner of his eye.

"All right then, what's the manpower situation?" Hamilton asked the relieved colonel.

"Good, we've got forty-six cops here including the two of you. I expect a lot of civilian volunteers shortly. The phones have been ringing off the hook at the office with concerned community members. I figured we'd give the dogs their due though. After they've had first crack at it I'd planned on taking on the civvies for a line search."

"Excellent. How long have the dogs been at it?"

"Maisy, our dog, a female Shepherd, has been sniffing around since dusk this morning. She's going on four hours now. The city dogs arrived at about eight, so about and hour and fifteen minutes. None have picked up anything of value..."

"All of them are working off of the same sample?" Wilder asked.

Sheridan nodded. "The roommate gave us a pair of the girl's socks, as well as a pair of running shorts and leggings, all used, she said. She dug them out of the missing girl's laundry hamper. Each dog got a snoot full of each article before hitting the trails."

"Good, let's start to think about how we want to cover the park then," Wilder said. "How many acres are we looking at?"

"One hundred and six," Sheridan replied instantly.

"Where would you suggest we start?"

"The runners and bikers skirt the lake side of course, but there are some trails up toward the north. The north is much wider though so I suggest we begin very tight to the south and then fan out as we head north. The later in the day the more volunteers we'll have I expect."

"We'll give the dogs until noon, then we'll start the line search," Hamilton decided.

Nobody disagreed. It seemed a sensible course of action. The dogs could, after all continue sniffing around despite an ongoing search. The dogs would simply work before or after the line, it was that simple.

In the meantime the officers had nearly two hours with which they could scour the park themselves. Riding quads, state park police slowly rode the trails looking for discarded clothing, footprints and any signs of a struggle.

While those officers already posted at entrances remained in position, the other cops, including Hamilton and Wilder, started from the south of the park on foot and picked their way north as they would do for the volunteer line search later if need be.

Only twenty feet from one another initially at the narrow south end they covered the ground quickly without finding anything to clue them in to the girl's disappearance. As the park unfolded to the north and the officers spread out the search slowed to a crawl. Now walking with over a hundred feet between each officer there was much more ground to survey. With less than perfect eyesight, many of the officers stumbled along just hoping to run into something.

It was nearly eleven o'clock when the relieved colonel received a call from the officer of his K-9 unit. The radio strapped to Sheridan's epaulet chirped twice and then a low, metallic voice rumbled. He adjusted the squawk button, clearing the frequency and advised, "This is base commander, come again."

"I've got an earring, Ray. Maisy found an earring," the voice came.

"Where are you, Pete?" Sheridan asked, all radio formalities forgotten.

"All the way north, just west of Gateway Boulevard."

"On the way. Good work," Sheridan replied.

Minutes later a state park four by four picked up Sheridan, Hamilton and Wilder and headed north through the park toward the K-9 unit. Rumbling to a stop on the rugged, rarely travelled trail, the park police truck shuddered as its engine died. Against all odds it was Wilder who was first out and running toward the K-9 officer and the German Shepherd. Excited as he was he had the tact and good sense to let the colonel question his own man.

"What can you tell us, Pete?" Sheridan asked approaching the officer with the dog sitting at his feet.

"I...well...Maisy found this earring", the officer replied, holding a plastic bag containing a small silver hoop in his left hand. He handed the bag to Sheridan who held it up for Hamilton and Wilder to see.

"Where exactly?"

"Right here," the officer replied pointing at a weedy patch of growth sprouting from the gravelly trail.

"It's hers?"

"I guarantee it is! Never seen Maisy act like this before. She picked up the scent probably thirty yards that way," he said pointing toward the south, "and practically dragged me over here."

"Nice work, Pete! And nice work, Maisy!" Sheridan said leaning down to scratch the shepherd between the ears. "Find anything else of interest?"

"Sure did," the K-9 cop answered. It rained the morning before our missing person is assumed to have gone running and that's good news for us."

"You've got tracks?" Hamilton asked.

"Sure do. Right over here," the cop said leading the colonel and the detectives back a few feet away from the trail. "Mud is nature's original cast maker and these prints are nearly perfect. You'll have to get the forensic people out here to nail it down, but I'd bet my paycheck these here are the missing girl's shoe prints. See the pattern there," he pointed at the print. "It's the sole of an Adidas cross-trainer. Did she where Adidas?"

The colonel and the detectives looked to one another for answers and when none came Wilder said, "We'll talk to the roommate about it."

"And here," the K-9 officer pointed to the right and slightly behind the footprints, "is another set of prints, considerably larger, and look how much deeper they've Sunk in. Look, this second set of prints is deeper, considerably deeper in fact. Now we know she was a runner and was presumably running right here. Her own prints are pretty deep for a small footprint, but she was running so it checks out fine. Her prints end abruptly right here," he said pointing at a stretch of moist soil which seemed to have been scratched or scuffed, but only slightly. The scuff marks were thin and short, less than two feet each, but following in the same direction as feet would have if they were being dragged. Now the second set of prints sink deeper into the mud here as if the person who made them had suddenly gained a hundred or so pounds."

"Or was carrying someone over their shoulder," Wilder interjected.

"Exactly. So whoever grabbed this woman had run up from behind her. Whoever got her is in pretty damn good shape and very strong. This guy caught her, most likely knocked her out, and carried her away in a single fluid motion. There are no other signs of any struggle. No additional scuff marks, no clothing, no hair, no blood, no nothing. This guy's good at this, not a first timer. According to these prints, the perp wears Nikes, size eleven I'd say. But again you have to have the lab folks weigh in on all of this. After all, I'm only a dog guy with an active imagination."

The ensuing line search comprising of twenty-five police officers as well as over fifty volunteer civilians slowly combed the park from south to north with the K-9 units heading in the opposite direction. By two-thirty in the afternoon the dogs were exhausted, done for the day. They were unable to turn up any other evidence. The line search went on until nearly dusk, but also came up empty. Although the volunteers found a varied assortment of sneakers, shirts, underwear and the like, none of the items belonged to the missing woman. The park got a good thorough cleaning at least. The park police called the sanitation department to send a truck to pick up the garbage bags full of litter, bottles, cans and condoms, both used and still packaged which had been gathered.

* * * *

While the search in the park was under way Hamilton dropped by Stadtler's apartment to speak to the roommate again. Abrams was certain Stadtler did in fact wear Adidas cross trainers for jogging. When asked if she knew what size shoe Stadtler wore Abrams motioned the detective into the bedroom in the rear of the apartment. Hamilton entered the room, it was obsessively neat and clean, typical of its occupant. Seeing no shoes upon the hardwood floor Hamilton turned the knob on the closet door and peered inside.

Carefully lined up against the left-hand side wall of the closet, was Stadtler's shoe collection. Heels, flats, pumps, mocassins, boots, snow boots, loafers, and closest to the door a pair of Adidas cross trainers. Bending down, Hamilton picked up the sneakers to have a closer look. They were beat up pretty good and worn thin on the sole. *Probably the emergency backup pair for when the others get wet*, Hamilton thought. She walked out of the closet into the brighter light of the bedroom and brought one of the sneakers up toward her face. Holding her breath, out of sheer instinct, she peered at the bottom of the shoe's tongue upon which she hoped there would be a tag informing her of the shoe's size. The tag was there, but all of the information on it was worn away by use, it was rubbed blank. She sighed and brought the other sneaker up to eye level and lifted up its tongue. The tag was badly smudged, almost unreadable, but not quite. Just below where the tag read " ade n C na" she found " m n's iz 5." *Same size as the tracks*, Hamilton thought to herself and then she bagged the sneakers to take them with her.

* * * *

At nine o'clock that night Wilder sat at his desk thumbing through more photos of the missing woman. He'd spoken to her parents a half an hour before on the phone. They had flown up from Long Island and were stopping in at police headquarters as soon they retrieved their luggage and picked up their rental car. He didn't have much to tell them, but steeled himself to let them know what had been discovered so far, as compassionately as possible. It was the worst part of the job and he wished Hamilton was with him, to provide the soft woman's touch she could give when the need arose.

He thumbed through more photos, both color as well as black and white, before tossing them on top of the missing girl's life story. "Pretty girl too, a damned shame," he muttered to himself when the phone rang.

"Parents are on their way?" asked Hamilton.

"Should be here any minute."

"I'll be there in five."

"Thanks Marguerite, you know this isn't my strong suit. I owe you."

"Don't mention it," she replied and then added, "Need anything while I'm on my way?"

"No thanks, but listen to this. I was still a little confused about Colonel Sheridan, giving up the case without so much as a peep."

"Yeah?"

"I spent some time with a few of the park guys and asked about it."

"And?"

"Turns out his own daughter was abducted when she was three."

"Really?"

"Right outside the stadium after a Bill's game. Sheridan had offered to help some woman with a flat tire, and while he's jacking it up and changing it for her somebody ran up and, boom, snatched the kid."

"Good God, that's horrible!"

"He was lucky though, the kid was found at a homeless shelter the following morning. Case of mistaken identity. Turned out the woman with the flat was in on the whole thing. The woman, one Jaime Little, never snitched on her accomplice. The feeling was, a divorced husband had hired the couple to abduct his estranged daughter, but it could never be proven."

"Probably a big payday after the joint."

"She did ten years at Auburn."

"Should have been more," Hamilton replied.

"It should always be more."

"Amen to that."

"Anyway, the girl is fine, doesn't remember a thing. She's thirty-seven now with three kids of her own. According to Sheridan's guys though, he was pretty well rattled and came away from the experience changed a little."

"No wonder he handed the case off so easily. As briefly as she was missing, it must have been hell for him."

"I've got a feeling we'll never see Patricia Stadtler again," Wilder said sullenly.

"Speaking of whom, I just pulled into the lot. I see a couple walking toward the front steps. It's gotta be her folks. I'll see you in a minute," Hamilton replied and ended the call.

Hamilton sprinted up the front steps of police headquarters and headed down the hallway to where she and Wilder shared an office. Wilder was seating Stadtler's parents when she walked in. Mrs. Stadtler's eyes were red and puffy, it had been the longest one hour flight in history probably. Hamilton shut the door behind her and took a seat beside Wilder. The crying from within was heart wrenching.

Chapter Three

Having made his special deliveries to destinations throughout the American mid-west, usually to Chicago and Cleveland, Gant most often flew to southeastern Canada. The Canadian healthcare system provided the perfect opportunity for him to carry on his trade. The sluggish socialized health care of Canada routinely required patients in need of transplants to wait years before being matched with donors. The waiting lists were so long and the bureaucratic paperwork so involved, very often needy patients died while waiting for the organs they so desperately sought. Many Canadians were literally dying for transplants. Those wealthy enough eagerly sought out organs trafficked illegally. Their reasoning was simple and sound, they preferred to pay in cash rather than with their lives. Canada offered Gant, and a handful of men like him, a rare occasion to exploit the failure of socialized medicine on a national level.

Gant had what he considered to be his "safe airports" where he knew people, he was never questioned. His departure point never changed though, it was always Taylor Johnson Airport which he could ride to on his bike if need be. Ninety percent of the time he flew to the Montreal International Airport at Dorval also named the Pierre Elliot Trudeau International Airport. He was on his way there now. Cruising at two hundred and thirty knots at ten thousand feet, it would take him about an hour and twenty minutes with favorable wind conditions, a bit longer otherwise, to reach Montreal. His people were gratuitously awarded for their exceptional treatment of him. Not one of them knew of his deliveries and not one cared, nor pried. All were taken care of handsomely.

With the Sun slightly off to his right he winged over the sparkling blue expanse that was Lake Ontario. He reviewed the current price list in his mind as he went. *Twenty thousand for each kidney, ten thousand for the eyes, the heart will cost fifty grand on the market, the pancreas another twenty thousand. The liver was worth at least thirty-five grand with all the alcoholics up there, and the lungs will bring in fifteen g's a piece. Grand total,...cha-ching...one hundred and eighty-five thousand dollars, U.S.. No surgeons, save me. No middle man to take his cut, pardon the pun. This is the way it should be. It's too easy!*

For Gant though it really wasn't about the money. He was financially set thanks to his father. He looked at his deliveries as, flights of deliverance. He envisioned himself as an angel of mercy providing life to those who needed help. His ulterior motive he brushed aside as merely the price for happiness and self-fulfillment. As facts would prove out, he really didn't need the money from the organ deliveries, he was rich by birth. He'd gladly give the organs away for free, but it would surely raise suspicions about how he came upon his supply. Even in the shady underworld of organ trafficking nobody was above turning informant, they only had to be arrested once to be flipped. He therefore charged full price and then donated most of his profits to various agencies, the largest beneficiaries being foundations devoted to cancer research. The remainder of the money was put aside for "gifts" for his contacts at the airports he used.

Beginning his descent some fifty minutes later Gant inhaled deeply and looked ahead as the plane approached Montreal. As the Cessna buzzed onward the snaking waters of the Saint Lawrence River beckoned him, he followed the natural guide as if it was sent from heaven. Closer by the minute, he peered through the cockpit window soaking up nature's blue and green as it crept up to meet him. Approved for landing, ten minutes later the airport was within sight, he was flying at an altitude of only two thousand feet. The wide tarmac spread out before him, a massive grayish-black blight on the otherwise pristine landscape.

A crystal clear day, he gazed out beyond the airport toward Mount Royal for which the city was named. A dense city having no true skyscrapers, the mountain dominated Montreal, lying immediately north of downtown. Atop the mountain stood the Mount Royal Cross stretching just over one hundred feet into the air. Gant squinted slightly to catch sight of the revered landmark. Illuminated at night, the Cross made much more of an impression, in his opinion. Nonetheless, he glanced back and forth from his instruments to the Cross until he banked slightly north and Mount Royal's peak swung out of his peripheral vision. Two minutes later the plane touched down with a barely noticeable squeak and Gant taxied toward his hangar.

Parked outside of the small grey-green hangar was a truck, a navy blue Chevy Tahoe. As Gant cut the engines outside of the hangar, a man in a red jumpsuit got out of the Tahoe and walked to the back where he raised the tailgate. He then turned toward the plane, its propellers dying, and approached it.

Gant was up and out of the Cessna before the man in the red jumpsuit had closed to within fifty feet. "Graham," he yelled above the roar of a commercial jet thundering overhead.

Graham Nystrom was about Gant's age, but looked years older. The two men had hit Montreal's bar scene quite a bit together when Gant first supplied Nystrom Aviation with parts. A heavy smoker and slave to Maker's Mark, the mechanic slept little, worked a lot, and drank even more. He held out a grease-smudged hand to Gant who cheerfully accepted it.

"Great to see you, Graham! It's been years, three at least. Where've you been."

"Well Phil, you know how it can be working for your own dad. He's had me working up north at Goose Bay," Nystrom replied sheepishly.

"What, is it some kind of punishment? Why'd he exile you?"

Nystrom took a deep breath and said, "The old man thought it would be good for me to get away from the nightlife here."

"So, it was exile."

"It made it worse. Always cold up there, very, very short summer. Nothing to do but drink."

"Well, you're back now, right?" Gant asked.

"Trial basis. He's got to see how I work out."

"I'm sure you'll be fine. Listen I'd like to speak to you all day, but the fact is I'm on a tight schedule."

"Gonna hit the tenderloin," Nystrom smiled alluding to Montreal's red light district.

"No, no those days are long gone. I'm practically married now. She's pushing for it, but I'm trying to hold it off."

"Years are passing by if you want kids."

"It doesn't matter for men, and besides, she's only thirty-three. She's got some time yet. But anyway, I've got a meeting up town in less than an hour so I need to get moving."

"You need a ride?"

"I've got a car coming for me, but thanks."

"Say no more," Nystrom responded holding up a greasy paw. "Let's pack it out."

Within minutes the boxes of airplane parts were unloaded from the Cessna and lay in the rear of the Tahoe. Nystrom signed off on the shipment and handed Gant a check for twenty-one thousand dollars. Gant provided his old friend with a receipt and patted him on the back. Nystrom slammed the gate shut and jumped in behind the wheel. He pulled out and seconds later the Tahoe disappeared behind the hangar and out of sight. Gant walked back to the plane, retrieved the cooler and then disappeared into the hangar.

Less than five minutes later a maroon Jaguar XF with diplomat plates pulled up next to the hangar. A middle-aged man with boyish looks stepped out into the mid day Sun. Like the kid from next door he walked into the hangar his Hawaiian shirt flapping in the mild breeze. Finding the hangar empty he noticed the bathroom door was closed. He sat down at a small table to wait for Gant.

Upon opening the door Gant welcomed the man, "Luc, how are you?"

"You bring that into the bathroom," Luc Monceaux asked with a frown.

"Of course, it goes everywhere with me. Who knows who might make off with it if left unattended?"

"That would be unfortunate, wouldn't it?" Monceaux replied.

"There'd be much explaining to do, that's for certain. An unassuming cooler thief would be quite surprised upon popping it open I should think."

"Can you imagine the look on the scoundrel's face? Hoping for free beer and getting livers and kidneys instead," Monceaux mused.

"Then again, perhaps someone desperate enough to steal a cooler would be in dire need of such things," Gant offered blithely. The two men shared a lighthearted laugh before getting down to business.

"So, all is present and accounted for Carl?" Monceaux asked as the moment quickly faded.

"Of course, as always," Gant, known to Monceaux as Carl Heydrich, replied curtly.

"Very good, most dependable. I'll be right back then," Monceaux said turning on his heel.

Watching Monceaux walk back to the Jaguar, Gant slipped his hand into the back pocket of his jeans to where a twenty-five caliber Beretta double-action Model 21A Bobcat auto rested. The handgun was on the large side for a pocket carry, yet still manageable. He'd been loading it in the bathroom when Monceaux pulled up.

As Monceaux returned he slid the hangar door shut behind him. He was back inside in less then a minute with a cooler of his own, a wide smile cracking his boyish face. He placed the cooler atop the little table he had briefly been seated at earlier and plopped down again. Gant joined him at the table, but remained standing, his hands behind his back as he often did when conducting business Monceaux noticed.

"As agreed upon?" Gant asked.

"Certainly, Carl," he replied lifting the lid of his cooler. Inside the cooler were stacks of bundled one hundred dollar bills. "You get what you want and we get what *we* want," Monseaux added, pointedly reminding Gant that he had numerous accomplices who would be sure to miss him if he failed to appear shortly.

Gant peered into the cooler and asked, "All U.S.?"

"As specified. *We* greatly value your business. You're dependable and most discrete. And productive I might add." Gant enjoyed the fact Monseaux always made it clear he wasn't working alone. His compulsive need to reference his partners showed a deep respect for Gant. It showed a healthy fear which Gant liked. "*We* purchase more product from you than either of our other two suppliers combined. Some of *us* wonder where you get such a steady supply from, not that any of *us* care."

"I could never let that out, could I? You'd go straight to the source yourself. I'd be left out in the cold," Gant said smiling.

"I don't think any of *us* would be able to tap your source. *We* think that you have special skills. But again *we* don't care."

"As long as they're healthy and fresh, right Luc," Gant clapped Monseaux on the back.

"Exactly, and yours are the healthiest and freshest to be found."

"OK, then. Let's finish this, I've got to get back to a rather pressing matter."

More pressing than pocketing almost two hundred grand in an afternoon, Monseaux thought to himself, and then asked, "Would you like to count it, Carl?"

"No, no need. I trust you, Luc."

Gant bent down to grab his red Playmate cooler and then heaved it up on top of the table. Monseaux reached into his cooler and began taking the bundles of hundreds out of it, he stacked them neatly next to the Playmate. When Monseaux was finished and his cooler was empty Gant pulled on a pair of thick rubber gloves. He thumbed the lock release on the Playmate and slid the cover to the side, ghost-like tendrils of dry ice smoke drifted up into the warm morning air. Gant snapped up the dry ice from the top and placed it into the bottom of Monseaux's cooler. He swiftly transplanted the contents of his Playmate into the cooler of his business associate. After the ice he switched the cardboard. The lobster, he left on the table momentarily as he moved the organs. When the organs were safely inside of Monseaux's cooler, Gant rested the lobster on top of them. Then he placed the other layer of cardboard atop the lobster, and then poured the dry ice from the bottom of the Playmate on top. Within a minute and fifteen seconds Gant had unpacked and repacked Patricia Stadltler. He closed the lid of Monseaux's cooler and smiled thinly at his partner.

Monseaux stared at Gant with a certain sense of disbelief. The two men had made similar transactions many times and Monseaux felt, he'd become more and more accustomed to Gant's icy calmness and disconnected demeanor. *I'm a cool customer, a fucking organ trafficker, but this guy, he's fucking creepy cool,* he thought. Monseaux found himself lost in Gant's different colored eyes. *What's behind those eyes? Does he have a heart? Does he have a mother?*

"Better get going now Luc," Gant said snapping Monseaux out of his fugue. "The ice only lasts so long, you've got to get to your customers, and the sooner the better."

"Right, right," Monseaux replied rising from his chair. "So you'll get in touch with *us* again in six months or so?"

"Probably so. Could be sooner though, you never know what you might run into."

Monseaux nodded and wordlessly headed for the hangar door with his cooler at his side. Stepping into the sultry morning he inhaled a great lungful of air and then breathed out slowly as he walked to the Jaguar. He popped the trunk, nestled the cooler into a corner and wedged it in with a box of books. Gently closing the trunk he got in behind the wheel. Once inside the car he pulled a pack of DuMaurier's out of his shirt pocket and lit up. Exhaling a plume of blue smoke he started the engine, shifted into drive and then gave the car some gas. He wiped a sheen of sweat from his forehead as he pulled away toward the city.

Gant had never intended to use the gun, but trusted nobody. *Better safe than sorry*, he figured. He knew to be most careful in his line of work. He unloaded the Beretta, placing the cartridges in the front pocket of his jeans while the gun he returned to his back pocket. He never flew with a loaded gun, he wasn't crazy after all. After rinsing out his lucky cooler Gant wiped it dry with a wad of toilet paper. He tossed the soaked wad of toilet paper into the commode and flushed it down. After washing his hands he filled the Playmate with the bundled cash and slid the cover closed.

He then contacted the control tower for permission to take off. He routinely spent less than an hour at Dorval before returning to Buffalo, it was the single greatest benefit of flying your own small aircraft, he thought. The convenience and quality of service enjoyed by the small craft pilots who used the outer, perimeter runways was unparalleled. The big jets could sit a long time waiting for clearance. Not Gant though. He was eager to get home and was delighted when the air traffic controller informed him that he would have to wait only ten minutes to take off. As soon as the money was laundered and wired to one of his offshore accounts he would make a large anonymous donation to the Cancer Research Institute, it was his habit.

Heading east from the airport Monseaux skirted the north side of the river on the *Autoroute du Souvenir* for five miles smoking one cigarette after another. Despite being in a hurry he was extremely careful to obey the speed limit, the Jaguar never exceeded forty kilometers, or about twenty-five miles, an hour. By the time the roadway swept to the northeast he had pushed his instincts regarding Carl Heydrich to the back of his mind and regained his composure. With the initial transaction of the trip behind him he looked forward to the completion of the day's business. Bearing onto *Autoroute Ville-Marie*, Monseaux continued on for a few miles before turning left onto *Rue Guy* and following it to the hospital at its end.

Twenty-five minutes after leaving the airport Monseaux placed a call on his cell phone and pulled into a reserved parking spot not far from the hospital's emergency room entrance. The Jaguar displayed a parking permit for the space, it was renewed annually by Monseaux's partner on the inside. He lit another cigarette and patiently waited. Within three minutes a security guard appeared at the pedestrian entrance. Monseaux watched in his rearview mirror as the balding, middle-aged guard briskly made his way toward the car with a navy blue duffle bag swaying at his side. Remotely popping the trunk, Monseaux finished his cigarette and stubbed it out in the ashtray as the guard settled the duffle bag into the trunk and then removed the cooler. The guard then placed the cooler on the black top and shut the trunk with a muffled thud. The guard never set eyes upon Monseaux, in fact never had, not once in the five years he'd been making the swap for the doctors within the hospital walls. Without exchanging a single word Monseaux doubled his money within half an hour.

As soon as the guard re-entered the hospital Monseaux backed out of the parking spot and headed south toward his home in Westmount. He figured that after the guard delivered the cooler of organs to the doctors the man would be erasing the tapes the surveillance cameras were sure to be recording. Monseaux wondered how many surgeons were in on the business. Briefly, he wondered what kind of cut the security guard got and then dismissed it as trivial, he really didn't care.

Monseaux smiled to himself as he neared home. Business was good, booming in fact. He justified his work as performing a service, like any other job. He was simply providing the sick with a remedy for their afflictions, if he became rich doing it, so be it. *If people were dying for transplants in the United States they were willing to kill for them in Canada,* he thought with a twinge of guilt. Again Heydrich seeped into his conscience threatening to ruin a perfectly good day, a great day, a most lucrative day by most standards. As he pulled into the driveway of his vintage Victorian any qualms he had with his work flew away with the breeze as his wife and two daughters ran from the side yard to smother him with hugs and kisses.

Chapter Four

After providing the Stadtler's with what scant information they had on their daughter's disappearance, the two detectives led the couple out and walked them to their rental car. They promised to update them with any new findings and made certain they knew their way to the hotel they were staying at. The detectives then left the couple and returned to the office which they had shared for three years.

"Never gets easier, thanks Marguerite," Wilder said.

"Nice people, despite all the money," Hamilton replied. "Maybe they'll get a ransom note."

"We should have heard already. Kidnappers looking for money aren't generally sadistic as a rule. Most make contact with the bread holders within twenty-four hours, usually less. They don't get their kicks by holding the person they nabbed."

"I know, I know. It's not likely, but you never know."

"Who can really tell what will happen?" Wilder frowned.

"If nothing breaks within a few days, the chief's gonna call the Feds in."

"Maybe it's for the best. This girl is the fourth person to go missing in the greater Buffalo area in what, a year?"

"Ten months to be exact."

"Two women, in their early to mid-twenties and two men."

"Boys really, one was fifteen and the other sixteen," Hamilton said.

"The common thread?"

"All young."

"What else?" Wilder asked pushing pictures of the missing persons across his desk toward his partner.

After thumbing through the photos for the hundredth time Hamilton replied, "They're all pretty good looking, what some ordinary looking people might call 'beautiful people'."

"They certainly are. Also, they're all in fine physical condition. The two boys were high school athletes. One on the cross country team, the other played lacrosse. The women were active, one a compulsive jogger and the other an avid cyclist."

"Lean and muscular."

"Uh huh, that's what I noticed after the first two, Andrew Spahn and Elizabeth McPherson, went missing. Everybody felt, and still feels all those disappearances are unconnected. Normally serial killers abduct or murder victims of one sex."

"It's all men or all women."

"Aha," Wilder grunted. "Neither were our case, but early on I felt those two were in some way the work of the same person or people, I'm not sure why. Just a hunch I guess. Then we have the lacrosse player and our latest, Stadtler, the jogger vanish. I think this last pair is connected to one another and also to the first pair."

"Pretty speculative, especially with no bodies. There's no dump site for any of them. No murder weapons. There's no way to tell how they were killed."

"Who says they were killed?"

"Well, we do, at least I do," Hamilton replied.

"I did too, initially. But now I'm not so sure."

"What are you getting at?" Hamilton asked.

"Four young, even youthful, people abducted in ten months. All athletic and attractive. The boys were muscular, yet thin, and still young enough to be subdued by a larger, stronger adult male. The women well," Wilder paused and attempted to choose his words carefully so as not to offend Hamilton. "Let's say all women aren't as skilled in the martial arts as you."

"Go on," she said, accepting the slight of her sex knowing it to be true.

"No ransoms for any of them."

"Right?"

"No calling card taking any credit for the disappearances or assumed murders."

"Right?"

"No bodies found," Wilder went on.

"It's still early, often twenty or thirty years go by before somebody stumbles upon remains. Sometimes they're never found at all."

Wilder held up his pudgy hands in a gesture of mock self-defense. "I think they're still alive."

"Really?" Hamilton mocked him right back. "So what are they doing then?"

"Sex trade," Wilder replied curtly with a grimace. "I think they've been abducted and are now sex slaves."

Sometimes predisposed to insomnia, Hamilton had toyed with this idea in the back of her mind during the early hours of the morning on a few occasions, but quickly dismissed it as being the manifestation of a nightmare or some sort of paranoia. In the thin light of the office she shared with the man sitting across from her it suddenly didn't seem so far fetched any more. Clearly rattled, she took a deep breath and then looked to Wilder for more.

"It would be difficult yes, but definitely possible. It does happen after all."

"Saudi Arabia, Thailand, they could be anywhere right now," Hamilton said.

"Including right under our noses, like say New York."

"Do you really think so?" she asked.

"Remember that freak a couple of years ago in Austria who kept his own daughter locked in the basement for over twenty years and fathered a slew of kids with her?"

Hamilton shuddered at the memory.

"After reading about him I believe anything is possible," Wilder replied. "Humanity is the sharpest of double-edged swords. We can at once be uniquely intelligent, sensitive, and compassionate, but are also capable of the most unspeakable evils. It's disturbing, but fascinating at the same time. When I retire I'm gonna take some psych courses at UB."

"Sick and twisted, but it makes a lot of sense," Hamilton admitted.

"Let's keep this between us for now," Wilder advised. "Until we find some concrete evidence. Because you're right. Right now it's all speculation." Hamilton agreed with Wilder and the two parted company for the night.

* * * *

Heading in opposite directions the detectives cruised closer to home and what they hoped would be a refreshing night's sleep. As Hamilton pushed the department's Crown Vic along at a steady clip of seventy miles per hour northward along Interstate One-Ninety toward her home in Kenmore, Wilder drove south at a more leisurely pace toward Lackawanna in his own Volkswagen Jetta Wagon. In the tough financial times detectives were no longer issued their own cars, they shared when partnered up. Every other week Hamilton and Wilder would drive their personal cars to the station while the other took the Crown Vic. Within minutes of one another they were nearly home.

* * * *

As Hamilton made her way through Kenmore her thoughts drifted toward Chauncey, her four-year-old German Shepherd, who would be dutifully waiting for her at the door. It was well past his time for a walk and she feared finding a mess to clean up when she got in. She pulled off of Tremont Avenue and into the driveway on the side of the modest cream colored ranch she had purchased for less than fifty-thousand. Built in 1912, the little two bedroom, one bath house encompassed just over seven hundred feet and was really little more than a bungalow.

She slammed the car door shut and took the three steps to the front porch in a single graceful leap, landing beside the front door. There was no fancy alarm system installed in the house. Hamilton had figured between Chauncey and what she carried on her hip, she was pretty much safe from any intruders. She jiggled her house key into the single lock and turned it clockwise opening the door to Chauncey who stood up on his hind legs with his leash in his mouth. She knew right away that the dog had held fast, but was now about to burst. Chauncey was well-trained and could hold his bodily functions for a long time, but he was so excited to see her that he might go any time.

"How's my good boy?" Hamilton asked the dog. Chauncey barked enthusiastically, tail wagging back and forth.

She patted the dog atop the head and gave him a good rub between the eyes before affixing his leash. She grabbed two of the plastic shopping bags she kept on a half Moon table by the door, tossed her keys onto the little end table beside the couch in the living room, which doubled as the dining room, and opened the front door to follow Chauncey as he led her out into the still warm night. Moments later the shepherd relieved itself two doors down from her little ranch. Hamilton left the mess temporarily, making a mental note to bag it before returning home. First she'd take a nice long walk with her best friend to stretch both of their legs.

Twenty minutes later Hamilton and Chauncey were on their way back home, both looking forward to a late dinner. It was far too late to cook and there was not much in the house to make anyway, she realized. She settled on leftover roast chicken breast, mashed potatoes, and green beans for her and dry kibble with some chunks of her chicken mixed in it for the dog. Hamilton and Chauncey always shared meals. After a day like the one just passed a nice meal, a shower and then some light reading before bed would be a welcome reward.

Approaching the house with a bagful of Chauncey's droppings Hamilton saw that the front door was wide open. Her thoughts instantly reverted to the Stadtler case, her stomach knotted up and she all but forgot about eating. Recognizing his master's unease, Chauncey began to growl, a low rumble deep within his chest.

"Shh Chauncey, quiet boy," she commanded as she threw the bag of dog poop toward the garbage cans in the alley beside the house.

She then un-holstered her Glock. The dog obediently hushed up, its chocolate eyes glistened with interest. She checked the road for strange vehicles, but found none. Only the usual assortment of neighbors cars filled the driveways and overflowed onto the shoulder of the road. Bringing the nine millimeter out before her in her right hand she advanced on the house. On the porch she loosed the dog, it tramped headlong through the open door. With both hands now on the gun Hamilton followed close behind sweeping the weapon from side to side searching for the intruder.

Expecting to hear a furious row from within the house Hamilton was shocked to hear nothing save the clicking of Chauncey's nails on the linoleum floor of the kitchen and the high whine of what she knew to be mosquitoes. After a harried room by room search turned up nothing but Chauncey waiting patiently by his food bowl Hamilton sat down at the kitchen table, placed the pistol on top of it, and exhaled as she rubbed her eyes. *This case is gonna kill me*, she thought to herself as she remembered rushing out the front door with the dog. Apparently she had simply failed to pull the door hard enough to close it behind her and then it swung open in the breeze.

* * * *

Dan Wilder's home in Lackawanna was infinitely more spacious than Hamilton's bungalow, and it had to be as he shared it with his wife, three daughters and son. For over a hundred thousand dollars the detective had owned the five bedroom, two bath colonial for nearly eight years. Built in 1960, the house boasted over two thousand three hundred square feet of living space, and featured a dual sided wood burning fireplace, the family enjoyed from the living room and the dining room. A second fireplace in the partially finished basement went largely unused, but Wilder had grand plans to build a bar down there to entertain his buddies. Then it would be used plenty he dreamed. A large covered front porch looked out onto East Milnor Avenue and the neighborhood playground a short distance down the street.

Wilder arrived home about 10:30 and stumbled out of his car and trudged up the steps, his breathing labored and raspy. On the couch in the living room was his wife of twenty-two years, Carol. A bowl of mint chocolate chip ice cream resting in her ample lap, she was entranced by an episode of *Desperate Housewives* which she had recorded earlier.

"Late tonight, Danny," she said hitting the pause button before shimmying forward to get up.

"Stay, stay," Wilder replied waving her back to the couch.

"Don't want to talk about it?" she asked.

"No, not yet. Too much going on, but thanks. What's for dinner?"

"There's pizza on the counter, I saved you two slices. Junior almost got them, the boy can eat and eat," Carol Wilder said, referring to their fifteen-year-old son who had sprung up two inches in the last year, and seemed to be a bottomless pit.

"Well he can afford it. Better him than me."

She nodded in acknowledgement and said, "All the same, you've got to eat. Go ahead now. We'll talk later if you want."

"I'll get changed first. Then I'll come back down and eat here in front of the show with you."

"Suit yourself, but no snide comments about how stupid my show is," she warned him.

He held up a pudgy hand and climbed the stairs to the second floor where the master bedroom was flanked by the girl's bedrooms. Dan Junior had moved down into the basement earlier that year much to Wilder's chagrin. It would be difficult to extricate him from the basement, but it would have to be done if the bar was ever to become a reality.

Wilder switched his khaki trousers and short sleeved button down for a pair of gray sweat shorts and a white T-shirt with yellowed armpits, his usual summertime lounging attire. He began his descent on the stairs when he stopped suddenly on the third stair from the top. He knew Junior and his older sister, Katie who was seventeen, were still sure to be out with their friends on this warm summer evening. The thought of Katie and Junior out in the night sent a chilling shiver up his spine. *My babies are out there in the same night in which a lunatic lurks hunting for his next mark*, he shuddered. *A curfew is what we need. A curfew for the whole damn area until this bastard is caught*, he thought unrealistically.

Then reason won out, *No, not in this day of civil liberties. Damn fools would rather risk their kids getting taken than infringe on anybody's right to move about unsupervised at all hours.* "Starting tomorrow we'll have a curfew in this house," he said aloud to himself. *Well, I'll just go in to check on the others.* It was past bedtime for Carrie, Susan, and Chrissy, ages eleven, nine and seven respectively. These last three of the brood had come upon the scene after Wilder had been promoted to detective and received the commensurate raise that went with the title.

Wilder pushed open the door to Carrie's room and peaked into the darkness, she no longer felt the need to sleep with a nightlight anymore. After his eyes adjusted to the darkness Wilder saw an empty bed and his heart jumped up into his throat. Pivoting to his right he pushed open the door to the room shared by Susan and Chrissy, the youngest Wilders. He was shaken by the dark abyss he stared into. The two little girls were still afraid of the dark, particularly Chrissy. His heart racing, Wilder flipped on the light switch beside the door jamb. Instantly bathed in soft white light the twin beds were conspicuously empty as well. A wave of hot nausea raced through Wilder, cold sweat sprang from his pores. Wilder turned back toward the stairway and while thudding down them he screamed out to his wife, "The girls! The girls Carol! Where are the girls?"

Carol Wilder yelled a reply, but he was unable to hear it, such was the state of his excitement. He burst into the living room almost tripping over the ottoman which had been there ever since they moved in shouting, "They're gone! Gone! Not in bed! Did you leave? Where are the girls?"

Carol Wilder held up a hand to calm him and after he stopped yelling and settled down she simply said, "At Mom's for a sleep-over. They've been talking about it for three days now, Danny. Mom had dinner here with us and then took them back to her house."

Wilder slumped down on the couch next to his wife with one fat hand on his chest. His belly shook beneath the stained T-shirt as he struggled to catch his breath. When he finally began breathing normally Carol Wilder asked, "You're sure you don't want to have that talk now, Dan?"

Chapter Five

Gant had no interest in the sex slave trade. His sex life was far better than most men half his age. It was mid afternoon when he was back in the basement eager to work on what was his passion. For the afternoon's activities he selected the early 1970's album *Brain Salad Surgery* by the rock band Emerson, Lake, and Palmer. He cued up the CD and raised the volume to eight. He stood still to listen to *Jerusalem*, an adaptation of a Hubert Parry hymn mixed with lyrics from the preface of William Blake's *Milton*. As the thrum of the Hammond organ and the thunderous pounding of drums shook the basement and reverberated off of the cinderblock walls Gant smiled in rapture. When the regal voice joined in he walked into the rear room of the basement to the refrigerator.

He opened the refrigerator door to retrieve the object of his fascination. Staring up from the bowl of saline was the eyeless visage of Patricia Stadtler. Gant carefully picked up the swimming face, its hair tethering out like the tentacles of a jellyfish, in both hands and closed the door with his elbow. He walked back into the onslaught of progressive rock, and placed the bowl atop the same table on which he had harvested it less then five hours ago. He flipped on the Medline surgical lamp and slipped on a pair of latex gloves.

With Stadtler's face in both of his hands, Gant gingerly depressed the nose inward with his thumbs while carefully pulling the flesh behind the ears toward him with his fingers. In this fashion he turned her face inside out. It took a great deal of patience and nearly ten minutes before he was satisfied and gazing upon the delicate tissue and capillaries which lined the interior of her face. It was as if he were looking at a burn victim who had a thick mane of brown hair for a brain.

He selected a very fine scalpel and went to work at the throat. Using short, quick strokes, he stripped away the subcutaneous fat layer and tiny capillaries. Layer after layer he shaved until he reached the dermis which he left intact. Using this method he worked his way upward toward the hairline and thence downward to the nape of the neck. Half an hour later a regal voice sang out, "Welcome back my friends to the show that never ends..." as *Karn Evil 9: First Impression, Part Two* was underway. Gant's right hand was cramping up a bit and not wanting to slip up so close to the end he decided to take a five minute break and give his full attention to the song. He sat back on the metal stool, took a sip of water from a paper cup and then opened and closed his hand several dozen times to aid circulation and loosen it up.

As the first impression transitioned into the second he was again shaving away the fatty tissue and by the time the third impression had rolled around he had finished scraping away all of the tissue he deemed unnecessary and potentially harmful. He put the scalpel down on the instrument tray and slid the pile of fatty tissue scraps into a plastic freezer bag. Always keeping his working surface as clean and clear of debris as possible he strode to the back room and deposited the tissue atop Stadtler's bodily remains inside of the freezer.

Back at the table, Gant manipulated the woman's face so that the epidermis would once again face outward as would be normal. Careful not to tear the fragile tissue, he took his time, her hair slowly trickled out from the cavern where her brain should have rested. When he had turned her face right side out once again he held it up to the lamp for closer inspection. *A perfect mask*, he thought marveling at his work.

Gant peeled off the gloves and from his shirt pocket he took the sheet of paper he'd jotted down Stadtler's personal information on. The Moog synthesizer, booming gong and knightly voice had faded away, gone until the next time he summoned them. He unfolded the paper and reviewed the woman's answers to his questions. After a minute or so he refolded the paper and replaced it in his pocket. Later, when time permitted, he would type it out for posterity.

It was his time to commune with the deceased, to honor her for the sacrifice she'd made. Gant picked up the mask he'd finished carving and slid it over his head. Stadtler's eyes were narrower than his own, but not by that much. He shifted the death mask slightly to the left providing him with an almost clear view of his surroundings. It was always a little disorienting to literally slip into someone else's skin, but he adjusted quite quickly. Gant walked to the wall by the stairs where a full-length mirror hung. With Stadtler's head resting on his shoulders he was astounded at how truly beautiful she was. Moving closer to the mirror he gazed at his own eyes within her face. The green, dilated eye had a clear, unobstructed view while the blue eye peered out from behind a flap of skin. He stuck his tongue out through her lips and licked them back and forth. Gant was far from a cannibal, he had no stomach for that. He did nonetheless have a strong urge to experience his victims as viscerally as possible.

He turned from the mirror and retrieved the metal chair that rested beside the operating table. He carried the chair over to the mirror and took a seat. Mentally reviewing Patricia Stadtler's responses, he sought to live her life as if it were his own. Comingling their experiences, he intertwined his life with hers as he traveled an imaginary journey through her childhood, adolescence and early adulthood. Gant caressed the fine skin of her cheek and ran his hands through her thick, lustrous hair as he became her and she transformed into he.

He swam at the beach in the town where she grew up as a child, he walked the halls of her high school, sat in the lecture halls she'd sat in through college, and dated her lovers. Her favorite scents, foods, songs, sights, and feelings, he smelled, tasted, heard, saw and felt as if they were his, for a short while anyway. As Gant felt Stadtler progressing toward the end of her life, as most would consider it, he became excited rather than sad. Her death exploded in a flood of color blinding him to the vision held in the mirror. In her death, he reasoned, she provided life to so many others who so desperately needed her help. She lived on in them in glory and triumph, a shining beacon of life and hope.

Euphoric with what he considered to be an out-of-body experience, Gant returned to the real world after a half an hour living as Patricia Stadtler. A half an hour was all the time he could afford for the dead woman's memory. He still had work to do to memorialize her adequately. He went back to the table.

Gant peeled the mask off of his face and placed it back into the bowl filled with saline. He cleaned his face with wet naps and then dried it with paper towels. He re-gloved his hands with fresh latex and was ready to go back to work. From the instrument table he took an empty plastic bowl and put it beside the steel bowl containing the death mask. He took the face in both hands and placed it in the bottom of the plastic bowl and retreated into the rear room once more.

Beside the refrigerator was a stainless steel slop sink. Gant ran the water cool and thoroughly rinsed the face and hair beneath the softly flowing stream. He then stretched the mask out and placed it atop a dish drainer which rested on the sidebar of the sink. As the mask dripped off the excess water he pivoted to the left of the sink to where he kept his supplies.

Gant opened the glass doors of the wall mounted cabinet next to the sink and took stock of his chemicals. Neatly arranged on the adjustable shelves were quarts of Knobloch pre-tan bactericide, gallons of McKenzie tanning solution, gallons of softening oil, pints of Enzol B rehydrater, pints of finishing deodorizer, bags of dry preservatives, pounds of citric acid, tubes of flesh colored Epoxy sculpting agent, cans of gold leaf foil flake powder and a wide assortment of paints, dyes and a box full of prosthetic eyes. He reached for a quart of bactericide and closed the cabinet. Spinning around he took two steps to his work table.

Gant poured half of the bactericide into a stainless steel bowl and went back to the sink to retrieve the mask. He tied Stadtler's wet hair back into a pony tail and returned to his work table. Beginning with her throat he slowly submerged Stadtler's face into the solution until it was completely covered, he stopped just shy of her hairline. As it had already been rinsed, her hair was clean enough he reasoned. From experience he knew hair lasted a very long time, longer than he could ever expect to live.

Gant was somewhat of an artist in the field of taxidermy, though his artwork was viewed by no one but himself. On this afternoon he began a process that would take weeks to complete. After the new mask was cleaned, tanned and treated with cleansing and preserving chemicals it would be left to dry. Once the mask had completely dried Gant would begin his finishing work. The finishing work was his favorite step in the process, as it was more artistry than anything else. Using acrylic paint he would restore her face to its natural color and beauty. When he first began his hobby he'd relied on a picture of his subject to duplicate its visage to his exacting tastes. As he became better and better he forsake the photos as he committed each face to memory. Besides, he reasoned, photos had a way of turning up at the most inopportune times, even for the most discreet.

He left the face to soak for a few minutes while he selected a pair of stunning light blue prosthetic eyes from the box on the top shelf of the cabinet. He wouldn't need them until much later in the process, but felt much better that he had them in stock and did not have to worry about ordering them. Satisfied, he closed the box of prosthetic eyes and placed the chosen pair on top of it.

Back at the work table Gant removed the face from the bactericide and held it to drip into the bowl for a few minutes before placing it into yet another bowl again with the hair safely draped over the side. From the cabinet he brought a gallon of the tanning solution which he poured over the face until it was completely submerged. He'd let the mask sit in the tanning solution for a few hours. He de-gloved, and ever clean, hand washed all of the bowls and instruments which he used. He then went upstairs to shower and have a bite to eat.

Chapter Six

Back in the station the next morning Hamilton and Wilder exchanged their stories about returning home the previous night. Wilder hadn't drawn his gun, but his heart was thumping just the same. Both agreed they'd never before been so on edge due to a case.

"I'm not paranoid, you know that, Dan," Hamilton said.

"I know, I know, neither am I. I panicked up there in the girl's room. It took Carol ten minutes to get me calmed down."

"I feel like we're very close, but don't know it. It's like this guy is right under our noses only we don't know where."

"I'm not sure about that, but I was definitely creeped out last night."

"We need to start looking at the obvious. We should…"

Hamilton was cut off by the phone on Wilder's desk.

Wilder looked at the caller I.D. and saw the number was inter-office, it was Chief Detective Harry Salerno's extension. "Wilder, chief," he answered the call.

"We've got prints off of a water bottle that came back from I.A.F.I.S.," Salerno said.

"We'll be right up," Wilder replied hanging up the phone. "They've got a hit on some prints, let's go," he said to Hamilton.

Wilder and Hamilton took the stairs outside of their office to the second floor. Salerno's office was directly above theirs. His door was open and they walked right in and took a seat before his desk.

In his early sixties, Harry Salerno was a thirty-four year veteran of the Buffalo Police Department. Many of his colleagues believed he would have been chief a decade ago if he'd wanted it. For Salerno though, true police work involved solving crimes not playing to the cameras. Fit and trim, and with a full head of curly salt and pepper hair, he looked a full decade younger than he was. In a grey short sleeved button down shirt and charcoal grey trousers he sat in a swivel chair behind his desk.

"Here's the story in a nutshell kids," Salerno said. "The techs were able to find Stadtler's DNA on a bottle of Mountain Valley Spring Water. They ran tests on every bottle or can found within a mile of where we believe she was taken."

"Not likely a runner would drink from a can," Hamilton said.

"Of course not, but better safe than sorry. We'll chase down anything we can for this one," Salerno replied. He continued, "Out of some forty-seven bottles and cans we examined…"

"People are pigs," Hamilton interjected.

Salerno ignored her. "We found the missing girl's DNA on said bottle. Minute particles of lip and gum tissue were found on the mouth of the bottle."

"Her DNA's on file? With a doctor, gynecologist, a dentist?" Wilder asked.

"Hair sample from her mother. Before the Stadtler's flew up from Long Island I asked Mrs. Stadtler if she had any keepsakes of her daughter, say a lock of baby hair. She assured me she did, she only had to find it. She thought for sure she'd put it in the victim's baby album and she was right. She brought the album here with her."

"So we know the water bottle was Stadtler's, what about the prints?" Wilder asked.

"There are two sets of prints on the bottle. One set is all over the bottle. Lots of smudges, remnants of uric acid, everything associated with sweat and exercise. It's most likely those prints are Stadtler's. Her baby prints are being sent to us from the hospital she was born in as we speak. I imagine the prints will be a match."

"And the other set of prints?" Wilder asked.

"A thumb, index and middle finger, all partials, but enough to get a hit on I.A.F.I.S."

I.A.F.I.S., the Integrated Automated Fingerprint Identification System, is a national automated fingerprint identification and criminal history system, maintained by the F.B.I. The fingerprints and criminal records of anyone having been convicted of committing a felony are included. The system provides automated fingerprint search capabilities, latent searching capability, electronic image storage, and electronic exchange of fingerprints and data. I.A.F.I.S. maintains one of the largest biometric databases in the world, containing the fingerprints and associated criminal histories of more than sixty-six million subjects.

"What's the name?" asked Hamilton.

"Subject is one Walter Thibodeaux," Salerno answered pushing a file folder over his desk toward the two junior detectives.

"Arrested in 2004 for drug trafficking, cocaine, but the charges were dropped. He was never caught with the goods in large quantity. His daddy knew somebody high in the D.E.A. and pulled some strings, sort of oiled the machine you might say. Arrested again in 2007 for domestic abuse, but again the charges were dropped. The girlfriend refused to press charges. Not a nice guy, and also a slippery son-of-a-bitch."

"When are we picking him up" Wilder asked.

"Right now. Any guess where he lives?"

"Here in the city?" Hamilton guessed.

"Right on Lake Shore Road, less than a mile from the park. His address is in the file there," Salerno nodded toward the folder. "Take two uniforms with you and make sure it's by the book. Don't provide any room for this prick to wiggle off again. No technicalities."

* * * *

Hamilton looked at the mug shot of Walter Thibodeuax, as Wilder drove the Crown Vic south on the Buffalo Skyway with a cruiser in tow. Thibodeaux was of medium height and build, with sandy blond, hair and hazel eyes. She actually thought he looked handsome. The photo was four years old, taken when he was in his late thirties. She sighed and slipped the photo back into the folder.

"He doesn't look like a killer does he?" she asked half-joking.

"What does a killer look like?"

"Grizzled, and dirty, and grungy."

"They should all look that way, then it'd be much easier to spot them."

"This guy looks like he could be the friendly neighbor from next door who borrows a cup of milk from time to time."

"He was somebody's friendly neighbor, he still is somebody's friendly neighbor most probably."

"Scary shit," she replied.

"No time to be scared now, we're just about there. It's coming up on the right. There it is, number twenty-three thirteen."

"I guess his daddy kept on paying the bills."

"Gravy train never ends for some people," he replied.

Wilder pulled the Crown Vic into the circular driveway, which was paved with bluestone. He parked directly before the front walkway and radioed to the officers in the cruiser to block the driveway from the road in case anything unforeseen occurred. The uniforms blocked the escape route and walked over to the detective's car. When they were within earshot Hamilton and Wilder got out of their car.

"Let's do this quick and clean. No rough stuff, right guys?" Hamilton prompted the two officers.

Wordlessly they both nodded.

Wilder and Hamilton walked to the front door with the uniforms spread out some forty feet behind. Hamilton rang the bell and put her hand on the butt of her Glock. Within seconds a pretty brunette answered the door. Her eyes went wide when she saw what greeted her at the door.

"Is this the residence of Walter Thibodeaux?" Hamilton asked.

"Yes, yes it is. Is he all right? What's happened?" the women asked.

"We're hoping you can help us out with that Ms.?" Wilder asked.

"Thibodeaux, Nicole Thibodeaux."

"Is your husband home?" Hamilton asked.

"No, he's at work."

"Where's work?" Wilder asked.

"Well, it's hard to say. He's at one of the stores."

"What stores?" Wilder asked.

"Convenience stores, we've got six of them. He's at one of them, I'm sure."

"Can you give him a call and find out which one he's presently at?" Hamilton asked.

"Sure, that's no problem. But what's this about?"

"We have to question him about a robbery that occurred. He may have seen something," Wilder offered. "Please don't mention that we're here, we'd like to question him fresh. Sometimes people recall things better that way."

"I don't know about this. I'm not comfortable calling my husband for you. Is he in trouble?"

"Should he be in trouble?" Hamilton asked.

"Of course not, Wally's a good man."

"Well then, this should be no big deal."

"What if I don't call him?"

"You'll be arrested for hindering an investigation and spend some time in jail," Hamilton bluffed without blinking

After a brief hesitation the brunette woman acquiesced. "Sure, all right, I'll call him then."

"Just find out where he is and how long he'll be there," Wilder advised. "And put us on speaker phone, please."

She walked into the kitchen and auto dialed her husband's cell phone. She feigned indifference as she waited for him to answer. After three rings he picked up the call.

"What's up, babe?" Thibodeuax asked.

"How long before you're home Wally?"

"You know this is a busy day, ordering day. Why are you calling so early? It's not even noon yet. You know I'll be awhile."

"I'm bored."

"Go for a walk. Knit some mittens. Hey, I've got a great idea, cook me some fucking dinner."

"I'm lonely Wally. Where are you now?"

"Genesee Street."

"Do you have to make another stop?"

"Three more, but I'm gonna break for lunch here," Thibodeaux replied.

"All right then. I'll see you when you get in."

"Yeah you will," Thibodeuax replied and then ended the call.

Mrs. Thibodeuax rested the phone back in its cradle. She sat at one of the chairs at the kitchen table and rested her head in her hands. Hamilton approached her.

"These officers will be staying with you to make sure you don't call your husband again. If he calls you are to put him on speaker so the officers can hear you're conversation. Do not mention the police at all or you will be prosecuted to the fullest extent of the law. Do you understand me, Mrs. Thibodeaux?"

"Is this legal, what you're doing here?" the woman asked.

"Do you understand what I said," Hamilton pressed.

"We'll be calling our lawyer."

Wilder ignored her. "What's the name and address of the store?" he asked.

"Wally's Way, fifteen twelve Genesee."

* * * *

The detectives left Mrs. Thibodeaux in the care of the uniformed officers and returned to their car. Hamilton immediately called for another cruiser to meet them at the Genesee Street store and gave Thibodeuax's description to the dispatcher. Wilder raced north using side streets and arrived at the store fifteen minutes later. A blue and white cruiser was parked across the street. As the detectives stopped in front of the store the new set of uniforms crossed the street to meet them. The four of them entered the store together. Thibodeaux was behind the counter talking to the clerk who manned the register. He was recognizable from his photo, but had packed on at least thirty pounds since it had been taken. Skinny arms and a pot belly, he didn't look capable of abducting anybody.

"Walter Thibodeaux, we'd like to have a word with you," Hamilton said.

Thibodeaux looked from the clerk to the detectives and then the uniformed officers behind them. "What's this all about?" he asked.

"Can you account for your whereabouts for the last seventy-two hours?" Wilder asked.

"I'm all over the city every day. I own a bunch of these places, there's always a fire to put out somewhere."

"So it's your claim that you've been at one of your stores for the past three days?" Hamilton asked.

"Usual routine, either at a store or at home, mostly sleeping. What's this all about? Am I under arrest for something? Should I be talking to you people? Do I need a lawyer?"

"Do you?" Hamilton asked him.

"Maybe in the past, but not any more."

"Have you ever seen this woman," Wilder asked as he pulled out a photo of Stadtler and waved it in front of Thibodeaux's face. Wilder was sure he would deny any knowledge of her.

"Sure, I've seen her. Pretty girl, you don't forget a face like that easily."

"How do you know her?" Hamilton pressed.

"I wouldn't say I know her. I'd say I see her from time to time. I'm only here once or twice a week popping in for inventory or to cover a shift sometimes. Hey Roger?" Thibodeaux said to the clerk. "How often do you see this girl?"

The clerk looked at the photo. "Hey, that's the picture of the missing girl in today's paper." he said. He took a closer look and then added, "She looks familiar, a lot like the one that stops in for a bottle of water sometimes."

"Yeah, she's a jogger," Thibodeaux chimed in. "I've seen her running by before. Now I think of it I covered Roger's shift three days ago. He was sick with a stomach virus he said. Right, Roger?"

The clerk nodded.

"She was in that day. Sold her a bottle of water and a bag of Sun Chips and something else, maybe a Chapstick or something. Put it into a bag and watched her ass as she walked out the door."

"You're a real charmer, aren't you Wally?" Hamilton said.

"Hey, I just call 'em as I see 'em, that's all."

"All right then," Wilder intervened. "We'd like you to come with us for an interview?"

"Am I under arrest?"

"No, not at all," Wilder said. We'd just like you to tell us everything you've noticed about this woman. She is the one who is missing and any help you could give us would be appreciated."

"I don't know anything about her other than she's a daily customer according to Roger here."

Again the clerk nodded.

Seeing a dead end for what it was Wilder relented. Thibodeaux's prints on the bottled water checked out as he'd said, he sold her items and then placed them into a bag at the counter. The guy was scum, or used to be at least, but there was nothing to bring him in on under the circumstances.

"Okay then. But if you remember anything or hear anything please give me a call," Wilder said, handing Thibodeaux his card.

"Will do officer, of course," Thibodeaux replied. Then he gazed at Hamilton and looked her up and down. "How about your card?" he asked.

"Not on your life," she replied giving him the finger.

"Feisty, that's the way I like 'em."

"Watch it or I'll lock you up for being an asshole," Wilder said as he ushered Hamilton toward the door.

Outside once more Hamilton said, "He's a real piece of shit, but not our piece of shit."

Getting into the car Wilder said, "I agree. Forget him, he's not worth the time. Let's have some lunch and then get back at it."

"Okay, but I'm eating real light. I'm meeting my cousin Lydia for dinner later, she thinks her boyfriend is going to propose to her. I don't see her often, she's the only family I've got up here."

"You eat whatever you want, I feel like some wings. How about the Brew Pub?"

"Can do, let's go."

Wilder started the Crown Vic and headed for Main Street in suburban Williamsville. Wilder ate heavy while Hamilton ate light. By one-thirty they were back at police headquarters with nothing to show for the first half of the day.

Chapter Seven

In his office Gant leaned back in his most cherished chair. Much too lithe for a bulky piece like an EZ-Boy, he relaxed in complete comfort in a vintage World War II parachute chair, which he'd purchased in Buenos Aires some twenty years back. According to the dealer, and supported by scrupulous research of his own, Gant found the chair had belonged to Heinrich Himmler, the notorious commander of Hitler's SS. Originally fitted within the belly of a Focke-Wulfe Fw 200 Condor, Gant had the chair reupholstered to original quality. He had briefly considered installing it within his Cessna but then logic won out and he placed it behind his desk, the central command post.

Skimming through the pages of *The Buffalo News* he made sure to keep tabs on the progress of the search for Patricia Stadtler. With each dead end story his heart truly went out to the parents of the missing girl. Always though, he became grounded in his sincere belief in the benefit of the greater good. So many lives saved for the sacrifice of a single one, he reminded himself over and over. After all, it did make perfectly good sense.

According to the paper as wells as the news outlets, the police had no leads in the case of Patty Stadtler. She had disappeared without a trace. With the authorities clueless and providing absolutely no information to the public Gant felt as if he had been given a free hand to do as he wished. He was more confident than ever, he would never be caught for the murder of Stadtler nor any of the others.

He booted up his computer and logged on to the site for *New York Newsday,* to catch up on the ongoing investigation concerning the discovery of human remains on Long Island. Ten bodies, mostly prostitutes, had been found dumped on the south shore along Ocean Parkway. For more then a year police from Nassau and Suffolk counties had been combing the dunes and marshes, along the desolate ten mile stretch of the seaside parkway. They found more and more bodies which in turn brought up more and more questions.

The seemingly picturesque landscape was nothing more, than a beautiful graveyard with an ever increasing population. As the body count piled up the investigation received national attention on all of the television news outlets. As it seemed there might be a breakthrough in the case, it suddenly went cold with no conclusion in sight. As the investigation stagnated the media furor died down, there were, after all, tornados, tsunamis, and nuclear meltdowns to cover. Week after week crime scene detectives trod over and through the dune grass and marshes with cadaver dogs, and when they thought they had uncovered all that they, would another body popped up and the media blitz began anew.

There's more there than meets the eye gentlemen, Gant thought to himself, as he read the latest article entitled "Police Focusing on West Islip Man." His interest in whores aside, the man in question would turn out to be entirely innocent of committing anything more than being horny. He was cleared of any charges regarding the murders, nonetheless his life lay in ruins. Disgraced, his wife later left him and his children became estranged from him, and he fell into a deep depression.

Gant checked the current weather conditions in his home town of Watch Point, it was partly cloudy and eighty-one degrees with a fifty percent chance of showers. He logged off of *New York Newsday* to check the long range forecast for Buffalo, to compare the two when his secretary buzzed him on the land line.

Gant picked up the phone, "What's up Sherry?"

"Ken Marcanti on line one, Lenny," the secretary informed him.

Marcanti was one of Gant's friend's from home, the only one he really still kept in touch with. Now a very successful attorney Marcanti asked no questions regarding Gant's use of an alias. Gant had told him many years ago that he felt more independent when not using his real last name in business dealings. His father had created the business, Gant explained, and he didn't feel right riding the old man's coattails. He preferred to expand the business on his own terms, with no mention of the Gant name. Marcanti chided him that it was odd, but pushed no further. He suspected that the alias was used for different reasons, but cared not to know what they might be. He was interested only in partying with his buddy.

"Kenny," Gant answered.

"Philly, I mean Lenny," Marcanti's voice echoed as if in a tunnel as he rolled out the l's.

"How's everything, my man?" Gant asked.

"Same old, same old. A few dates here and there and still no ring. Just the way I like it," Marcanti laughed. "How about you, brother?"

"Nothing's changed since we last talked."

"You're still with that chick, the drug dealer?"

"She's a pharmaceutical rep, and yes I am."

"Dum, de dum dum," Marcanti hummed. "Do I hear wedding bells?"

"Don't jump to conclusions quite so fast my friend, but I won't rule it out." Quickly changing the subject Gant asked, "So what do I owe the honor of this call to?"

"Well my handsome friend, I'm hosting a blowout, a hoe down, get that one, a hoe down?"

"Very funny."

"The bash is in three weeks. You've got to come down for it!"

"Hmm," Gant murmured into the receiver.

"Don't hmm me, say 'yes' and be here. We'll hit the beach during the day and the babes at night. Don't say it's too long a commute, you can be here in a couple of hours, so I don't want to hear any half-assed excuses."

"I'm most probably in," Gant replied. "Let me check with the old lady to make sure it's kosher. Looking at the calendar I'm pretty sure she's out of town. I'll get back to you tonight."

"Excellent! Make it happen, it's gonna be an all out bash, pig roast, full bar, ladies…"

"I hear you, let me call her right now, I'll get back to you."

"Good enough, call me. Later!"

"Later, Ken."

Gant decided that the phone call from his friend was providence, a divine intervention on some cosmic level. He dialed his girlfriend as soon as he hung up with Marcanti.

"Hey, baby," she answered.

"How's your day going?"

"Taking it easy, just some calls is all. Why what's up?"

"Listen Lyd, are you out of town the week of June twenty-seventh? I think you are.

"Yeah, I'll be in Cleveland, Indianapolis, Chicago and on and on and on," Lydia Bergstrom replied sullenly.

"Such is the life of the jet setting business woman."

"Car driving you mean. It's getting old. I'm ready to settle down and become a librarian or something mellow like that," she laughed into the phone.

"All right then, I'm going to go down to Long Island to visit my Mom, some friends, maybe mix in a little business as well. Since you're gone I think I'll make a week of it, hit the beach, maybe do a little fishing too."

"Stop it! Stop it right now," she teased. "You'll be basking in the Sun on a white sand beach, while I'm carting samples around from doctor's office to doctor's office. It's bad enough I have to live with it, don't rub it in."

"Thanks Lyd, we need to plan a trip down there for the two of us. I guess it's time you met my mother."

"I've got three weeks of vacation. Name the date."

"We'll make one soon."

"I'm waiting."

"I hear you." He quickly changed the subject, "I'm going to make a couple of calls now, but I'll be home before dinner. Would you prefer I cook or pick something up?"

"I went shopping this morning and picked out two beautiful porterhouses. I bought some asparagus and baked potatoes too."

"You are fantastic! I'll call when I leave and you can fire up the grill."

"Done."

"I love you, Lyd."

"Me too! Can't wait to see you, Lenny!"

"Good then. Bye bye," he said ending the call.

Gant immediately dialed the number of a business associate on Long Island who worked out of MacArthur Airport in Ronkonkoma which was centrally located on the island. After a brief conversation Gant confirmed the man was interested in purchasing some nuts and bolts in bulk at a reduced price. The men agreed on the terms of the order and Gant cradled the phone once more. He looked out the window of his office into the expanse of green that spread out before him. *Life was indeed good*, he thought.

He picked up the phone and dialed another number, this time his mother's. He waited patiently knowing it would take some time for her to answer the call. On the seventh ring she picked up.

"Hello?" Mrs. Gant answered.

"Hey, Mom," Gant said.

"Philip? Is that you sweetheart?"

"Yes Mom, it is. How are you?'

"My arthritis is killing me, the blood pressure pills have me all woozy, and my varicose veins are bulging, but besides that I'm doing fine. How about you, dear?"

"I'm doing great Ma. Listen, I was thinking I'd like to come for a visit in a few weeks. You'll be around right?"

"Where am I running off to dear?"
"One never knows with a spry one like you, Ma."
"Cut the crap! When are you coming? I'll make sure my calendar's clear."
"I'll be home by June twenty-seventh or eighth at the latest."
"Oh! That's great honey! How long will you be staying?"
"At least a week, but maybe longer, I'll have to play it by ear."
"Are you bringing the girl you told me about?"
"No, not yet, Ma. Maybe in August. We'll see," he replied while thinking, *No, I'm bringing another girl.*
"If I see any of your friends I'll let them know you're coming."
"Thanks, Mom. I'm going to wrap up work for the day and get back home. I'll be in touch."
"I love you, Phillip."
"I love you, Mom," he replied and then hung up.

Gant wished his secretary a good evening and walked out of his office in the Crosby Building not far from police headquarters. He got into his Volvo and drove northeast toward his home in Amherst. He left before rush hour, which was not much more congested than at any other time in Buffalo, and made the seven mile journey in fifteen minutes.

* * * *

Pulling into the paved stone driveway of Two Hundred Lebrun Road he parked before the mansion he called home and surveyed his domain before making his way to the front door. Built in 1915, the massive center hall colonial boasted seven bedrooms, five full baths, two wood burning fireplaces with boxes big enough for a grown man to stand in, an in ground pool, a tennis court and a private guest cottage located toward the back of its one and a half acres. Located in one of the most historic and prestigious neighborhoods of suburban Buffalo, Gant's oversized house sometimes overwhelmed him. That was part of the reason he'd asked his girlfriend, Lydia Bergstrom, to move in with him.

When he entered the kitchen she had her back to him her curly brown hair falling over her shoulders. Standing in front of a burgundy streaked, gray granite counter, she was busy rubbing herbs and seasonings onto the steaks she'd purchased that morning. She was wearing a snug, silk bathrobe that barely covered her heart-shaped rear end. Sneaking up behind her he goosed her behind and she spun around startled.

"Oh! You shit, you scared the hell out of me!" she shouted playfully.
"Wearing that getup, you're lucky that's all I did to you," Gant said.

She rinsed her hands and offered him a glass of pinot noir which he gratefully accepted.

"The baked potatoes are in the oven, the asparagus will only be a few minutes, so we can wait to turn them on. The steaks will be eight minutes or so. I'll throw them on whenever you want," she told him.

"I think you've got what I really want," he replied.
"I was hoping you'd say that, Lenny," she said, opening her robe to him.

Deciding dinner could wait, he caressed one of her breasts tenderly for a moment and then took her in his arms and picked her up. Cradling her in his arms like a groom carrying his bride over the threshold he whisked her into the living room where he gently laid her down on the couch. They knew how to please one another; it was the real reason he had asked her to move in with him.

Chapter Eight

Gant was once more in the basement of his home away from home, at Seven Mile Strip Road in Orchard Park, New York. He'd purchased the run down farmhouse and its thirty-three plus acres, for a little over three hundred and fifty thousand dollars in the late nineties, when he'd decided he was in need of more room as well as some peace and quiet with which to pursue his interests.

Built in 1909, the white clapboard farmhouse stood upon a disused apple orchard, its rickety wrap around porch and its vintage rockers, were the only welcoming feature in the otherwise stark structure. Sometimes after a long session in the basement or up in the attic, Gant would sit in one of the rocking chairs sipping a hot cup of coffee or a short tumbler of bourbon depending on his mood and the season. Gant had no neighbors remotely within earshot and knew nobody within Orchard Park or the surrounding environs. Only sixteen miles, and a comfortable twenty-five minutes from the house Gant shared with Lydia Bergstrom, the farmhouse may have well as been in Iowa. Nobody, save Gant, knew about the dilapidated property, nor was anyone aware of his interests in South America.

As the Stadtler mask was in need of time to dry and cure, Gant decided it was high time for a road trip. His anticipation for the completion of the mask approached the type of expectancy a child would have for Christmas morning. He badly wanted to view the finished project and was prepared to make notes regarding his creation's quality, both positive and negative. To be sure, he became increasingly impressed with his work with each and every procedure. Nonetheless, he knew there was always room for improvement, and ever the perfectionist, he was highly critical of his work.

When first viewing new creations Gant was prepared with a legal pad on which he scribbled copious notes and skillfully sketched drawings of the subject in question. Knowing he had a few weeks of waiting ahead of him, he tore himself away from the mask and got ready to leave. The mask would be ready and waiting for him when he returned.

His desire to remain at home with Lydia in Amherst or by himself in Orchard Park was strong, but he had a pressing urge to leave as well. Deep in his heart he knew it was time to set Stadtler's remains free, to put her to rest. Furthermore, it was good policy to get rid of any evidence as soon as possible. Gant toured the house making certain all of the doors and windows were closed and locked, with the exception of the basement door and then he went out to the garage.

Gant pulled the redesigned 2008 Ford Econoline van out of the detached garage beside the farmhouse and backed it up to the rear door that accessed the basement. Windowless except for the front windshield and the driver and passenger front seats, the steel gray van was nondescript, thousands of contractors, plumbers, electricians and other tradesmen drove similar vehicles in New York State alone. He pulled the back doors open and disappeared down the steps into the basement. Thirty seconds later he emerged with a large plastic ice tote, which measured four feet by three feet at its base. Its sides were two and a half feet high, it was well suited to contain fluids and large enough for his cargo. He slid the tote into the back of the van and headed back down into the basement.

He opened the freezer, smoky tendrils of frozen air wisped upwards to meet his face. He peered into the freezer and when the frosty mist had cleared a little he saw the heavy duty garbage bag which contained Patricia Stadtler's remains. With both hands he hefted the bag out from the freezer and carefully laid it at his feet. He shut the freezer door and then clutched the bag in both hands. Using his legs he crouched down and lifted the bag until it was at a comfortable height, about thigh-high, for him to carry to the waiting van. Quickly walking sure-footed, Gant shuffled up the stairs to the van without stopping. With a grunt and a sigh he dropped her into the ice tote with a thud. He then secured the tote with bungee cords to keep it from sliding and slammed the rear doors shut. He locked the basement door, started the van's ignition and cranked the air conditioning to high.

Leaving at noon he planned on arriving at his chosen site between eight and nine that night, around the time darkness would fall. He allotted an hour for dinner although it would take less time. Before starting out on the four hundred and thirty mile trip ahead of him Gant went through the CD organizer in the passenger seat. In alphabetical order by artist, the CD case held fifty of Gant's favorite albums, a mix of classical composers, progressive rockers, and classic rock. Past Bach, The Beatles, and Beethoven, he eyed David Bowie's *Scary Monster's (and Super Creeps)*. He took the CD from its case and placed it into the player in the dashboard. With a final look over his shoulder he slowly meandered down the dirt road that led to the farmhouse and headed toward Saratoga Road. By the time Gant was travelling east on I-90 the album's fourth song *Ashes to Ashes* came on. One of his favorites he turned the volume way up and sang along with the androgynous looking singer of fame.

* * * *

Gant had never even considered flying to Long Island with Stadtler's remains, he'd done it twice before and found it to be an incredibly difficult as well as nauseating experience. His first dump vehicle had been an old Chevy van with shitty air conditioning. Often when he arrived at his chosen dump site the corpse was sometimes thawed, the smells associated with death and decay had already begun to seep out. The bed of the van went slick and oily as fluids defrosted and dripped onto it. He'd learned early on to have the body in a waterproof container, hence the ice tote, as it solved the bodily fluid problem. One fateful day, the old van failed to start when Gant was desperate to rid himself of a body. Seeking an alternative dump method, and as money was no object, he decided to fly the remains of a teenage boy to one of his favored sites on the island.

On that dreadful trip he'd landed at one o'clock in the afternoon, on a balmy day in mid-June on Long Island. Waiting for a rental car at Macarthur Airport was enough for him to regret flying.

Then there was the awkward proposition of transferring the tote containing the thawing boy from the Cessna to the rental car, a 2002 Dodge minivan. He had to wait until nightfall to make the switch under the cover of darkness. It was nearly nine o'clock at night before he could safely make the switch. The boy's remains had been sitting in the plane for eight hours, more than enough time to thaw completely in the sweltering sun. When Gant opened the plane's door to retrieve the tote, the fetid stench of rotting meat slapped him in the face. He quickly shut the door against the ghastly stink. For a moment he actually wondered to himself if what he was doing was wrong. After briefly evaluating his conscience his survival instincts kicked in, right or wrong, he couldn't get caught with the corpse of a sixteen-year-old boy. He took a deep breath and pulled open the door again. Holding his breath he seized the ice tote, its grisly contents sloshed around in a stew of muscle, intestine and blood as he moved it. He placed the tote in the back of the mini van, which he'd backed up to the plane and slammed the gate down in disgust. As time was short he jumped into the mini van, rolled down the windows and took off for his chosen site. The only upside was the airport was only a half an hour's drive from the site. Gant made the dump and then stopped at a roadside tobacconist on Sunrise Highway. Not a smoker, but knowing the finer brands, he bought a Dunhill cigar with which to fumigate the mini van. He lit the cigar, rolled up the windows and fogged the minivan.

If the rental agency questioned the smoke, well fuck them, he reasoned. *Better smoke than corpse*. He was prepared to pay for any smoke damage. He got out of the Dodge and let the thick, blue smoke circulate and seep into the fabric of the seats. He then drove to a roadside convenience store where he purchased a can of Lysol which he emptied into the mini van and then drove to his mother's house with the windows down.

Upon arriving safely at his mother's home, he promised himself he would never fly a body out again. The moral question of his devious interests never again entered his mind. He thought about the collection, he was after all a collector, much like an art collector, he reasoned. He provided life to many while taking only one, he justified his motives. With any fears of wrongdoing alleviated he climbed up the front steps to his mother's house and walked in the door. He found her seated in the den on the couch dozing off to a *Lifetime* movie. He gave her a hug and kiss.

Only on one other occasion Gant brought a body aboard the plane. It was two years after his first harrowing experience flying the dead; and his Chevy van had died of old age. He had a corpse in the freezer that to be disposed of to make room for a newcomer, he was getting the itch for new blood. Calling the control tower he said he'd had an unexpected call from a friend in Ithaca, who needed immediate service back to Buffalo, it was nine thirty at night. Nobody would ask why, but he'd say the friend's daughter took ill he needed to get home as soon as possible. The tower confirmed he could fly into Ithaca Regional Airport, an unfamiliar airport where he knew nobody and would certainly be treated as only another pilot. Nonetheless, Gant agreed as he knew upon reaching Ithaca Regional, he would have nothing incriminating on board anyway.

The ice tote, with the remains of a young woman, barely fitted into the back seat of the Volvo as he moved the passenger seat all the way forward. He threw a beach towel over the top of the tote, in case a busy body in a high vehicle pulled up beside him. He placed a beach chair in the seat beside it for good measure. Fortunately for Gant, this occurred before nine-eleven, there was no guard stationed at all, it would be years before Mick the security guard came on the scene. He simply drove through the unmanned gate and backed up to his plane. He loaded the tote onto the Cessna and within twenty minutes he was airborne. With more than one hundred and forty miles between Buffalo and Ithaca, the vast majority of it rural if not downright forest, Gant had plenty of territory to work with.

Flying at five thousand feet Gant waited until the last twinkling lights of civilization had blinked out and there was only darkness below him. According to his instruments he began to fly over Seneca Lake. He decreased his speed to a minimum, put the plane on autopilot and shot up from his seat knowing he would pass over the lake within five minutes. He slid the ice tote next to the door of the plane and then unlatched the door, a very risky move in flight. He pushed the door outward as the drag of the headwind pushed it closed once more. Settling the ice tote at the foot of the door he shoved it forward with all of his might until the door crept open and the tote began to inch its way out. After two minutes of pushing and angling the tote this way and that the weight of the frozen young woman won out and gravity took over. Like a stone, the tote fell from the plane. As the tote tumbled through the sky the corpse fell out of it and plunged into the lake some twenty seconds later. It took the tote a few seconds longer to hit the water about a half a mile away from the body.

Gant remembered reading about the discovery of a waterlogged body in Seneca Lake a week or so later. According to the *Buffalo News* the corpse was visually unidentifiable as most of the skin on the victim had sloughed off as the result of being in the water for a prolonged amount of time.

That or it was blasted off by the impact, Gant thought. The newspaper went on to report that the victim was female, and suffered numerous broken bones, lacerations, and gashes. *Not all from the tumble*, he knew thinking his neat incisions were most probably ragged gashes of torn flesh by that time. The face being shorn off was to be expected, by the elements as well as predatory fish. The paper made no comment on any missing organs he noticed. He assumed the authorities were keeping it to themselves for the time being. Gant put the paper aside and reflected that while being extremely efficient in terms of time, the in flight dump was foolhardy and risky to say the least. Knowing with one slip of the hand or one mass of turbulent air,he could have easily joined the young woman in Seneca Lake, and he wouldn't have looked any better than she did. He swore to himself then, from this point onward any dumping would be a driving operation.

* * * *

It was right after the airborne dump that Gant purchased the Econoline he was now driving south on Interstate Eighty-One. Unlike most work van's his was equipped with a Blaupunkt Toronto 410 BT audio system as well as an upgraded air conditioning system that approached the quality of a refrigerated Boar's Head truck. When he slid the cargo door behind him shut he was able to drive comfortably in a T-shirt while his freight, on this run Stadtler, remained frigid if not frozen. Cruising along at fifty-five miles per hour throughout New York and Pennsylvania he was careful to obey the speed limit. He enjoyed the ride as he relaxed and listened to his music which was soothing and tranquil, it eased his mind. Most importantly it was always best to be prepared and the van kept him ready for anything.

Four hours after leaving Orchard Park he found himself on the outskirts of Scranton, it was shortly after five o'clock and he was hungry. He pulled the van into the parking lot of the Rider Diner, which was locally famous for its hot roast beef sandwich and mashed potatoes smothered in a rich, brown gravy. He'd eaten there once before and had liked it very much. He walked inside and waited patiently at the hostess station.

Glancing around the diner his eyes were drawn to the red, faux leather bar stools at the counter. Of course the upholstered booths matched the stools. He was admiring the vintage 1950's décor and the juke box in the corner of the place when a woman walked through the double doors of the kitchen and apprised him with a smile.

Languid and graceful the blonde haired woman was fit and trim as the muscles of her lean biceps suggested. Her knee length, rose-colored dress revealed the shapely legs of an athlete. In her late twenties, her face was exquisitely beautiful; a strong jaw line, warm brown eyes, a straight nose and full lips which were painted a ruby red that nearly matched the faux leather of the stool and booth cushions.

She walked up to the hostess station, Gant was about five feet away from her. He breathed in deeply attempting to attain her scent, but was unable to do so as the diner smelled mostly of french fries, coffee, and their famous roast beef. He stared at her as she wrote something on a note pad atop the lectern that was her workspace and glanced up at him. She could feel his eyes upon her, but seemed to like it.

At last she looked him straight in the eye. "Hi there," she said. "Only you tonight?"

"Unless you'd like to join me, Tammy," replied Gant looking at the woman's name tag.

"Oh, my," she blushed and then added, "It would be nice, but I don't think my boss would approve."

"Maybe another time perhaps," he suggested.

"The boss is also my husband, but thanks for the offer. You made my day."

"I'm sorry should have figured you were already spoken for as pretty as you are."

Blushing crimson again she laughed nervously and looked at him out of the corner of her eye. "Where are you from, mister?"

"I'm from upstate New York," he replied knowing that if she were to look at his van she would see the New York plates on it. "Not far from Niagara."

"Oh, I love the falls!" she gushed. "My parents took me there when I was little, me and my older sister."

"Tammy!" came a gruff voice from within the kitchen as the door cracked open a bit and a pot-bellied man in black and white checkered pants and a red, grease stained apron leaned out.

She spun around like a child caught with her hand in the cookie jar.

"Less gabbing, sweetheart! Give the man a menu for God's sake," the cook ordered her before slipping back into the kitchen.

She turned back toward Gant, rolled her big, brown eyes and held out her hand for him to follow him. "A stool or a booth, its' still on the early side. I could squeeze you into a booth before the dinner rush."

"I'll take a menu and stand here for a minute, I've got to order to go." He had to keep the engine running and the body as cool as possible. He'd wasted enough time with small talk already.

She handed him a menu and tapped her fingernails, also ruby colored with white tips, on the top of the lectern and then the phone rang. She answered the phone and began to jot down a takeout order while Gant perused the menu. She handed him the specials list as she wrote. She finished with the order and then hung up.

"Anything look good to you…?"

"Mike," he offered.

"Well?"

"We've already been through that. What I want doesn't appear on the menu."

She rolled her eyes again, this time at Gant.

"That's the boss I suppose," he said.

"Yep, that's my darling."

"He's hardly your better half," Gant couldn't stop himself from saying. "Kind of on the old side too, I might add."

"You know the old story, young girl falls for older man with some money," she replied.

"That's a shame, you've got a lot of potential," Gant said.

Unsure what he meant and a little put off she replied. "Really, I was flattered the first time, but I do have work to do, Mike."

"Very well, then. I can't go wrong with the hot roast beef with mashed potatoes and gravy, can I?"

"That's a home run every time."

"How long do you think?" he asked.

"About five minutes," she told him.

"Thanks Tammy, I'll pay you now."

The hostess rang up the check and Gant handed her cash. When she attempted to give him change he waved it off leaving her with a large tip. He smiled at her and she at him.

"I'll be back," Gant said and turned toward the door to leave.

She watched him as he went. There was something strange about him she felt. Strange, but beautiful she thought as she watched him climb into the Econoline. She didn't expect him to leave, but he started up the engine. The hostess held up putting in the order thinking that Gant had decided against the roast beef and had decided to go elsewhere. After a couple of minutes when the van just sat there idling she stepped into the kitchen and put it through.

Five minutes later Gant was about to shut off the engine and go inside to get his dinner when the pretty hostess came through the front door with a medium sized brown bag in her hands. She approached the van with a purpose that Gant found appealing. He watched intently as the cleavage of her perky breasts jiggled atop the low cut dress.

When the hostess stepped up beside the van's window Gant rolled it down. "Now this is real service. Thank you very much, Tammy."

She handed over the bag and leaned in close to him putting her hands on top of the door making sure to give him an eyeful of her breasts and said, "You're too damn charming. I had to speak to you again."

Outside of the aromas of the diner Gant could smell the cigarettes on her breath, his nose wrinkled in disgust.

"I gave you real silver ware, not the plastic stuff. You seem like a man who enjoys the finer things in life. I threw in a slice of apple pie from me, I hope you like it." A mixture of dying lung and nicotine blasted Gant's sensitive nostrils.

"You are too good to be true," Gant said with real conviction cocking his head away from her upturned face.

"And there's something at the bottom that maybe you'll use later, I hope."

Tiring of small talk with the hostess, she was now reduced to that in his eyes, Gant put the van into reverse and thanked her once more before backing out of his spot. He drove through side streets for a few minutes disgusted with his own poor judgment.

Tammy the hostess being a smoker was a huge disappointment for him. He couldn't fathom how someone so beautiful and so healthy looking could be abusing their body in such a horrendous way, but she was. She was most certainly not his type after all. She was not worthy of his attentions. There was no way he would ever consider harvesting her organs for others in need of help. At least he saw the truth of her before acting. Ironically, smoking probably saved the life of the unsuspecting hostess, at least for the time being.

After regaining his appetite he pulled into the drive through of a Dunkin' Donuts and ordered an iced coffee and then backed into a space to eat his dinner. The hot roast beef sandwich was now merely lukewarm, but just as delicious as he remembered it being. Eating at a leisurely pace Gant devoured his meal while watching the foot traffic in and out of the busy store. Finishing the roast beef and mashed potatoes he reached into the bag for the apple pie. He tasted the pie and grimaced, preserved apples, not fresh. He put the pie on the passenger side seat.

Remembering Tammy's surprise he reached into the bottom of the bag and withdrew a folded napkin. On the napkin was scribbled the hostess' cell phone number as well as an imprint of her lips in that rich, ruby lipstick. Initially, Gant was aroused, but then repulsed. He fought the urge to vomit. His evaluation of the hostess had been severely skewed by her outward beauty. "Good God! What a slut!" he said to himself out loud. He quickly realized that any married woman willing to give her phone number to a total stranger after a two minute conversation was most certainly a whore. *She was in all probability riddled with venereal diseases* he thought. Her internal organs were sure to be a disaster which he would never provide to anyone else.

Disappointed in his own failure to recognize her for what she was immediately Gant again felt nauseous. The fact that he let his lust overcome his morals appalled him. He crumpled the napkin up, grabbed the pie and shoved them both into the brown paper bag. Alarmed that he could have such a serious lapse in judgment, he slid out of the van and walked over to the dumpster behind the doughnut shop and tossed the bag into it. Then he leaned into the bushes beside the dumpster and threw up. Gant walked back to the van and reached for a bottle of water in the center console. He rinsed out his mouth, spat on the black top and got back in. Within four minutes he was heading south away from Scranton on I-81.

With a minimum of three hours of driving ahead of him he needed to get his head straight. Classical music worked best for him. He selected Vivaldi's *Four Seasons* and turned it up loud. The violin concertos did the job wonderfully. Within minutes he was whisked away back into his own private world where everything made perfect sense. Three hours and several CD's later, he had crossed the George Washington and Throg's Neck bridges, and found himself motoring along on the Cross Island Parkway in Queens. His old stomping grounds beckoned, he would shortly be on the Southern State Parkway in Nassau County and then on to Suffolk where he would lay Stadtler to rest as gently as he was able.

As Gant passed the county line around Linden Street in Massapequa he switched the Blaupunkt from CD to radio mode and tuned into WBAB, a local classic rock station in West Babylon. The station played the same songs over and over, but that was the norm for the industry. WBAB did broadcast a fair amount of Pink Floyd which happened to be his favorite band, but again the same five or six songs again and again, nothing ever obscure or cloudy. He tuned in to the station mainly because he was not yet positive where he would discard his friend in the back of the van, and was curious to see what the police were up to out on Ocean Parkway. WBAB was sure to have the most recent developments in the so called "Long Island Ripper" case as most of the rest of the country had come to know it.

* * * *

Gant had dumped bodies on the Ocean Parkway before, five times as a matter of fact. It was a most convenient site as the lonely stretch of oceanfront was largely devoid of people particularly in the winter; which was when he'd made his drops there. With the exception of the tiny beach communities of West Gilgo Beach and Gilgo Beach and the scant populations of Oak and Captree Islands, the barrier beach was quiet, peaceful and devoid of people. City dwellers would call it bleak and lonesome. Besides being desolate the picturesque parkway was bordered by salt marshes and bays, both salt and brackish, to its north not twenty feet from the roadway. The salt air alone was suited to accelerating the decomposition of flesh and bone. There were also a good many hawks, ospreys, gulls, crows and raccoons that would not pass up a free meal.

Gant felt the Ocean Parkway was a nice place to be laid to rest. Despite the extreme cold, and windy winters as well as the hot, humid summers the narrow spit of sand stretching fifteen and a half miles from Jones Beach in Nassau County to Captree in Suffolf County was paradise as far as he was concerned. The Atlantic Ocean and the Great South Bay less than seventy feet from one another at many points seemed like heaven to him. When he died he thought he wouldn't mind being left somewhere out there, the waves crashing on the shore as terns flitted over the bay.

As the body count grew Gant couldn't help but wonder how many other murderers used the parkway to dispose of corpses. It was more than one he felt, probably two or three others. Deep down, he believed the parkway had been used as a disposal site for years, like seventy at least. He was pretty sure the mob had used it for dumps as early as the 1930's, but had no proof of it, only childhood stories passed down from generation to generation in his hometown. He was completely sure of one thing though, the police had failed to uncover a single corpse he'd left there. All five of his victims lay within feet of one another, on the north side of the parkway. His bodies were in a secluded salt marsh three miles west of Hemlock Cove. The local crabs assisted with the disposal process quite nicely. Any discovery of bones or bone fragments would have been all over the media.

Gant knew it was a long shot to leave Stadtler on the parkway. First of all, it was high summer, the parkway was easily seeing its most traffic as beachgoers flocked to Jones, Tobay, West Gilgo, Gilgo, Cedar, and Overlook beaches for a respite from the scorching New York summer, not that he would ever be crazy enough to dump a body in daylight. Even at night it would be a risky proposition as a beefed up police force patrolled the parkway. State park police as well as state troopers cruised the roadway looking for speeders and drunks. Many nights there was a concert at the Jones Beach amphitheater, Gant had been to many there himself. He remembered the first "real" show he'd ever seen it was The Kinks at Jones Beach. On a concert night the parkway was crawling with cops. Secondly, there was the matter of the ongoing investigation. He felt certain his hope to return to the parkway was a pipe dream, it would surely be too hot to go there.

* * * *

His instincts were verified by a smoky voiced disc jockey after *Pour Some Sugar on Me* by Def Leppard finally died away. *Thank God for small favors*, Gant thought to himself, he couldn't stand hair bands. With perfect timing she informed listeners, "Thanks for rockin with me tonight Long Island. This is Bella updating you on the latest about the Gilgo Beach Killer."

Gant's eyebrows rose a bit. *They were now calling the killer the Gilgo Beach Killer,* he found it interesting and turned the volume up. "As the police officers being looked at for the murders have been cleared, Suffolk PD searched eleven spots of interest in and around Captree. These highly specific spots were originally spotted by an F.B.I. fly over in April. As of this evening no new remains have been found. To date, ten sets of human remains have been found, eight in Suffolk and two in Nassau. Police will resume the search tomorrow morning."

That was enough to jolt Gant out of any fantasy he had of visiting the Ocean Parkway. He was not the kind of killer who killed for the thrill of pulling one over on the authorities. He was no daredevil begging to be caught. He killed because he liked what he reaped from his victims. He was a Cheerful Reaper, of sorts, and intended to keep killing until the desire left him. As such he was very careful. With the investigation heating up once again there would be Suffolk and Nassau cops on the parkway in addition to the ever present state park police and troopers.

He turned the sound system off to consider his options, while listening to the hum of the air conditioner. It would have to be the Pine Barrens, a truly desolate place of haunting beauty, he decided. Gant continued east on the Southern State Parkway until he reached the Sagtikos State Parkway which he took south to Sunrise Highway. Heading much farther east then he had hoped he motored down Sunrise Highway formulating his plan. From here on out it would be silence in respect for the dead woman in the back of his van.

The Long Island Central Pine Barrens was an immense area of protected pines encompassing more than a hundred thousand acres of eastern central Long Island. The area was effectively the island's last remaining wilderness as well as its largest. Besides being home to a vast variety of wildlife including deer, foxes, rabbits, raccoons, opossums, ospreys, hawks, loons, snakes, and turtles, the preserve hosted a wide array of rare flora such as bladderworts, huckleberry, and sheep laurel. Some of the only Dwarf Pine Plains anywhere in the world grew there. The barrens over-laid and recharged an aquifer for all of Long Island's drinking water. Two of the four largest rivers on the island, the Peconic and Carmans Rivers as well as their watersheds were located there. With its coastal plain ponds, bogs, marshes, swamps and streams hidden by lush complexes of pitch pine and oak communities, the pine barrens was a naturalist's dream. It was also a fine place to dump a body.

Gant was nearly to his destination when he saw the sign for Manorville. He hadn't thought about the Manorville murders in years and it took him back in time. In 2003 the Suffolk County police were investigating whether the same killer was responsible for the murders of two women, whose mutilated bodies were found in the same wooded area of Manorvillle, the previous murder had occurred in 2000. Going back further the authorities uncovered a third mutilated corpse, this one near Hempstead Lake State Park in 1997. The heads and hands of the victims were severed. The women were the same race and around the same age and height. Gant was absolutely innocent of these murders. What intrigued him, was the body of a woman found in 2003 was positively identified by DNA testing, as being that of Jaime Tate. That in itself was no big deal. The fact that Tate's head and hands were found eight years later, on the Ocean Parkway interested him very much. The two dump sites were forty miles apart, he found that curious. Gant considered himself to be supremely logical, especially when it came to his dark hobby. He couldn't figure out why anyone would go to the trouble of dumping their victims in two, or maybe even more, different locations. He shook his head in confusion and then dismissed the method as being bush league. Then again whoever had been butchering the girls in central Long Island had not yet been caught, so maybe there was more there than met the eye. After careful consideration Gant saw little upside to dismemberment. Interred properly, he believed, a corpse should never be found, the need to avoid identification should not be an issue. He was confident he'd tallied many more kills and surely for a much greater good.

Gant had visited the Pine Barrens to dispose of his handwork three times prior to this trip. He had his spot staked out well in advance, actually years in advance, as he had decided upon it some four years earlier when he'd made his first trip out there. The salt marsh vegetation beyond the Flanders Bay wetlands was his chosen site. It was difficult to get to. He would have to do some serious humping with the corpse, but it was worth the peace of mind it afforded. Four freshwater tributaries flowed through the marsh complex into Flanders Bay. He chose the dense underbrush bordering the coarse sand banks of Goose Creek as his victim's final resting spot.

With no oncoming traffic before him Gant glanced in his rearview mirror and was happy to see nothing but blackness, he was alone on Sunrise Highway. He switched off his lights and slowed to ten miles an hour as he approached the turn-off to the service road he had sought out. Making the hard right turn onto the unmarked road, which was really little more than a path, he slowly drove south toward his destination. A half a mile before the path was swallowed up by the salt marsh vegetation, he pulled into a shallow ravine and parked the van obscuring it from anyone who might happen by, although it was most unlikely to happen.

Moving quickly Gant affixed a miner's hat atop his head and switched the bulb on. Timing was everything he knew. He wanted to get to his spot and back to the van within thirty minutes at most, hopefully less. The great advantage of Ocean Parkway was its relative convenience. His dump sites there were less than fifty feet from the roadway. Dumping in the Pine Barrens, on the other hand, was arduous work, but worthwhile in the long run. Not a single body, with the exception of the

Manorville murders, was ever pulled from the barrens and Gant suspected there were plenty of remains lying around.

He opened the rear doors of the van and slid the ice tote toward himself. Touching the amorphous shape within the garbage bag he ascertained that Stadtler had thawed a lot despite the air conditioning. Fortunately, she was not yet at the stage when her arms and legs would swing freely, or her intestines would slide around within the bag. She was still one pretty solid chunk of meat, but he would have to hurry. Gant slid the tote onto its side, the bag slipped into his waiting arms. He gripped the bag carefully with both hands and gained a firm purchase without ripping it. He took a deep breath and hefted Stadtler over his right shoulder. He walked with his head angled toward the ground into the beach grass.

Trudging through the grass Gant thought to himself that it might have been nice to be armed while disposing of the body, in case an interloper were to intrude upon his privacy. He dismissed the thought almost immediately after it popped into his head. His little Beretta was locked in a safe at the farm house. He only took it when dealing with the organ traffickers, whom he did not trust in the least. He'd never been seen before, a testament to his careful ways. He always rid himself of his victim's corpses under the cover of darkness. There was slim to no chance that anyone would be out here in the barrens in broad day light, much less the middle of the night. Besides, if anyone was to stumble upon him he would simply run for it, he was fleet of foot and positive he could make it back to the van before he could be apprehended. Gant had never killed in anger or as an act of passion. He had also never killed for self-preservation or to elude capture. He killed only to feed his own insatiable hunger and to provide a means to give life to others. *Small sacrifices are acceptable if they serve the greater good.*

It took Gant eleven minutes to walk the two-thirds of a mile to the chosen location. Switching shoulders four times along the way, he trudged through shallow ponds, over low dunes, and through thick underbrush before he came to the sandy, pebbly banks of the creek. Exhausted and drenched with sweat he laid the corpse into the creek with a splash. He untied the top of the bag and took a glance inside, at the remains of Patricia Stadtler one last time. He blessed himself, said a quick prayer and thanked her for her donation. He kissed the tips of his fingers and placed them atop the crown of her skinned head and then bid her farewell.

With Stadtler back on his shoulder Gant waded out into a nearby marsh pond, stepping carefully so as to not turn an ankle on the rocks and depressions on the bottom. A twisted ankle would prolong his return trip and seriously complicate the situation. About sixty yards into the pond he was thigh deep in mossy, brackish water. He slipped the bag off of his shoulder and into the murky pond. Holding the open top of the bag with his left hand he scoured the bottom for sizeable stones with his right. Stone after stone, he loaded the bag. After five minutes he had weighed Stadtler down enough so that she sank to the bottom on her own. Then, with a tear in his eye, he left her.

Chapter Nine

"I'm young enough, and I'm fit," Hamilton said. "Why not me?"

"There's no question of your fitness or age, it's a bad idea, and besides Salerno will never go for it anyway," Wilder replied in between bites of waffle.

The two detectives sat at a diner discussing what their next move would be, it was nearly eleven on Friday night. The profiler had left them with more questions than answers, so the pair were frustrated and confused. A new strategy was in order, but what the new strategy was eluded them.

Hamilton picked a strawberry from her fruit cup, popped it into her mouth and slowly chewed. After a moment she said, "Listen Dan, we're not getting anywhere at all with this case."

"Or the other missing person's cases for that matter," he added, while slicing into a sausage.

"Exactly! It can't hurt to troll the areas where the disappearances occurred, you know that old axiom about the killer always returning to the scene of the crime and all."

"Not the smart ones."

"It's worth a shot, we're turning up shit as it is. The Feds were useless."

"Confusing's more like it. Instead of narrowing the focus he blew it wide open. For God's sake. The man had me wondering if my own grandmother wasn't some type of mass murderer. She was very austere you know," Wilder smiled having never met his grandmother face to face.

"So what's there to lose then?"

"Maybe you?"

"No, no way. I can handle myself just fine. This creep would rue the day he tried to grab me. Balls," she made a squishing sound as she squeezed her hand into a fist, "right off."

Wilder rolled his eyes and shoveled a heaped forkful of hash browns into his mouth. After swallowing he said, "Come on Marguerite, you know that plain clothes cops have roamed those areas before with nothing to show for it."

"All guys, no women though. We obviously don't have any youngish boys available, so that leaves a woman, and I'm the best-prepared for it."

"That Donaldson guy just out of the academy looks pretty damn young, maybe..."

"I could kick his ass," she replied without letting him finish.

"Probably so," he agreed.

"And Salerno doesn't have to know about it anyway."

Wilder held up his hand. "If you think I'm gonna let you use yourself as bait for this nut, you're a nut too!"

"Dan, listen. We'll be in radio contact, you'll be in the car, never more than a mile away from me. I'll be armed, this guy will never know what hit him. Besides, if it's like you say, a waste of time then you have nothing to worry about."

"What if I refuse?"

"I'll do it alone."

"I could report you to Salerno, get you taken off of the case entirely," Wilder bluffed.

Hamilton smiled at him and then burst out laughing. "You'd never do that to me Dan. I can't believe you're trying to bullshit me, I know you too well."

"All right, all right, uncle, uncle," Wilder relented. "What's our story then?"

"Canvassing the prior scenes, nothing more and nothing less. It's simple and it's actually the truth."

"Yeah, we're only leaving out the part where you're legging it out there alone, while I sit in the car."

"Can't risk being made. No offense my friend, but you scream 'cop' from head to toe," she ribbed him.

"Sure enough," he grinned taking a long sip of his egg cream. "So, what's the plan then?"

"We'll start with Stadtler first, she being the most recent. Then we'll backtrack to Cory Nichols, Andrew Spahn, Elizabeth McPherson, in that order."

"So, we start at Woodlawn Beach and then on to Riverside, and Delaware for the boys. McPherson went missing first. It's thought she disappeared along either Red Jacket Parkway or McKinley Parkway, both of which connect Cazenovia Park and South Park. Lot of running, will you hold up?"

"I've always wanted to run a marathon. This is my chance to train for it."

"Better you than me sweetheart."

"That's pretty obvious," she chided him.

* * * *

At eight-thirty the following evening, Wilder found himself reading the *Buffalo News* in the air conditioned comfort of the unmarked Crown Vic, while Hamilton jogged the trail upon which Stadtler had been abducted. Equipped with wireless microphones and earpieces loaned to them from a surveillance technician, the two were in constant contact. Parked behind a gray Subaru in the parking lot, Wilder felt a little like a perv having a one-sided session of phone sex as Hamilton's rapid, shallow breathing made him uncomfortable at first. After a few minutes he got more used to it and the feeling of guilt subsided.

"See anybody that looks good?" he asked her.

"You'll know...as soon as I do," Hamilton panted.

Capable of maintaining a considerably faster speed, Hamilton held back a bit. Intent on conserving her strength while also leading any would-be attackers to believe that she was fit, yet still attainable quarry, she jogged along the mile long stretch of sandy Lake Erie beach front at a leisurely pace. Any faster, she felt, would scare off any prospective perpetrators. Wearing reflective Nike cross trainers, lime-green running shorts, and a hot pink tee-shirt with a florescent runner's vest over it, she could not be missed, she was like a homing beacon in the gathering gloom as twilight gave way to darkness.

"I'm just gonna shut up for the time being then," he said.

"Good idea," she agreed.

"Just be careful, okay?"

"Always."

Sweat dripped from the elbows of Hamilton's pumping arms and poured down her thighs as she emerged from a thick stand of oaks and began her third circuit of the trail thirty-five minutes later. An owl off to the right startled her a little, as it commenced its nightly vigil searching the ground for mice. With a crescent Moon low on the horizon she turned her attention back to the trail. Once again she was on the lake side of the woods, distant lights twinkled warmly off of the water. Her first lap through she noticed a single jogger besides herself and a pair of cyclists, apparently people were taking the latest abduction very seriously. During her second lap through there was nobody exercising, only a man seated at a bench staring at the rippling water before him. She ran within ten feet of him drinking in his attire, build and features. This time through the same man took a good, long look at Hamilton. As she jogged closer he stood up, her heart wavered in her chest.

"Dan, got a guy, too dark now. Saw him earlier, mid-forties, in good shape. Eighty feet away. Be ready," she whispered into her mic.

"Keep your distance Marguerite," Wilder advised.

"Yep."

She jogged on, the distance between the man and herself shrank, fifty feet, forty feet, thirty feet, twenty feet, and then he pulled a pack of cigarettes from the front pocket of his khaki shorts and sat back down on the bench. As she passed him he lit up a butt and inhaled deeply. Hardly noticing she was there he seemed to be content to watch the gently lapping waves of Lake Erie as they broke on the shoreline.

"Nothing, just nerves I guess. Didn't think I'd be nervous, but I am."

"Good! Are you ready to call it a night then? My wife's waiting on me. We're not getting overtime for this you know."

"I'll be back in fifteen minutes, it's early yet. Keep your pants on."

"Stay in touch," Wilder said opening the entertainment section of the paper.

"Will do."

On her last lap Hamilton saw nobody other than an adolescent couple walking arm-in-arm in the Moonlight. She completed the third circuit of the lake front trail and had run approximately six miles in a little over fifty minutes. She ran toward the parking lot and the waiting Crowne Vic. She smiled to herself looking at Wilder's profile within the dimly lit car, he looked haggard. Mischievously, she did an end around and snuck up on the opposite side from where she'd come.

I'll just give him a little scare, she thought to herself. As she was about to tap on the passenger window Wilder put the paper down and stared at her with a knowing expression. Then he pulled the paper back up to his face. Deflated, she got in beside him.

"That's not funny," Wilder said folding the paper and tossing it into the back seat. "You could have given me a heart attack, you know?"

"You're pretty slick old man. Hard to pull one over on you, even when you look like your about to doze off."

"I only sleep in my own bed. You should know better than to try to get me, we've been partners for years now and you've never come close. I'm serious about the heart attack, I'm getting older and rounder, too. Or suppose I shoot you one of these times?"

"Sorry, you're right. It's very childish of me," she answered.

"You disappointed?"

"No, I didn't expect anything tonight."

"What now? Same place, same time tomorrow?"

"Same bat channel," she replied.

"You're too young for that show. How could you know about the 'Caped Crusader'?"

"When the movies came out I did some digging and found DVD's of some of the original television episodes."

Wilder considered this a moment and realized he liked Hamilton more and more, in a purely plutonic sense, in reality he felt a fatherly bond toward her. "I suppose that's the only way you're little trap will work. You have to make yourself accessible on a regular basis, establish a pattern, make yourself predictable."

"That's what these freaks feed on. Once they've got a potential vic's routine down they feel comfortable, then they strike."

"All right then, you've got me for an hour every night until you've grown tired of it," Wilder shook his head.

"What's wrong Dan?" she asked.

"I get this feeling—this sense that we're not gonna get this one. Seems to be too careful, too experienced. We need a big break and we can't make it ourselves. I think this guy needs to make a mistake, do something out of his normal M.O. for us to have any chance at him. I feel like if we ever do get him it will be because we stumbled upon him, not because we caught him."

Wordlessly Hamilton gazed out the window toward the dark woods beyond. Deep down she felt the same way. Nonetheless, the partners returned to Woodlawn Beach State Park every night at the same time for the next two weeks. Despite their best efforts they came away none the wiser. At Hamilton's prodding they agreed to change their venue to Riverside Park where the Nichols boy was last seen with his lacrosse stick around the World War I Memorial.

Chapter Ten

As Gant motored south from Sunrise Highway onto the Meadowbrook Parkway at Freeport, he instinctively turned off the van's air conditioning and rolled down the windows to soak up the refreshing salt air, he could taste home. Onto the Loop Parkway he veered driving in silence towards his mother's house. Obscured by clouds, the thin Moon offered nearly nothing in the way of light, it seemed appropriate to him at the time.

With three bridges to go before reaching Watch Point he slowed to forty miles per hour to glance at the running lights of the commercial fishing boats as they made their way through Jones Inlet on their way to Freeport or the small marina in Watch Point. Driving over the last bridge he saw the Dead Eye Dick, a charter boat most probably returning from a striped bass trip. He also noticed the slip assigned to the Miss Watch Point II, a party boat, was empty. Gant had worked on the original Miss Watch Point as a mate throughout high school. There was little doubt the Miss Watch Point II was still miles offshore on a "Night Blues" trip. As luck would have it the light at the end of the parkway turned green for him. He turned left onto Lido Boulevard and dropped down to fifteen miles per hour, the town speed limit.

He briefly considered turning left into the town's east marina to clean the tote and himself up, he'd done it in the past. The bathrooms nearest the landed bulkhead had hot water showers. Many fishermen cleaned their equipment with a dockside hose and then showered off before getting in their cars or trucks to drive home.

Gant had used the facility on three occasions in the past, always tossing his clothing and shoes into the restroom garbage before stepping into the shower. In a plastic bag he would have a fresh change of shorts, a T-shirt and a pair of flip-flops. After dressing the plastic bag also went into the garbage. He could have used the showers, but something insisted that he not. Gant was blessed with eerie intuition that never failed him, and tonight it was telling him to steer clear of the marina's bathroom. As it was mid-summer it was unlikely, but perhaps there were teenagers partying in there like he'd done himself on cold windswept winter nights. Maybe it was because he felt like he had worn out his welcome there and needed a place that was completely safe. For whatever reason, he decided against the marina showers and coasted slowly into town. He caught a red light in front of the deli, the only traffic light within the tiny, one square mile town, and gazed around at the familiar landscape of the boulevard.

Surrounded by water on three sides, Watch Point's southern shore was pounded by the Atlantic Ocean, its eastern tip bordered Jones Inlet, and its north side faced Reynolds Channel. Originally called Nassau-by-the-Sea, Watch Point was renamed in the mid-1940's as it was used as a lookout station for the U.S. Navy during World War II. After the war the name stuck, nobody seemed to mind.

Not much had changed since his visit the previous summer. The New York yuppies had continued to buy up houses and build huge monstrosities right on top of one another, seemingly unaware they were diminishing the charm of the little seaside town. Beginning in the late 1980's, Wall Street found out about the hidden oceanfront gem and the land grab was on. Far easier than trekking from the city to the Hamptons, the city-dwellers hopped a train at Penn Station and could be on the beach within an hour, beer in hand. Instigated by opportunistic and in some cases, unscrupulous real estate agents, the property values became so inflated the county reassessed every property in town to make certain that the property taxes reflected the bloated values.

Overnight people's property taxes doubled and in some instances tripled. Families who'd summered in Watch Point since the 1950's suddenly found themselves unable to pay their property taxes and were forced to sell their bungalows. While it was true they sold those bungalows for exorbitant prices, it was also true they hadn't wanted to sell and would probably never have enough money to buy back into the community in the future. The only real winners were the affluent buyers who had money to burn and the realtors who collected a very healthy fee on every transaction.

One realtor sold the same house three times within a four year span collecting a cool one hundred and thirty-five thousand dollars in the process. It was a shame what the new money was doing, yet the town still maintained an essence of its nature and purity.

Growing up, the Gants and their neighbors took pride in the fact that the community had always been a summer town, most of its fifteen hundred residents arrived as school let out in late June and packed up for winter quarters like Manhasset, Forest Hills, or Manhattan right after Labor Day. It had been a real community in which everyone truly knew one another and looked after one another's interests. Large families had been fairly common back then, the Hendrickson's had nine kids, six boys and three girls, the Costello's had eleven, the O'Leary's had thirteen. The population wasn't necessarily affluent but upper middle class, without the snobbery that often accompanies it. Most of the houses had been one story bungalows with the exception of the big families, which crammed all their kids into modest two story capes.

Paved with blue stone streets the Watch Point of Gant's youth had one grocery store, a deli, two landlocked gas stations as well as two gas docks on the bay side. There was a little breakfast place, two pizza parlors, a pharmacy, a dry cleaner, and two restaurants, one being waterfront, the Bay View Inn. Affectionately nicknamed "Cirrhosis by the Sea", the quaint little town did boast eight bars, four on the bay side, within its single square mile.

The only public buildings in the town were the firehouse which kept three engines and a library annex which held no more than a thousand books total. Any kids attending public schools were bussed to Long Beach five miles to the west, most of the Watch Point children attended private schools. There were two houses of worship, Our Lady of the Sea Roman Catholic Church to which the overwhelming majority of the community were parishioners and the Community Church which had a token congregation of about forty people.

The largest structure in town by far was the Bishop McGinley Recreation Center which was owned by the Church. The Rec Hall hosted morning summer camp for the little kids, pick up basketball games for the teenagers and young adults and parties, both public and private. A sand filled playground and two baseball fields occupied the easternmost tip of the town along Jones Inlet.

The white sand beach and crystal clear water of the private, resident's only beach was the reason for being there of course, but the little town had a lot of character as well. There was money, but those with it were not the type to forget who they were or where they came from.

Gant turned south onto Cedar Dune Avenue and a third of the way down the block he pulled into the driveway of his mother's house. It was after eleven by then, so he knew his mom would be dozing off if not sound asleep. He killed the engine, stepped out of the van and walked to the back door. Opening the doors, he grabbed the ice tote, a scrub brush, and a bottle of bleach, then quietly shut the doors. He tossed the bleach and scrub brush into the tote and walked around to the back of the house. Gant's mother's back yard was all polished stones, he put the tote in the corner of the fence and emptied the gallon of bleach into it. He scrubbed the tote furiously for about five minutes, then tossed the brush into the garbage can on the side of the house. He uncoiled the hose by the rear door and hosed it down, diluting the bleach as he did. When the tote was filled with a hazy bleach-water mixture he tipped it over, so the milky liquid ran out over the stones and settled in a pool close to the walkway leading to the front yard. He then rinsed out the tote and returned it to the back of the van to dry.

Gant opened the back door to the house and took all of his clothes off, including his sneakers and under wear and tossed them into the washing machine by the back door. Naked, Gant walked out into the back yard to the outdoor shower. He closed the door of the cedar shower behind him and scrubbed himself clean for twenty minutes, making sure to get beneath his fingernails. Dripping, he sat naked at the circular deck table in the center of the yard to dry off. After five minutes he stepped back inside and walked in the darkness to his old room.

By a sense of feel he would never lose, Gant made his way through the darkness to his room. He'd made the same dark trip many thousand's of times before, so he knew every square inch, every contour of the ground level abode. Nicknamed "The Cave" by his friends, Gant's old room was a dim abyss even in broad daylight.

When he'd turned fifteen and began partying, he'd suggested to his parents that rich mahogany colored shades would really compliment the dark pine walls of the lower level, they agreed. As a result of the chocolate shades that were installed on all six windows which the bedroom, the bathroom and the laundry room shared, the noon day Sun was eclipsed. When home from boarding school he was able to party all night and sleep all day if need be. No objections about his lifestyle were ever seriously raised. Probably due to the guilt they shared because of their long term neglect of the boy, the Gants enabled his vampiric existence. Their opposite hours also limited the amount of time they came into contact with one another.

Once in his old room, Gant flipped on the light switch beside the door. He walked to the closet in the far corner of the room, opened it, grabbed a towel, and soaked up the remaining moisture on his skin. He then opened the dresser at the foot of the bed, selected a pair of boxers and a pair of shorts and slipped into them. The dresser was stuffed with his summer wardrobe; bathing suits, shorts, golf shirts, T-shirts, everything he would need for a nice summer vacation. Although he hadn't lived in the house for over twenty-five years "The Cave" remained his. It was still decorated with a variety of old license plates from different states, beer signs and posters of bikini-clad women, all things a teenage boy would find interesting. Barefooted and shirtless he climbed the stairs to the main floor to see how his mother was faring.

Tip-toeing into the den Gant watched as his mother's eyes fluttered back and forth, she was not yet in a deep sleep, but quickly approaching it. He turned on his heel and was heading for the kitchen when he heard her murmur his name. He looked back to face her and her eyes opened wide.

"No kiss for your old ma?" Eleanor Gant asked with a wry smile on her lined face.

"I'm sorry Mom, I didn't want to wake you," Gant replied crossing the room to his mother. He bent down to where she sat in a leather La-Z-Boy recliner and planted a big kiss on her left cheek. Straightening he asked, "How are you feeling tonight old girl?"

"Old, that's how I'm feeling. It'd be a blessing to join your father, I'll tell you that. The damned arthritis in my knees is unbearable, I'll be stuck in a wheel chair soon."

"Don't say such things."

"It's the truth Phillip, the doctors say so too. The knees are too far gone and getting worse every day."

"What about physical therapy?"

"Oh, it helped at first, but not so much anymore."

"What medication do they have you on now?"

"Etanercept, I think. That's the latest. All of them work for a while and then lose their magic. What I need are new knees."

Gant's eyebrows rose at the suggestion. "So let's do it then. The knee replacement surgeries they're doing now have fantastic success rates even among the elderly."

"I'm not sure I can go under," his mother replied.

"That's something we'll have to look in to. From what I hear it's a fast surgery, only about an hour and a half at most."

"For one knee, that is," she countered.

"That's right mom, for one knee. Maybe if we're willing to pay enough they would agree to have two surgical teams work on you at the same time, one for each knee," he replied.

"Let's look in to it then, my good boy."

"First thing tomorrow, no wait second thing tomorrow. We'll have breakfast first and then I'll make some calls to your doctors to see what they have to say."

"You're a good son Phillip, thank you," she said yawning.

"Let's get you up to bed, Mom."

"How about something to snack on before you turn in?"

"I'll get you upstairs and then help myself. I know where everything is."

"You're sure you don't want any company?"

"I'd be happy for the company, but you look tired Ma. Let's get you upstairs, we'll catch up in the morning."

"I won't argue," she replied struggling to rise from the recliner.

Rather than use her walker, Gant tenderly grasped his mother under her elbows and slowly pulled her from the recliner. He steadied her and then spun around so his back was to her. She reached up and placed her bony hands upon his shoulders. Like a train engine leading the way for his mother the caboose, Gant shuffled forward, the little two car train slowly crept toward the stairs leading to the second floor.

At the base of the stairs waited a motorized chair lift which Gant gently rested his mother into. She hit the "up" button and the chair whirred to life, its chain pulling her up toward the landing that overlooked the living room. Gant trailed the rising chair by a few steps and when it had stopped he held out his hands to her. Seizing his hands in hers she gained her feet once more and balanced her weight. Gant did his spin move again and the Gant Express churned into her bedroom where it dropped her off on her bed.

After kissing his mother good night Gant went back downstairs into the kitchen and made himself a buttered bagel. Still amped up from the day's activities he walked down to the beach and waded out into the dark water. After a ten minute swim beneath the Moonless sky he walked back to his mother's, took another outdoor shower and went to bed.

* * * *

The following morning was rainy and cool when Gant rose at five-past seven and decided to visit Palamino's, the local breakfast place, to put in an order. He jumped onto his Schwinn Hornet beach cruiser, complete with a basket, and peddled slowly down toward the boulevard. He was about to turn right toward Palamino's when he thought better of it and went left toward the beginning of town, where the deli was located. The deli had chicken cutlets not to be duplicated anywhere; he ordered a chicken cutlet hero with melted cheddar, tomato, lettuce and extra mayo.

The forecast was for continued rain, but like many people, he had little trust in meteorologist's predictions and sought to be properly prepared for a day at the beach. He prepaid and told the clerk he'd be back within ten minutes. Back on the bike he coasted down the boulevard toward the breakfast place. Fifteen minutes later he was back at his mother's house, with two large coffees as well as an order of pancakes for her and a bacon, egg and cheese on a roll with ketchup for himself. Considering her condition he figured he would be bringing breakfast home regardless of the weather. To think she would go through the agony of getting into the wheel chair and then her car for breakfast was a pipe-dream; torture was reserved only for doctor visits and special occasions.

After breakfast the mother and son caught up over their coffees. They sat at the kitchen table for over an hour until the rain ceased at around nine o'clock. Gant went to the front door and picked up the copy of *New York Newsday* which the delivery boy had thrown up onto the front stoop, then settled into the rocking chair in the corner of the den. An hour later the Sun began to peek through the clouds and Mrs. Gant urged her son to take a walk down to the beach to see who was around.

Instead he went down into the cave and put a call into a friend who was a hospital administrator at Winthrop University Hospital in Mineola. The friend gave him the numbers of three surgeons that he highly recommended for any type of knee procedure. With his friends assistance, Gant then made appointments to meet with two of the doctors later in the week, the third was on vacation.

After doing as he promised for his mother, Gant packed a cooler full of beer and the chicken cutlet hero and then changed into a pair of blue swim trunks which were emblazoned with tropical flowers of orange and yellow. He draped a towel over his neck, took a beach chair from the backyard and with the cooler in hand, walked out to the driveway to where the yellow Hornet waited. Laying the cooler in the bicycle's ample basket, he grasped the chair in his right hand, hopped onto the Schwinn and pedaled shirtless and shoeless down to the beach, with the towel flapping lazily between his torso and arms. A minute later he drove through the gate at the end of the block and was walking the Hornet toward the bike rack by the beach house where the bathrooms were located.

Gant slid the bike into a slot; there was no need to lock it, nobody even bothered to lock their doors at night in Watch Point. He set his course for the Sun shelter he and his friends had called The Pavillion growing up. The Pavillion was a sturdy structure constructed wholly of concrete and steel; it was designed to be hurricane proof. Three black steel arches jutted fifteen feet up from the concrete base to serve as the support for the shelter's heavy steel roof which measured thirty by twelve feet. The triple arches were visible from three miles on the island's flat south shore.

He had no desire to stay there long, just long enough to take in the slightly elevated view and reminisce a bit about old times. Walking up the concrete ramp to the Sun shelter Gant strode to the middle bench in the center of the shelter and hopped up onto it to get a better view. He looked out on the vast blue horizon to the south as the Sun's rays glittered off if its surface. As the morning had been wet, there were very few boats on the water as yet.

That would change by late morning as the local fishermen would be out hoping to hook striped bass or fluke. Gant stared far out to the shipping lanes where big freighters lurched to and from New York to Europe. The Pavillion held many memories for Gant, most of them good. The first time he'd smoked pot he'd been fourteen right there on the shelter. He had his first kiss in a dune not far from the shelter; the girl had been quite drunk and almost vomited in his mouth, he remembered with a shudder.

He thought back to being chased off by the police after refusing to leave when the security guard requested that he and his gang of friends leave. Kegs, cases, or beer balls, like most other teens, Gant and his buddies put away quite a lot of beer on this very spot. He took a deep breath in and beneath the salt spray of the breaking waves he got a whiff of beer. Nothing had changed.

Gant ambled slowly down the front steps of The Pavillion and onto the white sand beach below. He skirted the dune directly before the shelter veering to its left and out toward the center of the beach. At this early hour families with small children were excavating holes, making sand castles, frolicking in the surf and digging for sand crabs. He took in the scene with serene satisfaction, it was always good to get home. He'd done these things as a youngster.

He smiled as he saw a boy of two, or maybe three, topple headfirst over his castle and land with a splash in the mote his father had dug out for him. Gant wondered how these kids would turn out. *Like me? No, probably not.* He walked by the families, but recognized no one. Searching for some prime real estate, he realized the tide had started to go out. He found himself a semi-secluded spot right on the shoreline about fifty feet from the west side jetty; there was nobody within sixty feet of him to his left. He dropped the cooler on the sand, unfolded the beach chair and took a seat.

It was past twelve-thirty, Gant was on his second can of Heineken when a familiar voice called out, "Holy shit! Do my eyes deceive me or is that the one and only Phillip Gant!"

Gant looked up from he novel he was reading, something called *It's a Woman's World,* and saw Donald Murray, a summer friend looking down at him.

"Donald," Gant said getting up from his chair. "How are you?" he added flipping the book onto the seat of the chair and extending his hand.

Murray took Gant's hand and pumped it vigorously, his great belly jiggled as he did so. "I'm great! A little big around the middle, but you know it's a sign of good living."

Gant laughed while Murray rubbed his gut and eyed Gant's beer.

"Lots of those I tell ya," Murray said, nodding at the can of beer. "Looks like the beers don't have the same effect on you Phil. You look great," he said gently poking Gant in the ribs.

"Lots of exercise is all."

"It's been a long time, I think at least five years since I've seen you."

"I don't get down here too often and when I do its hard to find the old timers."

"Yeah, most of the summer people have sold out by now. My folks are one of maybe twenty or so summer people from the sixties."

"It's a shame the way things went around here, but that's life. My Mom knows hardly anyone anymore. The old names are pretty much gone, the history with them," Gant said. Then he asked, "Where're the wife and kids, Donny?"

Murray's smile faded quickly. "We're divorced, three years now. She's up in Westchester with the kids."

"And you're..."

"A Beach bum! Murray brightened. "Living at the folks for the summer. It's been a blast. Took some time off from work, I don't have to go back until mid-August."

"What then?"

"An apartment in Stuy Town, small but good," Murray replied settling his beach chair next to Gant's. He grabbed a can of Bud from his cooler and then hid the cooler in the shade behind his chair. He popped the tab and flopped down beside his old friend who he had known so very well thirty odd years ago.

After many more beers and several dips into the ocean the old friends decided to take a walk down to the public beach for a change of scenery. While stretching their legs the public beach had two main attractions the private beach had never offered.

First, the women on the public beach were very often scantily clad, there were thongs aplenty as well as the occasional topless Sunbather. Such attire, or lack of attire, was considered unseemly by the upper middle class, heavily conservative residents of Watch Point. Although the families had drastically shrunk, Watch Point was still very much a family-oriented town. The public beach was crowded with throngs of "outsiders" from as far as Queens.

Second, the public beach was further away from Jones Inlet and had much better waves. While Watch Point was all shore break, west of the town's private beach was a surfer's paradise. With no boards, Gant and Murray body surfed for the better part of half an hour before setting out on their return trip and its delights for the eyes.

On their way back they passed by the east mall concession stand, a two story red brick building with a terrace facing the ocean. Beside the concession stand were two bath houses, one male and one female which rented out lockers to day trippers. The concession stand had been closed for twenty years, but the bath houses were still in use for those who wanted to shower off before getting into their cars to drive home.

Murray looked to Gant with a sly look on his face. "I can't believe we missed it on the way there," he said.

"I didn't, I just didn't say anything," Gant replied.

"That was some heist, huh?"

"Unbelievable really, never happen that way today."

"What? The skateboards?"

"That and the timing. What kind of odds would you give that six kids could load over ninety cases of beer onto their skateboards and push the beer a half a mile home, making three trips, over the course of two and half hours, and go completely unnoticed?"

"Free beer for the summer, and some of it was imported too!"

"What odds?" Gant asked again.

"None, nil, you're right. Couldn't be done again," Murray laughed. He was about to go on when his eye was caught by a man waving to them from further down the shoreline toward Watch Point. Walking toward them the man smiled as he splashed through ankle deep water. "That's Billy O'Sullivan."

"No way, that guy's bald," Gant said.

"I'm telling you it's him. I saw him two years ago. He'd lost most of it by then."

Gant was still uncertain until the man was within shouting distance of them. "Donny, Phil!" Billy O'Sullivan yelled down the beach. The men smiled at one another as they drew closer.

"What's happening boys?" O'Sullivan asked fist bumping Gant and Murray at the same time.

"Taking the obligatory tour of the flesh," Murray answered happily.

"Yeah I figured as much," replied O'Sullivan. "I saw that cooler of yours by the shoreline Phil. I can't believe you've still got that thing. It's got to be twenty years old."

"Try twenty-nine," Gant said.

"Oh, come on. I don't want to hear that. We're getting older and older quicker and quicker."

"It sucks!" Murray added.

"Anyway, I saw the cooler, the only vintage Playmate on the beach, and knew you were around. With the empty seats I figured you were on the walk. Great to see you guys. How long are you in town for?"

"All summer," Murray responded.

"A week or so, maybe longer. I'll see how I'm missed at work," Gant said.

O'Sullivan nodded and said, "I'm on a three day leave from the wife and kids. You guys remember Noreen MacLaughlin, right?"

"How could I forget that rack?" Murray responded.

"I remember sneaking out her window on a few occasions," Gant added with a sly wink.

"Hey, I almost forgot about you and her. You hooked up with nearly all the girls at some time or another, huh Phil? I'll bet you never married, right?"

"That's true."

"Still playing the field, good for you. Anyway, I keep in touch with Noreen a little. Her husband's a big shot lawyer, her last name is Dwyer now. They own the old Lombardino house on Inlet Avenue."

"I believe that Philly here knows a little bit about the ins and outs of that house too," Murray interrupted.

Gant smiled sheepishly.

O'Sullivan continued, "She emailed me about a month ago telling me that she was having a party tonight. The barbeque starts at five o'clock. She said to show up whenever. Then we can walk to the marina for the fireworks and then back to her house for some more partying."

"Sounds like a plan," Gant said. "I originally came down because Ken Marcanti said he was having a big party, but he cancelled. He mentioned something about Thailand, I'm not really sure what that's all about. So yeah, I'm free. It's only three now, let's head back and have a few beers before we leave the beach."

"You guys are running a little low at the moment," O'Sullivan informed his friends. "I took a seat for a little while and had a few beers while I waited for you to show up."

The three men began to slowly trod through the foamy surf of the shoreline back toward the private beach. The Pavillion was about a third of a mile distant, its three black arches leading them home. The afternoon boaters had shown up in mass out on the ocean.

"But you knew we were down here," Murray said.

"It was too good to pass up. White sand, clear water, free beer! Would you have been in a hurry to go anywhere?"

"Nah, I guess not," Murray agreed. "How many are left?"

"Three Buds and two Heine's," O'Sullivan answered.

"Christ Billy! You drank ten beers just sitting there waiting for us? We were only gone an hour!"

"There were some pretty young ladies I felt obligated to share with, they kept me company for a while. I think I found the rookie of the year."

"I hope she's still around," Murray replied.

"So do I," Gant added.

"Remember that one girl who was rookie of the year for like six straight years," O'Sullivan laughed.

"Sure do," Murray responded. "Gorgeous blonde, all legs with a nice top, but nothing huge. I think her name was Meredith."

"I think you're right on the name you dirty old man. Anyway, this chick today, blows her away."

"So who's going to the store?" Gant asked his two friends.

"I think it should be you Billy, we'd still have beer if you didn't give it all away," Murray stated.

"Stick it, Donny Boy! You'd have done the same thing!" O'Sullivan shot back. "I buy you fly."

"I'm not walking up there, fuck that."

"I'll fly," Gant offered. "And buy. I want to check on my Mom anyway."

"That'll take a long time," Murray said with a hint of concern in his voice.

"I'll be back in fifteen minutes, I've got my bike."

"You still got that old yellow Schwinn?" O'Sullivan asked.

"You bet I do."

"Old coolers, old bikes! You're like a pack rat Philly."

"If it's not broke, don't fix it. And don't throw it out. The bike is like a collector's piece. I've had it since I was twelve."

Within five minutes the three men were again back at the chairs with beers in hand. To their dismay the new rookie of the year and her two friends were nowhere to be seen. Gant and Murray slumped into their chairs while O'Sullivan sat on a towel. "I'll go after this beer," Gant said raising a can of Heineken to his lips. "You guys can stay here and finish off the rest of these while I'm gone. I'll be back before you're done with them. You won't even lose pace."

"Thanks Phil," Murray said.

"Yeah, thanks Philly. You getting a twelve or a case?" O'Sullivan asked.

"With your track record I better go for the case to be safe. Any requests boys?"

"I'll drink anything you buy," O'Sullivan answered smiling.

"Your money, your call, Phil," Murray added.

With that Gant walked past the Pavillion to the bicycle rack and slid the Hornet from its slot. Walking the bike past the outdoor shower, there was no riding within the confines of the beach's gates, he saw what surely must have been O'Sullivan's rookie of the year. His friend had been right, the women, a college age girl probably, was a near perfect ten. Standing beneath the shower head she preened knowing she had an audience, she was used to having one, it appeared. Tall and muscular at five feet seven inches, she had long, naturally curly blonde hair that fell past her shoulders in loose ringlets. Her lime green bikini was cut to showcase her lithe, athletic body which was tanned a golden brown, but not too dark. With defined biceps, thigh and calve muscles, it was evident that she was an athlete of some sort, perhaps a soccer player. Despite her musculature she was wholly feminine as her breasts and heart-shaped rear end testified. With her sinewy build Gant couldn't grasp how she had breasts at all let lone the rather perky B-cups she was endowed with. As he edged to within five feet of her she suddenly turned the water off and reached for her towel which was on the wall beside the shower. She raised her head and looked Gant in the eyes as she wrapped the towel around her torso. Her emerald eyes gleamed warmly and her full lips rose in a smile. With no makeup she was strikingly beautiful, model good looking in fact with a straight nose, high cheekbones, and an angular jaw line. Gant smiled back and walked past knowing that he wanted her badly.

His heart pounding, Gant exhaled deeply as he walked his bike past the main entrance of the beach. He had to make contact with the woman, he would make it his mission to do so. There was time for her later though. Now it was time to check up on his mother. First though, he went to visit his father's bench.

Heading east along the concrete walkway Gant made his way toward Jones Inlet. Benches of wrought iron and cedar construction lined the walkway all the way from the west entrance at the corner of Cedar Dune Avenue, Gant's mother's block, to the east entrance at Inlet Avenue. While the benches on the ocean side were on the ocean, they had no view as they were blocked by the dunes in front of them. Mrs. Gant insisted that her late husband's bench have a water view, and so it did. Arthur Gant's body was laid to rest in Calvary Cemetery in Queens, but his heart still resided in Watch Point. Besides flying there was nothing the elder Gant enjoyed more than the sea and spending time at his beloved beach with his wife. Arthur Gant's bench was the fourth from the last before the entrance and the view from it was extraordinary. In the center of the bench was a simple iron plaque engraved with:

IN MEMORY OF ARTHUR GANT
LOVING HUSBAND
DEVOTED FATHER

Unlike some of the other plaques on some of the benches Mrs. Gant sought to keep her husband's simple and to the point. Rather than list the commendations he was awarded for his military service she put the two most important things in the man's life. She deliberately left off his birth and death dates, deciding they were irrelevant. Gant couldn't help but laugh a bit at the "devoted father" piece of the inscription as it was largely bullshit. Nonetheless, he had loved his father in his own way.

Gant flipped down the kickstand of the Hornet and sat down on his father's bench. He wouldn't stay long, just long enough to take in the view and say a prayer for his father's soul. Gazing out over the churning blue inlet toward the mile long jetty of Jones Beach some eight hundred feet distant, Gant blessed himself and prayed for his deceased father and also for his own soul. He knew in his heart that he was what many would consider to be a monster, yet he was helpless to stop himself. He prayed to God to give him strength and failing that to have mercy on him when his time came. As tears welled up in Gant's eyes a mother with a stroller appeared at the east entrance; the stroller was a double, she had twins. Realizing that his bike was partially blocking the walkway he got up from the bench and kicked the kickstand up and walked the bike through the sand providing her with plenty of room.

Outside the gate he hopped onto the Hornet and was off to the races. Gant cut west at Beach Street in order to avoid Noreen MacLaughlin's house on Inlet Avenue, as he was sure she would be outside preparing for her party. There would be time to speak with her later, he wanted to check in with his mother and then make the beer run quickly so as to get back to the beach as soon as possible. Flying down Beach Street he waved to the McDonough clan as they were departing for a late beach day. Hooking a right onto Cedar Dune Avenue he pumped his legs for five houses and then coasted to a stop in his mother's driveway.

Running up the front stoop, he almost tripped on the second to last step. Regaining his balance he carefully walked to the top and pulled open the door. From within the kitchen he could overhear his mother on the telephone. He walked into the kitchen and waved hello, she waved back from her chair at the table. At the counter he took a pen and pad of paper and scribbled:

"Will be eating out tonight. Met friends at beach. Going to market. Need anything?"

Mrs. Gant shook her head "no".

He kissed her on the forehead and bolted for the door. Within forty-five seconds he was inside the store and strolling toward the beer case. After selecting a twelve pack of Heineken cans as well as a twelve of Bud he grabbed a bag of ice from the freezer. The store was drastically low on everything and Gant wondered why and then realized the firework show was that evening. After quick pleasantries at the counter with the owner's cousin he was back on the bike and heading for the beach.

As Murray cracked the last Budweiser Gant walked up behind him and nudged the bag of ice onto the back of his neck. Startled, Murray popped up from the chair. He spun around to find Gant grinning.

"I didn't figure you could still move that fast," Gant teased him.

"Very funny Phil! Let me get that cooler for you," Murray replied opening Gant's Playmate. He then took the Heineken from Gant and stacked it inside and then took the Bud for his own cooler. Gant ripped open the bag of ice and poured half onto the Heines and the other half onto the Bud.

Consulting his watch Gant saw that the trip took him slightly less than twenty-five minutes, more than he had anticipated but still very good considering all he'd done. He eased down into his chair and popped a Heineken as the Sun fell closer to the horizon. "I saw your girl Billy," he said.

"Huh?" O'Sullivan asked.

"The new rookie," Gant replied.

"Oh, yeah. Am I right or am I right?" O'Sullivan mused.

"You're right, that's for sure. I wish I was twenty years younger."

"Is she really that hot?" Murray asked.

"Really that hot," Gant assured him.

For the remainder of the afternoon the three friends slugged beer down beneath the wavering, tangerine Sun. Shortly after six o'clock when the horn at the firehouse blew all the beer was gone, they'd given a few away as was par for the course. After one last dip in the ocean the three parted ways to shower up and regroup.

Chapter Eleven

Lydia Bergstrom was on to her last stop of the day, Northwestern Memorial Hospital on Chicago's north side. The mid-west heat was oppressive and the air conditioning in her rental car, a 2009 Chrysler 300, was struggling to keep pace with it. She'd just turned onto East Huron Street when her cell phone chimed. If it had been anyone but her family or boyfriend she would have let it go to voice mail.

"Hi, Lenny," Bergstrom spoke into the phone.

"Hey, baby! How's it going? Where are you?" Gant asked.

"It sucks! I'm in Chicago, also known as the armpit of the mid-west. I didn't realize it got this hot here, and sticky. It's gross!"

"It's on the lake. Where there's water there's sure to be humidity sweetheart."

"I've been to five hospitals and eleven doctor's offices today. This is my last stop for today. At least I have that going for me."

"How've you been received?" Gant asked, nobody would ever have known he'd spent the day drinking on the beach.

"Very well, as usual. The products really sell themselves. I'm sick of the work. The driving, the in and out of the car all day, and lugging around the sample cases. It's wearing me down. It's worse in the winter when I can slip and fall on my ass if I'm not careful. I want a new career, the kind where you work from home as say, an aircraft part supplier's assistant. Can you help me with that?" she asked playfully.

"Patience my dear. All in good time. Things will work out, I promise."

"How about you? What have you been up to?"

"Do you really want to know?"

"No, not really, but tell me anyway."

"I got in late last night and had breakfast with my Mom."

"How's she doing?"

"Not so good, it's hard for her to get around. I'm looking into knee replacement surgery for her."

"Oh, Lenny. I'm sorry to hear that."

"She's tough, she'll be fine," he replied.

"That'll be general anesthesia, can she handle it at her age?" Bergstrom asked uneasily.

"I sure hope so."

"Lenny?"

"Yes?"

"When will I meet your Mom? I've never even talked to her on the phone."

"She's a very private person Lyd. We haven't been dating all that long. She's old-fashioned. I'm sure she'd like to see an engagement ring before she meets you," Gant replied searching for some bit of truth in his statement. He wished he had introduced himself as Phillip Gant rather than Lenny Schenk, but he didn't, he couldn't. That ship had sailed. He still hadn't figured out how he would bring the two women in his life together without alienating one or both of them.

"That makes two of us then," Bergstrom responded deadpan.

"All right, then," Gant ignored her response, "after breakfast I hit the beach and ran into some old friends. We spent the day on the beach and I came home now to shower and go out to a party a few blocks over that another old friend is throwing."

"Beach and party, anything else?"

"Then the fireworks, then bed, hopefully," he replied.

"Alone I take it?"

"Of course alone. You know you're the only one for me Lyd. I miss you terribly."

"I'm sorry, I miss you too, Lenny."

"Listen, I'll call you in the morning. The guys will be here in twenty minutes and I haven't showered yet, I have to go. I love you!"

"I love you too my mystery man! Bye-bye," Bergstrom said, ending the call.

* * * *

Two hours later Bergstrom sat before a half eaten chef's salad, the solitary diner in the hotel restaurant off of the lobby. Saturday nights were desolate in the little restaurant as seemingly all of the guests had made reservations at the Cape Cod Room, Gibson's Bar & Steakhouse, or Table Fifty-Two for their dining pleasure. Bergstrom was too tired to go anywhere and felt she would be uncomfortable dining alone in a posh eatery. The salad was actually pretty good she thought as she took another forkful.

Lonesome, her thoughts naturally drifted to Gant, or as she knew him, Lenny Schenk. Bergstrom truly loved the man, she loved everything about him. He was over ten years older than her, but didn't look it for a second. Fit and trim, he looked better than most twenty-five-year-olds. His age also provided him with vast experience, both in the bedroom and out in the world in general.

A world traveler and man of unerring taste, she'd never met anyone quite like him. He was tender, loving, affectionate and could be very funny in a dry sense when he chose to be. Taking a sip of San Pellegrino from a wine glass she recalled calling him "her mystery man" at the end of their conversation late that afternoon.

She had never referred to him as that before, but it seemed to fit all right. There was much about her lover she didn't know. She'd never spoken to his mother who was, according to him, his only living family. He'd told her practically nothing about his upbringing or schooling. She'd never met any of his friends other than neighbors. She did know he'd served in the Navy. She knew he was a pilot who frequently flew. She'd been up in his plane, they had actually flown to New York for a long weekend in the city the previous spring. She knew he owned his own company and made very good money as was evidenced by the gorgeous house, it was really more of a mansion, in which they lived together. *He'd said his mother was a very private person, well the character trait surely runs in the family*, she thought, taking another bite of her salad.

Lydia, on the other hand, had told Gant everything about herself within the first few weeks they'd been together. An open book, she recalled the events of her life as if they'd happened yesterday. She related her childhood, how she had a twin sister and two older brothers. They had all attended public school through high school and then went on to college. Meeting their future spouses while at college, her sister and brothers had all moved out of the Buffalo area relocating south to Virginia, Florida, and Ohio. With the exception of her cousin whom she rarely saw, she had no family in the greater Buffalo area.

She was the only one of her siblings to not get married early on, and now at age thirty-three she was worried about becoming an old maid. It certainly wasn't for lack of looks she'd not been betrothed. She hadn't found the right man for her, until now that was. She was sure, Lenny Schenk was the man she wanted to spend the rest of her life with.

Schenk had met Bergstrom's parents within two months of their relationship. Mister and Mrs. Bergstrom, like their other children had grown weary of Buffalo winters. Peter Bergstrom, an amiable man in his mid sixties, worked for the Buffalo Water Board where he acted as a liaison between the water authority and the consumer public, he hated it, but it paid the bills.

Upon retirement he and Jane, his wife of forty plus years, sold their four bedroom ranch and moved to sunny southern Florida where they purchased a two bedroom condo in Lauderdale Lakes. Lydia's parents were up visiting their daughter and some friends for a few weeks over the summer when Schenk met them. The new couple and the Bergstrom's sat down together in Lydia's tiny dining room for a meal. The Bergstrom's seemed as taken with Schenk as their daughter was. A Vietnam vet himself, Lydia's father immediately took a shine to the decorated pilot while her mother gushed over his good looks, soft-spoken voice and fine manners.

As her plate was cleared Lydia thought back to the first time she'd laid eyes on Schenk. She'd been in the parking lot of the Catholic Health Hospital on the city's south side when he pulled up next to her in his Volvo. He was out of his car seconds after she was out of hers and graced her with a warm smile and a nod of the head. Then he turned and broke into a fast-paced walk toward the entrance. *Good looking*, she remembered thinking to herself as she popped her trunk to get to her sample cases.

Temporarily distracted by the stranger's appealing aura, Bergstrom took her eyes off the case in her right hand to have another look at him while her left hand came up to grasp the case more firmly. Missing the handle, her left hand brushed the latch atop the case hard enough to loosen it. Now ajar, the latch caught on the interior rubber lining of the trunk and the case yawned wide open spilling dozens of medication samples. Taken by complete surprise Bergstrom panicked and tried to close the case before its entire contents poured out onto the pavement, but succeeded only in dropping the case which landed heavily on the ground with a hollow thud.

Schenk spun around at the sound of the crashing case. Seeing the mess at Bergstrom's feet he ran to her. Blushing with embarrassment Bergstrom felt like crawling into the trunk and slamming it shut on herself. She stood her ground though and attempted to regain her composure. As Schenk drew closer his disarming smile returned and she actually relaxed a bit.

"Let me help you with that," Schenk said squatting down to pick up the now empty case. He laid the case on its side and began to gather up the samples and place them back into it.

Still a bit taken back it took Bergstrom a few seconds to join him, in retrieving the boxes and containers of medication that were strewn about.

"Oh, God! I'm so clumsy! The case got caught inside the trunk and whup! Everything went everywhere! Thank you so much for helping me with this, it's so embarrassing!"

"No need to be embarrassed. Accidents happen all the time," Schenk replied while tossing box after box into the case.

Bergstrom joined him in collecting her wares and within a minute or so they had everything back in the case. She stood and expected Schenk to do the same, but he didn't. Instead he peered under the car and placed his left hand on the bumper and leaned in underneath, with his right hand splayed out before him. Feeling around blindly his hand came out with another box that was wedged against the tire.

"Thank you, thank you so much," she said.

"Not yet, there's one more," he replied leaning back in. His hand reappeared again with a box of samples. "That should do it," he said rising from his crouch.

Now with both standing, Bergstrom got a really good look at him and her heart fluttered. He struck her as being completely masculine, but more beautiful than handsome. She couldn't take her eyes off of his. One a deep, rich blue and the other almost emerald in the noon day Sun, his eyes sparkled with warmth and intelligence. He'd seen the look in her eyes before and had learned to accept it as a compliment, she could tell. Still, he looked away from her.

"That's a lot of pills," Gant remarked awkwardly.

"I'm in sales, pharmaceutical sales," she replied.

"I see."

"Thanks again," she said. Then she added, "My name's Lydia," and offered her hand.

Schenk took her hand and gently shook it. "I'm Lenny. Pleased to meet you Lydia."

Schenk's warm hand and pleasant manner instilled confidence within Bergstrom. A beautiful woman who rarely had any trouble conversing with members of the opposite sex, she rode the wave of self-assurance and went out on a limb. "Lenny, huh? You don't look like a Lenny."

"What does a Lenny look like?"

"When I think of Lenny's I think of Leonard's, little mousy guys with big goofy glasses. That's certainly not you."

"No, no that's not me, I hope not anyway," he replied. He went on, "I'm going in to visit a friend. It looks like you could use some help. Can I give you a hand with them?"

The two cases in Bergstrom's trunk and the one at her feet contained nearly identical stores of samples, she needed only one per stop to show the doctors her products. She took the opportunity though to enlist the help of her new and very interesting friend.

"That would be great. If you really don't mind."

"Not at all."

Schenk hoisted the two cases out of the trunk and rested them on the pavement. He softly shut the trunk and picked them up again. "Away we go then," he said, now staring into her eyes. "Lead the way Lydia. I'll see you to your first prospective buyer and then take my leave to visit my friend."

"There's nothing 'prospective' about it, they all buy," she said, her confidence building.

By the time Schenk had escorted Bergstrom to the administration wing and departed to visit his friend the two had agreed to a date. At her suggestion he would pick her up on Saturday at seven, she would make reservations at Hutch's on Delaware Avenue. With two days to go before the weekend she felt like a giddy school girl again. That been over a year ago, now they lived together.

Back in the here and now Bergstrom declined the desert menu at the hotel restaurant and asked the waiter for the check. Her recollection of their first chance encounter filled her with a familiar warmth. While it was true she didn't know very much about her live-in boyfriend, she truly loved what she did know.

Somewhere in the pit of her stomach she had an empty feeling though. Instinct told her Lenny Schenk was too good to be true, there must be something wrong with him. Her heart whispered he was the perfect man, her soul mate. As her gut and heart played a game of emotional tug of war with her, Bergstrom surrendered, as she invariably did to her heart. The gnawing suspicion which she felt was locked away for the time being, until it resurfaced like some mutant phobia. Silently lurking beneath her bliss was the sinking feeling that the love of her life was hiding something from her. It was a trivial thing she thought for sure, but she was unable to understand why he would keep a secret from her.

Chapter Twelve

    Burning tiki torches bookended the gate to Noreen Dwyer's backyard, while a most patriotic windsock of red, white and blue fluttered below the stars and stripes upon her flagpole in the front yard. The day was drawing to a close, dusk was coming on, and the light would be squeezed from the day within an hour. It was the last weekend before the Fourth of July, but for all of the residents of Watch Point this was their Independence Day. As Grucci, the self-proclaimed "First Family of Fireworks", was busy in Manhattan and other high profile locations on the national holiday, lesser displays, like that of Watch Point, took place the weekend before. Although the parade would occur on the traditional date most of the town's residents had decorated their houses accordingly.
    Gant walked through the gate into the backyard, the tang of ribs and roasted corn teased his nose. He walked further into the sandy yard to find his old flame dancing on the patio to Van Morrison's *Brown-Eyed Girl*. Pushing nearly thirty years since their teenage dalliances, Noreen looked remarkably well especially given the fact she'd delivered five children. While it was true her waist was a little thicker, who's wasn't by their mid to late forties. In the soft glow of the flickering torches, which bordered the Dwyer's gated property at every ten feet or so, she looked young and energetic bee bopping to and fro with a much younger woman who Gant assumed could only be her daughter. He looked from Noreen to the other woman in awe, they were almost identical. As he approached the dancers Noreen looked up and her face lit up with surprise.
    "Phillip," she shouted above the din while spinning toward him.
    Gant smiled and silently offered the bottle of Veuve Clicquot he had in his hands. She snatched the champagne, laid it down on a table beside the grill and took his hand in hers. Now with two dance partners she resumed her gaiety. Up close Gant was able to notice the beginnings of crow's feet at the corner of her eyes. These were offset by prominent laugh lines which creased her cheeks agreeably. Her hazel eyes were alight with life and joy; she was, and had always been a truly happy person.
    When the song melted away she introduced the other woman Gant had been dancing with, "Phillip, this is my oldest, Katie. Katie, this is Mister Gant, an old friend."
    Katie Dwyer shyly grinned.
    "I might have guessed. She's your spitting image Noreen," he replied smiling at his host. "It's a pleasure to meet you Katie," he then added looking at his host's younger version.
    "You too, Mister Gant," she replied. Then to her mother she said, "I'm gonna go find Pete. I'll leave you two to catch up."
    "She's going into her senior year at B.C.," Dwyer told Gant.
    "Good for her and good for you and your husband," he replied. "One less tuition soon."
    "Oh, she's only the beginning. Rory is going to be a sophomore at Holy Cross

and then we've got three more in high school."

"It's a lot of money these days."

"Money's not so much the issue, Patrick makes a good living."

"I've noticed," Gant responded looking out through the backyard over the gigantic boulders and to the swirling darkening waters of the inlet beyond.

"It's just that it all happened so damned fast. It seems like yesterday that Katie was splashing along the shore in a diaper."

"Life is fleeting, that's for sure," Gant said.

"Come, let's get you a drink. Patrick is behind the bar, at least for a little while," she said picking up the bottle of champagne.

Gant followed Dwyer over to the bar where O'Sullivan and Murray were seated sipping strawberry daiquiris through straws from hurricane glasses. Noreen handed the bottle to her husband and then left to greet other guests who'd just arrived. He scanned the bottle reading the label and looked towards Gant, the two men locked eyes. Dwyer held up the bottle, nodded, and stuffed it into a cooler behind the bar.

Turning back toward Gant, Patrick Dwyer extended his hand and said, "Any friend of Noreen's is welcome here…"

"Thanks for having me!" Gant uncharacteristically cut in seizing Dwyer's outstretched hand. "This place is terrific. Better than I ever remember it being."

Dwyer nodded and then finished his sentence, "no matter what has happened in the past."

Gant was expecting worse, he feigned insult. "I can leave if this is uncomfortable for you."

"No, no, not at all. I must admit that I wasn't wild about watching you dance with my wife and daughter, but upon objective consideration it was harmless. Please stay, Noreen would be upset with me if she thought I made you feel unwelcome. Besides, I must thank you. If not for you I may have never landed Noreen. When you did your…whatever it is you did, she fell to me. Thanks!"

O'Sullivan and Murray sat sipping their drinks pretending not to hear the exchange.

"Like I said, it's all behind us. So, what can I get you to drink? I get your first and then you're on your own."

"Those daiquiris look pretty good," Gant replied nodding toward Murray's which was complete with a tiny umbrella and a sliced strawberry upon the rim. Pat Dwyer happily made another daiquiri and then excused himself to get more ice and check on the grill.

"Wow! That was awkward!" O'Sullivan muttered as soon as Pat Dwyer was out of earshot.

"Sure was. I hope that's the end of it," Gant replied. "Otherwise, I'll be hitting the road."

"Pat's a good guy. He just needed to get that off of his chest I'm sure," Murray said.

"Saw you cutting the rug out there Philly," O'Sullivan re-opened the can of worms.

"Noreen's still got the moves," Gant replied.

"Looked like a mother-daughter dance until you showed up."

"Then it looked like a "guy who bagged the mother and now had eyes for the daughter" dance," Murray said.

"Maybe even a Philly-Mommy-Daughter threesome," O'Sullivan added.

"Oh, come on guys, that's disgusting. Enough!" Gant replied, truly repulsed.

"Are you telling us that the thought has never crossed your mind?" Murray asked.

"That's the first time I've ever met her daughter, she seems like a nice kid. No, I didn't think about jumping into the sack with her and her mom."

"Must be slipping Phil," O'Sullivan replied.

Gant, in fact, had no such intentions. His thoughts were altogether entirely different. He wondered briefly how he could lure Katie Dwyer away for his own purposes, none of which entailed hanky panky. Almost as soon as he entertained this fantasy he dismissed it. The young Dwyer was too close to home, to abduct her was asking for trouble. The primary reason that Gant had succeeded at going undetected for so long was because he never preyed on anyone he even remotely knew. All of his victims were complete strangers with which he shared absolutely no ties. After stalking them for a matter of weeks, or months, he would make his move. On very rare occasions when the circumstances were optimal he moved on victim's within days, even hours, but he'd done that only twice in his life.

Never shit where you eat, Gant thought to himself, a little pearl of wisdom one of his C.O.'s was fond of saying regarding matters much different.

Although she embodied all that Gant looked for, Katie Dwyer was out of the question also because it would destroy her mother's life. As teenagers Gant had broken Noreen's heart once and he would not do it again. A late bloomer, by age seventeen Gant's sexual prowess was legendary in the tiny town. A month after young Noreen MacLaughlin had willingly surrendered her virginity to Gant at the age of sixteen, he dumped her for an eighteen-year-old with experience. MacLaughlin was devastated. Despondent she fell into a deep depression, her grades suffered and it was rumored she'd considered suicide. It was seven months before she recovered from the breakup. It was two years before she could look Gant in the eye without feeling embarrassment and shame.

It took Gant many more years to realize the deep implications of what he'd done. When he was twenty-seven he sought out the now married woman to formally apologize to her. Always an understanding soul, Noreen Dwyer granted her forgiveness and the two parted once again on amiable terms. As it turned out she'd married the man of her dreams in Patrick Dwyer. Smart, good looking, and kind, he was a fantastic provider and wonderful father. She had re-found happiness and her youthful smile had returned after years of simply making it through the day. Gant had no intention of destroying Noreen's life again.

His thoughts turned toward the rookie of the year once again. He was disappointed not to see her at the party, but also relieved. Her not being there informed him she wasn't friendly with the Dwyers and that was good, very good. As dozens of parties raged all over town Gant wondered which one she was at. He hoped that she ran in different circles than anyone he knew well. The fact Murray had never seen her before was a positive sign. In a town as small as Watch Point to not be known was a rare feat. Knowing it was a long shot Gant set his sights on the unknown wild card in a deck of familiar faces. He hoped she was a friend of a friend from out of state visiting for the weekend.

Gant punched O'Sullivan in the arm good-naturedly and then sampled the daiquiri and grimaced. He put it down and grabbed a Corona instead and then suggested that they hit the buffet table. Beside the grill was an eight by three foot picnic table. Covered with platters of grilled marinated skirt steak, baby back ribs, pork tenderloin, barbecued chicken, cheeseburgers, hot dogs, roasted corn on the cob, and salads including potato, macaroni, and three-bean, the red and white checked table cloth beneath was obscured from view.

As dusk settled in cloaking the auburn sky in purple darkness, Gant helped himself to a second helping of the succulent ribs; Murray was already nearly finished with his third plate. Fireflies flitted about the sea-scented yard as the guests finished up their meals and the grill was shut down for the night. By eight-thirty the buffet table was cleared and dessert was put out. Much too full Gant passed on the strawberry shortcake, baked Alaska, water melon and vanilla ice cream. Murray and O'Sullivan had snuck off to get high. Gant could smell the sweet tang of cannabis nearby, apparently they'd not snuck off far enough. Soon after the stoned duo had returned Patrick Dwyer announced it was time to trek down to the marina for the show.

Dwyer rolled a kid's radio flyer wagon out of the driveway and into the street. Loaded into the wagon was a seventy-two quart Igloo cooler filled with a variety of iced bottled beer, wine, and wine coolers. As Dwyer lead the way the guests fell in next to him most carrying beach chairs and some smaller coolers of their own. The streets of Watch Point were rumbling with movement.

As seen from above, the festive parade of revelers looked like a migration or, under dire circumstances, an evacuation. Like hordes of wildebeests they thronged west toward the marina using the streets as their sidewalks, automobile traffic was non-existent as the parkway had been shut down since six o'clock. With nobody entering or leaving town for close to three hours it was safe to walk freely wherever one wished. The only wheels were those of kids riding bicycles helter skelter down the avenues.

Ten minutes later the Dwyer party had arrived at the east marina. Finding an open space on the lawn just south of the main dock they staked their claim spreading out their beach chairs and settling in. Waiting for the show to begin they drank, laughed and traded stories, old and new, while gazing west toward the last remnants of the dying Sun, as it shimmered a bruised violet from beyond the horizon. Despite a large police presence the drinking went on unabated, the aroma of reefer wafted by in dribs and drabs. As the sky darkened dozens of boats tied up in the marina and anchored out in Reynolds Channel blew their horns in anticipation of the display. Gant searched the crowd hopelessly for the rookie and was not surprised when he didn't find her.

At nine-twenty-five total darkness had enveloped the area surrounding Watch Point, the first mortar shell thumped, its reverberation pounded off of the spectator's chests, and then streaked silver into the sky. Half a mile up the shell burst forth first a red flower, then a white flower and lastly a blue one. The accompanying concussions shook the ground, the spectators roared their approval, and the show began. Volley after volley, shell after shell shot up from the barge in the channel and exploded over the water less than five hundred feet from those comfortably seated in the marina.

As the sky was illuminated by spectacular iridescent greens, blues, reds, oranges, purples, silvers, and golds, the crowd of better than twenty-five thousand "oohed" and "ahhed," with each successive blast. A blitzkrieg of peonies, chrysanthemums, willows, horsetails, palms, spiders, rings, fish and crossettes gleamed high overhead their thunderous reports echoing off of the water. Gant placed his hand over his heart as a telltale *whump* signaled a series of what he called "Big Bangers" took flight from the barge. Bursting lower and with multiple reports the concussion from these shells was staggering, he felt their pounding thump ricochet within his chest again as they exploded in quick succession.

By 9:50 the grand finale was in full swing, the sky scorched with blooming flashes of light. Lasting a little over five minutes the final barrage incorporated all the different types of effects and was particularly heavy on the "Big Bangers". As the last light of the eruption faded from the dark sky, a darker cloud of smoke stretched out for a mile or more from Watch Point into the marshes toward Freeport and Baldwin. The ovation was enthusiastic and long lasting as the spectators on shore clapped and shouted while those on boats blew their horns with long, honking toots.

The crowd surged out of the marina all laughs and whistles heading back toward the parties from which they'd come. Walking slowly back toward the Dwyer's Gant happened upon Mary Maniscalco and Lisa Dent, two women he knew well from the old days. As they were on their way to the Bay View Inn they invited him to join them.

Eager for a change of scenery he gladly accepted.

* * * *

Home on leave in his early twenties, Gant had spent a lot of time at the Bay View Inn, known simply as the B.V.I. to the locals. Many of them still referred to it as "Red's", the original owner being Red Beckett, a lobsterman turned restaurateurs who'd made a fortune selling lobster wholesale and retail back in the 1960's. Beckett owned his own fleet of eight lobster boats, and had the means to store and process his take, on the premises of his twelve thousand square foot, bay front property. A simple operation, Red's boats docked up behind the storage facility and off-loaded their catches. He owned the boats, the docks, the lot, and the building that stood on it, in short he owned the whole shebang. Rumor had it that Red's dad, Ernst, had been a rum runner during prohibition.

Ernst Beckett was said to have run his illegal cargo in a speedboat from the Atlantic Ocean through Jones Inlet and into Freeport, effectively providing the port village with its name. He was free to make port as local authorities were said to look the other way as the Canadian whiskey or West Indian rum came in. When the elder Beckett passed away in 1959 he left the whole of his inheritance to Red, his only surviving kin.

With his lobster business booming Red decided, a waterfront seafood restaurant could only add to his fortune, and he was so right. Beckett began construction on the Bay View Inn in the early fall of 1963, it was finished in time for the summer crowds that year. An instant success, people came in droves from all over Long Island to feast on Red's shellfish while overlooking the pristine channel behind the restaurant. With a seating capacity of over two hundred and fifty people, Red was in the black by the end of the first summer. An interesting feature which Red made sure the architect incorporated into the plans was a double wide door in the basement of the building. Facing the bay, the door swung outward opening up onto water and nothing else.

After Red sold the business in 1999, close friends let it be known that the old man was quite superstitious and sought to keep his father's spirit alive in the bones of the new building. Beckett's superstitions combined with his distrust of the government prompted him to put the door in place. He reasoned, if the government ever enacted a state of prohibition again he would be ready for it. If the day were to come he would simply load his lobster boats with booze and run it straight into the basement under the cover of night. A solid plan, but the day had never come. Nonetheless, Gant had heard of the wait staff and kitchen crew taking part in all sorts of illegal activities in the basement right under his feet as he stood there at the bar.

* * * *

Following Maniscalco and Dent down the long hallway which led from the main entrance to the bar and dining room Gant peeked into the private party room on the right hand side and saw a number of old acquaintances. Seated at the head of the table was George Bluthe whom Gant was not overly friendly with, but remembered very well.

Bluthe was temporarily banned from the B.V.I. for exposing himself, among other things, at the bar. Some twenty years prior, Bluthe had arrived by boat and ignoring the "No shirt, No shoes, No service" sign, walked into the bar in a bathing suit and nothing else. He'd been very friendly with the bartender on shift and thought nothing of it. He took a seat at the bar, ordered a pina colada with a Meyer's floater and started drinking.

Seven pina coladas and six shots of Cuervo 1800 later, Bluthe thought it would be a good idea to get really comfortable, so he did. Stumbling out of his bathing suit he stood naked at the bar asking for another drink. Gant remembered vividly, Bluthe was nothing to brag about below the waist, yet he admired him for his balls. It was after midnight, there were no children in the restaurant, the bartender was slow to give Bluthe the boot as the naked drunk was a most generous tipper, usually good for at least fifty dollars a night. With yet another pina colada and another shot of tequila Bluthe sat down at his bar stool and continued his binge.

All probably would have worked out well enough if Bluthe had not relived himself right there at the bar. A half an hour or so after peeling off his swim trunks he lurched off of the bar stool onto his feet. Swaying back and forth he leaned against the bar rail with his left elbow while fiddling down below with his right hand. The woman standing with her back to Bluthe screamed in shock as she felt the warm spittle of his urine splash off of the hardwood floor onto her ankles and calves. The woman's husband knocked Bluthe out and dragged him out into the street, where he laid in the gutter for ten minutes until the police arrived.

Decades later, here was George Bluthe, once a pariah barred from the bar, now the guest of honor, or the host of the party, in the very same establishment. Gant couldn't help but laugh to himself thinking back on it. He caught Bluthe's eye as he walked slowly down the dim hallway. Gant gave him a wave and Bluthe raised his glass of red wine. On the opposite side of the hallway from the party room was the coat room which had been the location of the original bar until the restaurant was renovated in late 1999 when Red Beckett sold it to out-of-towners. Further down the hallway, Gant and his lady friends, both of whom he'd slept with at one time or another, passed the bathrooms and then walking up a slightly inclined ramp, found themselves at the head of the dining room, the bar a rectangle measuring fifteen by eight feet was to their right.

Gant wedged his way through the three deep crowd thronged at the bar and made his way to one of the two bartenders. He ordered a Johnnie Walker Black and soda for himself and two Heineken Lights for his company. Emerging again from the scrum he gazed about the bar and dining room in hopes of locating the rookie. Neither the rookie nor his old conquests were present. Knowing the girls habits he waited, his back against the wall not ten feet from the women's bathroom. Within a minute Mary and Lisa emerged hand in hand from the bathroom, both of them glassy eyed and smiling.

"You're still doing that shit, huh, Lis?" he asked Dent, handing her a beer.

"Oh, come on Phil. Don't knock it until you try it. It puts a spring in my step," she replied with a wink of her right eye.

"It's not like we're addicts, we have a little fun sometimes," Maniscalco added taking a sip from her bottle.

"It's your life," was all Gant said.

"You want to try some?" Dent asked him.

"No, no thanks. This is bad enough," he responded holding up his scotch and soda. "But here's to seeing you girls. You both look great, despite the shit. Cheers!"

The three clinked their drinks together and then rehashed old stories for a time, until Dent began sniffing and her itch renewed. Back into the bathroom the girls went while Gant strolled out onto the deck adjoining the bar to have a look outside. A blue heron sat perched atop a piling, staring down into the dark depths below. Intent upon catching a late snack the bird paid no attention to the drunks on the deck. With only a few exceptions all of the thirty or so people out on the deck were smoking. Many of them were sniffing as well. After quickly scanning the scene and finding the rookie lacking, he went back inside making sure to close the glass door behind him.

Back at the bar he was ordering another round when he heard cheering coming from the front of the restaurant. Seconds later the cheering had broken into a chant Gant knew well. "Billy! Billy! Billy!" the crowd shouted as Billy Perelli staggered into the bar. Gant smiled at the old man, astonished he was still alive, and by the looks of it functioning rather well.

Perelli owned a Ford dealership in Hempstead, about a half an hour from Watch Point. Living in Garden City he didn't own a house in town, he rented one for the outlandishly expensive summer months. No more than five foot seven and maybe a hundred and fifty-five pounds, Perelli had that deep, throaty voice that only years of scotch and cigarettes provided. Always wearing a blue Brooks Brothers blazer and slacks in various hues, he looked like a character out of *Goodfellas*. Generous to a fault, Perelli would give a stranger the shirt off of his back if asked.

Everyone in town loved the man especially the bartenders. He was famous for buying drinks for the entire house. It mattered not if there were three customers in the bar or a hundred and fifty, Billy Perelli would always buy the house a round. After making sure that everyone had received their cocktail of choice Perelli would settle up with the bartender, always paying in cash, and then tip him with a hundred dollar bill. If there were two bartenders working he would tip them a hundred each. Gant recalled, Perelli, randy at age sixty-three, had put the moves on a trio of girls who'd moved into town. As the story went the women, all in their late twenties were still unpacking when Perelli knocked at their front door with a bag of lobsters and two magnums of Dom Perignon. Unfortunately for Perelli, nothing came of his offer, but Gant was sure other such offers were repaid in kind or services rendered.

Billy Perelli stumbled into the bar, the sea of people parted as if he were Moses. A man around Gant's age immediately rose from his stool overlooking the liquid blackness of the bay as the tide ran out. Perelli shook the man's hand and sat down. As one of the bartenders rushed over toward Perelli the old man pointed his index finger out before him and swung it around in a circle indicating that he was buying for everyone. The crowd cheered while Gant estimated there must have still been over a hundred people in the bar. It didn't take a genius to figure that including the customary tip Perelli's tab would push toward a grand.

Gant waited for the rush to die down before ordering another Black and soda, he had lost the girls, they were probably in the bathroom again. He picked up his drink and weaved his way toward Perelli who was entertaining a group of bodybuilders who he'd befriended on one of his rare winter visits.

Approaching Perelli from behind, Gant tapped him lightly on the shoulder. The old man spun around on his stool and craned his neck backward to see who it was. When he saw Gant his eyes bulged behind his thick, oversized glasses.

"Philly, baby!" Perelli croaked while gaining his feet. The two men hugged and then Perelli whistled to the bartender closest to them and signaled for two more drinks. "Come, have a drink with me."

"I am right now," Gant replied. "It's somebody else's turn to buy Billy." When the bartender approached with the Dewars on the rocks for Perelli, Gant said, "I'll also need a Black and soda for myself and a round for the gentlemen with the muscles."

In a flash the bartender brought the drinks—the muscle-heads were drinking merlot. Gant handed the wine to the four bodybuilders, all of whom Gant had met at some time and genuinely liked. They voiced their thanks holding up their double-fisted hands.

"How's everything, Billy?" Gant asked.

"Same old shit, kid! The last divorce was a hard pill to swallow, but I'll live."

"I see money is still no object."

"No fucking government bail out for us!" Perelli roared. "We have quality cars, not like that other shit coming out of Detroit."

Gant nodded and laughed.

"What are you laughing at? What are you driving these days anyway?"

"A Volvo, very safe," Gant answered sheepishly not wanting to disappoint his old friend.

"You prick! I oughtta take that drink back!" Perelli bellowed and then laughed from down deep. The deep, coughing laugh thundering out of the old man made Gant wonder if he was going to have a heart attack or stroke. He pictured the man's lungs bouncing off of one another inside his chest. "Born from jets my ass! Smart guy like you should know better," Perelli went on.

"Those are Saab's," Gant corrected him.

"What?"

""Born from jets, those are Saabs. I've got a Volvo."

"Same thing. What the hell do those Scandinavians know about cars? Cars were invented right here!"

"Okay, okay." Gant held up his hands to stop the assault. "It was a gift."

"A gift? Who's giving you cars these days?"

"My Mom, she wants me to be safe."

"Good enough," Perelli answered before sipping from his rock glass. He put the heavy glass down on the bar with a thud, both bartenders looked his way. "Gimme two bottles of that Rodney Strong cabernet and one, two, three, four, make that six glasses," he said taking a head count. "I can't drink this stuff all night," he said nodding toward the scotch, "it'll kill me."

The wine came, the bartender popped both bottles to let them breathe. "Just pour it Sammy," Perelli grunted.

The bartender did as he was told and then turned to go.

"Hey Sammy, sorry! Get a couple glasses for yourself and Pete! And another bottle!" Perelli shouted over the din of the jukebox which was cranking out U2's *Beautiful Day*.

"I need some broads, Philly?" Perelli said Gant.

"There are a few good ones around," he answered careful not to mention the rookie. "I know two who will party with you Billy," he added pointing toward Mary and Lisa who were finally not in the bathroom any longer.

"Been there, done that!" Perelli roared. "But I could go back for more. Why don't you go invite them over for us?"

"This is strictly you Billy, I'm out," Gant replied.

"Out? What do you mean out? You turned fag on me, Philly?"

Gant laughed and then said, "I'm pretty serious with a girl back home, almost engaged."

"You better get your head examined. What are you, crazy? You're what, forty-seven?"

"Close, forty-five," Gant corrected him.

"I was already divorced once at your age. Live it like you've been boy! Keep the good times rolling while you still can."

Gant tried to wave Mary and Lisa over, but they were deep in conversation. To Perelli he said, "I'll go get the girls. You'll get reacquainted." He slipped through the crowd to the other side of the bar. The girls both smiled and waved over to Perelli. A minute or so later they were seated on either side of him drinking his wine.

Everything was going very well. Perelli had the girls laughing, the wine was flowing, the music was loud, but good. The bar began to empty out a bit, it looked like one, or both, of the women would accompany Perelli home. Then the old man ordered a seventh bottle of wine.

The bodybuilders, who had been downing shots of Bacardi 151 on the beach, hit the wall. One of them drained his full glass of cabernet in a single gulp and then smashed the empty glass over his own head, shards of glass burst off of the top of his head and showered down over his wide, tan shoulders. Monkey see, monkey do, the other three bodybuilders also gulped down their wine and shattered their glasses over their heads laughing all the while.

Perelli thought the whole spectacle was so damned funny, he too finished off his wine and smashed his own wine glass over his bald pate. While all of the bodybuilders sported thick heads of lustrous hair, Perelli was almost completely bald. The jagged wine glass lacerated his scalp, blood spurted from the wound and poured down his neck as he laughed oblivious to the damage he'd done to himself. Rather than going to bed with a woman, or women, much younger than himself, Perelli found himself heading to the hospital for seventeen stitches.

By the time the ambulance carted his old friend away, it was past one-thirty. The B.V.I. had become largely empty. It was obvious to Gant that the rookie would not be showing up there. Mary and Lisa were nearly out of blow and sought to find some more. There was one last place to go.

They decided to walk a hundred and fifty feet down the street to see who was hanging out at Captain Sal's Anchor Bar, the late night spot. Also known simply as Sal's as well as Dalia's, Dalia being the widow of the deceased Captain Sal, the Anchor Bar was a fixture of the Watch Point bay side bar scene and a familiar haunt of Gant's. Since the 1950's Watch Point residents had imbibed, most often in the summer, at the Anchor Bar.

Walking into the Anchor Bar was like walking back into history, like walking into someone's living room as a matter of fact. To the right of the front door an upright piano which badly needed a tuning sat idle below the lone television. To the left of the door was an entryway which housed an old coin operated phone booth; it also led to the bathrooms. Stairs ran up from the entryway to the apartment in which Dalia, now ninety-eight years old, still resided. The bar itself stretched twenty-five feet to the door in the back. It was beaten and battered and in dire need of a good cleaning and coat of polyurethane. There were tap heads, but no tap beer was served, only bottles and cans. The soda guns were inoperable as was the ice machine very often, the bartenders sometimes brought bagged ice with them when they went on shift.

The crowd at the Anchor Bar had spilled out onto the front stoop, most of them smoking cigarettes and many others pot. On the heels of other late night carousers hell bent on ruining their next day, the threesome squirmed their way through the door and entered the fray as the ancient jukebox against the wall warbled out *Tell Him*, the 1962 hit by the Exciters. The girls headed for the back deck while Gant shouldered his way up to the bar.

While waiting to catch one of the bartender's attention Gant noticed Robert O'Grady, an old friend and retired city cop, slumped back in a bar stool in the corner next to a vintage 1950's lamp. Gant called over to O'Grady but was unable to rouse the man from his drunken slumber. O'Grady went by many names such as "Bobaloo", "Big Bob", "Boner Boy" and a host of others. Well endowed, O'Grady referred to his member as "Bob's Big Boy". Unfortunately for O'Grady's wife, he often passed out and forgot to wake up when relieving his big boy as was evidenced by the yellowed, drying mattress on their back deck every month or so. A real pistol, while still on the force back in the 1980's, he shot his service gun through the roof of one of the neighborhood bars while he was drunk.

Sober or drunk O'Grady was one of the funniest men Gant had ever encountered. Looking over at the man, Gant instantly recalled one of the best one liners he'd ever heard. It was during the fall of 1991, by then O'Grady was retired on a three-quarters pension. He was working as a bartender at Prudente's, a bar which had once been a very respectable Italian restaurant right up on the main boulevard. It was coincidentally the same bar in which he had discharged his gun. Gant was home on leave, it was late, around three-thirty on a Tuesday morning in mid-November.

Unable to sleep and out for a walk, Gant noticed the lights on inside Prudente's so he tried the door, it swung wide open. Inside, the place was dead quiet, no jukebox, no patrons, no bartender. Gant wondered if somebody forgot to lock up or maybe there was a very stupid burglar sneaking around. Tip-toeing around the hostess station he spied the back of O'Grady's head, he was sitting with his back to the door.

Moving closer, Gant heard O'Grady moan once, twice, and then a third time. Now ten feet behind O'Grady, Gant peeked around the unsuspecting man's shoulder. Bobbing up and down between O'Grady's legs was a curly blonde head of hair. It was then that it happened. Having no idea anybody was in the bar with him and the women, O'Grady groaned once more and calmly said, "Don't ignore the balls young lady." Gant thought he would piss himself. Cupping a hand over his mouth he backed away and then ran for the door and out into the chill night air.

Still reminiscing about the great one liner, Gant paid for his beers and walked toward the back deck. It took some time to make it back there as the bar was full with old time Watch Point people, most of whom he knew on a first and last name basis. He chatted with a number of old acquaintances, the whole time keeping an eye out for the rookie, before he made it to the back door. She was nowhere to be seen. Finally making his way outside, he saw Mary and Lisa sitting at a table overlooking the bay by the bulkhead.

The night sky was cloudless, twinkling stars shimmered down from above. The red and green running lights of a party boat returning from a bluefish trip danced on the rippling, black water.

By that time, Murray and O'Sullivan had left the Dwyer party and were also on the back deck of the Anchor Bar. They, too, were by the bulkhead, on the opposite side from the girls, leaning on the railing with beers in their hands. Gant looked from the girls to his buddies and then back again.

Right between the two couples was the rookie. With her chest thrown out and her right leg bent at the knee toward her left, she posed model-like with a beer in her hand and the other hand on her hip. Nestled between two tables of younger men it looked as though she were holding court. Instinctively looking to separate himself from the wolf pack he walked over to the girls, gave them their beers and settled into an easy conversation with them. He would wait patiently for his opportunity.

As it turned out he waited for a very long time. After making the rounds and mingling with the crowd he always inevitably ended up back with Mary and Lisa, a signal to all that he was in demand, not desperate. The rookie took no notice of him. After an hour and a half Gant lost his patience as happened with him when he became drunk. He left the girls and walked past the rookie slightly brushing her shoulder as he went by. "Oh, excuse me. I'm sorry," he said flashing his charismatic smile.

As if waiting for his ploy she replied, "That's the best you could do?"

With a sheepish grin he responded, "Very amateurish, I'll admit. You're very difficult to make eye contact with."

"I saw you trying," she replied flipping her golden curls away from her face.

"Then why not?"

"Well, really, you're probably old enough to be my dad," she blurted out seemingly with no thought for his feelings.

"Ooh, that hurts. I thought I'd held up pretty good."

"Oh, don't get me wrong, you're hot, but just a little bit too mature for me," she said winking her now glassy emerald eyes.

Not used to rejection Gant was slightly taken back at her rebuff. He glanced around and noticed that the two of them now had an audience. Men, and some women too, gawked at them as they spoke.

Gant instantly realized it was no good. The rookie was a mere pipe dream. Even if she were to be receptive to his advances everyone in town would be talking about it the following morning, probably for the rest of the summer the way she looked. It was time to call it a night and go home. Still, he couldn't resist asking her, "Where are you from anyway?"

"The city," came her reply. "My friend from Amsterdam is a nanny here. I came out for the weekend. Beautiful place."

"That it is," Gant agreed as he walked away.

Back inside the Anchor Bar Billy Hayes, an old friend, was banging out *Lady Madonna* on the poorly tuned piano. Despite the instrument's condition and Hayes's vocal limitations, it actually sounded pretty good to Gant. Either that or he was too drunk to not know any better. He did know he'd done well to cease and desist, as he'd remained within the proper boundaries of logic and reason. Admitting to himself he had set the bar too high, he left the bar feeling confident. He was glad he'd been wise enough not to push the envelope as that could lead to a possible disaster.

Regardless of the fact the rookie had no real ties to anyone in town, it was too risky to attempt his craft with such a high profile player. He realized he'd never taken anyone from Watch Point, and with good reason. The town was too small, too compact. People living on top of one another knew everything about one another. Satisfied the night was a learning experience as well as a good deal of fun, he began his walk home. The following day was forecast for thunder storms during the day but clearing at night. He planned to go fishing in the evening.

Chapter Thirteen

A phone call startled Wilder from a peaceful slumber shortly before seven o'clock on Sunday morning. Still in a dream state he struggled to find the phone on his nightstand before it woke up the rest of the family. His hand brushed the water glass by the phone spilling its contents onto the hardwood floor beneath; he was fortunate to grasp the glass before it too found the floor. Groaning, he picked up the phone and answered, "Yeah?"

"Is this Detective Dan Wilder?" a calm voice asked.

"Yeah, who's this?"

"This is Inspector Dreyfuss of the Royal Canadian Mounted Police."

Wilder pushed himself up onto an elbow, he was suddenly wide awake.

"I apologize for calling on you so early," the Mountie went on, "but it seems we've recovered the body of one of your citizens."

Wilder scratched his head and replied, "My boss is out in California visiting relatives. I need to get in touch with him, chain of command and all that."

"Chief Detective Salerno advised me to call you directly and give all the details to you. I woke him a little before four o'clock in the morning, but he was deeply appreciative of the call."

Wilder was out of bed and heading into the kitchen with the phone to his ear. "Me too, me too! It's something I wasn't prepared for this morning."

"There's never a good time for this type of news, is there?" Dreyfuss replied sadly.

"You've gotten a positive I.D.?" Wilder asked, now with a legal pad and pen in his hands.

"We have. We checked with the National Missing and Unidentified Persons System and found the young man's name is, well, was Cory Nichols, age fifteen according to our information."

Wilder's heart sank, he was hoping the kid would eventually turn up alive somewhere.

"We've got nearly two hundred unidentified bodies in Ontario, but this one came back very quick for us," Dreyfuss informed him.

"Two hundred?" Wilder gasped. "It's not exactly New York up there!"

"Some have been around for decades. The oldest unidentified body in the Ontario Provincial Police database traces back to 1956 when a man was found on the outskirts of North Bay. Very sad."

Not knowing where North Bay was and not really caring Wilder got back to the case at hand, his case. "Picture I.D. and prints for Cory Nichols?"

"Well, prints—yes. A picture I.D. would be impossible," Dreyfuss responded.

"Waterlogged, or bloated?" Wilder asked.

The Mountie paused, "There's no face at all, really. Nothing left on the skull but a thin layer of fatty tissue. It looks as though this boy has been scalped from the throat to the back of the neck."

"Could be scavengers, weasels, raccoons, birds. You have wolves up there?" Wilder asked.

"Could be, but the rest of the body is pretty much in tact," Drefuss replied, and then added, "except for the organs."

"Come again please, inspector," Wilder asked.

"The organs are all gone. It's as if the kid's been gutted. Outside of a morgue after a body has been dissected I've never seen anything quite like this."

After digesting this grisly piece of information Wilder asked, "When did you find him?"

"The body was discovered by some kids yesterday afternoon at around four-thirty our time. It took until now to get a positive match on the prints."

"Where did you begin?"

"Well, we searched the database for missing persons worldwide, paying especially close attention to those missing from here and the states. The victim is obviously male so that helped to cut down the pool of candidates. Using medical birth records we ran matches for all males between the ages of twelve and thirty and we hit on Cory Nichols. Our medical examiner took some x-rays as well. The fact that there is a titanium plate fusing his wrist together only validates the I.D. Apparently the kid was a hockey player and had an accident two years ago which shattered his wrist. It's him."

"Where was he found?"

"He was in a river just outside of Alliston, it's about fifty miles northwest of Toronto. The Nottawasaga River runs east of Alliston. The land in the area is being cleared for development. It seems that the body was uncovered by land movers, but went unnoticed until these kids came upon it. It scared the hell out of them."

"Probably won't be going back there any time soon."

"I wouldn't," Dreyfuss agreed.

"How long has the body been there, do you know?"

"It's hard to tell without an official autopsy and we're leaving that matter to you since he's a U.S. citizen. If I had to take a guess though, I'd say that the boy's been there for at least half a year."

"Anything else?"

"Well we know the who, the what, the where, and the approximate when. What we don't know is the why, or how. I promise we'll do our very best to assist you in getting to the bottom of this. It's very disturbing to all of us."

"So his family hasn't been notified, I take it," Wilder presumed.

"Again that's going to be your job, like the autopsy," Dreyfuss replied. "We think that it's best coming from your department."

"I agree," Wilder lamented.

"So then, the next logical step is for you to make arrangements to retrieve the body. I'd suggest you drive up yourself to see the site, it will only take you about two and a half hours. You should get here ASAP, preferably before it rains, as well as for the family's sake."

"Of course, I'll be there this morning," Wilder replied. "I'll call my partner and head straight up. I need the closest available address and directions from there."

"There's a convenience store less than a mile from the dump site. Call me when you get to it and I'll give you further directions from there." Dreyfuss provided the address of the store as well as his cell phone number. "I'll be waiting at the site.

We'll go to the morgue as soon as you've checked it out."

"I'll see you within three to four hours depending on traffic which should be light, early on a Sunday morning."

"Very good then, goodbye detective," Dreyfuss said warmly.

"Thank you inspector, I appreciate all of your help," Wilder ended the call.

He speed dialed Hamilton to rouse her. They made plans to meet at the station house within a half an hour. With a certain degree of anxiety he then picked up the phone and woke the chief of police, to ask him to contact the Erie County Medical Examiners Office to request a transport north over the border. Wilder was told the van would be ready by eight-thirty. Wilder and Hamilton left for Canada shortly after eight o'clock, the van would proceed on its own directly to the coroners building in Toronto.

* * * *

Motoring north in the Crowne Vic, Hamilton took a sip of coffee and asked, "All of the organs are gone, you say?"

"That's what the Mountie told me," Wilder answered.

"Crazy, maybe it's some weird voodoo ritual," she offered.

"I'm not thinking there's a big Caribbean population up here," Wilder replied.

"I'm brain storming Dan, this is nuts! Whoever did this is not your normal run of the mill psychopath."

"I'd have to agree with you."

"Plus the face is gone."

"Also the hair," Wilder added.

"What could he possibly want with the face and hair?" Hamilton asked.

"You said 'he'. We don't know if the killer is a 'he' yet although the deck is stacked in favor of it."

Hamilton shot him a knowing look as if to say only a man could be capable of such course brutality. "It's like a sicko movie, like the *Friday the 13th* series. We've got to think in the bizarro world."

"Well then, maybe it's part of a ritual sacrifice. Some of the native populations up here still adhere to the old ways," Wilder halfheartedly proposed. "Maybe the kid ran away from home and then found trouble."

She shrugged, and said, "The face and hair is the strangest part. I mean the organs can be explained."

"Please explain," Wilder asked.

"Some people consider certain organs delicacies. Look at Jeffrey Dahmer."

"The hair is obvious, you can make wigs," Wilder said.

"This kid had a buzz cut when he went missing," Hamilton countered.

"Could have grown out, it's been eight months," he replied.

"Not enough for a wig, maybe a toupee," she said.

"Again you pick on the men," he responded which earned him another annoyed glance.

"I have no idea what anyone would do with a face," Hamilton said.

"A mask?" Wilder joked.

"Shut up Dan!" Hamilton backhanded him on the arm.

Hamilton and Wilder were delayed as they ran into an accident, a fender bender involving a local farmer and a teenage texter. They pulled up to the dump site about twenty minutes after the van from the Erie County Medical Examiners Office arrived at the coroners building at Twenty-Six Grenville Street in Toronto. While the detectives got out of the Crowne Vic and walked the five hundred or so feet into the ravaged forest the driver from the Erie County ME's office was signing for the remains of Cory Nichols. By the time the detectives reached the actual location where the body was found Cory Nichols was already loaded into the stainless steel shelf in the rear of the Erie County Ford Econoline panel van. The driver started the ignition, the van's industrial power refrigeration system hummed to life and the dead boy was on his way to being repatriated.

The Buffalo detectives approached a pair of Ontario Provisional Police cruisers, black with white doors, their red flashers blinking in the mid-morning Sun, and took out their credentials. Waved through, they ducked under the yellow police tape and made their way toward the river to where the inspector was overseeing a crime scene investigation team of four. Dreyfuss got the heads up from the patrolmen on the perimeter and left the investigators to do their job.

The inspector turned toward the detectives and strode forth in their direction. A big man with a bulging belly, Charles Dreyfuss moved surprisingly quickly. He stepped up to Wilder and held out a large, freckled hand, "Detective Wilder, thank you for your expediency."

Wilder nodded, took the burly Mountie's hand and replied, "This is my partner, Detective Hamilton."

Dreyfuss smiled, his red handlebar mustache arching upward as he shook hands with Hamilton. "Pleased to have you here to help us. The more heads, the better I always say."

Hamilton instantly liked the fatherly older man.

"Well it seems we were in error until quite recently," Dreyfuss began running his thumb and index finger through his mustache.

"You mean it's not ours?," Hamilton asked hoping it was the case.

"Oh, no. Sorry. I should have been more careful prefacing that. The body is yours, but I was told twenty minutes ago this is not the dump site, it's merely where he was found."

"Okay," Wilder said. "So, what are we looking at now?"

"Come down here," Dreyfuss said, ushering them toward the river.

Hamilton and Wilder followed Dreyfuss down into a trench created by the developers hewn into the soil for electric and water service. Climbing out of the trench they found themselves looking at a ravaged and gnarled landscape. Tree stumps yet to be ground and dislodged rocks, littered the until recently pristine woods. The developers had not cleaned and graded the land as yet. Carefully navigating the terrain they found themselves at the banks of the Nottawasaga River. The riverbank had been ripped up despite strict government regulations against such crude land usage. Tree roots, displaced boulders and old pilings, mixed with the mud to create an inhospitable shoreline.

"The body was found right here," Dreyfuss told them pointing to a culvert in which the limb of an oak tree and some rose bramble were stuck. "The boys, three of them, ages nine to eleven, were out doing what boys do when one of them saw what he thought to be a nice piece of driftwood. It turned out to be the deceased's elbow and forearm sticking out of a ripped up burlap bag. Upon closer inspection the boy recognized it for what it was and ran off screaming for his friends. Terrified, they took off for home. We received the call within a half an hour of them finding it."

"What's changed then?" Wilder asked.

Dreyfuss held up his hand and said, "Give me just a second. Robby," he shouted, but good-naturedly toward the team of investigators.

A young black man sporting a puffy, 1970's style afro, slowly raised his head from his work sifting through mud and looked in Dreyfuss's direction. "You need me, Charlie?"

Dreyfuss nodded his head. "Could you some up here and explain to these detectives what your thinking is?"

Trudging through the muck, the investigator joined the detectives and inspector. After introductions he said, "The burlap bag has big holes in it as you'll soon see. It's my belief those big holes were created when the bag was dragged along the river bottom for miles maybe. This isn't where the body was dumped. If the body was dumped here the holes would not be in evidence."

"Unless the killer used an old, holey bag to begin with," Hamilton suggested.

"It doesn't check out. The bag is as clean as can be. There's practically no sand, silt, or mud residue on it or in its fibers. If that body was dumped here and then unearthed by the land movers it would have been caked with mud."

"Could the current have washed the bag clean?" Wilder asked.

"Very unlikely. We've had a drought for the last six months. Look at the flow of the river," the young man replied.

Hamilton and Wilder stared at the river which was indeed barely trickling by. The banks on the opposite side featured easily perceptible high tide markings. The high tide line indicated that the river was flowing more than three feet below normal.

"This river flows south to north, its headwaters being the Niagara Escarpment. If you ask me, the body was dumped upstream, maybe as far as a hundred miles upriver, and slowly made its way up here. If it got caught up from time to time it could have taken it months to reach here, many months."

"It's unlikely the killer dumped the body into the falls though," Wilder presumed.

"Very. If that body had been dumped into the falls it would have incurred a massive amount of trauma. Lots of broken bones and contusions. There are none."

The young investigator's theory seemed sound. Needing some time to mull his findings over the detectives thanked him and he returned to his work. It was evident to them and the inspector, the body had only recently come to rest here.

"He does very good work, don't you think?" Dreyfuss asked.

"He's a sharp kid alright," Wilder replied.

Dreyfuss sighed deeply and fingered his glasses up on his nose, "So now, it's up to us to search the river from here up to its headwaters. We'll look for anything out of the ordinary, tire tracks, remnants of the bag, clothing and such. But I must be honest with you, the chances of us finding anything that will lead us to the original dump site are near nil. There's too much territory, too many elements involved, and it's been far too long."

"We appreciate your efforts on the boy's behalf," Hamilton said to the inspector.

"You'd do the same I know. It's our lot in life after all. Let's head for the morgue so you can have a look for yourselves."

"That's already been taken care of," Wilder informed the inspector. "One of our M.E. vans picked up the remains and is on its way back to Buffalo."

"Timely, very good! I will call with any new developments. You do the same, please," the inspector said.

"We will, and thanks again," Wilder replied.

* * * *

The ride home to Buffalo was somber to say the least. There was no hypothesizing, no brainstorming, practically no conversation at all between Hamilton and Wilder. Both had their minds on what awaited them at the medical examiner's office.

With two lanes in each direction Kensington Avenue was dotted with billboards, scrub trees and open fields of scorched grass on one side and mostly abandoned, boarded up houses on the other. What was once a residential district had fallen upon hard times and had degraded into not such a nice neighborhood. With number Five Hundred and One in sight, Hamilton eased up on the gas and turned into its narrow driveway. Coasting into the parking lot behind the small two story structure, the detectives saw three vans parked side by side. The van closest to the receiving bay was still knocking and pinging from its recent trip. Wilder rang the bell at the door and after providing his name via an intercom system an attendant opened the door. Wilder held the door as Hamilton entered the rear entrance of the Erie County Medical Examiner's Office. The attendant slipped by them and into the parking lot eager to get back to his weekend activities.

The chill air of the morgue was a welcome respite from the soaring temperatures of the late June heat. Doctor Herzlich's office was immediately to the right; the door was closed. Wilder knocked, the chief medical examiner failed to answer so the detectives moved on, the cold tile floors click-clacking beneath their hard soled shoes. A wall of stainless steel pull out shelves, the cooler, lined the right side of the office. Within these frigid, forty degree storage shelves those of dubious demise lay until they were autopsied or, that having been completed, were moved on to the funeral home chosen by their next of kin. File cabinets lined the left side of the office; there was also a water cooler and a coffee maker. Past the cooler was the autopsy room, then the X-ray room, identification room where the deceased were fingerprinted and photographed, and finally the lockers where their personal effects were stored until they were claimed. The offices of the other two M.E.'s were side by side toward the front of the building on the second floor. The second floor housed the labs as well as the doctor's showers, and lockers.

Wilder peeked through the small observation window within the steel door to the autopsy room and saw Doctor Herzlich, his back stooped over a gleaming silver table. The doctor was being assisted by Doctor Beryl Flatley, the office's second in command. A high profile case, the two were summoned in to work late Sunday morning. Wilder gently knocked on the glass; both doctors looked up from the table and peered toward the door, Flatley went to the service bank at the head of the table, flipped a switch and then waved him in.

Upon entering Hamilton and Wilder immediately donned blue surgical masks to fend off the stench they presumed would be wafting off of Cory Nichol's remains. Having been inside the room a number of times, Wilder walked directly over to the table upon which the boy's body laid. It was only Hamilton's third time in the morgue, she took a few seconds to adjust and get her bearings. All of the equipment in sparkling stainless steel, the room contained six identical autopsy tables on rolling wheels. Each table had its own wall mounted service bank consisting of sinks, hoses, solution feeders, scales, surgical instruments, a pull down overhead lamp, and cabinets containing supplies. Stretching the length of the three service banks on the left hand side of the room was a large observation window from which aspiring med school students were given the opportunity to view an autopsy live, many of them asking and answering questions. There was nobody permitted in the gallery today.

Hamilton joined Wilder and the doctor's table side. The sheet was off of Nichols as they were already well in to the procedure. As the Mountie had told them, the boy's face and hair had been stripped clean off. What was left covering his ivory skull were mere strips of graying, rotted fatty tissue. The eye sockets were empty, tendrils of water soaked gray matter feathered forth from them as if seeking light. The body was indeed intact though woefully empty. Seeing the victim for the first time Hamilton winced, her heart plummeted with intense fear and revulsion, yet it never surfaced on her face. Wilder glanced toward her and then back away, satisfied she was all right. Horror turned to pity and then she regained her composure and resolve, she was here to do her job.

Herzlich, a tall man at six foot six, stood erect as the doctors and detectives exchanged greetings.

"I'll speak people speak, right Dan?" Herzlich assumed.

"Please," Wilder replied. Wilder had always liked Herzlich. He'd known him for over twenty years and found him to be a regular guy despite the stigmatisms sometimes associated with medical examiners.

"Thanks, when speaking to college students and the occasional high school anatomy class I'm always careful to speak in purely scientific terms, they are here to learn after all. It's nice once in a while to, as they say, let your hair down." Herzlich did, in fact, have a foot and a half long pony tail of reddish gray curls tucked neatly into his surgical cap. "At any rate the complete procedure from start to finish, with correct terminology, will be on tape. We just turned off the camera when you came in."

The detectives nodded their understanding and waited for him to go on.

"Well then, unfortunately this will be one of the fastest autopsies ever, there's really not that much to look at. There was no need for a y-incision, whoever did this took care of it themselves."

"Inspector Dreyfuss told us he'd been gutted," Hamilton broke her silence.

"This boy has been harvested," Doctor Flatley corrected Hamilton. She went on, her warm brown eyes conveying a sympathy, only another mother could feel, "Nearly all of his organs have been carefully removed. Whoever did this has real skills, knows what they are doing. I'd be surprised if there aren't six or seven people walking around with this boy's parts right now."

"That's highly probable," Herzlich agreed. "The lungs, liver, pancreas, heart, kidneys and eyes were all taken out with extreme skill by the looks of it. The incisions are clean and distinct. If an amateur where to have attempted this it would be easily noticed. The incisions would be ragged, there would be chipped bones, there are all sorts of indicators. There's no doubt in my mind, either of our minds," he said nodding toward Flatley, "someone with training harvested this boy to sell his organs on the black market."

"Is it possible the water and river bottom wore any ragged scraps of flesh away leaving the incisions smooth?" Wilder asked ."Plus polished chipped bone too?"

"I suppose it is possible, but not in this case. Here look for yourself," he said, peeling back a flap of abdominal tissue exposing the rib cage. "These ribs are all flawless, not a scrape, a chip or an abrasion on any of them. The same is true for all of the bones. Water can't buff out imperfections and then replace the bone as if it were never gone. It simply can't happen. This kid was carved up by a steady, experienced hand."

"So you're saying maybe we should be looking for a doctor?" Wilder asked.

"I'm not saying it's definitely a doctor, but did you ever read *The Devil in the White City?*" Herzlich asked.

Wilder shook his head no while Hamilton replied, "Yes, the doctor at the Chicago World's Fair."

"Exactly!" Herzlich clapped his hands. "The book is non-fiction so we know anyone is capable of anything when the right or, in such a case, the wrong circumstances present themselves. Could be a doctor, or a pathologist for that matter," he said wryly. "It's almost certainly someone with in depth anatomical knowledge as well as true hands on skill and experience. It could be a vet or military medic, maybe a farm boy whose grown up to find there are more lucrative ways to make money than slaughtering cows and pigs."

Wilder searched Hamilton's stare; the two were thunderstruck. All of their half-baked, grasping theories flew out the window with the retrieval of this body. Suddenly it all made sense and neatly tied the four victims together. All were young and healthy consequently their organs were in prime condition meaning they could be sold for a premium.

"What about the face and the hair though?" Hamilton pressed.

"That's anyone's guess really," Flatley answered. "It's my feeling anyone capable of doing this to another human being, has obsessions other than getting rich. To understand why the killer would want to scalp and skin the face of his victim you should probably speak to a shrink. Your best bet would be a forensic psychologist."

Herzlich nodded his agreement, "Could be as simple as a trophy or a souvenir, who really knows what goes on inside the minds of these types."

"Can you recommend someone?" Hamilton asked.

"Doctor Viscardi, Thomas Viscardi. We'll contact you with his number when we're done here," Flatley replied.

"Now then, let's get to the cause of death which is very unusual," Herzlich continued spreading the slack jawed mouth wide. "Now I'd like you to take a look up at the roof of the mouth." He pulled the overhead lamp down and tilted it at a ninety degree angle so that the beam of light illuminated the oral cavity and throat of the corpse.

Wilder leaned down and peered into the maw of the dead boy using a magnifying glass which Herzlich handed to him. "Look up at the roof," Herzlich instructed him. "You see that circle there? It's about the size of a ten-penny nail head."

"Yeah, I see it.

"Well that's what it is. I checked it out with a microscope and it's definitely not a slug, there's no evidence of tumbling that occurs when a slug enters flesh. This goes straight through as if it were driven in like a stake. I'm pretty certain that when we crack the skull we'll find a nail in the brain."

"You're sure about that?" Hamilton asked taking the magnifying glass from Wilder and peering into the boy's gaping mouth.

"Like I said, once we saw the skull in two and take out the brain we'll know for sure, but I'd bet my house on it."

"So whoever did this drove a nail through this boy's brain to kill him?" Hamilton inferred aghast.

"No, more like shot it through. The killer likely used a nail gun as the murder weapon," Flatley countered. "A framing gun by the looks of the wound. Nail guns leave tool marks consistent with a solitary mechanized blow, very much like the firing pin impression on a shell casing. Look at the perimeter of the entrance wound here," she said. "See how the flesh is bruised and abraded?"

"I do," Hamilton replied. "It's discolored too, I mean darker than the flesh surrounding it."

"Nail guns most often leave primer residue, usually lead or barium, like gunshot residue. After being submerged it's unlikely any of the residue would remain near the wound, but nail guns slightly singe whatever they are fired into so the residue has been burned into the flesh," Flatley explained.

"That's sick, it must have been so painful," Hamilton said.

"Actually, he probably didn't feel a thing. We're confident, and again we'll have the evidence as soon as we open the skull, that the nail was fired from a nail gun. They're so powerful, the nail most likely penetrated the brain causing almost instantaneous death," Flatley finished.

Herzlich added, "It's really a most effective weapon and completely impossible to trace. Unlike the slug from a gun which has its own unique signature and can therefore be traced back to the gun from which it has been discharged, a nail from a nail gun has no distinguishing features. The nails come in strips, mass produced and boxed in factories. Billions of nails are used every month. The guns themselves are sold by the tens of thousands each year. Nobody needs a scrap of I.D. to buy a nail gun. They're available at many hardware stores."

"Of course, you'll have all of the physical evidence shortly," Flatley said.

"What else can you tell us then," Wilder asked after mentally readying himself.

"We know that the vic was, of course, held against his will as is indicated by these ligature marks here," Flatley said, pointing at the boy's wrists, "and here," then at his ankles. "We're thinking he was most likely bound with zip ties, or cable ties whichever you want to call them." Wilder and Hamilton examined the bloated, gray flesh at the boy's wrists and ankles and saw the purplish, bruised abrasions indicative of debilitating, prolonged pressure at those areas.

"Anything else we can use?" Wilder asked.

"This is a stretch, but we think the murderer may have used chloroform or another anesthetic to subdue the victim," Herzlich said. "It's extremely difficult to say with any real authority, because we don't have any lungs to examine. We did though find slight trace elements of an anesthetizing agent in the boy's windpipe. The amounts are minute, but that is most probably attributable to being submerged for months. At any rate the trace amounts are there and the lining of the trachea shows mild inflammation. Sometimes a mild allergic reaction will manifest itself in that way."

Flatley added, "Now an alternate reason for this could be, the boy had visited the dentist prior to his disappearance to have a cavity taken care of. Novocaine would cause similar inflammation. If he didn't know he was allergic to Novocaine he wouldn't object to having it administered."

"Better than a drill cold turkey," Wilder said.

"Yes, and the boy has only one cavity and it looks as though the dental work has been done recently. We'll be in touch with the dentist shortly," she finished.

"You'll have the full report and accompanying tape by tomorrow morning at the latest," Herzlich assured them. "If you hang around for fifteen minutes we can tell you with one hundred percent accuracy, what type of projectile killed him. We're about to crack the skull now. It won't take long to splice the brain. Why don't you walk up to the viewing gallery and have a seat. There's coffee outside by the file room."

"I think we'll pass this time, thanks doc," Wilder replied looking to Hamilton who shook her head in agreement.

The detectives thanked the pathologists for their time and Doctor Flatley turned on the video camera. She then engaged the circular bone saw, it whirred to life, a high pitched whine like a dentist's drill. The detectives turned toward the door in a hurry. Seeking to avoid the scream of the saw as it bit into the skull of Cory Nichols, they scurried out of the autopsy room and into the hallway.

The first ever Gant victim had been recovered and had provided a wealth of information. The detectives had a reasonable profile for the killer with which to move forward. They had a logical, money-driven motive to work with. They now knew something about how the assailant operated. Yet, the feeling they were no closer to catching their quarry pervaded their thoughts.

Chapter Fourteen

Shortly after two o'clock the detectives left the morgue and headed toward police headquarters.

Gant was waking from a fitful night's sleep, he never slept well when he drank a lot. He'd come home to his mother's house by four-fifteen in the morning. He took some aspirin and chased it down with two large glasses of water and was in bed by four-thirty. Five and a half hours later he woke, bleary eyed and head pounding. He rolled out of bed and in the dim light of his cave stumbled toward the bathroom. After relieving himself of the previous night's libations, he washed his hands and tramped up the narrow stairs to the kitchen.

Squinting back unexpected light as the Sun glinted through a dense layer of clouds, he noticed his mother was fast asleep in the living room rocking chair, her midmorning nap well underway. Counting his blessings he went to the refrigerator and rummaged around before finding two slices of leftover pizza which he ate cold. Two more aspirins and a big glass of milk helped to ease his pain. He padded back down the stairs and into the safety of the darkened cave. He planned to rise for good at five o'clock and go jogging on the beach to sweat out the toxins he'd ingested the night before. Then an outdoor shower, a quick bite for dinner with his mother, and then he'd catch the seven o'clock boat for a night's worth of fishing.

Thank God for the cave, Gant thought to himself, as he quickly succumbed to the room's benighted enchantment.

* * * *

As it was a Sunday night trip the boat was only half full, about twenty-five anglers were aboard. Gant had been down at the marina early and staked out a prime spot back in the stern. After paying his fare he claimed the stern's port corner by placing his rod in the rod holder and tying an old, ragged T-shirt on the handrail. He placed an empty bucket and his well travelled Playmate cooler on the deck beneath the rod. Gant then disembarked and walked through the marina parking lot and across the boulevard to the deli where he bought some beer and ice. He also ordered a chicken cutlet hero for the cruise back inshore later that night. He returned to the boat at ten to seven to await its departure.

Diesel fumes hung heavily in the evening air as the twin Cats of the Miss Watch Point II belched out dark clouds, her deck rumbling beneath the fishermen's feet. With the engines running the captain made one last check of his instruments and then made a radio check with the Coast Guard station at Jones Beach. With all at the ready the captain blew his horn signaling his deckhands to untie the seventy-seven foot party boat. Its lines cast off, the big bi-level boat reversed out into Reynolds Channel clearing the east marina's docks. Then the captain threw her into forward and the Miss Watch Point II churned east toward Jones Inlet. It was ten after seven when the boat cruised by the Bay View Inn. The Sunday evening dinner crowd had spilled out onto the back deck to have cocktails and watch the boats drift in and out. Some of them waved to the fishermen on the party boat, Gant returned the wave.

The captain of the Miss Watch Point II was named Tomas Brecht. Short and squat, with a prominent belly and a jet black mustache, Brecht was the son of Gunter Brecht, the man for whom Gant had served as mate on the original Miss Watch Point during the summers of his high school years. Upon seeing the captain Gant instantly recognized him as being the old captain's son as he was the spitting image of his old man. Gant wondered why he'd never met this son before. It was certainly curious. He'd met the old captain's wife, the other son and both daughters, yet he'd never crossed paths with Tomas, who appeared to be in his early thirties. The elder Brecht had died of heart disease at the age of fifty-four and it looked as if young Tomas was following in his father's footsteps. Besides the captain, who would have no association with Gant, Gant recognized nobody on board, and that made him most comfortable.

As the boat cleared the channel the mates checked the rental rods to make certain they were appropriately rigged with hooks, sinkers, and wire leaders. The bluefish they had caught the night before were called "gorilla blues." These fish had big chompers that bit right through monofilament, the wire leader eliminated that problem. There were two mates as was customary on a night blues trip. Working from the bow to the stern each took a side and examined each pole. Working the starboard side was a kid of about seventeen, Gant estimated. Golden tanned, with Sun bleached dirty blonde hair, he was heavily muscled, and of medium height.

Gant noticed a cigarette dangling from the corner of his mouth as he chatted up a man and his wife. On the port side was a younger kid, probably no more than fifteen. Tall and lanky he was a bit clumsy, he hadn't yet grown into his frame it seemed. He pushed a shock of chestnut hair out of his eyes before smiling at a couple of middle aged men and asking them if they wanted in on the pool. After collecting some pool money from them he moved on to the next rod. He re-rigged a couple of rods, tying on heavier sinkers, and then moved on. Finally making it to the back of the boat he saw Gant had brought his own set up. He checked it visually without touching it and gave Gant the thumbs up.

After making sure everyone aboard was properly rigged for the trip the mates, in sneakers and shorts, went below deck into the hold. They reappeared minutes later wearing orange bibs, sometimes called skins by those who fish for a living. The waterproof bibs would keep the mates dry from chest to ankle. From experience Gant knew the boots they now wore went to the knee; the two boys were virtually impervious to water. The waterproof boys met at the filet station beside the stairs in the stern. From the freezer underneath the cutting board they took a flat of butterfish, a flat of mackerel, a dozen whole bunkers, and a can of chum. The baitfish were tossed into ten gallon buckets and hit with a hose to thaw. The younger mate softly sprayed the chum to loosen it up a bit, the seventy degree air would do the rest of the work as the night went on.

Gant caught a whiff of cannabis and saw most of those aboard had already cracked their first beer. *That's why I loved working these trips. People were drunk and stoned and tipped me out the wazoo*, he remembered. *There were no annoying mothers with their screaming kids always tangling their lines. Those that went out at night knew what they were doing, and even when they got shit-faced they were usually somewhat manageable and almost always generous.*

Gant reached into his cooler and grabbed a can of Bud. He popped it open and wondered if the mates would eat for money. Thinking back to his nights working the bluefish trips, he recalled customers daring him to eat the frozen bait for money. *How stupid I was*, he thought. *On a nightly basis I'd swallow a chunk of butterfish or sometimes a sardine for five dollars. The Sun hits the shit during the day trips, it thaws out, and if it's not used, is refrozen for the night trips. Could have, probably should have ended up in the hospital getting my stomach pumped for a lousy five bucks! I got lucky.*

As the two mates began to carve up the bait a smattering of men, some with their adolescent sons and even daughters, gathered by the filet station to watch as the mates did their best imitation of Japanese hibachi chefs. Flipping fish heads and tails up into the sky where vigilante gulls and terns patiently waited, the mates filled small pails with a variety of the baitfish. When the pails were stocked the mates hosed in a little sea water to keep the bait fresh and then walked the deck placing them at the foot of each groups claim. Returning to the filet station the younger mate stuck a ladle into the semi softened can of chum and stowed it safely in the corner next to the men's bathroom door.

Gant was about to declare dirty sushi eating a lost art form when one of the fishermen, an older guy who was wearing tattered green bibs of his own, called out, "Ten bucks for the mackerel!"

Ten bucks, Gant thought to himself. *The art has finally been formally recognized. I guess that's the cost of inflation.*

With the cigarette hanging from the corner of his mouth, the older mate didn't wait for the offer to be rescinded. "Let's see the cash first!" he called back before taking a long drag off of his Marlboro Light.

"Here you go," replied the fisherman, holding a crumpled up ten out for the mate to see it. "But you have to swallow it, no hiding."

"Do you want it chewed or swallowed whole," the mate asked. Apparently he was quite experienced in such bets and didn't want any technicalities to get in the way of his payday.

"That's your choice, but I get to pick the chunk," the fisherman replied.

"Make him chew it, make him chew it," the fisherman's friend said elbowing him in the chest.

"All right, chew it then," he said. "And it's got to be done within thirty, no wait, twenty seconds."

The mate rolled his eyes and replied, "That will cost you another five. But no heads or tails, they hurt like a bitch."

Gant liked the mate, he was a hustler.

"Fifteen; you got it," roared the fisherman after taking a gulp from his beer. "Doesn't count if you puke though!"

"Don't worry about that," the mate said flipping his cigarette butt over the side. "Pick away!"

The younger mate quickly carved up a mackerel, slicing the body into six chunks. With the blade of the knife he scraped the head and tail off of the table and let it drop into a bucket at his feet. The fisherman leaned over the cutting board and selected the largest chunk.

The mate picked up the chunk of mackerel and gave it a sniff for effect, the assembled gaggle waiting in quiet anticipation, and then tossed it into his mouth.

The crowd began counting, "One Mississippi, two Mississippi, three…"

The mate chomped down hard, oily blood squirted from the corner of his mouth. He shifted the fish to the other side of his mouth as the count reached seven. The fisherman grinned and rubbed his stubbly beard as the mate forced back a grimace. When the count got to fourteen the old salt clapped his friend on the back thinking he would hold on to his money. Then the kid swallowed the chunk and stuck out his tongue for inspection. He rolled it back so that the fisherman could have a look underneath and then he held his hands over his head as if he'd won a prize fight. Everyone roared in delight. The fisherman counted out five singles and added it to the twenty and handed it to the mate.

With the cash in hand the kid said, "Double or nothing?"

Having just lost fifteen dollars the fisherman merely shook his head.

"Anybody else?" the mate shouted to the crowd, but there were no takers.

Good for him, Gant thought. *One a night is enough. You have to know when to draw the line. Kid was probably bluffing anyway.*

A woman in her mid thirties wearing a pink sweatshirt that read "My Husband, The End" surged toward the filet station. "I'll give you twenty for a whole butterfish, head, tail and all."

The mate considered it and said, "I'll eat two bodies for twenty. I'll do a whole fish for twenty-five."

The crowd had doubled, they howled with beers raised.

"Whole fish for twenty-five? Done," she agreed. "One minute time limit. I don't care if you chew it or swallow it whole," she added quite generously. "I pick it."

"You're on," the kid said. He glanced a bit uncomfortably at the younger mate who was shaking his head.

The woman picked her butterfish and handed it to the kid. "You're sure about this sweetheart," she asked.

"I'll do it, just watch."

The kid slipped the butterfish head first into his mouth, the onlookers started the countdown. With his eyes closed he tried to swallow it whole but found it impossible. The fish was thin and flat, but broad, too broad for his throat to take. Gagging he reached into his mouth with his thumb, index, and middle fingers and yanked the fish free. He tossed the fish onto the filet table, the crowd groaned in disappointment. Rallying the mate grabbed the fish and bit the head and upper body off, oil and blood ran down the front of his bib. Chewing with great urgency his jaw ground the fish into pulp and he muscled it down. With twelve seconds to go he placed the remainder of the body and tail into his mouth and swallowed it whole. The crowd yowled with excitement. The woman took his hand and raised it above his head in congratulations.

Euphoric the kid jumped up and down in a jubilant victory dance. He'd made a cool forty dollars in about five minutes. The woman counted out the cash and was about to hand it to him when his face went pale. A gout of vomit spewed from his mouth as he bent to his knees. The crowd shuffled back away from the filet table as if he were radioactive. He retched a second time and then a third and then after half a minute or so straightened up and stood, an embarrassed grin crossing his face.

The crowd boomed with laughter, even the younger mate was unable to control an outburst.

"I'm giving you an E for effort. Here's ten bucks, kid," the woman said handing the cash to the embarrassed mate.

The kid gladly accepted the money and wiped the corner of his mouth with the back of his hand.

"Hey, I saw some mackerel in there," the old fisherman mumbled.

"Oh, have a heart. He'll probably be heaving the rest of the night. Let him keep it," said the woman walking up toward the bow.

The old man acquiesced and walked toward the bow on the opposite side of the boat. The younger mate hosed the puke out from under the filet table washing it over the side into the sea. The older mate already had another cigarette burning.

All in all it was a pretty good deal, Gant thought. *He made twenty-five dollars and now his stomach is empty, he probably won't really get sick. They wouldn't have let me keep that back when I was working.*

After the rotten sushi show was over the two mates climbed the ladder to the upper deck and joined the captain in the bridge. With another three miles to go before they reached the wreck they'd be fishing off, they had about twenty minutes of downtime. With the setting Sun a blazing burgundy ball of fire behind them, the younger mate replayed the sequence of events for Captain Brecht's enjoyment. Laughter echoed forth from the bridge, Gant smiled to himself guessing the cause of it.

The boat hovered over a wreck in ninety feet of water some eight miles southeast of Jones Inlet when the captain let the anchor go. It caught on the sandy bottom and as there was no perceptible wind on this balmy night he decided against throwing the other hook. The younger mate retrieved the can of chum from the stern and brought it up into the bow. He set up on the port side and began ladling the watery mixture of ground mackerel into the water. The oily, fish gut stench drifted slowly down the length of the boat where it reached those back in the stern. Some of those around Gant complained of the wretched stink. Gant's nostrils flared initially in revulsion and then recognition and finally comfort. It was an aroma he knew well, it set him at ease like a soothing bath, it was the smell of home. He had, after all, smelled much worse.

The mates advised the anglers to let their lines out about thirty-five feet and when the captain blew his horn the reels spun out sending baited hooks down into a school of bluefish. Captain Brecht switched the boat's hull lights on, the black water sparkled with ghostly luminescence. A school of phosphorescent squid thronged toward the boat attracted to the light like moths to a flame. Within minutes the rich scent of blood and gore brought the fish up from the depths. Drags clicked as lines went out, the bluefish taking the hooks. Reels screamed as anglers waited for the right moment to set the hook and then the rods bent down toward the water as the fights commenced.

The first fish brought to the boat was a big one, at least ten pounds. As the woman in the pink sweater struggled to keep the fish from diving the younger, seemingly gawky mate sprang into action. He dropped the chum ladle and seized the gaffe which was amid ship in a rod holder. The kid sized up the situation and rammed the ten foot long gaffe down into the water. Angling it beneath the flailing blue he jerked it up, the sharpened hook tore into the fish's belly and held firm. Hand over hand the kid brought the flapping fish up to the boat and heaved it over the rail giving the gaffe a brisk shake.

Freed from the cruel hook, the fish flopped onto the deck with a thud, splashing blood all about. The kid then pulled a burlap sack from inside his bib. He pinned the slippery, squirming fish down on the deck with the sack and quickly dislodged the hook. While the woman re-baited her hook he shoved the bluefish into the sack and kicked it under the bench where her belongings were stowed. He went back to his chum station and waited for more action to break.

Gant's line dipped up and down in the water with the ebb and flow of the gentle swells for almost twenty minutes without any takers. Nearly everyone on board had already taken a fish, some even two or three. He was beginning to wonder if his bait had been stolen when his reel screeched and the line ran out. Calmly adjusting the drag he waited letting the fish run a bit and then yanked the tip of the rod upward hooking it. The fish dove for the cover of the bottom.

Gant struggled to keep it from going any deeper. It felt like a shark, and perhaps it was he reasoned, with all the blood in the water and all. With line still running out Gant sought to avoid a snapped line, he gave the fish some slack. Giving the fish about thirty feet he slowly began to reel it in until the line was again taut.

Deciding that it was now or never, he carefully raised the rod up from a thirty degree angle until it was at a forty-five degree angle. He let the rod fall back down while quickly reeling in the line he had gained. That's when the fish moved horizontally toward the bow. Raising the rod over the ducking heads of his fellow anglers, he slowly made his way the length of the boat along the port side before he was able to settle again, he was practically in the bow. Playing it safe in this fashion, he had the fish boat side within ten minutes. It was no shark, but a monster bluefish, at least fifteen pounds, maybe more.

"Gaffe!" Gant shouted, a bit winded.

The young kid came running up toward the bow with the gaffe in his hands. "Holy crap! That's a big one," he shouted upon seeing the fish. He rammed the gaffe into the water and began dragging it toward the fish.

"Take it easy, buddy. I've seen what you do and you do a good job. But let's try gaffing this guy in the head this time, all right?" Gant encouraged the kid with a wink.

"Whatever you say, it's your fish," the kid replied, while positioning the gaffe below the snapping mouth of the great blue. With a sudden pull the hook pierced the jaw of the fish and came out below its right eye.

"Bingo!" Gant yelled. "Nice shot, buddy!"

The kid wrangled the bluefish from the water and dumped it spattering onto the deck. He quickly sacked it in burlap and wiggled the hook free before looking over to Gant who was seated on the bench beside someone else's tackle box. "Why'd you say to gaffe it in the head?" the mate asked.

Gant looked at the boy and recognized the natural beauty inherent in the kid's face. Warm brown eyes looked out from above rose colored, lightly freckled cheeks. The wavy chestnut colored hair fell down upon a fine high forehead of unblemished creamy skin. "Do you eat fish?" Gant asked him.

"No, I actually hate the stuff," the kid replied.

"If you gaffe the fish in the body you often damage the filet. Fish flesh is very delicate you know?"

The kid nodded.

"Now if you gaffe the fish in the head or even the tail, you get a perfect filet, there's no wound in it from the gaffe puncture," Gant explained.

"Oh, cool! That makes sense. I'll do it that way from here on out," the young mate replied.

"Heads are easier than tails," Gant offered, but the kid was already racing down the deck as another customer had a fish on.

Unlike most people, even seafood lovers, Gant enjoyed the taste of bluefish. While others turned their noses up at the mere thought of eating bluefish, he found them to be robust and full flavored. The flesh of a striped bass was certainly meatier and more appealing to look at, all fluffy and white, but he found them lacking in taste and by extension character. A bluefish, on the other hand, was bursting with a natural briny seasoning he found delicious. Gant also liked the fact that pound for pound the aggressive bluefish was one of the finest fighting fish in any ocean. In his book, that was character.

When Gant had returned to his spot in the stern he placed his pole in the rod holder and then stepped up to the filet table. With his trophy bluefish in hand he went to his hip and brought out a long filet knife. He laid the fish on the table and gutted it. He had it filleted, throwing the head, tail and entrails overboard before the older of the two mates saw what he was doing.

"Hey, why'd you do that?" the kid asked, marveling at Gant's work.

"I like to clean them and get them on ice as soon as possible," Gant replied.

"That could've been the pool winner. Now we can't even weigh it," the kid said.

"Oh, well. Maybe I'll catch another one, a bigger one," Gant replied, smiling.

The rotten sushi eater looked at him as if he were stupid or insane, or both and walked off along the starboard side.

Gant sat down to enjoy a beer. Parched by the fight, he slugged down half of it at a gulp, sighed and slumped back against the wall. He was content to sit there and watch the action play out before him. He'd already caught his fish, maybe he'd hook a few more, but he planned on releasing anything else he caught. To take any more was wasteful in his eyes. He had more than enough for dinner with his mother and it had to be eaten fresh. *Waste not, want not!* He remembered his grandparents always saying to him when he was a little boy.

He was nearly done with his beer seemingly lost in thought staring up at the stars when the man next to him said, "That was some fish, and some job of getting it to the boat. You come out here often?"

"No, just visiting," Gant said.

"My name's Henry," the man said offering his hand.

"Nice to meet you," Gant replied shaking the man's hand.

"Where are you from ?"

"Near Galveston, down in Texas," Gant replied.

"You don't have an accent," the man noticed.

"I've been around a lot. Lived in lots of places."

"Good fishing down there?"

"You bet," Gant used a popular Texas phrase. "Red snapper and grouper are big down there on the Gulf Coast."

The fisherman was about to ask Gant another question when his rod bent toward the water signaling another fish on.

* * * *

Four hours later it was nearly one in the morning, all on board had tired of wrestling with the big blues. Some anglers kept fifteen fish, the limit, while most kept three or four and were catching and releasing by this time. At one past ten Captain Brecht blew the horn, calling for all lines to be pulled up. The Miss Watch Point II turned northwest and began the hour and fifteen minute run home.

About half of the anglers gathered once again before the filet table for the weigh in. The woman in the pink sweat shirt was pitted against a chubby boy about eleven or twelve years old. Her fish was longer, but his had considerably more girth too it. The older mate hung a steel balance scale equipped with hooks at either end of its bar from an eyehook screwed into the base of the top deck. Holding her fish upright by the gills the woman gave it to the younger mate who slipped one of the scale's hook through the gills.

The bar of the scale fell horizontally, the big bluefish hung there teetering alone. The boy then gave the fatter fish to the younger mate as the older mate righted the scale and held it steady. The younger mate slipped the fish onto the hook and let go. The bar seesawed up and down the two fish vying for the crown as the crowd watched in silence. Just as it seemed that there would be a draw, the scale tipped ever so gently in the direction of the fat fish. Much to the chagrin of the mates the boy won the pool. They knew they wouldn't be seeing any of that money. The payout was one hundred and ten dollars. The boy pocketed it and skipped happily back up to the bow.

As soon as the weigh in had been decided the mates were side by side cleaning and filleting the night's catch. This was where they made the bulk of their tips. They worked efficiently, the older boy filleting the bluefish while the younger one skinned and bagged the fillets. Time was of the essence. The faster they got the fish filleted the more customers they got to and therefore the more tips they made. They also had to wash down the boat. Gant, and many others, watched them as they worked.

After gutting the bluefish and pushing its innards into a bucket waiting at his feet, the older mate quickly sliced the delicate flesh away from the bone up toward the fish's spine. Cutting the filet free he flipped it to the other side of the table where the second mate grabbed it and skinned the scales off of it. After he had a pile of filets belonging to the same person he dipped them in salt water and bagged them. Upon presenting the filets to the customer, the mate was rewarded with a tip, usually the more filets the bigger the tip.

Gant observed the duo with a critical eye. They were fast, but not very thorough. The older kid who was filleting the fish wielded his knife haphazardly, leaving a lot of meat on the bone. Likewise, the younger kid skinned off a fare amount of meat along with the scales. Gant was dying to show these kids how it was done, but refrained as he did not dare bring any attention to himself. *At least the birds will be happy*, he thought.

After all the fish had been filleted the mates cleaned and stowed the rental rods below deck and then began cleaning the boat. Both had a bucket of soapy water, a long handled scrub brush, and a hose. Beginning up in the bow they hosed down and scrubbed the deck clean of blood, scales, beer and debris. Then, each taking a side, they worked their way down the length of the boat back toward the stern. The younger kid plowed straight through and was done with his side in about twenty minutes. Working with a cigarette, it took the older kid longer to do a less thorough job. He also stopped now and again to swizzle down some beer. The second mate walked across the stern to help the first who had finished little more than half of his side. After they had completed both sides they finished up with the stern and than disappeared below decks to get out of their bibs and boots.

In shorts and sneakers once more, the two climbed up top to chat with the captain, the older one with a beer and cigarette, the younger one a bottled water. Twenty minutes later they were back down on deck as the boat was pulling into the marina. The captain eased into the slip, reversing the boat enough to insure a smooth docking. On either side the mates were careful to keep clear of the pilings, that's how hands got crushed. In neutral now, the big boat floated slowly beside the portable ramp resting atop the dock. The mates deftly looped the lines over the pilings securing the boat in the bow and then ran back to the stern to do the same.

Disembarking, happy anglers streamed off of the Miss Point Watch II and flooded into the parking lot, their coolers heavy with iced bluefish. Within ten minutes the lot was empty save for the captain's 2000 Dodge Ram Wagon and the older mate's Chevy Trailblazer. From the doorway of the marina bathroom Gant watched the second mate unlocking his bicycle at the rack by the marina's main office west of the parking lot. As soon as the kid had hopped on his bike and peddled toward the marina entrance the captain and first mate drove out onto the boulevard.

The entire crew headed west, none were townies. The captain and first mate headed north over the bridge onto the Loop Parkway destined for Merrick, Freeport, Baldwin or maybe another town further away. The second mate pumped his legs furiously through the red light at the end of town and continued west toward Long Beach. At nearly two-thirty Gant was the last to leave for home.

* * * *

Gant spent the next week with his mother, occasionally visiting friends, and spending a few hours each day at the beach regardless of the weather. His mother's consultation with the orthopedic surgeon went well as did the meeting with the second. Both had agreed that knee replacement was a realistic option for Mrs. Gant. Gant made the arrangements and planned on returning in mid-August when the surgery was scheduled.

On Sunday night, a week after his fishing trip, Gant bid farewell to his mother after dinner and headed for home. He preferred to drive through the city at night, he told her, as there were less morons on the road, which was true. It was nearing ten-o'clock when he turned the Econoline into the marina parking lot. Driving past the main office he saw the bike belonging to the second mate, it was the only one in the rack. Gant turned the van around, drove back into town and headed down to the bay.

From shortly after ten until one a.m. Gant sat on the back deck of The Anchor Bar sipping club soda watching the light boat traffic on the channel. He left the bar and drove back to the boulevard parking in front of the gas station which had a clear view of the marina. He locked his doors and walked to the marina making sure no one was around. Confident he was alone, he made directly for the bicycle rack reaching into his shorts pocket as he went. Quickly walking toward the kid's Trek mountain bike, he bent down as if he were picking up a quarter and pushed a thumb tack into the side of the bike's rear tire. With any luck the tire wouldn't deflate until there was some pressure put on it. He returned to the van to wait.

At 1:45, Gant alertly rolled down his windows to listen for the incoming boat. By 2:05, he heard the low rumble of the Miss Watch Point II as she made her way through the channel. He turned his attention to the marina and waited for the boat to dock. Five minutes later the boat was secure in her slip. A minute or so later people began to disembark, and ten minutes after that the parking lot was empty again with three exceptions. As the kid got on his bike the captain and the first mate motored out of the lot, eager to get home and into bed. Gant started up the van and slowly rolled toward the kid on the bike.

It was a quarter of a mile past the traffic light, to the south of the water tower, when the rear tire of the kid's bike blew bringing his race home to a halt. When Gant pulled over onto the narrow shoulder of the boulevard the kid was kneeling down spinning the tire in anger. Gant looked at him and pulled the van forward so that the kid was positioned within five feet of the van's rear doors. He turned his hazards on and got out.

"Need a hand there," Gant asked the kid.

"I've got a couple of miles before home," the kid answered despondently. Looking at Gant, his face lightened in recognition, "Hey. You're the guy who told me how to gaffe."

"That's me," Gant replied, not the least bit uncomfortable.

"You weren't out tonight."

"Prior commitments," Gant answered and then added, "Your parents let you ride a bike on the road at this time of night?"

"My Mom's alone, she's just happy I have a job."

"What's your name?" Gant asked.

"Jimmy," the kid answered after a brief hesitation. "What's yours?"

"Phillip," Gant replied.

"Well Jimmy I'm heading west, so if you'd like a ride throw the bike in the back and hop in," Gant offered.

The kid hesitated and then said, "Maybe I'll just call my Mom." He pulled a cell phone from his short's pocket.

"All right buddy, suit yourself. I hope you won't be waking her up."

The kid knew his mother had finished her waitress shift at ten o'clock, Sunday night's were early, and she would be fast asleep on the couch. He eyed the New York plates on the van and after a few moments consideration agreed, "Okay, I'll take a ride."

Gant turned away from the kid and opened the back doors. The ice tote was moved all the way toward the front of the cargo area, there was plenty of room. "Be careful now, just lay it in there nice and easy." Gant looked down the boulevard in both directions; there wasn't a headlight to be seen.

The kid grabbed the bike by the handle bars and front wheel while Gant watched for any traffic. When the kid turned his back to guide the front wheel of the bike into the van Gant reached around with a chloroform-soaked rag in his right hand and cupped it against the boy's mouth and nose from behind. Gant reached up with his left hand pinning it firmly against the back of the kid's head as he briefly struggled. As the bike hit the pavement the kid's legs withered and he fell backwards into Gant's arms. Gant cradled the boy up into the van and hopped in beside him shutting the doors as he went. From his back pocket he took two, heavy gauge foot long zip ties and quickly bound the boy's ankles and wrists. Inside the ice tote was a roll of masking tape. Tearing off an eight inch piece with his teeth, Gant taped the boy's mouth closed. He then slid out of the back and slammed the doors shut. With no oncoming headlights in either direction he got back inside and killed his hazards. Calmly he made a legal U-turn heading back toward the Loop Parkway. Unbeknownst to anyone including himself James Geignetter was on his way to western New York, to Buffalo.

Chapter Fifteen

Nearly four decades earlier, six-year-old Phillip Gant had sat beside his paternal grandmother, Elsa, on the top step of the back porch of the Gant family farm some twenty miles east of Riverhead on Long Island. The boy had finished his breakfast of warm rice and milk which his grandmother had sweetened with generous spoons of sugar. It was late June and, as was customary, he was spending six weeks of the summer with his grandparents. Gant's father was busy with his infant aeronautical enterprise, his mother had a full social calendar, and neither had time for their son. Gant cherished his time with his grandparents, but was no dummy. Deep down he knew he was sent out east because his parents wouldn't make time for him, and it hurt the boy.

The Sun had just peeked out above the horizon, its gleaming rays shimmering through the cornfield beyond the vegetable garden, spreading luxurious yellow light onto their faces as they huddled against the slight chill brought in with the ocean breeze. By ten o'clock the morning would warm to seventy degrees, and by July it would be hot and humid as summer would seize control until mid September. Young Phillip loved his grandparents and their farm more than anything else in the world, even his own parents. Every day, even the rainy ones, were special. The air smelled of sweet corn on the farm, the sky looked clearer, and the symphony of crickets at night and chirping of jays and chickadees during the day, were music to his ears. This was the life little Phillip envisioned himself living.

Grandma Gant was in her mid-seventies, but appeared and lived much younger. Thin yet muscular, she ran a short sprint faster than most people a quarter of her age. She was still able to catch Phillip when he attempted to escape punishment for some naughtiness he'd gotten up to. Punishment consisted of a single, and gentle, swat on the backside with a ping pong paddle when she caught up with him. Phillip's response was gleeful laughter, which made the old woman shake her head and join him. Although her weathered face was wrinkled and her fine hair, which was set in a bun, had the bluish tint that many older women's hair had, she was the picture of vitality. Her hazel eyes sparkled with intelligence, affection and curiosity. A nurse as a mere girl during World War I in Germany, she was a tough old lady who saw quite a bit in her lifetime. After immigrating to the states in the late 1920's, she graduated from nursing school. As her superiors noticed her enduring patience, she was recommended for work with "difficult" patients. She nursed primarily at Creedmoor Psychiatric Center in Queens and, to a lesser extent, Bellevue's psychiatric ward in Manhattan from the early 1930's through to the early 1950's when she and her husband sold their home in Springfield Gardens and headed out east to raise corn.

"Where's Sunshine, Grams?" Phillip asked his grandmother inquiring of the neighbor's dog.

It was Grandma Gant's habit to feed the neighbor's dog any leftovers from the previous day's meals for breakfast. Having lived through the Great Depression, Grandma Gant was not one to waste. Whether it was hot dogs, fish, or pork tenderloin, the dog got its cut. If there were no leftovers she would make corned beef hash for her dear friend the Border Collie. This was fine with Sunshine's owner, as he was off the hook for the dog's breakfast every morning. On this morning breakfast consisted of hamburger, rice, and lima beans which were from her own garden. She had mixed it up in Sunshine's shiny metal bowl, which she left on the second to highest step right at their feet.

"She's probably sniffing around after mice and squirrels, she'll show any minute, she always does," Grandma Gant replied setting her coffee mug down beside her on the step.

Phillip deeply inhaled the rich aroma of his grandmother's coffee and sighed with satisfaction. Grandma Gant took her coffee very light with lots of cream and sugar and he loved the way it smelled.

Grandma Gant knew the boy's tastes and asked, "Would you like a sip?"

"Can I, really?"

"Sure you can, but just the one," she said handing the mug of warm coffee to him.

The boy carefully accepted the mug and cautiously sipped from it, the warm creamy coffee warmed him inside. "Mmm, that's good, Grams. Can I finish the rest?"

"Go ahead," she said tussling his wispy, blonde hair, there was only another mouthful anyway. "Now where is that Sunshine?" Grandma Gant leaned forward and tapped the dog's bowl with the inside of her wedding band. Seconds later the black and white Border Collie streaked along the deer fence beside the garden, through the backyard, and up to the porch steps. She looked up at the grandmother and grandson with glistening brown eyes and seemingly smiled, her mouth open and tongue wagging.

"Up Sunshine!" Grandma Gant commanded.

The dog scampered up the steps, bypassing the breakfast bowl with its tasty treats, and sat down beside the old woman on the top step.

"Good girl," she cooed into the dog's furry ears as she rubbed her under the chin. "Say good morning to Phillip."

Sunshine gave a low, rumbling bark to greet the boy. Unless she smelled a deer which she tried to herd or sensed danger in the form of a raccoon or rat, the dog never barked until commanded to do so; the Gants had trained her since she was a puppy. She looked at Phillip and rose from her haunches and approached him.

Phillip beamed with delight as he ran his hands over the dog's soft coat over and over. He had no pets at home, this was the only exposure he really had with dogs. Rubbing the fur on Sunshine's chest, Phillip asked, "Should I let her eat now, Grams?"

"Whenever you're ready," Grandma Gant replied.

"Okay, Sunshine! Ready to eat?" Phillip asked the dog.

Sunshine rose and descended two steps below the bowl of food, her bushy tail wagging furiously back and forth which only widened Phillip's smile.

"Okay, Sunshine!" the boy repeated, raising his hand as his grandmother had shown him. "One, two, three, eat!" he squealed while pulling his arm down.

The Border Collie fell upon the bowl with relish and lapped up the hamburger, rice and beans within a minute. She looked up at Grandma Gant licking her chops and cocked her head to the side as if asking for more. She sat down before the empty bowl and waited.

Grandma dug into the pockets of her pants, she never wore shorts, not even in summer. When her hand came out she had a Milk-Bone dog biscuit in her hand. She handed it over to Phillip. "Why does she get a biscuit after her meal, Phillip?" she asked her grandson.

"To clean her teeth, right Grams," he shouted.

"That's right, my good boy!" she replied, patting him on the shoulder. "Go ahead and give it to her."

Phillip stood up with the biscuit held between his thumb and index finger and addressed the dog, "Okay, Sunshine! Treat? You want a treat?"

The Border Collie stared at him panting.

"Here you go girl," he said stretching his hand out toward the dog's muzzle.

Sunshine waited for direction.

With the biscuit an inch or so from the dog's mouth Phillip gave the command, "Open!"

Sunshine opened her mouth and let the boy place the biscuit on her tongue. She made sure that his fingers were clear before chomping down on her treat. Satisfied she pranced down the steps to the backyard and then turned around to look at Phillip. As he descended the steps she ran past the garden and into the cornfield beyond. With Phillip and Sunshine playing their own version of hide and seek in the corn field Grandma Gant took the dog's bowl inside to hand wash it.

Grandpa Gant came out onto the porch half an hour later cleanly shaven and smelling of Listerine. He'd been up since before dawn, it took him a very long time to shave, shower, brush his teeth, and complete the rest of his morning routine. "Cleanliness is next to godliness," the old man would often quote the Biblical proverb from the Acts of the Apostles.

If that's true, Grampa will be at heaven's gate the second after he dies, little Phillip thought to himself on more than one occasion while waiting on his grandfather.

Grampa Jack Gant was a decorated World War I veteran who managed to make it back home intact. While many of his buddies were killed or maimed overseas, he came home fit and ready to enter the New York Police Department academy. After spending three years as a foot patrolmen he quickly moved up the ranks and finally served as an inspector for twenty-one years until he retired in 1952 with over thirty years service. With two full pensions in hand the Gant's left Queens for literally greener pastures.

The country life had been as kind to Jack Gant as it was to his wife Elsa. In his late seventies by the time Phillip began his annual visits, he was lean and strong, often flexing a muscular bicep for anyone who dared challenge his fitness. Phillip asked his grandfather to flex on a daily basis as he got a big kick out of feeling the rock-like ball that bunched up beneath the skin in the center of the old man's arm. With glasses and a pug nose, he wouldn't be considered handsome, yet his still full head of hair took ten years off of him, providing verve that most others of his generation lacked.

The Gants grew corn commercially on their fifty-seven acre farm for twelve years before retiring for good. During those years they provided fresh, sweet corn to local restaurants, farmer's markets, and even operated their own farm stand on the side of Sunrise Highway. As they tired of the work they sold off most of the acreage, keeping a three acre parcel for themselves where their home rested. Behind their modest three bed room home was a sprawling backyard, it gave way to their vegetable garden in which they grew sweet corn, lima beans, strawberries, rhubarb, cucumbers, basil, and tomatoes.

Early on the Gants learned the deer would gladly eat anything and everything they could get to so they erected a ten foot tall deer fence to keep them out of the garden. Beyond the garden was an acre or so of corn they planted mainly for their viewing and smelling pleasure. Unprotected, most of this corn was gobbled up by hungry deer and the Gants wouldn't have it any other way. While growing, the rich scent of the corn floated down through the yard bathing the old couple in an aroma they held dear. Besides being visually appealing to them the "free" corn, as they called it, attracted hordes of deer which they loved to watch from their back porch.

In the middle of the acre of "free corn" stood one of the commercial farm's old tractors, a 1954 International Harvester Farmall Super C. The original Farmall was the first tractor in the country to use a tricycle design, which could be used on tall crops such as corn and cotton. Grandpa Gant had kept the one tractor as a memento of their time as true farmers. He sold the other two, larger and more modern versions, for parts and scrap. Once fire engine red with oversized jet black rear wheels, the mechanical dinosaur was the color of rust now, its tires shearing off in long, ragged shards. The tractor was young Phillip's most prized toy.

When his grandparents were on the phone or talking to neighbors and Sunshine was off adventuring somewhere alone, the boy could invariably be found perched in the weather-beaten bucket seat, of the International Harvester, his sweaty, dirty hands gripping the rusted steering wheel pretending to operate the metal beast.

"Come on Phillip, let's hit the bricks," Grandpa Gant shouted into the cornfield, it was his way of saying, "Let's get going." Knowing his grandson could be deep into the field he sat down in a folding chair with a glass of orange juice and patiently waited for the boy to appear.

A few minutes later Phillip romped out of the cornfield with Sunshine at his hip. He ran up the steps and jumped into his grandfather's lap, Grandpa Gant wheezed in, and then after ascertaining that no damage was done, breathed out.

"What are we doing today, Grampa?" Phillip asked, wide-eyed and ready for adventure.

"Well I thought we'd go down to the dairy and take a look at the cows. How's that sound to you?"

"Great! Is Grams coming too?"

"Well, probably not this morning. She likes to see the cows, but she said she's got some sewing to do. Anyway, we'll head to the mechanic's afterward to check up on my motor, and she would be bored to death."

Up until he was in his late sixties Grandpa Gant had done all of his own mechanical work, including boat and tractor engines. Thereafter, as good a shape as he was in, he lacked the brute strength necessary to do such work. If his son Arthur had not been so immersed in his fledgling aeronautics business, he would have helped the old man so he wouldn't be dependent on outside mechanics when things broke down. It was Grandpa Jack, after all, who'd got Arthur into tinkering with electronics, engines, hydraulics and so forth. If not for his father Arthur Gant may never have become an aeronautical engineer.

"Is the motor ready, Grampa?"

"It should be; it should be," Grandpa Gant answered, scratching the side of his head where a fly had landed. He shooed it away with a wave, Sunshine reared up on her hind legs in an attempt to swallow the fly, but it buzzed by her snout.

"Yea! We can go fishing then!"

"Probably tomorrow. If it's ready today, I've still got to pull the boat and have it fitted."

"When will you do that?"

"Later this morning, if it's ready."

"Can I help?"

"It's hard work and sometimes those boat yard workers don't use the best language. I'll drop you off here with Grandma. She'll like your help picking beans and tomatoes. By the time you're finished, it will be lunchtime, we'll eat and then see what we feel like doing. Say goodbye to Sunshine and let's get going, then."

Phillip scratched the dog beneath the chin and let her lick his face, the boy giggled with glee and then shot around the corner to catch up with his grandfather. Hand in hand, they walked toward the old man's glossy, tan 1972 Dodge Coronet four door sedan. Phillip buckled up in the back seat, Grandpa Gant started the engine, and with a low rumble they backed out of the driveway and pulled out onto Sunset Lane.

* * * *

The visit to the dairy was breathtaking literally, it took Phillip a fair amount of time to adjust to the overwhelming smell of manure. Once he was able to un-cup his hand from his nose he adjusted nicely and even took big, deep breaths of the fresh hay. The boy ran from cow to cow marveling at the way they accepted the vacuum like devices attached to their udders. With fascination he watched the milk stream through the yellowed rubber hoses, which were once clear, and fill up in shiny glass collection bottles. As the milking was almost done for the morning the owner, who was a good friend of Grandpa Gant, led them to the barn where he kept the new calves, there were six of them. Phillip's face broke into a beaming smile as the owner handed him a bottle to feed one of the calves with.

With the engine ready, Grandpa Gant dropped Phillip back at the house to help with the gardening and then met two boat yard workers at the marina to haul his boat. One of the workers hefted a nine horsepower Johnson outboard onto the transom of the seventeen foot Boston Whaler Montauk and steered it over to the boat ramp where the other waited with a pickup to haul it out and drive it back to the shop. Once the boat was refitted with its own seventy horsepower Johnson engine, it was launched with Grandpa Gant aboard. The old man skillfully guided it back to its slip and then joined his wife and grandson for lunch.

The day grew cloudy and windy. With a good forecast for the following day, Grandpa Gant decided to take Phillip into town to get a hat, to keep the Sun at bay while they went fishing the next day. Stopping at the five and dime general store beside the historic movie theatre in the center of the neighboring village, Grandpa Gant took his grandson's hand and led him inside.

On the back wall of the store were dozens of summer themed T-shirts, emblazoned with the logos of local restaurants, seafood stores, and farms. In the corner stood a revolving hat rack stocked with an assortment of hats with similar logos emblazoned upon them. Seeing nothing that interested him Grandpa Gant told Phillip to give the rack a spin.

As the boy spun the circular rack clockwise, his eyes suddenly bulged from their sockets, his face lit with a smile. "That one, right there Grampa!" young Gant burst out, pointing at a white Navy gob cap.

"That one? The Donald Duck hat?" the old man asked.

"Yes, please," the boy replied, his hands grasped together.

"You're sure you don't want this one, here?" Grandpa Gant asked, fingering the navy blue bill of a white captain's hat.

Philip admired the gold braid and the gold anchored insignia above the bill; he hesitated briefly before replying, "No Grampa, you're the captain. I want Gilligan's hat."

"All right then, first mate Philip, a Gilligan hat for you and a captain's hat for me," Grandpa Gant said pulling the captain's hat down over his forehead, it was a perfect fit. After rummaging through the Gilligan hats and coming up empty for the boy's size, he asked a stock boy for a small. As luck had it there were two left. The duo strode toward the counter, their new hats perched atop their crowns.

Grandpa Gant stopped short before the candy counter. Behind the counter a smorgasbord of hard candies and chocolates lay arranged in thick, glass jars. The old man tapped the top of the glass counter with his index finger and turned toward the boy. "What'll it be Phillip?" he asked.

Phillip knew exactly what he wanted, but needed to locate it. After a few seconds he spied his quarry and replied, "Malted milk balls, please."

"Excellent choice, one of my favorites, and Grandma likes them too. We'll have to double the order."

The clerk shoveled a pound of malted milk balls into a crisp, white paper sack and asked if there was anything else.

"The hats," Grandpa Gant said, pointing to his head and then to Phillip's.

The clerk had totaled the items when Grandpa Gant suddenly asked the boy, "How's your toothbrush?"

"Almost new, Grampa."

"How about your nail brush?"

"I don't have one. What's a nail brush?"

The old man reached down and picked up a little brush from a box next to the register. "This, is a nail brush," he explained holding the powder blue handled brush before his grandson's eyes for closer inspection.

"I've never seen one. Dad doesn't have one," the boy said.

"Figures. As much tinkering as he does I guess it's impractical," the old man responded.

"What does that mean?"

"Oh, it means it doesn't make sense for your Daddy to scrub his fingernails clean, because he'll only dirty them up again." The old man then picked up a small nail clipper and added that to his purchase.

"Is it important to have clean nails?" the boy asked.

"Well, I think it is. Here, look at mine," Grandpa Gant said, holding the backs of his hands out for the boy to study the nails. While other old timers often had thickened and yellowed nails, Grandpa Gant's nails were clear, clean, and perfectly trimmed, they gleamed as if there was polish on them. So shiny and polished were they that many people thought he paid a professional to manicure them. The boy looked at his own ragged nails, the nails of most young boys, and shrugged his shoulders.

"It's up to you Phillip. I live my way, other's live their way. The choice is yours, I want to give you every opportunity."

* * * *

The thunderstorm that night approached the ferocity of a tropical storm and would have been considered such, had the wind been coming out of the right direction. Sustained winds of forty miles an hour swept in from the west while random gusts topped out at near sixty. Grandpa checked the tide chart upon his night table and went to bed that night knowing there would be no fishing the next day. The bottom would be much too shaken up for the fish to see the bait. Nonetheless, he smiled to himself as he had a special treat in store for his grandson.

By 6:30 the following morning, the storm had abated. Its clouds formed a bruised, purple mountain range to the east as the Sun climbed into the sky. Grandpa Gant took Phillip, with his Gilligan hat on, down to a mile and a half stretch of beach upon Long Island Sound which the locals called Long Beach. Looking out the car's window Phillip could tell the tide was out. While white, Sun bleached stones made up the beach, on this morning a wide band of darker stones below them, those that were most often submerged, was clearly visible.

The narrow parking lot was empty, Grandpa Gant parked the Coronet closest to the entrance and popped the trunk. From the trunk he retrieved two ten gallon buckets, and a smaller red bucket.

As soon as Phillip got out of the car, he heard a curious click-clacking sound rising above the gentle crash of the incoming wavelets. He cocked his head to the side to get a better listen at the strange sound.

"What's that sound, Grampa?" he asked.

Pulling on his captain's hat the old man replied, "That, my first mate, is what we came here for. Wait and see."

With their buckets the old man and the young boy trudged down the shell strewn beach toward the source of the incessant chatter. Phillip broke into a run as he saw what was making all of the ruckus. Down by the rippling water line were tens of thousands of stranded bay scallops prattling clamorously in a near futile effort to launch themselves back into the life saving sea.

"What are they, Grampa?"

"These are bay scallops, buddy boy," Grandpa Gant said, bending over to pick up one of the jawing bivalves. "Now when you pick these little guys up make sure to grab them from behind. You want to pick them up by what we call the 'hinge' so they don't get a chance to snap down on your fingers." He held the scallop at his grandson's eye level so the boy could get a good look at the delicate striations inherent in the beige and white shell.

"Why are they doing that?"

"They're doing their best to get back into the water."

"Do all clams do that?"

"No, to the best of my knowledge they are the only ones that swim."

"Swim?"

"That's what they're doing. They were washed up here by last night's high tide and storm. Now they're trying to swim back into the water."

"They're striped," the boy noticed examining the fragile shellfish in his grandfather's hand.

"Open your hand," he directed the boy.

"Will it bite me like a crab, Grampa?"

"The worst that could happen is it might pinch you if you're not careful. As long as you grip it from behind you'll be fine. Even if it pinched you it would only feel like a little squeeze, they're not too strong," the old man explained, placing the scallop into his grandson's open palm.

Phillip accepted the scallop with a mixture of curiosity and trepidation. He peered at the mollusk which had drawn shut upon his grandfather's touch. "Will it open up again?"

"As soon as you put it down I'd bet."

Phillip placed the scallop on the pebbly shore and within a few seconds it began to chatter once again. He kneeled down, placed his hands on the stony, sandy shore and bent his head low to get closer. After clacking for ten seconds or so and finding itself no closer to water it stopped. Winded for the moment, the scallop yawned open leaving itself exposed.

"It's got a necklace on it Grampa, look!" the boy shouted with excitement, pointing at the tiny blue dots strung around the scallop's mantle like a string of beads.

"Those are its eyes, Phillip."

"Wow! So many! It must see real good!"

Grandpa Gant laughed, his right hand adjusting his glasses while his left hand rose to his belly. "Watch this," he said kneeling down beside his grandson. He extended his pinky finger and waggled it inside of the scallop's open shell, it immediately clamped shut on his finger. The old man wiggled his finger up and down, the scallop held tight.

"Doesn't it hurt?"

"Not at all. Like I said they're not very strong. Scallops are very delicate, not like hard clams." The old man pulled the scallop free and tossed it into the bay. "Off you go, then."

"This is great, Grampa!"

"It is. Now, let's fill up these buckets and get home as quick as we can."

"We're taking them?"

"Some of them."

"What for?"

"To eat. They're delicious. Grandma and I love them, so will you. Fill your bucket, Phillip."

Within ten minutes the old man had his bucket filled three-quarters with scallops. As par for the course, young Phillip was more interested in playing with them than collecting the shellfish. Grandpa Gant filled the little red bucket with salt water and poured it out over his scallops. After another half bucket of water all of the scallops were covered. While Phillip played he made the trek back to the Coronet. It took the old man longer to haul the scallops back to the car than it did to pick them. He placed the bucket in the trunk wedging it between the bump of the wheel well and a cinder block he had placed there earlier in the morning. Upon returning to the beach he saw Phillip running toward him at full tilt.

"Look Grampa! Look," Phillip shouted as he ran up the beach, his hands outstretched before him.

As the boy came closer Grandpa Gant burst out in laughter. Phillip had a scallop dangling off of every one of his fingers and his thumbs.

"You're right, they don't hurt at all," the boy said.

"Told you so. The only problem now is how are you going to get them all off?"

Phillip smiled and held out his hands.

"Down to your bucket, matey. You've been slacking. You've got to earn your keep."

After freeing Phillip from his bivalve buddies Grandpa Gant explained what "earning your keep" meant. Grandfather and grandson then filled the other bucket to three quarters in short order. He sent the kid off to play while he filled it with water.

"Now here's the plan, Phillip," the old man called over to his grandson when he had the scallops ready to carry. "While I carry this up to the car I want you to walk down the beach and throw as many scallops as you can back into the water."

"So they live, right Grampa?"

"Exactly! Waste not, want not."

"Should we leave some for other people?"

Grandpa Gant smiled and said, "You could spend all day throwing them back and there would still be plenty for anyone willing to come get them."

With that Phillip scampered off bent at the knee scooping handfuls of scallops up and tossing them into the water. When Grandpa Gant returned from loading the car he figured that the scallops in his trunk had a couple of hours before they would start to die off. He joined his grandson and for the next hour the two of them returned as many of the landed scallops to the water as they could.

Once back home Grandpa Gant called three neighbors to let them know about the bounty on Long Beach. With the scallops waiting he was quick on the phone and then went to the cutlery drawer to get his scallop knife. Phillip followed him through the kitchen to the sink where the old man had placed the buckets on the tile floor. Reaching up into an overhead cupboard his hand came down with a medium sized stainless steel bowl that he placed on the counter to his right.

"Do you want to help me, Phillip?"

"I sure do, Grampa."

All right then. You reach into the bucket and keep handing me scallops as I need them. As soon as I'm done with one, I'll need another. Just keep them coming."

"Got it," the boy replied, handing the first scallop to his grandfather.

In a single, quick motion Grandpa Gant pried the fragile, yet stubborn shell open, yanking away the slimy innards and slicing a thumbnail-sized chunk of delectable muscle away from the shell. The shell and the guts he let drop into the sink, the muscle he flipped into the stainless steel bowl beside him.

"Wow, Grampa! That was fast!"

Grandpa Gant winked down at his grandson and motioned for another scallop. Phillip watched the intricate workings of the blade intently as Grandpa Gant disemboweled and harvested scallop after scallop. He watched the reflection of the mid morning Sun as it glinted off of the flashing blade and twinkled across the kitchen ceiling. He was astounded at the speed at which his grandfather was able to shuck the clams and was intrigued by what could be accomplished by a seemingly simple piece of steel.

An hour and a half after he started, Grandpa Gant had five pounds of clean scallop meat and two buckets of shells and waste. Young Phillip had discovered the tool of his eventual trade.

After lunch Grandma Gant egged and bread crumbed the scallops and then whipped up her tartar sauce, which was heavy on the mayonnaise and lemon. With only three mouths to feed Grandma Gant called the neighbors to join them for dinner. The Yorks came to dinner at five-thirty bringing a bottle of white wine with them.

Besides the scallops which Grandma Gant had started to pan fry at four-thirty, dinner included homegrown corn on the cob, tomatoes from the garden, and baked potatoes bought from a local farm. Phillip loved the scallops every bit as much as his grandparents did. Grandma Gant made a rhubarb pie from her garden for dessert, the adults raved about it while Phillip had a bowl of vanilla ice cream instead.

* * * *

The following morning was clear and warm with no wind—perfect for fishing. The western horizon was still dark when little Phillip found Grandma Gant hovering over the stove stirring a pan of hash. The aroma of the onions and corned beef wafting through the kitchen made his mouth water. She poured him a glass of orange juice and put four slices of white bread into the toaster. With the toast on she cracked six eggs, spilling them into a large cast iron skillet coated with butter. As the eggs began to sizzle over the flame, Grandpa Gant came out of the bathroom; he was showered, clean shaven, and smelled of Listerine, his nails were immaculate.

"Today's the day, young mate," Grandpa Gant said, taking his seat at the head of the table.

"Yea!" Phillip cheered, putting his glass of orange juice down.

"We're looking forward to it as much as you sweets," Grandma Gant said. "Now eat up young man. A good breakfast will give you the vim and vigor to pull in some big whoppers."

"I thought a whopper was a hamburger, Grams?"

"Niehehehehe," Grandma Gant let go a squeaky laugh. "If you catch some of those we'll take them too!"

"As long as we have fun, right Phillip," Grandpa Gant said.

"You said it, Grampa."

"Now eat up and let's get going. The early bird catches the worm, you know."

"I thought we were going fishing," the boy said.

"We are, eat, I'll explain that one later," Grandpa Gant replied.

Ten minutes later Phillip impatiently paced back and forth upon the weather-beaten dock, his life vest already strapped on, as his grandparents loaded gas cans, fishing gear, bait, and a cooler onto the Boston Whaler. Grandpa Gant half filled a bucket with seawater and tossed a box of frozen squid and a box of frozen spearing into the bucket. With his right foot, he nudged the bucket up into the bow ahead of the center console. Grandma Gant submerged a plastic live well into the water and brought it, leaking water from its holes, back into the boat and laid it down in the stern to the left of the engine. As Grandpa Gant backed the little Whaler out of its slip Grandma Gant tied Phillip's Gilligan hat down, knotting a red bandanna under his chin.

As the first hints of light appeared on the eastern horizon the old man swung the boat around and headed for Noyack Bay. Once clear of the marina, he edged its speed up gradually until they were cruising along at a comfortable twenty-five knots; the bay was calm, lake-like even, the going was easy.

With Grandpa at the helm, Grandma and young Phillip sat astern of him on a wooden bench fitted with seat cushions which doubled as life preservers. While his grandfather steered them to his favorite spot, his grandmother pointed out the different gulls, terns, and cormorants that were working the bay for breakfast. After twenty minutes or so the seasoned captain slowed, scanned the gentle swells of the breathing water and then cut the engine with the infant Sun reaching out to warm their backs.

"Here's good, don't you think, Elsa?" he asked his wife.

"I think it'll give up some fish, John, I do," she replied rising from her seat behind the center console. "I'll freshen these a bit," she said grasping a rope tied to the handle of the live well. She lifted the bait container, dunked it into the water and then tied it onto the portside stern cleat. She turned toward her husband. "Calm as can be, I think three ounces should do it," she said.

"I'm thinking the same thing," Grandpa Gant replied handing his wife a three ounce bank sinker. Arthritic hands or not, within minutes the old couple had rigged three poles with double hook fluke rigs and sinkers. Grandpa Gant handed the shortest pole to Phillip and waited on his wife who was pulling up the live well.

"What will we use for bait, Grampa? Worms?" the boy asked.

"No, I'm not much for worms Phillip. Some folks use certain types of worms for flounder, which is a flat fish too, but we're going for fluke, a bigger flat fish that's in season now. Lotsa people use spearing and squid for fluke, and we will too, but I like killies the best."

"What's killies?" Phillip asked.

"Just a second now and Grandma will show you," the old man responded nodding in his wife's direction.

The boy's eyes moved toward his grandmother who was swinging the live well over the gunnel and back into the boat. Streams of salt water coursed from the tiny holes of the bait container as she brought it to rest on the deck. Phillip went to her side and peered down at the red and white live well.

"The bait's in there, Grams?"

"It is honey," the old lady said glancing at her husband with a hint of sadness in her eyes.

"Why?" the boy asked.

"To keep them alive, sweetheart. Take a look," she said pushing the door to the live well open.

Phillip peaked in through the small door of the live well and saw a swarm of tiny fish swimming circles within it. No longer than two inches each, and most of them smaller, the little minnows darted up and down and around one another in search of escape.

"Put your hand in there and see if you can catch one," Grandma Gant suggested.

Grandpa Gant turned his attention to the frozen bait. He pulled the thawed box of squid from a bucket full of seawater and began to slice the first of two large squid into long strips. He threw the strips back into the bucket and then tore open the box of spearing which had defrosted. He poured the little silver fish into the bait bucket to join the squid strips and remaining whole squid. He always liked to keep some whole squid in case he saw something big to go after.

Cautiously the boy dipped the fingers of his right hand in through the door of the live well. As soon as his fingers broke the water the little fish scurried every which way for cover of which there was none. The boy squealed with laughter as the tiny fish tickled his fingers and palm. After a minute or so of glee the boy grew a bit frustrated and looked up at his grandmother and said, "Grams, I can't catch one. Will you show me how?"

"Of course, sweetheart, move aside a little."

"Grab one for me too if you don't mind, Elsa," Grandpa Gant requested.

The boy watched as his grandmother's hand disappeared into the live well and lightening quick, it reappeared tightly cupped. "Let's see how I did," she said bringing her left hand up to form a bowl out of which she hoped the tiny fish would be unable to jump out of. Within her hands Grandma Gant had four killies.

"Niehehehehe!" she squeaked in her birdlike little laugh. "I've got an extra!" She chuckled.

Grandpa Gant had already baited one of the hooks on two of the poles with a shiny spearing and a long strip of squid. He looked into the rising Sun and waited patiently for the live bait. After Phillip had a good long look at the killies his grandmother walked over to her husband.

"We bait it the first time and then you're on your own, mate," Grandpa Gant said with a wink.

"Of course, we'll be happy to help you," Grandma Gant added.

Grandpa Gant seized the last pole to demonstrate for his grandson. "What you want to do with the spearing is hook them through the eyes, that makes it harder for the fluke, or whatever tries to eat them, to steal your bait. Then you take a strip of the squid and hook it so it lays parallel, uh, in line, with the spearing like this," the old man said showing the kid how to bait the hook. Now the killies are a bit more difficult as they do a lot of squirming."

"You mean we're going to put hooks into theirs eyes while they're still alive?" Phillip asked horrified.

"Well, yes, we are," Grandpa Gant replied. "Live bait is the best bait. Now then, what you do is take one of the killies," the old man instructed as he seized one of the wriggling little baitfish from his wife's hand, "and put the hook through the center of the eye like this, Phillip," he continued, piercing the fish's eye with the barbed hook and pushing it through until it came out on the other side with one of the fish's gelatinous eyeballs smeared on its tip. "Make sure you go through the center of the eye or down because if you go too far toward the top you might put it through their brain and kill them, and we want them alive."

"But that's not fair, Grampa! That's not right! That hurts them, it's cruel," the boy said with tears welling up in his mismatched eyes.

Grandpa Gant sighed and looked to the sky taking in a deep breath before answering his grandson's accusations. "Sure it hurts, but it's for the greater good. Phillip, that's life, little boy. They're just fish. We'll use the little fish to catch big fish which we'll eat. It's a concept, uh, an idea, I don't expect you to understand completely. Think of it this way. Bigger, or smarter animals eat smaller, less smart animals. We use these little fish as bait to catch big fish which we in turn eat. We don't eat them for the fun of it, do we? We eat animals because we need to eat to survive. Small sacrifices are acceptable, uh okay, if they serve the greater good, Phillip."

Grandma Gant returned the other three killies back into the live well and tossed it over the side again. Grandpa Gant left his wife to console the boy and got on with the fishing as the boat drifted lazily to the west. Within five minutes the old man's rod dipped hard to the bottom and he gave it a staunch pull upward.

"Come on over here, Phillip," the old man shouted. "We've got one hooked already. You're gonna be my reel man."

His tears mostly dried, Phillip shot from his grandmother's lap and stood at his grandfather's side anxiously awaiting instructions. Grandpa Gant placed the rod in Phillip's hands with the butt snugly fitted into the boy's armpit. He then reached around and grabbed the butt of the rod in one of his gnarled, yet nimble hands.

"Now then, matey, I'll keep the rod steady and upright while you reel this monster in," the old man said while passing a glance at his wife who nodded kindly.

Phillip cranked the reel in the wrong direction initially before correcting himself. His grandfather took him snapper fishing before after all, and he knew how the reel worked. The reeling was hard, more difficult than he'd imagined it would be. "It's a big one, Grampa, it's gotta be!"

"Take it slow and easy, I hooked it good, shouldn't get off, don't give it any slack."

Phillip reeled and reeled, the pole bent down at a sharp angle all the while. In childlike anticipation Grandma Gant seized the net from a starboard side rod holder and waited for the fish to come up. It seemed like forever although it only lasted a little over two minutes and then the fish was up on the surface, a big, beautiful flattie, at least three pounds. As the fluke hovered at the waterline Grandma Gant reached down with the net and scooped it out off the water. Grandma Gant turned the net upside down at her feet, the fluke hit the deck with a flat clap and flapped around, blood frothing from its mouth. Phillip watched as Grandpa Gant reached down and unhooked the fish.

"That's a beauty, Phillip! Let's take a picture Elsa," the old man shouted.

Grandpa Gant took his grandson's hand and guided his fingers into the gills of the flapping fish to gain a firm hold on it. "Now hold it up nice and high so Grandma can get a good shot, matey."

Young Gant held the now dithering fish upright as his grandfather had told him to and smiled for the camera. His smile was so natural, so innocent, and yet so knowing in another way. After Grandma Gant snapped the old Kodak Instamatic the boy's grandfather took the fish and opened the larger cooler which was filled with ice. He slid his hand along the backside interior of the cooler, making an entryway for the still slithering fluke and slipped the fish down onto the bottom of the cooler.

"Great job, Phillip! That's a nice start to the morning, huh, Elsa?"

"Sure is, sure is," Grandma Gant agreed, never getting overly excited. "We've got lunch now, let's all get after dinner then," she added.

Four hours later Grandma Gant dumped the surviving killies into the bay along with the rest of the unused bait. The Gants motored home with five large keepers, the largest, a seven pounder, which grandma took, in the cooler. All told they had boated twenty-three fluke, half were legal size. Also among their throwbacks were several porgies, many sea robbins, and one unseemly anglerfish, a rare and unwelcome catch in waters of this shallow depth. Phillip religiously kept count and knew he'd personally reeled in thirteen of the fluke. He also took note of how all of the larger fish had indeed gone for the live killies.

Within sight of the marina Grandpa Gant killed the engine and threw the anchor. He liked to clean his fish on the water, it was his habit to feed the birds of the air and the crabs on the bottom. He also liked to be close to the marina in the event anything unforetold occurred; one never knew when an engine would conk out or a hasty cut might open a finger rather than a fish, it made good sense to be close to home.

Grandpa Gant reached into a compartment below the helm and brought out, a leather sheaved, fillet knife and sharpening stone. After running the knife over the stone on either side several times the old man reached into the cooler and grabbed the first fluke he felt at the bottom. Fluke were slimy, bottom dwellers and not easy to grasp, but Jack Gant had been at it for some sixty odd years, he knew what he was doing.

Phillip watched, mesmerized as his grandfather's knife sliced through the flesh of the fluke, his concern for the lives of the killies long forgotten. Grandpa Gant cleaned, filleted, and skinned the fish while Grandma Gant rinsed and bagged the fillets. The squawking gulls and chirping terns hovered only feet above the old couple as they processed the fish.

With Grandpa Gant's blade glinting in the late morning Sun, the boy thirsted to hold the knife himself, to do his grandfather's work. When the boy asked if he could try the old man hesitated, Phillip was only six years old after all, and a knife was surely unacceptable in his tiny hands. Then his grandfather's face loosened a bit and he called the boy over to the fillet table. Hand over hand, with Grandpa Gant in complete control, the old man showed the boy how to properly clean and fillet a fish. Cleaning a slimy, flat fish was no easy feat. The boy started with the most difficult fish to clean, it would only get easier for him from then on. As it turned out young Phillip was an apt pupil.

Back on Sunset Drive, Grandpa Gant dropped a couple of fillets off at the Doxsie's house and a couple more at the Hochstedter's while young Phillip sat astride the old International Harvester thinking about the day's events, his life, and daydreaming about his future. While Grandma Gant was baking the fluke for their lunch he saw himself as a doctor helping people out. In the next instant he saw himself following in his father's footsteps and becoming a pilot. One thing he knew for sure was he was going to make a difference in the world somehow.

That evening the Andruzzis came for a dinner of fresh grilled fluke, tomatoes, corn on the cob, potato salad and for dessert, blueberry pie. The Addruzzis' had a granddaughter a year older than Phillip, it was nice for him to have a playmate about his own age. While the after dinner drinks were served the youngsters played dominoes on the couch in front of the television which got only the fuzzy networks, it would be five more years before cable reached the east end.

Phillip roused from sleep briefly as his grandfather carried him off to bed. With glassy eyes he looked up to the elderly man and smiled, a deep smile of warmth and satisfaction, a smile indicative of comfort and belonging. Drifting back off to sleep in his bed that night he grasped the nail brush that sat, as of yet unused, upon his night table. He'd make it a point to try it in the morning.

* * * *

The next six years were quite eventful for Phillip and his grandparents, as his own mother and father became more and more detached, and tended to pawn him off on the elder Gants as often as possible. The summer visit was extended from six weeks to the entirety of the summer. The boy was put on a train the day after Christmas and spent New Years with the old couple. His exodus to the east was fine with the steadily maturing boy, as it was with his grandparents. The elder Gants were glad to have him. They felt an obligation to fill the void in his life created by the shortcomings of their grandson's parents.

During those wonderful, carefree times Phillip learned how to butcher a deer. It was two days after Christmas, the boy, now twelve, and his grandfather were driving back from the IGA shortly after nine in the morning with milk, eggs and bread when they saw the deer, a yearling no less, upon the side of the road. Grandpa Gant pulled over to the side of the road and parked the Coronet behind the stricken animal. With his grandson's hand in his own he walked toward the poor beast. When they were within ten feet of the deer, a doe, it attempted to gain its feet. It pushed itself up with its hind legs only to topple forward and back down onto the ground nearly breaking its own neck. The hindquarters were fine, but both of the forelegs were shattered beyond repair.

"Strange to see one like this," Grandpa Gant told his grandson. "Usually the car hits them from the side or from behind. This one was caught flush on in the face, no time to react, I guess. She probably bounced over the car. Driver had to have been going damn fast, the bastard."

"Will it live, Grampa?"

"No, Phillip it won't. Let's get back in the car, quick as you can, now."

Grandpa Gant threw the car into drive and sped off for home. He had planned on leaving the boy home, but Grandma Gant was busy volunteering at the local thrift shop and the boy pled with him to take him back to help the deer. It was less than five minutes before the old man and his grandson returned to the fallen doe.

There were no other cars on the lonely stretch of road between the harbor and Shelter Island. Grandpa Gant opened the glove compartment and took out the .38 caliber service revolver he'd used as a detective. He loaded it with two shells and got out.

"Why do you have to kill it, Grampa?" the boy asked.

The old man leaned in through the driver's side window and replied, "If an animal's gonna die and it's in pain, the merciful, uh, right thing to do is kill it, Phillip. It's best to put it out of its misery. There's nothing wrong with mercy killing, it's the humane, uh, right thing to do."

When Phillip opened his door the old man put his hand on the boy's shoulder, "Stay here, son. There's no need for you to see this. I don't want you to see this."

The boy nodded and settled back into his seat.

Grandpa Gant quickly strode over to the deer and looked it in the eye. Its frightened brown eyes begged for aid, but its breathing was labored, the end was near, the pain must have been excruciating. Without further delay the old man put the barrel of the revolver to the deer's forehead and pulled the trigger. Although he was prepared for the gun's report, the explosion from the Smith and Wesson still startled the boy.

"Pop the trunk, Phillip," the old man called over his shoulder as he seized the yearling above the hooves of the hindquarters and began dragging it back toward the car. When he'd gone home for the gun, Grandpa Gant had lined the bottom of the trunk with a plastic mattress cover which they'd used on Phillip's full bed when the boy had been potty training; it was the best he could come up with on short notice. The doe weighed under a hundred pounds; the old man had plenty of strength to hoist it up and muscle it into the trunk alone.

After returning from the thrift shop Grandma Gant helped Grandpa Gant haul the maroon picnic table from the backyard into the garage. She then retrieved his knives and the electric sharpener from the kitchen. Having a sharpened boning knife, a cleaver, and a skinning knife, the old man took out a surgical scalpel with which he would conduct the finer work. Grandpa Gant's father had been a butcher by trade; he'd passed on a good deal of his skill to his son. Phillip watched as his grandfather went to work on the little doe.

Grandpa Gant quickly and efficiently disemboweled the animal and cleaned it of its organs. The slop he pushed off of the table into a bag-lined trash can. He was neatly slicing down upon the ribcage when he suddenly paused.

He turned toward the boy and asked, "Would you like to give it a try?"

Bright-eyed and eager, Phillip accepted the scalpel and under his grandfather's direction, began to cut the tender meat away from the bone. Impressed with the boy's dexterity, Grandpa Gant allowed his apprentice to work alone with the knife, something he would never have dreamed of doing with any of his other grandchildren. Phillip found butchering the doe was far easier than filleting the slimy fluke. The boy had plenty to grab on to with the deer as opposed to the thin fish; gripping dense fur rather than slippery scales made all the difference to him. The young Gant exhibited a natural aptitude with the blade his grandfather took pride in.

"You're pretty good at that, matey," the old man said. "Or should I call you 'butch' now?" he asked.

"I like it Grampa. It's fun," the boy answered, the "butch" comment sailing way over his head.

"Remember to keep those fingers away from the blade, little boy, or we'll both be in Dutch with Grandma."

Phillip failed to reply as he was immersed in the work before him. Grandpa Gant sat down upon the steps leading into the kitchen and watched on as the young cutter finished paring the flesh from the deer's ribcage. Phillip turned toward his grandfather, eyes alight, and asked, "What's next, Grampa?"

The old man looked at his watch, it read just before noon. He rose to his feet and walked to the refrigerator that stood beside the head of the stairs leading to the basement. The basement stored the old couple's jars of stewed tomatoes, and preserved raspberry and blueberry jelly. He opened the refrigerator and grabbed a bottle of Ballantine Ale, and reached for an opener which hung next to the light switch for the basement. Grandpa Gant popped the cap off of the green bottle and took his seat back on the stairs. He took a long pull from the bottle and fixed his eyes on his grandson.

"So, what should I do next, Grampa?" Phillip asked again.

Grandpa Gant eyed the kid curiously and said, "I think you've earned your keep for the day, Phillip, more than enough. Put the knife down, give your hands a rub and come over here."

Reluctantly the boy obeyed his grandfather and placed the scalpel carefully on the table. Despite the blood and gore before him his stomach rumbled for lunch. He wiped his hands with a dish rag which Grandma Gant would never see again and sat down on the stairs beside his grandfather.

Grandpa Gant slung his arm around the boy's shoulder and said, "Big day, huh Phillip?"

"Yeah, Grampa. I felt bad for the deer, but this is cool."

"Well, I don't know about that, but I'd say you're definitely good with the knife."

The boy smiled, pleased with himself.

The old man smiled back with measured weariness. "Would you like a sip?" he asked, holding the bottle of Ballantine's before the kid.

"Grams would kill us," the boy replied.

"She'd do no such thing, go ahead," Grandpa Gant replied.

Gazing at the shiny, green bottle, Phillip gave it some thought and then took the beer into his hands, both of them, cupped as if it were the Holy Grail. "Are you sure, Grampa?" he asked.

Grandpa Gant nodded. "Grandma won't mind at all. Just a taste though."

Phillip sized the bottle up, it was over two-thirds full. He rested the mouth of it on his lower lip and tilted it back to let it flow, expecting the sweet taste of soda, 7-Up, he hoped. He grimaced as the bitter ale stung his tongue. His empty stomach rolled in protest. He held back a retch and swallowed with considerable labor as he handed the beer back to his grandfather. "Yuck, how do you drink that stuff?"

Grandpa Gant erupted into laughter holding the beer against his lean belly. "Soon enough, Phillip, soon enough. I'm glad not now though," he said, placing the bottle between his feet on the garage's cement floor. "Why don't you go on inside and get cleaned up. I'll finish up out here."

"No, Grampa. I'd like to see the rest."

"I was thinking you could help Grandma with lunch?"

"Please, Grampa. I want to stay, I want to learn," the boy persisted.

Grandpa Gant was never one to stand in the way of education, so long as it was clean and moral. Phillip watched as the old man wielded the cleaver and whittled with the boning knife until the doe was a carcass of sinew and bones. The boy's grandfather wrapped the venison steaks, loins, tenderloins, ribs, and chops in plastic wrap before storing them in the refrigerator. Later in the afternoon he'd parcel the meat out to neighbor's and friends, and then freeze whatever they didn't choose to eat within the next few days. He made a big pile of scrap, much of it quite good, that he earmarked for Sunshine, the Border Collie. Grandma Gant would boil it up for the dog after lunch.

Phillip soaked up his grandfather's primal expertise, taking note of every angle of every slice, the force behind each cut, the smoothness of each stroke. Nothing was lost on the young Gant, he was to get better and better at this craft as he progressed in age. Back then, as a boy becoming a man, it was still healthy, even normal.

Grandpa Gant packed all of the offal and bones into two high density, biodegradable trash bags. Meticulously clean, he made certain nothing was leaking; the boy took note of the old man's obsessive cleanliness. Grandpa Gant hefted the bags into the trunk of the Coronet. In addition to the deer carcass the old man loaded the past week's newspapers, cans, bottles, and kitchen refuse into the trunk as well. Trailed by Phillip, he went inside to wash his hands. When he emerged from the bathroom he asked the boy if he'd like to accompany him to the dump. His grandfather's shadow, Phillip was right behind the old man as he walked to the car.

The dump was smaller than the boy had imagined it would be. Residents of the East End of the island tended to generate much less rubbish and trash than those living toward the city. Whether it was because many of them were weekend only residents, or the fact as a whole they were more frugal in their appetites, they left considerably less waste than most of America. Perhaps it was because there was no garbage pickup and they had to transport their waste to the dump themselves. People with large gardens like the Gants, as many of the East Enders kept, had very little to throw out. The Gants, like most of their neighbors maintained compost heaps or buried their vegetable waste in their gardens, it made for excellent fertilizer. The Gants also buried fish carcasses when the weather turned and Grandpa Gant was unable to filet onboard. Meat waste was most often offered to neighborhood dogs, cats, and the crows and starlings. Despite the tidy appearance of the dump, just like any other dump, it wreaked sufficiently to make one gag.

Grandpa Gant backed up to a mound of rotting bags and killed the engine. Quick as a fox he leapt from the car, a white bandanna tied around his face, western bandito fashion, and unloaded the trunk in seconds. Back in the car he keyed the ignition, peeled down the bandanna, and took off for home.

* * * *

Gant had exceptionally fond memories of his grandparents for seven magical years. When he turned thirteen everything fell apart. Phillip's father's business took off to the point where the family summered in Watch Point and wintered in the upscale town of Manhasset on Long Island's north shore. The north shore, being very hilly, led to Grandpa Gant's ultimate demise.

It was Easter in mid April of 1976, the elder Gants drove in from out east to spend the holiday in Manhasset. Grandpa Gant brought the Coronet to rest in the graveled black top driveway which pitched down to the street at a forty degree angle. Phillip and his father had unloaded the old couple's luggage and were shuttling it up to the guest room on the second floor of the slate roofed Tudor.

Grandpa Gant returned to the car to retrieve a picture of the boy that Grandma Gant took the previous summer. The boy had boated a doormat fluke, Grandpa had the picture framed. The old man reached across and flipped open the glove compartment. He took the picture out, admiring it as he slid back toward the driver's side.

He failed to notice his shirt was caught on the steering mounted gear shift. In his excitement to see his grandson, Grandpa Gant forgot to step down on the emergency brake. As the old man stepped halfway out of the car his entangled shirt yanked the gear shift into neutral and the car began to roll down the steep driveway. With one leg stuck in the car and his other leg and entire torso hanging out, the old man flailed helplessly attempting to pull himself back inside. Age had finally caught up to Grandpa Gant, he hadn't the strength he'd enjoyed in younger years.

Gravity overpowered him, he was unable to hoist himself back into the runaway car, he slid down the driveway with the gaining momentum of the Coronet, the entire left side of his body scraping along the cruel, black driveway. Once in the street the car gained speed as it ambled down Oxcroft Road at twenty miles an hour. The street slanted down at a forty-five degree pitch to the village pool some four hundred yards distant. The old man's clothes in tattered rags, the biting teeth of the gravel paved street tore into his bare flesh, as the car headed downhill with greater speed. Blood pouring from his left knee, hip, elbow, and shoulder the old man summoned the strength to reach up with his right hand and jerk the wheel sharply to the left. With no power steering, it took horribly long seconds for the car to take his direction and swerve to the left.

Halfway down Oxcroft Road, the car swerved in a long arching turn, shot up over the curb and crashed backward into a small oak tree. The oak split at the point of impact and tumbled down into the street. The car continued slowly up onto the front lawn and came to a stop almost parallel to the street as if its driver had just decided to park on the lawn.

Arthur Gant was the first to see the Coronet halfway down the block beyond the leveled tree. He yelled to his wife to call an ambulance and took off down the hill at a run toward his father. Looking over his shoulder Arthur saw Phillip taking up the chase some eighty feet behind him. He was about to stop and turn the boy back toward home, but was unable to justify it. The boy would see what he would see, there was no turning him back, it was inevitable.

Coming upon the Coronet, the car looked fine, the old Detroit product was heavy metal. It had sheared the oak cleanly, with only the back bumper suffering any significant damage, it was smashed into a long, gleaming frown. Grandpa Gant was another matter altogether. The old man hung limply from the driver's side seat, his pants and shirt torn to ribbons and dyed crimson with his blood. Unbelievably, his shirt was still hooked onto the gear shift. Arthur Gant cradled the old man's head in his arms and was at once relieved to see his father's eyes flicker.

Grandpa Gant shook his head in disgust and whispered, "God damned parking break. I forgot to set it. At least my insurance is all paid up," he joked and then closed his eyes.

Dragged downhill for nearly two hundred yards Grandpa Gant had survived his brush with death, he was a hard man to kill. A thick trail of dried burgundy ran down Oxcroft Road all the way to the fallen oak's stump. Phillip walked down the road every day inspecting his grandfather's blood trail. The trail lasted for nearly ten days until a hard spring rain washed the old man's blood down the hill.

Grandpa Gant recovered slowly from his accident, he'd had to undergo skin grafts to replace the tissue lost at his shoulder, elbow, and knee. Most attributed the long recovery to his age, but he feared that there was something else at work. He had pain in the right side of his abdomen to begin with. Attributing the pain to cramps, he ignored it and concentrated on his stretching therapy, seeking to soften the scar tissue. He'd endured far worse pain during the Great War and come out alive, he reasoned. Soon though, the pain he felt in his abdomen spread to his right shoulder blade, it was then he actually became frightened.

The old man felt fatigued, even early in the morning and then the fevers began. When her husband showed no interest in eating and vomited up what little she was able to get into him, against his wishes, Grandma Gant called an ambulance. A nurse who'd seen much ugliness and death in her time, she dreaded the worst and was unfortunately correct in her diagnosis. After extensive testing at Southampton Hospital it was determined the old man was suffering from advanced liver cancer. Emergency surgery followed that afternoon, the surgeon was sure he'd cut out all of the cancer.

The problem was, there was too little of his liver left to function effectively. After being held three days for evaluation Grandpa Gant was added to the long list of patients waiting for liver transplants and then sent home to die. *If only he could get a new liver,* Phillip thought to himself over and over.

As the nausea, fatigue and vomiting intensified the old man lost a great deal of weight. In six short weeks he lost over sixty pounds he was a mere shell of himself, weighing an anemic one hundred and twenty-five pounds. Still, Grandpa Gant greeted each morning with a smile and a renewed sense of hope, that by some miracle, he would pull through and last long enough until a donor liver had become available. Phillip's parents asked the elder Gants to come stay with them in Manhasset, but they declined. It was better to die in your own home they both reasoned.

It was mid June when Grandpa Gant developed jaundice. Phillip was allowed to take his final exams early and then head out east to stay with his grandparents. Phillip was shaken to see his grandfather's condition, the old man's skin had yellowed, his eyes too were glazed and yellowed, and shot with blood. Upon seeing his grandson his mouth broke into a wide smile. Phillip could tell it hurt him to smile like that, but he did it anyway. The boy's parents stayed the weekend and then left him with the old couple. Arthur Gant had business meetings he said he absolutely could not postpone any longer. Phillip's mother, Eleanor, claimed she had pressing matters to attend to at home as well, she never elaborated. The fact was she was too self-absorbed to care too much about the old man.

For nearly a week Grandpa Gant progressed nicely, his appetite returned, he was able to keep his medication down, his pain subsided; he thought he was on the road to recovery. The old warrior was able to dress himself and even walk short distances. Phillip shared his grandfather's optimism while Grandma Gant still held reservations.

After breakfast one cool, crisp morning during that wonderful week, the three of them quietly took a walk through the garden. The Sun was up, on the outside of the deer fence they found a family of rabbits contentedly munching away on the grass and clover. Grandpa Gant reached down and plucked a few carrots from the ground and tossed them through the holes in the fence for the rabbits. After watching the family gnaw down the carrots the Gants silently walked out into the "free corn" field in hopes of seeing some deer. In the middle of the tall, green stalks stood a pair of deer, a buck and a doe. Both were small, juveniles, the buck's antlers began to come in. Grandpa Gant wondered what it would be like to be young again. Inching closer and closer Phillip got to within fifteen feet of the doe before she raised her head and stared in his direction. She snorted delicately alerting the buck of their company. It took the deer a few seconds to register they were not alone and then they were gone. Their white tails a blur as they disappeared into the center of the maze of corn.

Phillip walked over to the old International Harvester and rested his right hand on one of its big, worn down tires. The old man joined him, patting his grandson on the head and then ruffling his hair playfully. Phillip saw Grandma Gant wipe a tear from the corner of her eye before joining them at the tractor. They stayed there by the rusted out tractor in the middle of the corn maze for some time before Grandpa Gant patted the iron beast on the hood as if to say goodbye.

The good week would be Grandpa Gant's last. Shortly after, his symptoms returned with a vengeance and blood appeared in his urine. His familiar smile was gone, the old man was a pale cornflower yellow once more. Incapacitated, he never got out of bed again, he was too weak. Knowing the end was near, Grandma Gant called her son to tell him to hurry out. It was half past ten, a full Moon glowered down through a cloudless sky. While waiting for his parents to arrive Phillip sat with his semi-conscious grandfather and cried. He hugged the frail old man as tears ran down his face, Grandpa Gant was capable only of murmurs and weak sobs. Phillip heard the door of his father's car slam shut; he said goodbye to his grandfather hoping with all his heart to see him once more in the morning.

Arthur and Eleanor had made it out east within two hours, much to Grandma Gant's relief, she hated to see her husband in so much pain. Upon their arrival, Grandma Gant advised Phillip's parents to say their good-byes, she felt sure her husband wouldn't last the night. Phillip's parents hustled into the old man's bedroom shutting the door quietly behind them.

Phillip eavesdropped intently from his upstairs bedroom, but was unable to make out much of any conversation. An hour later he did hear the door to the room his parents were sleeping in shut.

He crept down the stairs and stood on the landing beside the front door as he watched Grandma Gant walk from the kitchen toward the master bedroom, her face somber, but determined. Phillip tiptoed into the kitchen and turned toward his grandparent's bedroom, Grandma Gant had left the door ajar.

Peering into the open room he saw his grandmother sitting in bed with her husband's head cradled in her lap. The old man looked blindly up into his wife's eyes and nodded his head, a single tear streamed down his yellow cheek. Grandma Gant nodded her understanding and rose from the bed. Phillip ducked back into the living room where he listened, his head cocked toward the bedroom. Grandma Gant crossed the room and closed the door quietly. Straining to hear what was going on, Phillip heard only the gentle smack of a kiss that he was certain his grandmother had planted on the old man's forehead. After what seemed like hours he slinked back upstairs and climbed into bed. It was a long time before he slept, and when it came it was fitful and filled with fear.

If only he could get a new liver, were the boy's last thoughts before he finally drifted off.

The following morning Grandpa Gant was dead, his arms resting at either side of his emaciated body. Dying in his sleep was the best way he could go, Phillip's father had said to which his mother eagerly agreed.

Grandma Gant said nothing about her husband's passing away during the night, she shed not a tear in front of the boy. By the look of her bloodshot eyes, she had silently cried herself out during the night. She busied herself with funeral arrangements while the others mourned at the old man's bedside. Phillip was quite certain that Grandma Gant had smothered her husband as soon as she shut the door.

There's nothing wrong with mercy killing, Phillip remembered his departed grandfather's words. He walked out into the kitchen and stared at his grandmother who was now boiling water for breakfast. She looked at the boy, who was fast approaching adolescence, and then looked away, rubbing her nose with the back of her hand. Phillip understood her pain, he shared her pain. Phillip understood her decision, he really did.

* * * *

Beneath a warm, Sun-drenched sky in late May the Gant family gathered together at Calverton National Cemetery about half an hour's drive from Grandpa and Grandma Gant's home. As a decorated World War I veteran, Grandpa Gant received full military honors at his funeral. After the priest had finished with his final blessing an eight member honor guard, outfitted in neatly pressed olive dress uniforms with gold piping, visor caps, and shiny black shoes, marched before the flag draped coffin. The bugler played "Taps" while two of the soldiers ceremonially folded the flag into a triangle and presented it to Grandma Gant. The two soldiers saluted and returned to their line. The line of soldiers then raised their M-14 rifles and fired off three synchronized volleys in the old man's honor. As the soldiers marched away from the grave Phillip collected the spent shell casings from the grass and shoved them into the pockets of his trousers, he would never be without them.

* * * *

Grandma Gant lived out east by herself for another two years. Phillip's visits continued after school was out, now he stayed the entire summer as well as most vacations. With his grandfather gone Grandma Gant had sold the little Whaler along with its trailer. There was no more fishing, but still, there were good times. Besides tending the garden with the elderly woman, Phillip mowed the lawn every week which was a time consuming chore. Pushing the old green and white Lawn Boy along at a steady clip it took the healthy teen nearly two hours to cut the sprawling yard as he had to stop and refuel and sometimes wipe off the blade.

Of course, the grass clippings had to be bagged. Grandpa Gant would never tolerate a messy lawn and Phillip was constant in honoring the old man's ways. He was happy to do it, happy to do anything to help his grandmother. She always had a tall glass of iced lemonade waiting for him on the back porch when he finished. The two went for deer and rabbit watching walks, played pinochle on rainy days, and of course spent time with Sunshine. The border collie was old, plump, and gray by that time, but nonetheless playful and "full of vim and vigor" as Grandma Gant was fond of saying. The two never spoke of Grandpa Gant's death, it seemed as if they had an understanding about it.

Grandma Gant was eighty-three herself, but still full of life. While most elderly women packed on the pounds, the little old lady remained in excellent physical condition, she weighed no more than a hundred pounds, all of it sinewy muscle. Looking at her wrinkled, deeply creased face, Phillip saw only the beauty of her twinkling, childlike, hazel eyes. Phillip loved the way she smelled also, there was no old person odor clinging to her clothes or in the house. To the contrary, the old women had a new baby smell about her. Hugging her first thing in the morning or before bed, he was sure to take a deep breath, it made him feel safe.

Grandma Gant was healthy of body, but unfortunately her mind and senses were other matters. She suffered from the usual forgetfulness attributed to old age, but there was more to it than that. Her hearing had failed to the point, she was nearly deaf as well. Her eyesight began to go, too, but not as quickly. Noticing his mother's hearing and vision loss as well as her deteriorating memory, Arthur Gant pleaded with the old woman to sell her house and move in with them in Watch Point, they had sold the house in Manhasset preferring to spend their time on the ocean rather than the bay. Again and again she rebuffed the invitation. Arthur didn't want to force his mother to move. *It wasn't at that point yet,* he thought. She still functioned better than most people twenty years younger.

It was a mid-September morning, the Sun was bright and sharp, Phillip had returned to school; Grandma Gant was mowing the lawn, and actually enjoying it. She'd emptied the mower's bag of clippings into a garbage bag when she reached down to wipe off the blade. Her right hand under the mowers housing, she felt a jolt, as if she'd been shocked or stung by a bee. When she took her hand out from under the mower her thumb, index, and middle fingers were gone, she'd forgotten to turn the mower off.

Bewildered, Grandma Gant stared at her hand minus three of its five digits, the blood gushed and then ran crimson down her forearm and then dripped off of her elbow. She calmly turned the mower off and pushed it forward exposing her decapitated thumb and fingers.

As they lay in the grass, a June bug scampered over her index finger. Holding her mutilated right hand over her head, she bent down again and, with her left hand, gathered up her digits and then stood upright. Knowing that no neighbors were home she wasted no time in getting inside into the kitchen. She laid the severed digits on the kitchen counter next to the sink, there was no time for neatness, there were splotches of blood all over the kitchen floor already. With her good, left hand and her teeth she tied a tourniquet around her right arm, just above her elbow. She then opened the pantry door and grabbed a plastic sandwich bag. She shoved the fingers and thumb, along with some grass, into the bag and then filled the bag with ice. She snapped up the Coronet's keys off of the counter and stormed out the front door toward the car.

Willing herself to stay conscious Grandma Gant rolled down her window with her left hand as she steadied the steering wheel with the heel of her shredded right hand. She turned on the radio and blared music, heavy rock music, none of the Big Band melodies she so adored, she needed something to keep her alert. Half an hour later she arrived at Southampton Hospital. She parked the car legally and ran to the emergency room with her chilled bag of digits. As luck would have it the morning was a slow one and she was taken within five minutes, they skipped the paperwork. After over two hours of surgery her fingers and thumb were reattached. Her hand wasn't so pretty to look at anymore, the fingers and the thumb bowed out awkwardly and she never enjoyed the same dexterity, or anything close to it, but the digits were functional.

After the lawn mowing incident Arthur Gant insisted his mother sell her East End home and move in with them. The woman was proud, but no fool, and a month later she acquiesced to him. Her home was sold quickly as that area of the island was experiencing a boom in demand, denizens of the city with money were snatching up properties as quickly as they could. It was two months later when the Gants received a phone call from Grandma Gant's old neighbors. Sunshine, the Border Collie, had died, they told the old woman. They were sure the poor dog had died of heartbreak having lost her best friend.

* * * *

The first year of Grandma Gant's residence was good. Phillip had started at the Salzberg School, but he returned home every weekend to see her. He loved having her around and gave up playing any sports, attending dances, and any other extra-curricular activities to spend his time with her. Being absent from any school functions, outside of class, caused the other students to treat him as somewhat of a pariah. It mattered not to him if he was cast as an outsider, he yearned for two-forty on Friday afternoons so he could hop on a bus to the city. From New York he took the Long Island Railroad to Freeport where his father and grandmother picked him up.

Her forgetfulness taking a hold, Phillip had to repeat himself again and again, but it was a small price to pay for such cherished company. Grandma Gant still cooked during those first two years, the aromas of beef stroganoff, fried scallops, and baked chicken wafted through the kitchen up to the high ceilings of the house. On Saturday mornings she prepared rice and milk with lots of sugar for him, just like she had at her own home. Sunny days meant long walks on the soft, white sand of the beach down the block. Even on cold winter days with snow on the ground they bundled up, sometimes Phillip's father joined them, and strolled the beach providing it wasn't overly windy. Pinochle was, as always, reserved for rainy days, often in the den before a roaring fire.

Toward the end of his freshman year Grandma Gant's forgetfulness became more and more pronounced and she was diagnosed with Alzheimer's. Still with a healthy body, the old woman sometimes "escaped" from the house and wandered around the town. On one occasion she was found walking on Lido Boulevard in Lido Beach some three miles from home. The Gant's made stickers with their name and address printed on them. They affixed the stickers onto the back of her shirt every morning after she was dressed; otherwise she would peel them off and throw them away.

A month and a half later, her vision worsened considerably and it was discovered she had cataracts. After several procedures proved to be ineffective her sight dwindled quickly. Within a period of months the old woman was deaf and legally blind, she could make out shapes and see light, but she had no depth perception to speak of. With her auditory and visual senses cut off, the Alzheimer's kicked into high gear and by August, shortly before Phillip returned to Salzberg for his sophomore year, Grandma Gant failed to recognize her son or grandson, by sight or voice. A prisoner of her own human frailty, she turned inward.

By the following December, Grandma Gant was largely nonfunctional. Unable to see or communicate, she sat in the den staring blindly at soap operas she could not see nor hear and would have no interest in if she could. Two nights before Christmas Eve, Phillip and his father had helped her up to bed and said their good nights to her. Phillip and his parents turned in a few hours later. Half past three in the morning Grandma Gant rose from her bed and felt her way out of her bedroom, she unsteadily stood staring blindly at the second floor landing before her. The Gant's were in the habit of leaving the lights on their Christmas tree, a towering twelve foot Douglas Fir, on throughout the night.

Like a moth to light, Grandma Gant drifted toward the tree which her filmed-over eyes somehow detected. Edging down the step from her bedroom door she found herself on the landing at the top of the stairs. The landing overlooked the living room beyond in which the tree stood, its red, white, and green lights shimmering. It was probably the angel on top, a luminescent cherub with a golden harp, which really drew her in. She shuffled toward the light of the tree not seeing the waist high railing that bordered the landing. She reached out toward the magnificent tree with her hands, one normal, the other deformed by the lawn mower accident, and sought to touch it. It was then, her right slipper caught on the carpeted floor, her momentum swept her forward arms splayed out; she hit the railing waist high and tumbled over the railing into the tree. Somehow the tree remained upright, with just a few strings of lights torn off and some of its ornaments strewn across the living room floor.

Grandma Gant however lay beneath the tree with a broken hip. It wasn't her scream or cry that woke the house, because she did neither, she lay there with tears streaming down her cheeks, but emitted no noise, not even a sob. Whether it was due to her tough upbringing or the dissociative effects of the Alzheimer's, nobody knew for sure, but she remained silent. She would not have been discovered until the following morning having not been for the glassy ting of the shattering ornaments which roused Phillip from sleep.

Elsa Gant lay for three months in a hospital bed, recognizing none of her visitors. It seemed as if the broken hip had broken her spirit as well. Her strength wavered to the point she was unable to participate in physical therapy. Bed sores developed as she was largely immobilized.

Phillip remembered his last visit to her room, it was in the evening, a month before Easter. He laid down in bed with the dying woman cuddling up beside her so his face was level with hers. He cried for a long time, but when he finished crying his sense of smell was uncommonly acute. He deeply inhaled the old woman's scent. Even dying she smelled good, she smelled of new baby, he would always remember.

Grandma Gant died the morning after Phillip's final visit. The fifteen-year-old Gant was left all alone, it wasn't just that he felt that way. He'd lost the two people he'd loved more than anyone else in the world. Sure he loved his parents, but it was largely an unrequited love, particularly on the part of his mother. Returning to the Salzberg School, Phillip ceased to go home on weekends, but was still considered an outsider by his peers. He became more and more introverted, avoiding his classmates and his disinterested parents. Gant didn't completely shut down though, he immersed himself in his studies and took on additional work as well. He was most inclined to learning.

Small sacrifices are acceptable if they serve the greater good, echoed within the young man's brain. *Small sacrifices are acceptable if they serve the greater good*, a simple life lesson that would become Phillip Gant's mantra in later life. *Small sacrifices are acceptable if they serve the greater good*, a fundamental belief the young Gant took to heart hook, line, and sinker.

Chapter Sixteen

Early on in the trip James Geignetter had stirred in the rear of the van alerting Gant of his consciousness as they drove over the Throg's Neck Bridge. Having crossed the bridge, Gant exited onto Randall Avenue and pulled into a mostly empty parking lot beside a movie theatre. From a case beneath the passenger seat he took out a syringe and a vial of ketamine, he didn't like to use it, but felt the boy would fare better sleeping than awake and terrified. Gant slid the cargo door aside and joined Geignetter in the rear of the van. Seeing the kid was wide awake with tears in his eyes, Gant looked away from his face and concentrated on the task at hand. He crouched down toward the immobile boy and seized the flesh of his left thigh with the thumb and index finger of his left hand. With his right hand he stuck the syringe into the flesh and depressed its plunger. Minutes later Geignetter lapsed back into unconsciousness and Gant was back on the road.

There was pouring rain south of Syracuse when Gant heard the boy thrashing around again. Bound up with duct tape, he was buffered by pillows on either side of his body and had two more under his head, with another pair under his knees. Gant did want him to be as comfortable as possible for the ride. The young mate was securely pinned within his protective pillow cushion by the steel wall of the van and the currently empty ice tote, there was only so much he could really move.

Gant was unsure how long the boy had been awake, it could have been hours or simply minutes, it was the first he'd heard from him since they were passing from Queens into the Bronx. Needing to refuel, Gant pulled into a rest stop off of Interstate Eighty-One and contemplated dosing the boy again, but decided against it. He looked in on him before gassing up and continuing home.

It was still raining as Gant pushed westward on Interstate 190. It rained nearly the entire time he was gone. Some of the storms brought torrential downpours. The grass was a vibrant green in the early morning Sun, it had magically transformed during his absence. Storm debris littered the highway and the streams and ponds had overflowed their banks.

Gant felt as if he'd been living in a vacuum. Lost in a sea of relaxation, and the one night of overly indulgent drinking, he'd enjoyed his visit to Long Island very much. He hadn't thought of home, work, or Lydia, there were the nightly phone calls to her. During his entire stay he'd not once turned on a television or radio. Neither had he picked up a newspaper or logged onto the Internet. He suddenly realized he had no idea what was going on in the world, and it scared him a little. As the last song on *Candy-O* by the Cars wound down, Gant switched the Blaupunkt to radio to catch up with the news. He tuned in to WNED, nine-seventy on the a.m. dial. The station had a wide audience serving Buffalo and Toronto.

The straight, business-like voice of Kirk Newfield, the station's morning news man, droned on about skyrocketing gas and food prices, increasing inflation, rising unemployment, and then moved on to speak about Congressional gridlock. *Apparently nothing's changed*, Gant thought to himself. He was about to switch the radio off and cue up the Rolling Stone's *Sticky Fingers* when the reporter announced, "Now here's more on the human remains discovered outside of Marilla, New York."

Gant's eyes widened, his hands gripped the steering wheel tightly.

"This past Wednesday a body found by a hunter scouting a wooded area south of Marilla, a sleepy little town, twenty miles east of Buffalo, spurred investigators to search for additional remains," the announcer went on. "According to the hunter, he was scouting the area for the upcoming fall black bear season. On the only non-rainy day in nearly two weeks, he'd taken his dogs along for company. While nosing around the dogs began to bay and much to his surprise, uncovered what he believed to be a collar bone. He contacted the state police immediately. It was reported late yesterday the state police had found more remains. Authorities were slow to provide details, but did say the remains of two different people were recovered only a hundred and fifty feet apart on a two hundred and fifty acre parcel of land frequented by hunters. Further information we're being told will be made available after the remains are identified."

Gant could identify them, he was the last person to see them alive.

Newfield went on, "An anonymous source familiar with the investigation has indicated the condition of the remains is poor, but dental records should provide the identifications. The source provided no time line for identification though. The same source went on to say the bodies were buried in shallow graves and both were hunched in the fetal position."

The graves weren't shallow, it was the runoff from all the damned rain, Gant's inner voice said. *The rain eroded the soil to the point the hunter's dogs got a sniff of the body. Yes, I left them in identical positions. The fetal position takes up the least amount of space, it's most compact. Ask any pregnant woman. It allows for a smaller hole, less digging, a quicker job,* his inner voice added.

"Speculation the remains are connected runs high, although nothing has been corroborated by the police at this time," the announcer stated. "Crime scene investigators are at this moment scouring the area for more remains. Stay tuned for more information on this breaking story. Now, let's check in with Heather Helms to see when all this rain will clear out."

"Thank you, Kirk. In the wake of near record rainfall amounts and massive flooding it looks like the end is finally in sight—" the young meteorologist began when Gant shut the radio off.

They won't find any more bodies, those are the only two I buried there. If they find others, they're somebody else's, Gant thought as he edged closer to home.

Early on in his career Gant had buried a number, five to be exact, of his victim's at three different locations upstate. He quickly learned interring his victim's was altogether wrong. There were far too many ways in which a buried body could be stumbled upon. Excavation for land development, adventurous kids, hungry animals, simple erosion, and trained scent hounds all posed a significant risk. As a kid growing up on the beach Gant should have immediately recognized the nominal risk involved with water disposal. It was far better to sink a corpse than it was to bury one, he realized. After those first five which he put in the ground, all the rest of his victims were provided with watery graves, sometimes fresh, sometimes salt, and sometimes brackish.

* * * *

Gant thought back to the women who were exhumed. Tabitha Small had been a realtor, Gant remembered. She'd told him so while he interviewed her upon the cold, steel table in the basement of the house outside of Orchard Park. A real talker, she'd been very forthcoming which he found refreshing, yet at the same time somewhat disarming. Yes, Gant wanted to know about his victims so he could honor their souls after he'd taken their lives, but too much information was troubling. Too deep an insight into the life of a donor caused Gant guilt, it cost him sleep at night.

During his interview Gant had learned, Small was the only child of a local banker and stay at home mother. She'd attended a private prep school and excelled in gymnastics there, so much so she'd received a partial scholarship to the University of New Hampshire. She'd never been married, but was in love with a veterinarian. Gant found out she was an exceptionally successful real estate agent who owned a house in the ritzy section of Cheektowaga. She had told him of her grandmother who was dying of cancer, and her uncle who looked forward to her visits because she was the only one who really understood him.

In her thirties, Small was aptly named. She stood just over five feet and weighed no more than a hundred pounds after leaving an all-you-can-eat buffet. With fine, dark hair to her shoulders and darting hazel eyes, she was not beautiful, but not unattractive either. Her arms and legs were sinewy and tight, as one might expect a gymnast to be.

Gant took notice of her while he was jogging through the Losson Nature Trails early one autumn evening in 1998. The little woman was speed walking the trails within Stiglmeier Park in the town of Cheektowaga when Gant ran up behind her. He eased his pace to a casual walk some hundred feet back to admire her stride and ascertain if she was right for his purposes.

After discretely following Small for ten minutes he was satisfied he had a new donor. For the next two weeks Gant frequented the park at five o'clock every day, and each day the little speed walker appeared, sometimes she was a few minutes earlier or a bit later, but never more than five minutes either way. Gant routinely arrived at the park at the same time, but was careful to never cross paths with Small on the trails.

He was patient, he could wait, and wait he did. The fall of 1998 was a season of eternal waiting, it seemed for Gant, he bid his time patiently as the Sun sank earlier and earlier each day. Not knowing if the impending cold might cause Small to quit walking for the winter, Gant made his move in late November when dusk had fallen. Gant's nondescript, blue Toyota Camry pulled in to the lot adjacent to Stiglmeier Park and stopped nearest the main park entrance, two spaces away from the speed walker's Honda Civic. The park was deserted, all the kids and their mother's had already left, the season's first real nip chilled the air. Gant counted his blessings that winter had held off as long as it had. Most years by this time snow carpeted the ground, very often it snowed heavily in western New York before Halloween. This year though, unusually warm and dry weather had moved in from the south and had remained for a few weeks. Local residents considered the thirty-five degree lows at night an Indian Summer of sorts, it seemed as though fate was on Gant's side.

Gant stepped from the Camry donned in jogging clothes he'd never worn before and never would again. He walked into the trails and took a leisurely forty-five minute stroll returning toward the park entrance five minutes before the speed walker was due to return. From behind an ancient oak tree just inside the park, Gant spied the woman making the final turn on the near trail. With her still over a hundred yards distant on the straightaway, Gant hurried into the lot and crouched down behind her car.

Small approached the Civic casually pulling her keys out of her jacket pocket as she walked. She thumbed the unlock button on the key fob, the interior light brightened the car's inside. Gant shrunk lower on his heels as the glow from the interior light gleamed forth. It was instinct to duck, he knew the glare from the light only served to conceal his position all the better while blinding his intended victim to everything beyond her car. As Small's hand grasped the door handle, Gant crept out from behind the trunk with a chloroform soaked sponge in his right hand. As the woman swung the door open and lifted her right leg to enter the car Gant was upon her, his left arm pinning her arms down to her abdomen his right hand smothering her nose and mouth with the sponge. He held her tight until her legs buckled. Then he hoisted her over his right shoulder and carried her to the Camry. He reached into his jacket pocket with his left hand to retrieve his keys. He popped the trunk and laid the little woman inside. That was the end for Tabitha Small.

* * * *

Now, thirteen years later, Gant felt badly about Small, but still, it seemed to be worthwhile. *Small sacrifices are acceptable if they serve the greater good.* He had darker remembrances of Alona Ricketts, it was a very different experience altogether. For the first, and only time, he'd acted impulsively.

* * * *

Gant visited cemeteries regularly, most often at mid-day when he was able to read the headstones in the bright Sunshine. With a sincere respect for the dead and a most odd attraction to burial sites, he sometimes drove by a cemetery, sometimes two, before he returned home from work. It was after nine on a warm May night when Gant happened upon a black woman jogging on the shoulder of Harlem Road outside Holy Sepulchre Cemetery. Gant was still driving the Camry at this time, his dark hobby was in its infancy.

Gant noticed the twinkling reflective vest in the glare of his headlights a quarter of a mile distant as Alona Ricketts ran toward home. Creeping along at fifteen miles per hour the vest sparkled in the Camry's headlights as he edged closer, the runner's physique revealing itself. Recognizing the gait of the jogger to be obviously feminine, he slowed to ten miles per hour rolling up to within a hundred feet of her. Gant knew that taking action then was risky, but he was fairly new to this, and had decided to roll the dice.

Ricketts cocked her head toward the road peering into the Camry's headlights as the car slowed. Blinded, she turned away as the car sped up and disappeared ahead of her. Gant turned right onto Genesee Street about a half mile ahead of the jogger.

He parked the car in a weed strewn stretch of land, there were no houses within sight. Walking back toward Harlem Road he rubbed the chloroform soaked rag in the back pocket of his trousers. He waited at the corner until he saw Ricketts' silhouette appear in the dim light cast by the streetlight. He kneeled stock still, giving her time to pass before he jumped out from behind a still hibernating hydrangea and took pursuit.

An avid runner, Gant was upon the woman in seconds. Not bothering with subtleties, he wrapped his arms around her shoulders and threw her into the weedy grass beside the road. Ricketts hit the ground with a thud, her eyes instinctively searching for what she knew, could only be a rapist or murderer. Gant dropped down onto the woman, the chloroform rag gripped into his right fist. Ricketts threw her hands out before her, her left index finger caught Gant flush in the right eye.

Gant barked in pain, his eye watering, his vision blurred. Ricketts reflexively drew her hand back at Gant's outcry. Not interested in attaining any more injuries, Gant swung down hard with a hammer blow to the jogger's forehead. Dazed, but not out, the woman jabbed upward with a sharp left that split Gant's lip, his blood drizzled down onto her screaming face.

As the runner's hands searched out Gant's testicles, he seized her by the throat and kneed her in the stomach knocking the wind out of her. The chloroform rag was administered as she gasped for air, and within thirty seconds she was unconscious. It was a short walk back to the Camry and Gant had the heavily-laden woman in the trunk less than two minutes later. He'd learned his lesson though, he'd never take another donor on impulse.

Ricketts was tall for a woman, five foot eight, and solid, she weighed a hundred and fifty pounds, mostly muscle. Her thick thighs led to a wide trunk with small breasts. Her biceps were not large, but defined and powerful. She wore her hair short, in corn rows, which her daughter braided for her while they watched television after the child's homework was done. With a chocolate complexion and brown, red-rimmed eyes, the woman looked tired, and it wasn't the after effects of the anesthesia. Gant had a feeling the bloodshot eyes were the norm for her. Gant found her face to be not attractive, but matronly. The motherly face was badly mismatched with the body of a warrior. It wasn't until later during the interview phase of Gant's processing, he learned she took kick boxing lessons twice a week, her legs attested to the strict workout regimen.

During the interview Ricketts sobbed while telling Gant she was twenty-nine, and raising her twelve-year-old daughter alone, her boyfriend had left soon after she'd told him she was pregnant. She'd worked two jobs, one as a telemarketer at night, the other, as a hair dresser during the day, to pay her way through nursing school. She'd been an RN at Buffalo General Hospital for three years and begun to save money for her daughter's education when Gant had absconded with her.

Gant remembered the guilt pangs he'd suffered finding out the woman stretched out on his table was not only a mother, but also a nurse, a caregiver to the ill. Gant held nurses in high esteem, believing they often did more for their patients than the doctors.

It was criminal, he thought back then and still believed today, *to take this women's life.* Momentarily he'd wondered if he could let her go and quickly dismissed the fanciful idea.

There was no going back, Gant knew the inherent risk involved in such folly. There were simply too many ways to get burned when one played with that kind of fire. He respected the woman's fighting spirit, despite, or maybe because of the split lip she'd inflicted upon him. He felt deep remorse when he wedged the nail gun into the mouth of the woman, whose work it was to heal the ill and infirmed. It sickened him to the point he vomited immediately after he pulled the trigger.

As the rain washed away the world's impurities, so too Gant's depraved psychology washed away his guilt. He took consolation in reasoning it was a mistake, a poor choice to choose Ricketts, but her organs would save a great many lives. He hoped she understood his logic and maybe even approved of his methods. A fair amount of ugliness and heartache was to be expected when one was striving to improve the lot of the human race. A life was a small price to pay for the salvation of many. *Small sacrifices are acceptable if they serve the greater good.*

* * * *

Gant's lifelong creed snapped him out of his dark, yet fulfilling remembrances. He straightened up in his seat, he had work to do. The fifteen-year-old party boat mate produced a series of moans from behind his duct taped mouth. The kid probably heard some, or all, of the broadcaster's announcement and was in the process of shitting himself, if he already hadn't. Gant was relieved that he smelled neither feces nor urine to this point in the trip. Many of his victim's lost control of their bowels or bladder or both upon waking from the anesthesia and discovering their predicament. He hoped the kid could hold out another half hour.

Before ten in the morning the Econoline turned on to Milestrip Road. Shortly afterward Gant brought the van to a halt beside the steps descending to the basement door. He slid out from behind the wheel and threw his arms skyward in a long, deeply satisfying stretch. He felt wide awake and alive despite spending almost eight hours on the road. Keys in hand he hurriedly went to the bottom of the stairs and unlocked the door. After a quick search of the house he found it empty, so he returned to the van for the boy.

Gant pocketed the keys after unlocking the van's back door and then swung the doors open. Geignetter's oversized sneakers fell from the van's bed and hung out, almost touching the bumper. When Gant had gassed up the kid had been comfortably positioned exactly as he had been placed at the beginning of the trip. The boy must have been quietly trying to escape his bindings and inadvertently slid toward the rear of the van on the last leg of the journey. Gant sighed in pity and reached down and grabbed the kid by his ankles. Gently sliding the tall, gangly boy backward out of the van on his backside, he brought him to rest sitting on the bumper. Gant tried to avert his eyes, but it was impossible to ignore the kid's sobbing and tear-stained face. Gant looked into Geignetter's brown, bloodshot eyes and wordlessly nodded in sympathy.

He squatted down taking a deep breath as he did so. Pushing his right shoulder into the boys belly and seizing him by his skinny buttocks, Gant hoisted him off of the bumper and up onto his right shoulder. He carried the young mate over his shoulder, the boy's comically big sneakers out in front of him, the kid's head bobbing up and down behind in rhythm with Gant's steps. The kid's fine, chestnut hair hung out from his head as if he'd received an electric shock. Halfway down the steps to the basement Geignetter's bladder finally blew soaking Gant's side from shoulder to thigh.

Gant laid the boy down atop the cold, shiny table and ascended the stairs to lock the van. Panic-stricken, the boy watched the open door waiting for his assailant to return. Bright, morning Sunlight streamed down the stairway into the dank, lifeless basement. The boy watched the door with new tears dripping from his eyes as dust particles danced in the shaft of light afforded by the Sun. Gant's shadow came into view before the boy heard the man's footfalls on the steps. Then Gant appeared in the doorway and pulled the door shut behind him, the boy would never see daylight again.

After securing Geignetter to the autopsy table, Gant stripped off the boy's urine-soaked clothes and sponge bathed the kid clean. He covered the kid with a paper, hospital sheet and wordlessly left him. Gant then threw his own clothes and his guest's into the washing machine at the foot of the stairs and walked in the back room of the basement where he stepped into the shower. Twenty minutes later he was back table side with the kid in a fresh change of clothes. He'd wait to unpack the van later as he didn't want the kid to linger in false anticipation of escape or release. He had only a few questions for the boy. He removed the duct tape as gently as possible.

"Well, Jimmy, how do you feel?"

The kid looked at him as if he were the devil himself.

"I'm sorry I have to do this, Jimmy, but you'll be helping a lot of people out. Do you want to be a hero, Jimmy?"

Geignetter tried to speak, but his throat closed up.

"If you can't speak I understand," Gant said soothingly. "Know that you're a good kid, none of this is your fault. I hope you know what you're doing is good, it's noble. You'll be a hero to many people."

Geignetter looked at Gant with incomprehension.

"What happened to your daddy?"

Geignetter swallowed hard and then croaked, "Died."

"How old were you when he died?"

"Twelve," the boy muttered, tears and snot running into his mouth as he opened it.

"Did you love your dad? Was he good to you?" Gant asked.

The kid just nodded, his lips trembling too much to answer.

"You'll see him again, Jimmy. I promise."

The kid stared up into Gant's blue and green eyes as the chloroform soaked rag came up to meet his nostrils. Geignetter held his breath, trying to avoid the fumes, but it was futile as Gant pushed the boy's mouth shut with his left hand and firmly cupped the rag over his nose with his right. The boy's head shook back and forth violently at first, but then he lost strength. Thirty seconds later the boy was out and Gant disappeared into the back room to retrieve the nail gun and assemble his instruments. He swore to never again take anybody under the age of twenty-one, it had become too painful.

After Geignetter's organs were garnered, Gant flew to Montreal to meet Monseaux for the exchange. Securing his pay he took off for home. At four-thirty-five in the afternoon he touched down at the Clarence Aerodrome heavy of heart, but confident he'd done the right thing.

Chapter Seventeen

"Now that you have a growing body count of which all the victims have been disemboweled, or harvested rather, in a similar fashion, it does suggest you're subject is indeed a serial killer," Doctor Viscardi said, pushing his glasses up on top of his head. The chubby, white-haired forensic psychologist had provided testimony at court cases for over thirty years. He was especially adept at translating psychological findings and terminology into legal language that could be understood. For that reason he was very popular with the district attorneys of not only Buffalo, but also of Rochester and even Syracuse.

"So we thought earlier," Wilder poked at the doctor.

Viscardi had dismissed Wilder's earlier call citing the fact, "One mutilated corpse does not make a serial killer." After the other two bodies were found in identical states, the doctor was intrigued. Upon Wilder's second phone call, Viscardi was eager to meet with the detectives, he invited them to his office immediately.

Viscardi held up a small, boyish hand and said, "My apologies detectives. I was hasty to dismiss your earlier entreaties. I've been very busy though, I've been getting a lot of calls regarding the nonsense going on down on Long Island."

Wilder nodded.

Hamilton asked, "You're working on the case?"

"No, no. Not in any official capacity. They have enough doctors in my line of work down there, God knows they need them. I provide my two cents whenever I'm asked to."

"So what about our, guy, uh, subject?" Wilder pushed.

"Well, first off, you're most probably correct in assuming your subject is male, the overwhelming majority of serial murderers are. But for now we'll stick with calling the murderer 'the subject' to be fair, okay?"

"Fine, so what can you tell us, then," Wilder asked again.

"There's very little to go on as this is a very peculiar case. Here's what I do know. Your particular subject is an odd one, indeed," Viscardi stated squinting at Wilder. "The subject doesn't really adhere to the major indicators we've established over decades of research. You see, there is often, but not always, a sexual component to the murders. There is no evidence of sexual abuse in your three victims."

"The coroner says the last two victims may have been dead for five years or more."

"How can you tell?" Hamilton asked.

"I'm basing this on the Nichols boy who was found first, he was relatively fresh. There was no sign of sexual abuse to his genitals or his anal cavity. According to the M.E. there was very little bruising at all, which would indicate a lack of torture. The M.E. informed me this indicates the boy sustained the abrasions and contusions after he was already dead, most probably while floating down the river."

"I don't know if I buy that," Wilder responded. "Because the boy wasn't sexually assaulted, doesn't mean the two women weren't."

"I agree," Hamilton said. "Those women were pretty nearly skeletons. How could we know?"

"Legally speaking of course, if there is no evidence, there is no evidence. We all have our gut feelings, and my gut tells me the same person murdered these three people. I believe you feel the same way."

Both detectives nodded.

"My gut is one thing, but research is another. By definition serial killers repeat their offenses very often verbatim. It would be very out of character for a serial murderer to sexually assault one victim, but not another. These people are slaves to ritual, otherwise they don't get the desired high they seek," the doctor looked toward the detectives.

"You said a sexual component is not always involved," Hamilton stated.

"I did, indeed," the doctor admitted. "Let's assume for now, the subject didn't assault the victims sexually, okay?"

Wilder and Hamilton nodded.

"There's also no sign of torture on the boy—very odd. Additionally, the scant number of knife scrapes on each of the victim's skulls is remarkable. Whoever did this is very good at cutting. The few scrapes that have been found are nearly identical in terms of location, depth, and signature on all three victims, right behind the ears, a delicate area for even the finest of surgeons under optimum hospital conditions. There were also scrapes found on certain ribs, identical in all three. It is also certain a surgical scalpel did the cutting."

"So, this tells us what, doctor?" Wilder asked. "We already know all of this. We all think it's the same guy, right?"

"This tells me whoever did this was extremely patient, meticulous even, making the same strokes on each victim. The subject had plenty of practice doing this. This also tells me there are more bodies out there. Three is the tip of the iceberg."

Wilder rocked back in his chair, Hamilton's eyes widened.

The doctor continued, "This also tells me this same subject is undeniably responsible for these three murders, and probably many more, but more importantly, it tells me the subject is a rare bird in the world of serial murderers. While it's true these three murders have been completed in a similar fashion, the victims have very little in common. Most often a serial murderer's victims will be of the same sex, race or occupation, they will have something in common. You have three victims. Cory Nichols was fifteen, white, male, and a student. Tabitha Small was thirty-four, white, female, a realtor. Alona Ricketts was twenty-nine, black, female, a nurse. Very, very uncharacteristic for a serial killer to choose these three people. But what do they have in common?"

"We spoke about this before. They were all youngish, under forty anyway, and all were in good physical shape." Hamilton stated.

"Exactly! Those are the only commonalities shared by the three," Viscardi said.

"No offense, Doc, but we'd already had that figured out," Wilder stated.

"I know you did, I'm letting you know what you're up against. Serial killers sometimes have very high I.Q's, they're smart, and if they don't want to get caught, they often aren't. The vast majority though adhere to the two criteria we spoke of, but your subject bucks all of the trends. The person you're looking for is like a new breed of serial killer, certainly nothing I've ever read about. It's very possible the killer you're looking for is the first of its kind. I have some ideas, but they're really only conjecture. I don't have a solid feel for what motivates your killer. It's actually quite fascinating."

"I'm glad you're fascinated by this weirdo, Doc. So where do we go from here, then?" Wilder asked, clearly perturbed.

"I'll tell you what I think and what to look for, it's the best I can do right now," Viscardi replied.

"Let's have it then."

"This is what I do know. Power is the focus of these people's thinking, it's what drives them. This obsession with power stems from low self-esteem, neglect and very often child abuse. Children feeling unwanted growing up, may become violently assertive as adults. These people may appear to be normal, sometimes even charming, but they are usually very low key and introverted. You should be looking for a loner, most can't make a go of it in relationships. If they have had relationships, their partner is very often their first victim."

"We know that most of these killers start small, with birds, for instance," Wilder said. "I've heard animal abusers are twice as likely to abuse people. What else do they have in common as youngsters?"

"There is a theory called the MacDonald Triad which suggests traits common to these people in childhood. According to this theory there is a combination of three symptoms common to nearly all serial killers. These people torture and kill animals, as you mentioned. They are also pyromaniacs and bed-wetters."

"Bed-wetters?" Hamilton asked.

"Correct, any bed wetting past the age of five is considered abnormal. Some of these killers have the problem well into pre-adolescence, some even as adults."

"Gross," she said.

"Agreed, but true. Anyway, these symptoms are the product of abuse and neglect. These children are destined for sociopathic behavior. They may be extremely shy as kids, who then grow into outwardly reserved adults with bizarre concepts of life. Add in the incredible compulsion for violence and internal hostility and you have a big, big problem".

"All right," Wilder said. "Let's talk about motivation. Since you believe sex is out of the question, what are the remaining motivations?"

"Of course monetary gain comes into play, even with quote 'normal' human beings. The most sane person will kill for money as long as the situation is amenable. It's obvious we can rule this out easily as none of your victims thus far had any real money. You've got a kid, a nurse, and a real estate agent. Unless you're selling homes in the Hamptons or Beverly Hills you probably won't get murdered for it. I'm not advising you overlook people close to the deceased, but I don't think you'll find anything."

"So, we rule out sex and money," Hamilton said.

"I would. Racism is an easy out as well, your subject doesn't differentiate between the races," the doctor said.

"It leaves us with what?" Wilder asked.

"That leaves you with an incredibly difficult task unfortunately. To my knowledge the only other motivators for such behavior are killing for fun, thrill and pleasure. These are the worst killers because they tend to be the most intelligent. Still, I'm hesitant to say your subject falls into any of the categories, which makes it all the more perplexing."

"Our guy's motivation is the real key to stopping him," Hamilton said.

"Yes, your greatest chance of success is to uncover what drives your subject," Viscardi corrected her stressing his final word.

"Besides being crazed killers, are there explainable reasons why this happens?" Wilder asked.

"The overwhelming majority of serial murder's, almost all of them in fact, suffer from at least one mental disorder which quote unquote 'normal' people suffer from. Often they have obsessive compulsive disorder, schizophrenia, multiple personality disorder, bipolar disorder, antisocial personality disorder, any number of anxiety disorders, or a form of delusion. I could go on if you'd like, but the list is tiresome. They may suffer from many disorders at once. These people are not mentally well to begin with.

Alone these disorders are controlled with therapy or medication, usually a combination of the two, but when you add in deep-seeded feelings of inadequacy, a dysfunctional childhood, and warped social norms, or no norms at all, you get individuals with no sense of empathy or remorse. You get people who kill to either ease their own pain or feel good about themselves." The doctor paused and then added, "Don't think you can narrow this down to people who've been treated for some sort of psychological disorder. There are millions of them here in this state alone."

"Not that it really matters Doc," Wilder said, "but do you think some of these people were born into this?"

"If you're asking me the age old 'Nature vs. Nurture' question, I believe a very marginal amount of these people have a genetic disposition toward killing. It's not to say it doesn't occur, because it does. I'd say the odds can be likened to the 'Big Bang Theory' in my opinion though. With the infinite nature of space, we are the only 'discovered' life. It's wondrous to me that one big explosion gave rise to intelligent life, and yet, here we are. The odds were, literally, astronomically against us ever coming into existence at all."

Hamilton glanced at Wilder. Both were speechless.

"Nature creates disorders, but nurture makes monsters of those disorders, it's what I believe, anyway. The evidence bears this out, killers aren't born, they're made."

The detectives looked to one another solemnly.

"So, what about the organs then?" Hamilton asked.

"It's hard to say, I'd be giving you an educated guess based on what we know so far," Viscardi replied.

"Cannibalism?" Wilder threw out.

After a brief hesitation the doctor carefully said, "I think not. Cannibals will eat hearts and livers for sure, even kidneys, but lungs are rather difficult to digest. If this person was eating organs I'd think he, or she, would split open the skull and take the brain, it happens. For certain a cannibal would take the pancreas and stomach, the so-called sweetbreads. Also, cannibals tend to eat the truly meaty parts of any body, namely the arms, legs, and buttocks. No, I don't think you're looking for a cannibal as tempting as that may seem to you."

"So what, then?" Wilder pushed on.

"Two possibilities come to mind."

"Please," Hamilton said.

"I'd say the person you're looking for has a penchant for souvenirs, as most serial murderers do."

"He holds on to the organs?" she asked. "That's foul," she added.

"Yes, it is. In many cases these types keep mementos to relive the thrill of the kill. Individuals like this one have been known to hold on to their victim's underwear, jewelry, ears, whatever most bonds them to the experience of the murder. There have been cases in which killers have accumulated a number of victims and left the corpses within their residence, actually living with them as if they were one big happy family. An actual, physical item has the power to release a plethora of emotions in the people. They revel in reliving the events of their acts, over and over again. It's a kind of therapy for them, it soothes them, they get off on it."

"So, that takes us to the scalping and the skinning of the faces," Hamilton said.

"It certainly does. Often, these predators memorialize their acts by keeping collections of articles, or in this case organs or tissue of their victims. These collections, or shrines, as I'd prefer to call them, may be held sacred to these individuals. These shrines of their souvenirs memorialize their empowerment. In their twisted psychology, the killer commands the attention, recognition, and in some cases the adoration of their victims."

"So, it's normal if our subject is cutting off the faces of his victim's. He's keeping them as souvenirs?" she asked.

"It would be the most logical conclusion for a person of this mind-set, yes."

"What would he do with them, make masks?" Wilder asked, half-joking.

"Well, yes. I'd be looking for someone adept at taxidermy. I'd put taxidermists at the top of your list, that's my recommendation."

"With all of the hunters upstate and all of the fisherman on the island there are hundreds, maybe a thousand, taxidermists in New York State," Wilder said.

"Narrowed it down quite a bit, didn't we? We went from tens of millions of suspects to possibly a thousand or so," the doctor replied.

"This may not be right at all," Hamilton said.

"No, it may not, but it's better than where you were. At least now you have a point to start from."

"Okay, then. You said there were two possibilities which came to mind, what's the other?" Wilder asked.

"I believe your subject is selling the organs," the doctor said. "I'm confident of this."

"Selling, like for transplants?" Hamilton asked.

"The black market for organ transplants is a most lucrative one. Someone having the skills and connections could make a fortune in a few short years, enough to retire on for the rest of their lives."

"So, we should look for a black market organ dealer whose day job is taxidermy?" Wilder asked sarcastically, opening his eyes in mock surprise.

Viscardi thought to himself, *You're dealing with a new breed of serial killer,* before answering, "You may look for whatever you wish, I'm simply telling you what your best bet is, at least right now anyway. As I said before, until we have more substantial information, this is as good as it gets. I could be one hundred percent correct and you could conduct a perfect investigation and still not find this individual."

"Anything else?"

"You can most probably eliminate very large and strong persons from your search. As is normal with most predators, the types tend to prey on those smaller or weaker than themselves. You've got two women, one of them very small, and a teenage boy. Most adult males and many adult females would have been capable of abducting these victims."

"Do you think our subject might stop, or will we have more bodies?" Wilder asked.

"Your subject may have already stopped. The subject may be deceased for all we know. Whether or not there will be more remains unearthed is unanswerable, we don't know how many are out there, and probably never will. This subject may have stopped killing years ago, it doesn't mean he or she has not left behind many more victims. In reality though, if the subject is alive, we have to hope for a cooling off period during which he or she will be satiated and not look to kill again. Hopefully during a cooling off period, or before, we'll get lucky and find the subject. Most often these types continue to kill until they're caught or die themselves."

"Not an optimistic picture you paint, Doc," Wilder stated matter-of-factly.

"I'm not in the business of making lemonade out of lemons Detective Wilder. You've come here seeking my guidance and I've given you what I can."

"What do you suggest?" Hamilton asked.

"I suggest you work closely with the F.B.I. Their profilers are pretty good. They know what they're doing. I'm sure the bureau profilers are thinking the same thing I am."

"We meet with one of them later today," Hamilton responded.

"Can he be caught?" Wilder asked.

"I don't know if he can be caught if he doesn't want to be, but I don't think so. Honestly, you'll have to be very lucky."

Chapter Eighteen

With his booming business demanding ever more of his time, Arthur Gant relied on others to care for and educate his son. By the time the boy was one and a half the Gants had employed a live-in nanny who raised the boy. He would have a live-in caregiver, really a housekeeper, until the age of twelve.

Baby Phillip Gant's first nanny was Ane Dyrdahl, a vivacious young Norwegian woman, who had first come to New York as an exchange student in the late summer of 1963. Dyrdahl earned her undergraduate degree from Hofstra, which had recently gained university status, in May of 1965. Upon her graduation she decided that she liked New York so much she decided to stay, at least for awhile. Dyrdahl applied for citizenship and planned to study for her master's degree in social work. Looking for work she found the Gant's quite by accident while working at a cancer research fund-raiser which Arthur Gant had attended. The Norwegian woman had volunteered as a waitress for the event and happened to overhear Gant conversing with people at his table about how difficult it was to find a nanny that suited his needs. Nearly broke, Dyrdahl asked the aeronautics engineer for an interview for the position, right there at the table. Inspired by her assertiveness as well as her pleasant demeanor, he agreed to meet with the woman. He handed her his business card and advised her to call his secretary.

Dyrdahl's first meeting with Mrs. Gant did not go well at first. Eleanor was furious with her husband. Ane was striking, the stereotypical Scandinavian with straight platinum hair, blue eyes and a figure most twenty-year-olds would die for. Threatened from the instant she set eyes on the Norwegian, Eleanor envisioned her thirty-two-year-old husband humping the twenty-two-year-old student, there was only a decade between them after all. Not wanting to appear impolite, Eleanor decided to let the interview proceed, never thinking that she would agree to let this young woman invade her house. The interview was lackluster as Eleanor went on the offensive and Dyrdahl felt out of place and unwanted. As the young woman was about to leave, little Phillip cried out from the upstairs nursery. Eleanor quickly rose from her chair, bid Dyrdahl goodbye and tromped up the stairs. Dyrdahl too, rose from her chair, but then sat down as Arthur begged her to stay a minute to meet the boy.

When Eleanor reached the bottom of the stairs, she began a barrage of complaints at her husband about the prospective nanny. She continued, Phillip wailing away on her right hip, until she reached the living room and saw the gorgeous Norwegian girl still sitting on, of all pieces of furniture, the love seat. Eleanor's eyes flared with anger, but ever the gracious host, she composed herself and brought the crying child into the living room and sat down beside Dyrdahl on the love seat.

Phillip continued to cry no matter what his mother did to soothe him. Growing frustrated, Eleanor held her baby out to the stranger on her right and asked her if she'd like to try to calm him down. Dyrdahl gently accepted Phillip into her arms, rocked him back and forth slowly, and then began to sing. She sang *Byssan lulle barnet*, the Norwegian version of *Hush Little Baby* to the boy. Her voice was angelic, it poured effortlessly out of her thin-lipped mouth naturally, and with deep feeling. Little Phillip gazed into the stranger's cobalt eyes and shortly thereafter he grew quiet. He hadn't been hungry or thirsty. He did not need changing, he had cried out for love and affection. The little boy stared endlessly into Dyrdahl's eyes and found what he needed. Eleanor Gant's jealousy evaporated. As she stared into those same eyes, she saw only freedom.

Ane Dyrdahl didn't have much to pack, she moved into the Gant's Manhasset Tudor that very evening. Ane loved Phillip, doting on his every whim. Arthur was married to his business and Eleanor was happily ensconced in the posh social scene, often hobnobbing with the super rich of the Gold Coast. Now little Phillip had the mother he so desired. For two years Ane was Phillip's constant companion, most thought the wispy, blonde haired boy was hers. All was right in the Gant household, at least superficially.

Dyrdahl earned her masters by December 1966, and in between Christmas and New Years was offered a position in Baltimore. Dreading her loss and the stability she had brought to their family, the Gant's offered to double her salary. Given the fact she had free room and board with the family, she came out ahead monetarily. Putting the start of her career on hold, she agreed to remain with the Gant's, at least until Phillip started nursery school which was only half a year distant. As fate would have it Ane's mother fell ill back home in late July of 1967. She returned to Norway to take care of the ailing woman. While she was home she fell in love with a young dentist. Hoping little Phillip would not remember her, she never returned to the United States. The boy was an emotional desert once again.

The next nanny, Gladys, was a middle-aged Honduran woman, who'd already seen six of her own children to adulthood. Gladys turned out to be a much better housekeeper than caregiver. She'd had her children young they were all out of the house. Her husband had died, so she gave up her apartment to live with the Gant's in what most considered luxury.

Although Gladys kept the boy well fed, and dressed, she had no interest in him whatsoever. Having reared six of her own children, it was apparent she had no energy for play and certainly showed no love to the little boy. Coddling the boy when the Gant's were present, she largely ignored him as soon as they walked out the door.

Phillip sat for hours by himself as the woman went about her daily chores of cleaning and vacuuming, she did not cook at all as Eleanor Gant despised spicy food; the Gant's ordered most of their meals in. Upon completing the housework, the aging housekeeper preferred to sit on the couch watching *The Edge of Night* rather than engage Phillip. She neglected Phillip's needs and issued harsh rebukes when the child bothered her, asking for a bite of her muffin or a bottle of juice. A most convincing fraud, Gladys stayed with the Gant's for nearly a year until they noticed that the tot avoided the woman. By age five, the wheels of destiny were set in motion for Phillip Gant.

From ages six to twelve, the young Gant had a slew of nannies, none particularly bad like Gladys, but none very good either; certainly he never bonded with any of them. Unwilling to make the little sacrifices that can make real differences in a child's life, Arthur spent what little free time he had vacationing with his wife or on the golf course. Neglectful and irresponsible in family matters, Arthur kept his son at a distance. The boy had a father who made a lot of money and that was it. He had no real male role model. Eleanor Gant was frigid toward her son for some reason known only to her. It was obvious by her cold indifference toward the boy that she viewed him as a hindrance to her entertaining and likewise, being entertained. When Phillip grew older, and wiser, he realized his mother harbored feelings of resentment toward him.

Her pregnancy had been difficult. After his birth Eleanor's previously hourglass figure never returned to form, she remained thick around the waist and her breasts sagged due to all the breast feeding. Phillip recognized disdain in his mother's eyes, condescension in her voice, and near hostility in her dismissive gestures. Truly alone, the boy became more and more introverted. He grew silent and socially despondent.

The Gant's brought Phillip to see a child psychologist in an attempt to get him more socially involved at school. The doctor advised them, the boy simply needed a mother and father, a home life. The psychologist said Phillip was emotionally starved. Fearing a reprisal from social services the Gants claimed the boy was lying and they were the best parents a child could hope for. They never returned to the psychologist. Unsatisfied, under an assumed name, they went instead to a psychiatrist in search of the magic pill which would make the boy happy. The psychiatrist was terse and cold, as is often the case. He denied any medication finding nothing to warrant it. The psychiatrist too, saw something wrong with the entire family, not just the boy.

Despite his pronounced isolation, Phillip was an excellent student. Attending the Mumford Academy of Garden City from ages four to fourteen, he showed signs of brilliance and was at the top of his class year after year. It came as no surprise when he was accepted to the Salzberg School. Phillip made his feelings known that he preferred to remain at Mumford, it was an outstanding prep school, after all. His parents though, sought to rid themselves of the boy and his aggravating problems. The Salzberg School was hours away and for this reason they shipped him off to boarding school.

* * * *

The Salzberg School was, and remains, an independent boarding school located ten miles west of New London, Connecticut. Founded in eighteen-eighty-nine, the school's reputation for academic excellence attracted Arthur Gant, who wanted the best for his son, despite taking no real interest in the boy himself. As touted, the school provided an education of unsurpassed quality to some five hundred plus intellectually gifted students. Students at Salzberg came from across the United States and over twenty-five foreign nations. In four short years the school transformed students endowed with raw intelligence into young adults, commanding comprehensive knowledge and sophisticated opinions. Its graduates attended mostly Ivies or near Ivies. Some went on to one of the service academies.

Gant's roommate freshman year was a boy named Gil Rembert. He was from Austin, Texas. His father was an oil man. Rembert was tall for his age, standing at nearly six feet in ninth grade. The red-haired, freckly boy's gangly arms and legs suggested he would grow a good deal more in the coming years; he would eventually become the basketball team's captain. Friendly and easygoing, he was a godsend to the shy and introverted Gant. Nonetheless, Phillip's avoidance of his peers did not go unnoticed, particularly his habit of eating all of his meals in his dorm room. Rather than eat meals, which by most standards were very fine, he preferred to pack a cheeseburger or chicken patty sandwich into his bag, grab a few cartons of milk and head back to his room. While the other students dined on baked chicken with mashed potatoes, pepperoni pizza and on Thursday nights, steak, Phillip ate in isolation.

"Hey, Phil," Rembert called to Gant as he walked through the doorway into their room.

It was after lunchtime and Gant was hunched over at his desk eating roast beef and Swiss cheese on a roll, he looked up to see his new roommate smiling good-naturedly at him. "Hi," Gant waved, red-faced and almost dismissively.

Rembert thought he heard the shuffle of papers or the rustling of a book or maybe a magazine. He sensed Gant was hiding something from him. "Hittin' the books pretty hard already, ain't cha?" Rembert asked, noticing the algebra text Gant seemed to be pouring over.

Gant had not yet grown accustomed to the tall boy's slow drawl, he wasn't sure he ever would. "That's why I'm here."

"Got to have some fun though, don't cha think?"

Gant sighed, and replied, "Fun's overrated."

"Suit yourself, but yer missin out. You should see some of the girls."

"I see them in class every day."

"But you don't talk with 'em."

"Why bother?"

"Yer kiddin' me, arn't ya?"

"I'm not one to kid."

"You've got to be crazy, Phil."

Gant flinched.

"These girls are smokin'—some of 'em anyway," Rembert continued.

"That's great!" Gant replied sarcastically. "My name is Phillip, okay?"

Rembert held up his hands in apology. Gant could tell it was sincere. "How 'bout you come to supper with me tonight? They're servin' pork chops."

"No, thanks."

"You know, the hot food is real good and they serve it on real china. We use real silverware, too."

Gant was unimpressed. "Same with my old school, big deal."

"Did you eat with the other kids in the cafeteria there?"

"Yes, I mean no. I did in the beginning. Then I realized that I was just wasting time, I could be studying instead."

"Not sure I'd consider talkin' with girls a waste of time, but maybe I'm crazy."

Gant flinched again, more noticeably this time, as if he'd been avoiding a punch or slap. The term "crazy" shook Gant a lot, he looked away from Rembert. He dreaded words like "crazy", "nuts", "*loco*", "psycho", really any word that implied a psychological disorder. Deep down he knew he was battling a mental illness of his own, but he didn't like to think about it.

"You all right there, Phil...ah, sorry, I mean Phillip?"

"I'm fine, I'm fine," Gant burst out. "Just leave me alone. I'd rather be alone. I need to study."

"Good enough, then. If you want to talk, I'll be here for awhile. We've got class in a half an hour," Rembert said looking at his watch. "After school I'm meetin' some of the guys in the gym to shoot some hoops. You can come too."

Gant made no reply. He placed his sandwich down on his desk and buried his face in the textbook instead.

Rembert frowned and shook his head. He fell onto his bed and picked up a copy of *A Separate Peace*, which was required for freshman English, and began reading. Twenty-five minutes later both boys left for Earth Science class, their black and white composition notebooks and textbooks packed into their book bags along with pens and pencils.

After class, the roommates walked back to their dorm together. Rembert changed out of his school uniform of khaki pants, a white button down oxford shirt emblazoned with the Salzberg logo, black shoes, and a navy tie. He quickly debriefed and pulled up an athletic supporter. He grabbed a pair of red mesh shorts and a T-shirt which read "I'm with Stupid" and was dressed before Gant took his tie off. While lacing up his Converse high tops he glanced over at his roommate's desk. As Gant was preoccupied hanging his trousers in the closet, Rembert took the opportunity to really eyeball Gant's desk, but there seemed to be nothing there save the algebra text.

"Well, I'm gonna go to the gym then. Yer sure you don't wanna come along?" Rembert asked, giving up his search.

"Positive," Gant replied.

"I'm guessing you'll be heading over to the library?"

The boys had lived together less than a week and a half, but Gant's routine was not difficult to track. It seemed to Rembert that Gant was either in class, at the library, studying in the dorm room, or sleeping. If he went elsewhere or led some secret life, Rembert was unaware. Although Gant was always squeaky clean and meticulously groomed Rembert could not remember seeing him in the shower room or on his way to the bathroom to relieve himself.

"That's right."

"All right then. I'll be back around five o'clock or maybe five-thirty. Think about dinner, it'll be fun."

"Maybe," Gant mumbled while pulling up his corduroys.

"See ya later," Rembert said closing the door behind him. Walking down the hall to the dorm's front doors he thought to himself, *What a weird dude! Wonder what's wrong with 'em?* Rembert would never know what ailed his roommate, but not from lack of trying.

The basketball player got halfway to the gym which was situated between the library and the dining hall when he suddenly stopped. He walked directly across the quad to the visitors center and loitered in front of it long enough to watch Gant walk up the cobblestone path that led to the library. As soon as Gant disappeared behind the heavy oak doors of the library entrance Rembert sprinted back to their room.

Rembert had not a single malicious bone in his body, he was curious by nature, he wanted to find out a little about Gant's odd standoffishness. The tall Texan went to pick up the algebra text to see what was under it, but hesitated not knowing what to expect to see.

If Gant were like me, Rembert reasoned, *I bet he's hiding a stroke mag*. Based on their earlier conversation though, it seemed that Gant wasn't all that interested in girls. Suddenly Rembert grew flush with embarrassment as well as fear. *What if this guy's gay? What if I find some queer magazine under there? I'll have to move out, that's all.* He marshaled his courage and picked up the textbook. Beneath it he found a one page anatomical drawing, not even sex organs, that Gant had Xeroxed from *Gray's Anatomy* while at the library. He looked at the two dimensional rendering of the human muscular skeletal system, back and front, and frowned. *We don't take bio until next year. This guy is seriously hard-core*, he thought to himself placing the diagram back down. He briefly considered rifling through his roommate's belongings to see if he could uncover anything else, but decided against it. Rembert was curious, but not one to pry, he had his limitations. Rather than invade Gant's privacy any further, he locked the door behind him and ran back toward the gym.

Gant excelled at Salzberg even more so than at Mumford. He was at or near the top of his class in every subject and stood out head and shoulders above his counterparts in the maths and sciences. Surpassing all expectations of the faculty in biology and geometry, he was fast tracked on to chemistry and trigonometry while still a sophomore. Of course, Gant kept his secret studies all to himself. Unbeknownst to anyone, he continued his examination of human anatomy on his own time. He took a keen interest in taxidermy, not only reading from texts, but also visiting a local taxidermist and participating in workshops on Thursday evenings after the store was closed.

It was on Easter break, during his sophomore year, that his grandmother died. The fifteen-year-old was devastated. Seriously contemplating suicide, Gant took to reading about anesthesia and euthanasia. He indulged in fantasies about how to best end his own life. *There's nothing wrong with mercy killing.*

Later, there would be many people who wished he'd done so. Gant ceased going home on the weekends, there was nothing for him to go home to. Swamped in a dire depression he still managed to excel at his studies. His ability to immerse himself in work fended off the temptation to take his own life.

Toward the end of his sophomore year, Gant began to examine psychology in some depth. He clearly recognized there was something amiss with him, he had known for years, but had been unwilling to admit it. Seemingly insignificant events, like choosing when to clip his nails, had turned into major contributors of angst. Everything was magnified, it seemed. Not knowing if he was mentally imbalanced or genetically disposed to some rare psychological disorder which caused him to perceive ordinary events as being extraordinary, he dove into psychology texts and journals in an attempt to label his malady.

Unable to uncover a disorder or condition which suited his ailment, he made a self-diagnosis. Gant believed that he suffered from a form of cognitive distortion he coined "Negative Magnification Disorder." Although no such disorder was recorded he felt his symptoms matched those of other related disorders and together had snowballed into a unique disorder that he may very well be the first person to suffer from. Key to this belief was the fact that he catastrophized possible outcomes for simple, every day happenings. This type of thinking, he read, was based on arbitrary inferences, meaning he made assumptions, and dark ones, without any evidence.

He found he suffered from selective abstraction in which an individual focuses on their perceived shortcomings rather than their successes. Lastly, he felt for sure that he focused overwhelming on his mistakes, the cognitive error of magnification. Gant recalled remembering what he perceived as mistakes over and over again, replaying them in his mind like a movie clip. He had bits and pieces of these disorders and many more. Unable to find an officially recognized disorder he made up his own. Of course, he never told a soul. Gant questioned his own self-worth, his own fitness for living. *There's nothing wrong with mercy killing*, he remembered Grandpa Gant's words.

Attempting to find the true source of his unhappiness he really knew it all the while. Prolonged neglect from a very young age had gotten the ball rolling. Severe parental neglect nearly from birth had left Phillip Gant with deep-seeded feelings of insignificance and unworthiness. This abandonment coupled with his newly developed neuroses left the young man paralyzed with fear. Seeking recognition, young Gant was to grow into a monster, a beast demanding attention and respect on many levels.

To add to his psychological problems, Phillip Gant was a late bloomer. Only five foot three and less than ninety pounds at the age of fourteen, his meek character certainly could be attributed to his slight stature. Arthur Gant was no giant, but standing six inches taller than his son and more than doubling his weight, the elder Gant had his concerns. Eleanor Gant was tall for a woman and full figured as well, even more so after her son's birth.

Searching for answers, the Gants took young Phillip to a host of dieticians and developmental specialists to find out what was wrong with the boy. As none of these experts could shed light on Phillip's stalled development they investigated whether the boy suffered from a growth hormone deficiency disorder. The Gants consulted a pediatric endocrinologist to find out if human growth hormone injections would benefit the boy. After examining Phillip's blood work, the doctor urged the Gants to exercise caution. He told them there was no need to rush into anything yet, he advised that Phillip be given at least another year before such measures were taken.

Life changing events mold some people's lives. Shortly after Gant turned sixteen there were three such events which changed the course of the young man's life, and the lives of many others, forever. First, and possibly foremost, Gant went through latent puberty. Secondly, his parents finally took a shine to him. Lastly, Gant experienced a sexual awakening which is normal during puberty, but most pronounced life-altering for Gant. Always handsome, overnight he seemingly transformed into a social butterfly.

Arthur and Eleanor Gant were no fools. Eleanor's parents had died in their late fifties, her mother from ovarian cancer and her father of a heart attack. While Grandpa Gant had lived considerably longer than his wife's parents, he too died of cancer. That left Grandma Gant who toiled with Alzheimer's, and probably would have for another decade, if she hadn't had broken her hip while jumping into the Christmas tree.

Quickly approaching mid-life, the Gants realized their time was limited. When they eventually fell ill and needed care and compassion they wondered who they would turn to. Phillip was their only child, but he was so distant. Realizing that it was imperative to form a relationship with their son, the Gant's made a concerted effort to bring Phillip back into their lives. Phillip Gant gladly accepted his parent's long absent love, he craved their attention and encouragement.

Gant was a good son, he saw it as his duty to love his parents no matter how they had previously neglected his needs. He was a very bright young man though, and he never forgot their past transgressions, or more appropriately, their lack of action and effort. Deep down he knew they had envisioned him as their caretaker late in life. That was all right though, he could live with that.

The endocrinologist was correct in his diagnosis. Gant hit puberty toward the middle of his fifteenth year and shot up like a weed. As his voice deepened he packed on muscle as well. A year and a half after the visit to the endocrinologist the boy had grown five inches and gained forty pounds. He was no bruiser for sure, but he was on the same scale with his peers. With the onset of puberty it seemed Gant's various mental disorders disappeared as if he'd literally grown out of them. Perhaps it had been a chemical imbalance after all, he later thought. As is natural, along with his growth spurt came a new interest in the opposite sex.

Despite his roommate's odd aloofness, Gil Rembert requested the two be paired again for their sophomore year, and again for their junior years. The first dance Phillip attended at Salzberg was homecoming in 1981. At Rembert's prodding, the shy, introverted boy went stag, but soon had a bevy of girls milling about him. His body had matured and when combined with his always handsome face, he was the talk of the evening. After his first mixer he found himself in high demand having danced with four girls. That night Rembert and Gant discussed the night's events while lying in bed. Their conversation was excited and animated, they laughed out loud enjoying a truly bonding experience. For the first time since his grandmother took ill, Gant was able to smile and feel at least a little bit good about himself.

Throughout his junior year Gant dated many of the Salzberg coeds, never having sex with any of them. Still quite reserved, he was the consummate gentleman, never pushing his desires past necking. It wasn't that any of the girls said "no" or "stop", not a single one did. Gant simply never attempted to go any further, deep down he was afraid of their rejection. *Better to not try than to be rejected*, was his thought process on the whole issue of sex.

While other guys had bragged about making it to third base or even home, Gant was satisfied with mere kissing, as the company was most welcome. It all changed on the first day of his senior year when Kaydence Montgomery strolled onto the Salzberg campus as a transfer student. The school had never before accepted a transfer student past the sophomore year, but Montgomery came from an extremely affluent family with considerable political leverage in Connecticut. The fact her father, a partner at one of the big Wall Street firms, had donated a fortune, and not a small one, to the school's athletic program, made her acceptance very easy to understand.

According to the rumor mill on campus, the girl had been expelled from three other prep schools before arriving at Salzberg, but it wasn't yet known for what. Public school wasn't an option her parents ever considered, not with their money and pedigree. Her new roommate was Nancy Altsbacher, a notorious gossip, so it seemed the student body wouldn't have to wait long to find out the reason for her multiple expulsions.

Montgomery's curly blonde hair bopped about her shoulders as she made her way to class on the first day. Many of the girls looked away as the boy's lustily gazed at the buxom beauty. Hiking up her uniform khaki skirt to show off her Sun tanned legs, she slowly strutted along enjoying the buzz she'd created; she was in no particular hurry to be on time for her first class which was World Literature.

Sauntering into class a few minutes late, Montgomery was wordlessly ushered to her seat by the teacher, Mister Zhenlin. Gant, an advanced student in math and science, was encouraged to remain with his peers in history and English classes, the school administration asked him to peer tutor struggling students. The headmaster gained approval from the Gant's, explaining it would be good for the boy's social interaction. He further stated the top colleges were focusing in on individuals who were willing to give their time to assist others in the classroom.

The Montgomery girl sat down and surveyed the classroom as the World Lit class ground on. She was unimpressed until her big, brown eyes found Gant sitting slightly behind her to the left. As all eyes were on the girl she had eyes only for Gant. During the forty-five minutes class, of which she had already missed three, she spent most of the time peering over her shoulder at the handsome young man with the fair hair. Montgomery's head turning leers were embarrassingly obvious to all of those sitting behind her, even the shy and reserved Gant. Whenever her gaze fell upon him he looked down at the notebook he'd been scribbling in.

The overt interest which Montgomery showed in Phillip Gant was not lost on Mister Zhenlin either. Perhaps by blind fate, or quite possibly, by design, the teacher assigned Gant to be the new girl's study partner, really more of a one-on-one tutor. When reading the paired student list, Mister Zhenlin wore a thin grin while calling out the Gant-Montgomery pairing. The teacher liked Gant very much and figured he was doing the timid senior a favor. By this time pretty much the entire class had a good idea of why the curvaceous girl had been expelled from three schools. There were exaggerated sighs and some subdued giggling from many of the boys in the class, while the girls, almost to a one, rolled their eyes in Montgomery's direction, with contempt.

It was half past six in the evening when Gant personally confirmed his peer's suspicions. After dinner the study partners walked through the main doors of the library. At Montgomery's request for peace and quiet, Gant followed her upstairs where more secluded tables afforded a fair degree of isolation, apparently Kaydence Montgomery had been in the Salzberg library before and staked out the building. Gant remembered trailing up the stairs behind her,, breathing in her perfume, her scent. Gant had been unable to keep his eyes off the voluptuous blonde's rear end and seemingly knowing this, the girl slowed from one step to another almost causing him to rear end her several times before reaching the top floor landing.

Bypassing a number of tables closer to the stairs, Montgomery sashayed through the top floor before sitting down in the far corner at a small table set with only two chairs. Thinking back on it years later it was obvious to Gant, the girl had set the whole thing up. Sitting across from one another Montgomery had her back to the wall. Still too shy to make any type of move Gant opened the text to Kipling's *The Man Who Would Be King*, their assigned reading for the following class. He had planned to begin by sharing his thoughts regarding the plot when Montgomery flipped halfway through the book and, instead, selected Hemingway's, *The Three Day Blow*, explaining she was much more interested in that. Looking back, Gant marveled at his ignorance, it went right over his very brilliant head.

Growing impatient, as well as very horny, Montgomery kicked off her black loafers and ran her stockinged foot up the inside of Gant's right leg pausing momentarily at the knee and then pushing on toward his groin. Gant instinctively stiffened, but still resisted the urge to commit to an advance which could backfire and cause him embarrassment. *It's better not to try than to fail*, he thought.

Kaydence Montgomery had grown very short on patience. The playfulness and warmth had left her eyes, her red glossed lips had turned hard and demanding, a little mean even. She tossed her pen under the table and told Gant to retrieve it for her. Underneath the table Gant seized the pen and then, not able to help himself, took a peek in the girl's direction. Montgomery had lifted her skirt to her upper thighs, she was also without any panties. Gant gazed upon the light brown triangle between her Sun tanned thighs and gulped, he was instantaneously, and fully hard.

Montgomery smiled to herself as she asked him if he liked what he saw. Not needing any more hints Gant at once replied that he did, to which she told him to kiss her there. Gant buried his face between Montgomery's legs and after a few minutes she returned the favor. He would lose his virginity later that night. Gant knew for sure now, why the girl had been tossed out of so many schools, even before her own roommate, Nancy Altsbacher found out.

Gil Rembert struggled to control his curiosity when Gant finally came home before curfew at ten o'clock. After exchanging cursory greetings, Gant began to undress, the musky scent of sex rolled off of him. Rembert knew his roommate, still more reserved than most, would not be forthcoming with any of the sordid details of the evening's events. He did his best to seem uninterested, a chemistry text rested upon his chest, his eyes not seeing a single word or equation. After a few minutes of silence, the new captain of the basketball team dogged eared the book and tossed it carelessly onto his night table. Unable to hold out any longer Rembert asked, "So how was it?"

"No way, Gil. You know I'm not going to tell you anything," Gant responded. "I never do."

"You never spent hours alone with a girl like that. This is different, Phillip, c'mon."

"It's none of your business. Whatever happened or didn't happen is between her and I."

"Stop bein' such a fuckin' grownup, Phillip. You're only seventeen—you're supposed to fill your pals in on the dirt," the gangly Texan responded.

"Maybe so, but still the same, I won't." Gant was actually bursting to tell Rembert of his sexcapades with Kaydence Montgomery, but found himself unable to do so.

"C'mon, boy! Why not? I'm your best buddy, ain't I?"

"Yeah, you are my closest friend," Gant agreed.

"So confide in me, buddy. I won't tell a soul, promise."

"It's not that I don't trust you, Gil. It's because it's not the right thing to do. What two people do in private is their own business. It shouldn't be broadcast all over the place." Gant remembered another one of his grandfather's axioms, *Make someone happy today, mind your own business*. He'd overheard Grandpa Gant saying this only a few times, and always on or around the Fourth of July when the nosy neighbor across Sunset Drive complained about his fireworks. Besides upholding the gentlemanly principle of "Don't kiss and tell", Gant was embarrassed about what had happened more than anything else.

"In private? Where'd you go? As of 9:45, Nancy Altsbacher said she hadn't seen either one of you since before suppertime," Rembert replied with a gleam in his eyes.

Gant paused and then responded, "I guess it can't hurt to tell you, we were in the library."

"The library!" Rembert shouted. "You knocked boots in the library?"

Gant shook his head, "Let me finish, will you."

"Please do."

"We went for a walk out to the creek."

"Deepdale or Wabash?"

"Deepdale," Gant said.

"Go on," Rembert nudged him.

"With what?"

"Details, details, I need details! Did you hit a double? Or a triple, I'd bet."

Gant shook his head disapprovingly.

"Christ almighty! Did you make it all the way home?"

"I already told you, I'm not giving out any details."

"Aw, c'mon Phillip—you might as well spill it to me. By tomorrow afternoon the whole school will know anyway. Give me a first listen, why don'tcha?"

"You really think everyone will find out?"

"Of course, half of 'em already think it's a done deal. Some of the guys on the team started a pool taking guesses at how far you'd get the first night. Besides, that girl rooms with Nancy. Nancy's relentless, she's like a badger. She'd make the devil come clean. Once your girl spills her guts it'll be broadcast all right, you can bet on it."

"So, you'll get your details tomorrow," Gant replied.

"The problem is, it'll be Montgomery's story, and worse yet Altsbacher's version of it everyone will be hearing," Rembert said attempting to draw Gant in. "You want your story out there first so people know the truth. Suppose she tries to make you out to be some whiskey-dicked loser who has a dud pud. Worse, what if she says you got a little one?"

"This is all I'm going to tell you, Gil. Kaydence will tell the truth, I think she may love me. We had a great time. And anybody questioning the size of my...my pud can ask around, I've been in the locker room enough the last six months."

With Gant not taking the bait Rembert switched tactics. "All right, Phillip. How about you don't say another word, shake your head "yes" or "no" to my questions?"

Gant shook his head "no" to the request.

"Tell me somethin' at least. Somethin' that nobody else will ever know. That way you'll know I can keep a secret," Rembert nearly begged.

Gant hesitated, but then with great conviction said, "I love her eyes, I mean the way she looks at me. She gives me her full attention. I could stare at her eyes forever."

Rembert was correct in his assumption the entire Salzberg student body, would know about Gant's fling the following day. Montgomery provided vivid descriptions of the evening's activities to Nancy Altsbacher, even the gossip turned crimson faced during her roommate's lurid accounting of the tale. Montgomery knew from briefly speaking to her talkative roommate, Altsbacher would immediately grapevine the juicy details to anyone who would listen. Montgomery took pride in her sexual prowess, wearing it as a badge of honor. In that respect she was more like a man than a woman.

Lots of the Salzberg boys chased after Montgomery, but for three and a half weeks she slept only with Gant. In retrospect it was obvious to him she viewed him as a conquest and when she'd exhausted his innocence she moved on to a host of other boys. Girls like Montgomery had a nose for virgins. It seemed to Gant, they could sniff them out. After preying on a number of other virgins, Montgomery was again literally "bounced" out of Salzberg before Christmas vacation.

Gant was initially heartbroken when Montgomery dumped him. After a torturous week without her during which he almost backslid into his prior neuroses, he began to feel better. Taking some sound advice from Rembert, he saw the girl for what she truly was. He looked at his time with her as a learning experience, a sexual seminar of sorts, no pun intended. He made up his mind to appreciate Montgomery despite her whorish nature.

Although Kaydence Montgomery was something of a sexual predator, she had done a world of good for Gant. The girl had schooled him as none of his teachers could, she'd instructed him in the art of sex. An apt pupil in all of his studies, Gant was no different when it came to Montgomery's lessons. Ravenous as only the young are, Gant was very fortunate not to have gotten her pregnant. He had no doubt she'd already had abortions, but it was something he didn't want to get involved with. She had empowered him with skills he never knew he had. She taught him what the opposite sex sought, what it needed, and not just in bed. Montgomery had instructed him not only physically, but also mentally and emotionally. Gant was now privy to the subtle nuances so critical to relationships.

Despite her usury of him Gant was sad to see Montgomery go. She had, after all, freed him to pursue a life of normalcy. She had turned out to be quite the study partner indeed. Mister Zehnlin would be happy, Gant believed. Thanks to Kaydence Montgomery's sexpertise Phillip Gant had gained confidence, and a certain amount of swagger; he would never be a wallflower again. Her tutoring gave him newfound confidence which he enthusiastically put to use with many of the coeds on campus. After his brief relationship with Kaydence Montgomery, Gant had a reputation to live up to.

* * * *

While at the U.S. Naval Academy Gant's star rose higher and higher. Military life agreed with him, he liked the discipline as well as the early and very long days. He slept and ate better than he ever had in his life. Naturally trim he savored the demanding workouts which built the solid muscle he'd always desired. His five foot ten inch frame had filled out to a robust one hundred and eighty-five pounds by his twentieth birthday. The boy had blossomed into a strapping young man. Gant maintained many casual relationships while in the academy, it was difficult to become seriously involved with a woman under such circumstances; he had little desire for long-term commitment then anyway. Advanced in math and the sciences, the academy was decidedly less difficult for him than it was for most of his peers, he still found a little time to pursue his other, private interests. Gant graduated with merit cum laude earning a Bachelor of Science degree and was commissioned an Ensign in May 1986. After graduation, he attended flight school in Pensacola,

Florida and completed his training nine months before the outbreak of the First Gulf War. Now a United States Naval Aviator, Gant was primed for action.

* * * *

Captain Phillip Gant had never killed a human being before the war. He'd never even needlessly killed an animal, there was always a reasonable use for taking life, any life. While some men returned from war mentally unstable and a handful had ended up murderers, Gant was not one of them. It did enable him to disassociate himself from killing though, he found killing from the air to be easy. Flying an F-14 Tomcat from the deck of the U.S.S. Theodore Roosevelt, a Nimitz Class aircraft carrier, Gant soon became anesthetized to death, as many soldiers eventually become. Aboard the fighter/bomber, Gant loosed laser guided bombs which demolished bunkers thousands of feet below him; he never caught a glimpse of his adversaries.

Small sacrifices are acceptable if they serve the greater good. Shooting fleeing Iraqi fighters from the sky before they could make it into Iranian air space, he felt nothing at all, it was his duty. *There's nothing wrong with mercy killing.* Captain Gant felt neither remorse nor triumph, it was, merely his duty. The impersonal nature of the warfare made it easy for him to kill. The war didn't make him what he later became, it was his destiny.

Gant finished with his military service in May of 1998, and he assumed the management of *Generations Air Supply*, in order that his father could retire and play golf. He was handsome, intelligent, charming, well-travelled, socially adept, and had tens of millions of dollars coming to him. In short, he truly had it all. Still, he was damaged, murderously flawed, in fact. Late in the year he realized his true calling and his spree began.

Chapter Nineteen

Oliver Conrad landed at Dorval way overdue at 9:03. His flight had been delayed before takeoff due to a domestic disturbance up in first class, a woman and her husband had been escorted off of the plane by the air marshal. Sitting in coach himself he couldn't help but think money couldn't buy manners and he was more than a bit miffed, he would be late to his morning meeting. At half past nine Conrad stepped out of an unmarked car and walked up the steps of police headquarters on Franklin Street.

Hamilton and Wilder rose from their seats as the instructor from Quantico was admitted into their office. After exchanging pleasantries Salerno was called in to join them.

Conrad had been with the F.B.I. for more than twenty-five years. A field agent for nine years, he'd worked diligently to become a profiler. After cracking several high profile cases, he was selected to pass on his knowledge and methods to the up and comers at the training site. In his mid –fifties, he looked older, with silver hair surrounding his balding pate. His dull gray eyes matched his drab charcoal suit, both of which disguised his intellect and belied his ambiguity.

"So, we have no leads whatsoever I'm informed," Conrad opened the meeting after taking a sip of coffee from a mug Hamilton had given him.

"That's right," Salerno said. "As of now we're completely in the dark."

"We thought we had a lead, but..." Hamilton began and Salerno shot her a look which quickly quieted her.

"The detective means we thought we had a lead, but it was nothing," Salerno said.

Conrad raised his eyebrows in consternation and was about to question Hamilton and then let it go.

"After reviewing the case on the plane I feel you have a real problem here. Not to sound obtuse, but I think you have to think way out of the box to catch this one. No evidence, no leads, no inklings even, adds up to failure."

"What do you suggest?" Wilder asked, a little peeved.

"Well, up until now you've looked solely at men, is that correct?" Conrad asked.

"Yes, we had one man that seemed like a solid suspect. His fingerprints were on the victim's water bottle."

"Yes. Yes, we know that didn't work out. What I'm trying to say is, maybe you're not looking at the right sex. Maybe the perpetrator is a woman, or maybe more than one woman, or maybe a woman and a man."

"It doesn't fit the profile," Hamilton replied.

"When you look at enough of these cases you really can't count on a profile."

"Isn't that what you specialize in?" Hamilton asked.

"Yes, it is what I teach in fact, but it's hardly scientific. The individuals committing these types of crimes are so different in many cases, it's impossible to nail down a fast and sure concrete suspect-type. The person committing this crime may be deranged, depraved, or simply desperate. Each case is so unique in most cases it's very difficult to pigeonhole a type, let lone make an identification based on loose facts."

"So, what you're saying is that profiling is basically useless," Hamilton stated.

"No, no, I'd never say that. The fact of the matter is, profiling does have it's place and can work effectively, but not all the time."

"How often," Salerno asked.

"It's fifty-fifty," Conrad answered.

"Like a weatherman," Wilder said.

"Please, I'm here to help you. If you won't take my advice, that's fine, but don't belittle me. I've helped to solve seven cases in which seemingly simple abductions turned out to involve serial murderers. How many cases like that have you detectives been involved with?" Conrad looked around the room from Hamilton to Wilder to Salerno.

All were quiet.

He went on, "I could easily be wrong, but it doesn't hurt to look at everything. Let me tell you what I do know as fact. As coined by Special Agent Robert Ressler, a serial killer is defined as an individual who kills three or more people with sufficient time intervals between each, known as a cooling off period. These deviants have been divided into two groups: disorganized, asocial offenders and organized, non-social offenders. There can be no single precise profile for a serial killer. The basic profile calls for a Caucasian male between the ages of eighteen and thirty-two with a history of child abuse, bed wetting, animal abuse, and arson. Each serial killer has his or her own motives and personal agenda."

Nobody interrupted so he went on.

"Male serial killers are the subjects of the media because their crimes are much more horrific. They brutally kill their victims and desecrate the bodies. When committing their crimes, male methods most commonly incorporate a combination of firearms, about forty-one percent of the time, suffocation around thirty-seven percent of the time, stabbing under thirty-four percent of the time, and bludgeoning twenty-six percent of the time. There are cases in which all of these methods have been used, and others where only a single method has been used. Men most often seek attention for their crimes and do not attempt to hide them. Very often, the crime scenes are staged to provide clues for the police and to attract the media.

Most often the body count of a male serial killer is higher than that of most women serial killers. Some killers have murdered over three hundred victims. While female serial killers are not very common, they do exist and are quite different from their male counterparts. Women serial murderers are less visible and use methods such as poisoning in order to be discrete and remain undetected. Women are sometimes termed gentle killers despite their methods being gruesome, albeit less graphic in nature. Methods used more by women include drowning and neglect."

Without pause Conrad went on, "Overwhelmingly male serial killers are violent as children. Usually sexual predators, they rape their victims dead or alive. Sexual deviance and control are the major motivators in their urge to kill. The Boston Strangler, DeSalvo, is a good example of a sexual predator as he raped, murdered, and arranged women's bodies in grotesque, suggestive ways. Other motives men have for killing include control, money, enjoyment, racism and hatred, mental problems, cult-inspiration, and attention."

"Female serial killers are a much more complicated criminal with vastly diverse motivations. However, money is always the primary motivation for seventy-four percent of their killings. Besides money they kill for control, enjoyment, sex, drugs, cult involvement, and feelings of inadequacy. Most often the women are diagnosed with a psychological disorder called Munchausen Syndrome by Proxy. This illness involves the fabrication of symptoms or the infliction of injuries by the serial killer on dependent individuals, such as children, to gain attention or sympathy for themselves."

"Like that woman from Schenectady," Hamilton broke in.

"Exactly," Conrad agreed. "A well-known example is Mary Beth Tinning, who realized after the natural death of her first child that she received a lot of attention from others. Consequently, she chose to kill her other eight children. These types of serial killers are commonly called Black Widows because they kill family members, friends, and anyone with whom they have created a close personal relationship."

"That seems almost worse than what the men do," Wilder stated shaking his head in disgust.

"We've checked out the families and friends already. Nobody seems suspicious in the least," Salerno added.

"I'm sure of that Detective Salerno, bear with me. This type of killing is most common for women. They prey upon people who are dependent upon them and those with whom they are acquainted. The revenge killer is also a common type of female serial killer who murders people who have wronged them. They kill out of hate and jealousy. Unlike the Black Widow, these killers do not seek attention and sympathy, they murder purely for personal satisfaction."

"Males, on the other hand, have a common pattern of killing strangers instead. They most often tend to enjoy killing prostitutes and the filth of society. Jack the Ripper terrorized the East End of London for three months in the year of eighteen-eighty-eight. His savage and brutal cleansing of the streets of Whitechapel, where he mutilated and dissected the bodies of five prostitutes is legendary as we all know. Thus one of the main categories of male serial killers is the Missionary Killer, those "cleanup killers" that murder target groups such as prostitutes, homosexuals, and certain ethnic groups."

"What makes you think we're dealing with a woman here?" Salerno asked.

"I'm not saying your killer is a woman. I'm saying your killer may very well be a woman and we should not exclude females, that's all. Research on female serial killers is limited, but study on them has produced what was named the Kelleher Typology, which divides these killers into five groups: Black Widows, Angels of Death, Sexual Predators, Revenge Killers, and Profit Killers."

"We haven't received any ransom requests," Wilder interjected.

"Please, let me finish; I'm almost done," Conrad held up his liver-spotted hand. "There is only one member of the Sexual Predator category, her name is Aileen Wuornos, a prostitute who murdered seven men in Florida. She was executed by lethal injection. The Black Widows and Angels of Death are the most common type of female serial killer. Revenge Killers who are repeat offenders are rare because most are one time crimes of true passion. Profit Killers are rare as well, but they are considered to be the most intelligent and resourceful. They are usually contract killers or have devised scams to cheat victims from their assets and lives."

Conrad took a breath and seeing no questions were being raised, he continued on, "The Kelleher Typology for male serial killers divides them into four types which includes Visionaries, Missionaries, Hedonists, and Power Seekers. Visionaries react to psychic messages, godly commands, or alter egos commanding them to kill. Missionaries feel they have a job to do, a duty to clean up society. Hedonists are power oriented, often gaining pleasure from killing. Hedonists can be subdivided into lust killers and thrill killers. They are the most common type of male serial killer. The last type, Power Seekers, kill for pure excitement. For them, the more grotesque the crime, the greater the thrill and the more power they derive."

"So, what you're actually saying is, the person we're looking for could be anyone at all?" Hamilton asked.

"What I'm saying is leave no stone unturned. A large proportion of these types of crimes go unsolved, ever. Look at all the bodies we're finding on Long Island. We have no idea who's responsible. It's my assumption, bodies have been dumped there for decades, maybe even a hundred years. Long, lonely stretches like that are very inviting to these types of criminals. It wouldn't surprise me in the least if one of your Buffalo residents, turned up by the seaside further south. But don't limit your investigation to a man or a woman working alone."

"A partner? How is it two people that sick find one another?" Wilder asked.

"Many serial killers, both male and female, work as part of a team. Four classifications of teams exist. There are male/male, male/female, female/female, and family teams. A third of all female serial killers are members of a team. Male pairs are the most common team slayers representing thirty percent of the American total. Male/female teams usually commit crimes sexual in nature, with the males tending to dominate their younger female accomplices. These teams represent twenty-five percent of American team killers. Groups of males can form what is known as a wolf pack ranging from three to six members in number and represent ten percent of team killers in the U.S. Female/female teams are the rarest and tend to be active for two to four years and are usually older than other teams. Family teams have a short life span, about a year or so. Think of Charles Manson's family."

Seeing that Salerno was about to interrupt him, Conrad held up a bony finger and rambled on, "There are very few documented cases of female serial killers, however violence and killing by women is steadily on the rise. White women are much more likely to be serial killers than African-American, Asian, or Hispanic men. As their numbers grow, more information is being gathered to understand this phenomenon and to help us better understand how they differ from male serial killers."

"White women are more likely to be serial killers than minority men?" Wilder asked astounded.

"That's what the data indicates," Conrad responded.

"So, you're not suggesting our killer is a woman, but we should be open to that scenario?" Hamilton prodded.

"We all saw the movie or read the book *The Silence of the Lambs* where the villain was making a suit for himself out of women's skin. Who's to say something similar is not going on here. You may be looking for a woman seeking an alter persona, or possibly a woman unhappy with her appearance. Maybe a woman struggling with her sexual identity is responsible. Your killer takes both sexes."

"Masks, then?" Hamilton asked aghast.

"Worse has been documented."

"All of our victim's are young and trim," Salerno offered.

"Who's to say this individual doesn't drink the blood of the young?" Conrad countered. "We can't know what we're dealing with really until we catch the killer. I wish I could offer more, but with no clues whatsoever, we have nothing to work with. I will say the lack of clues is consistent with a revenge killer, which often turns out to be a woman."

"None of the victims knows one another. I find it difficult to believe the murderer killed these people based on revenge," Wilder stated. "He or she must have been wronged by quite a few people."

"That takes us to the biggest problem with this case. We've all assumed the missing people are dead. All of this may be pure conjecture. We have many missing people, but only three bodies. The others may have taken off for greener pastures."

They all knew better.

Chapter Twenty

Lydia Bergstrom received the call from Gant shortly after she finished dinner. It was after seven o'clock. He told her he was on the road and should be home within fifteen minutes. Like a puppy, she sat in the living room, staring out the front picture window, waiting for him to turn into the driveway. Right on time ,the Volvo pulled into the driveway and rolled to a stop in front of the garage.

"Oh, Lenny, I'm so happy to see you. I'm so glad you're finally home," Bergstrom said opening the front door for him.

"It's great to be home and even better to see you, beautiful," Gant replied setting his suitcase down to hug his girlfriend.

"I missed you so much. I love you."

"I love you, too. Now let's see those eyes. Let's see those beautiful baby blues I love so much." Bergstrom's slate blue eyes contrasted the ringlets of her chocolate hair with piercing sharpness.

Bergstrom looked up into Gant's mismatched eyes. He soaked up her gaze and inhaled deeply as if he could absorb the moment.

"I could stare at you staring at me forever, do you know that?" Gant asked her.

"Seems I've heard that a time or two before," she replied.

"It was a great trip, very productive…" he began.

"It was too long, Lenny. I know you love to visit your mother, but next time I'm going, no questions asked. I won't take no for an answer."

"All right, if it's what you want, you're welcome to come next time. But it may be awhile."

"Putting me off again, huh? First it was 'later, later, later', then it was 'it's not the right time' and now it's 'okay, but later!' I don't understand you, Leonard Schenk. Sometimes I feel like your hiding something from me," Bergstrom said, only half kidding.

"What you see is what you get, Lyd."

"What is that supposed to mean?" she asked.

"I can't give up all of my secrets. You'll have to figure me out for yourself, won't you?"

"I guess I will."

"Now enough with the arguing unless you have make up sex in mind," Gant said, seeking to change the topic. "I was thinking sex, but not of the make up variety."

"Me, too," she relented. "I wish you'd called earlier. I would have waited for you to have dinner. I finished, maybe half an hour ago.

"That's all right, I'm not hungry."

"Let's go upstairs, then," she replied moving toward the stairs.

The television was on in the den. When Gant was away she liked to leave it on as background noise, it seemed to fill a void for her. As she took the first step onto the stairs she heard one of CNN's anchors droning on about the recently found remains in upstate New York.

Bergstrom paused and lingered at the foot of the stairs. "You heard about the bodies right, Lenny?"

"I've been pretty much out of touch for the last two weeks, as you know."

"No shit. You should try calling more often." She shot him a look. "So, you really haven't heard?"

"I guess not, what's up?"

"It's horrible."

He failed to agree. Taking her hand in his he replied, "Tell me in bed," he began walking up the stairs.

She took her hand out of his and answered, "No way, I don't even want to think about this in bed, I might get sick."

"So, what happened, then?," he asked, walking instead toward the den. Old footage of police cruisers with their flashers on flickered through the dimly lit den. The talking head reported that no additional information had been provided as yet and then CNN cut to commercial.

"Great, I missed it," he said, falling down into the leather sofa.

"Some freak killed two women and buried them outside of Marilla—that's a short drive from here. Can you imagine it, right here in our own backyard?"

Freak? Hhm, Gant thought to himself. He was put off by her terming the killer a "freak". *She would no doubt have problems with the Geignetter kid's body in my freezer.*

"It probably happens more often than you think," he answered her matter-of-factly. "People disappear all the time, many of them are never found."

"You think?"

"I know. Look at the statistics, I have. In the U.S. alone two thousand-three hundred people, that is men, women, and children, are reported missing every day. The overwhelming majority show up alive and well, but if even one percent of those are never seen again it amounts to twenty-three people every day that go unfound."

"That's crazy!" Bergstrom gasped.

Maybe, he thought. "Of course some of these people may have wanted to disappear, beat debt, start fresh, who knows why. Still and all, it's an everyday, or nearly, every day occurrence. It's a big country." Then Gant added, "Imagine the numbers on an international scale."

"Yuck! How many of these weirdos are there running around?"

Weirdos? Gant really didn't like her ill informed use of terminology. "Hundreds for sure, maybe even thousands," came his cold reply.

"Why do you even know about this stuff? It's creepy."

"It interests me."

"You're pretty calm about it," Bergstrom commented.

"Can't get too excited, we really can't do anything about. We've got to live our lives, right?"

"Yea, I guess your right. It's disgusting to think that people actually get off on doing things like that."

"You'd have to speak to a shrink about it," he suggested. Then having decided he'd tempted fate long enough, he said, "Don't worry about anything. What happens, happens. We can't control fate, right?"

"No we can't, but I hope they catch the bastard, and execute him. I'm not for capital punishment usually, but it's what this sicko deserves."

Execution? Capital punishment? Sicko? Gant was rendered speechless. He slowly processed what she had said, carefully reviewing it searching for errors. There were no words to be minced. The woman he loved, and who loved him, had wished for his own death.

After a prolonged pause he said, "It doesn't affect us unless we let it. I'm going up to bed, it's been a long day."

"I'm right behind you, I've got the creeps," she replied taking his hand. "Maybe we should get a gun in the house."

"There's a twelve gauge shotgun in my closet. I'll teach you how to load and shoot tomorrow if it will make you feel safer," Gant offered.

"Yes, yes, it would. Thanks, Lenny."

"You'll never need it, I assure you, Lyd. Now about that sex we've been missing out on."

Bergstrom led Gant upstairs into the bedroom. Gant was frustrated and very upset with, what he perceived to be, Bergstrom's careless labeling of him, the man she allegedly loved. He resolved to forgive her as she surely did not know what she was talking about. The sex was good, but took on the guise of make-up sex for Gant. During copulation Gant stared into her eyes as he always did before his climax. What he saw bothered him. Her once caring and compassionate eyes all at once seemed empty and devoid of warmth. Bergstrom was not the same woman he'd fallen in love with. It took only a few remarks which he considered to be unkind to sway his feelings about her. He loved her, but was unsure if they were truly compatible. He suddenly questioned her worthiness. Disheartened, Gant lost his erection. Failing to orgasm he pulled out and rolled away turning his back to her. When Bergstrom reached for him he feigned sleep. Both of them lay in the bed wondering what had happened.

* * * *

Early the next morning, Gant sat at the kitchen table sipping a cup of coffee, wondering when Bergstrom would join him. After not seeing one another for two weeks they wanted one day together before going back to work. They' had plans to jog together and then drive up to Niagara, to do some shopping at the outlet malls. Afterward they would have lunch and then take a leisurely stroll around the falls. It was a gorgeous mid-summer morning and looked like the perfect day for their trip.

Gant was nearly done with his coffee when Bergstrom stepped into the kitchen wearing a high cut, silk robe and nothing else. She poured herself a cup, added cream and sugar and then sat down across from him at the table. She blew on the mug and took a sip and then placed the mug on the cherry wood table. She searched his eyes waiting for him to speak, but he said nothing.

After an awkward half minute she asked, "Are you all right, Lenny? You haven't been yourself since coming home."

"I've never felt better," he replied curtly.

"What was that about last night? You got off of me and went to sleep, you didn't even say good night."

"I'm sorry. I was so tired. It was a long drive. I feel much better now, though."

She brightened briefly and then asked, "Did you...finish last night? It was kind of weird. It didn't seem right. I didn't feel you."

"Sometimes it's not that important. I know you did."

She smiled, her cheeks blossoming red like roses. Still, it was the first time she'd ever heard of a man diminishing the importance of an orgasm. In her experience it was all her prior lover's really ever cared about. Something was amiss, but she decided not to press him any further.

"What's with the goldfish?" Gant asked tapping the bowl on the table in which a solitary common goldfish hovered.

"I was lonely, so I got a fish," Bergstrom replied.

"What's its name?"

"Speedy, she's quite quick."

"She looks lonesome in there. I never really got the point of keeping animals in tanks or cages," Gant replied.

Bergstrom laughed, not taking him seriously. "We'll buy her a playmate then, to keep her company."

Gant said nothing for a few seconds, he stared at the fish in its gallon sized home. "What happens when we're both on the road? Sometimes you're gone for a week at a time. I'm usually out of town for a few days every month. Who will take care of her? She needs to be fed. The tank needs to be cleaned or she'll die."

"That's why I bought a cheapie. It's only a feeder fish."

Gant was appalled at Bergstrom's callousness. "You mean you'll let her die?"

"I won't have much to say about it. I won't be home. If she lives, she lives and if she dies, I'll get another one."

Ironically, the man who murdered people for their organs felt true pity for the little orange fish. "I have to be honest with you Lyd. I don't like your logic on this. You shouldn't take ownership of anything if you're not willing to take responsibility for it. You're responsible for the care of this fish."

Bergstrom looked at him as if he were mad. She had no idea how close to the truth she was. "You're starting an argument with me because I was all alone and decided to buy a fish to keep..."

"It's selfish, Lydia," he snapped.

"It's a fish, Lenny," she shouted.

"It's still a life," Gant whispered. Then in a cold calculated voice he said, "Life is precious whether it be yours or a seemingly insignificant goldfish. Lives should be treated with dignity and respect, not subject to irresponsible whims."

Bergstrom was disappointed with Gant's behavior toward her since returning, and this little episode over a goldfish put the icing on the cake for her. Wordlessly she returned to the upstairs bedroom. Minutes later Gant heard the toilet flush and then the shower go on. There would be no jogging, shopping or walking at Niagara Falls today.

Gant sat at the table with his empty coffee mug watching Speedy dart to and fro in her tiny glass prison. He knew then and there Lydia Bergstrom was not the one for him. Her blatant disregard for life, coupled with her self-serving interests were too much for him to absorb. Resolved to end the relationship, he wondered how to best do it. He did love her, or at least he had, so he ruled out taking her life.

After a few minutes, he decided he would end the relationship gradually. He planned to be away as much as possible and when home, he would remain aloof.

If she refused to take the hint, he would then speak to her about moving out. Gant was sure he'd miss Bergstrom's undivided attention. He knew the breakup would be very hard for him, for both of them, but he couldn't envision happiness with her any longer.

Disappointed with the turn his life took that afternoon, he told her he'd been called away on business and didn't know when he'd return. When Bergstrom protested saying she wanted to talk things over, he told her he needed some time to think about things himself. Ten minutes later, he was in the Volvo heading back out to Milestrip Road where he had pressing work to attend to. He craved attention and recognition for his efforts. It was a short ride to satisfy his needs.

Chapter Twenty-One

Shortly after his discharge from the Navy in 1998, Gant had found himself speaking to a homely, middle-aged woman in a diner in Queens Village. Her name was Michelle Doughty. Gant had met Doughty fifteen years earlier, he'd hoped she wouldn't recognize him. He doubted she would, he'd aged and she'd probably had thousands of customers since he'd bought his fake driver's license from her.

* * * *

In 1983, Gant had just completed his first year at the Naval Academy, he and three of his buddies were in New York City for Fleet Week. It was the Saturday night of Memorial Day Weekend, many of the service men staggered around Manhattan in alcohol fueled dazes. Gant and his friends had been turned away from another downtown club. Although they were all over eighteen, there were many upscale clubs throughout major cities which required their patron's to be twenty-one. Age discrimination suits were still ten years distant when political correctness gained steam in the nineties. Seeking entrance into the trendy clubs in which the somewhat older, more mature women flocked, one of the sailors suggested they should look into getting fake I.D.'s. Generally not known to be a law breaker, Gant agreed and the little band of half-drunk sailors visited Times Square in search of I.D.'s, it seemed like the logical place to go.

Targeting seedy men on the sidewalks in front of the peep shows and sex shops, they were provided with many offers. The foursome were about to walk into a print shop when someone grabbed Gant by the shoulder. He spun around raising his hands ready for a fight. When he saw a burly Marine sergeant standing before him he let his hands fall to his sides. The Marine warned them against using the services of a rinky dink operation like the one they were walking into. He scribbled an address onto a bev nap he pulled from his pocket, and advised the four midshipmen to take the time and spend the money to get quality identification. He told them they would have to pay more, but the product was flawless—his eighteen-year-old nephew had bought one the previous night.

Not knowing the subway system, the four friends hopped into a cab and headed toward the Mid-Town Tunnel on their way to Queens. Back in Manhattan four hours later the midshipmen were out a cool one-hundred dollars a piece, but they gained entrance to any bar or club they wanted. Now, nearly two and a half decades later, Gant still had his fake I.D. He'd used it for six years, up until his twenty-fifth birthday. He kept it as a memento of his youth. Although ragged around the edges, it looked every bit as authentic as it had the day he bought it.

* * * *

There he was, fifteen years later, sitting across from Michelle Doughty who had granted him access to the truly adult singles scene. He wasn't surprised to see her still in the same neighborhood. Her business was steady and lucrative. She had etched out a large area, about twenty city blocks, which was her turf; it was her monopoly. Doughty was a year or two older than Gant, but time had not been kind to her. She had never been anything to look at, but now she was fatter and more unattractive than when he'd first met her.

I'm glad I don't have to kill her, she looks like she's about to die, Gant thought to himself glancing at her across the table, he found it hard to look her in the eye. Though dazzlingly talented, Doughty had dropped out of the School of Visual Arts in Manhattan, her major had been graphic arts.

The short, plump woman was accompanied by a brute of a man named William, he looked every bit the hairy knuckled enforcer that he was. Her muscle, he was there to collect money, Gant couldn't imagine anything else going on between them.

Gant came prepared with a thick envelope of one hundred dollar bills safely stowed within the right interior pocket of his jacket. He recalled watching a story on the evening news about how the price of illegal documents had recently skyrocketed. The case occurred in the late 1990's, when the U.S. Immigration and Customs Enforcement Agency (ICE) uncovered a Mexican family,which operated a false document business that stretched to many major cities all across the U.S. The Castorena family had well over a hundred employees working for them. Officials reported the family was linked to millions of counterfeit ids. At a raid on one of the family's operations in Los Angeles, ICE agents seized false documents with an estimated street value of twenty million. On the other side of his jacket Gant wore a shoulder rig which held a Glock nine millimeter pistol.

"You're not a cop?" Doughty began the conversation.

"No," Gant replied.

"How do I know?"

"If I was a cop I'd arrest him for the blow caked around his nose," Gant replied nodding toward the body guard. William glared at Gant and wiped his nose with the back of his hand.

Doughty snorted like a pig laughing. "Yeah, that's a bad habit William, you should quit that junk."

"It keeps me sharp," William mumbled more to himself than anyone else.

"How did you hear about me?" Doughty asked.

"Anyone and everyone looking for a fake I.D. knows your name," Gant replied hoping to stroke the woman's ego. "According to the locals you're the best there is."

"What locals?"

"I asked around at the Patio, a guy named Frankie told me I could find you here. He told me what you look like, William too." This was true, it was not difficult to find the woman.

"You're looking for a driver's license?" Doughty presumed, lifting a cup of tea toward her lips.

"Passport, and social security card as well," Gant responded.

Doughty's eyebrows arched up, she pushed a strand of stringy hair out of her eyes. "You're really looking to go unnoticed, huh?"

"I figure I may as well go all the way, make the illusion complete."

"No green card or work visa I take it?"

"No, I won't need those."

"If you change your mind they're really cheap to make."

"Thanks, but no."

"Licenses go for five grand a piece. Passports are six thousand, so are the SS cards. I'll throw in a birth certificate for free."

Knowing he would probably never need the birth certificate, Gant ignored the offer and replied, "Prices have gone up, huh?" Gant said.

"You've bought before?"

"Oh, back in college," he responded.

"That's seventeen grand for everything."

"Don't you offer a package deal for good customers?" he asked, tongue in cheek.

Doughty ran her hand through her greasy hair and took a sip of her tea. "I'll do it for sixteen."

"Thirteen," Gant countered, watching William out of the corner of his eye.

"Fifteen, take it or leave it."

"Done," Gant said.

"Do you have any name in mind?"

"I do. I'd like the name to be Leonard Schenk."

"Not real Hollywood, are you?"

"Why would I want to be? The whole idea is to be nondescript, right?"

"Just making an observation," she replied.

"Do you ghost?" Gant asked. He was alluding to the form of identity theft in which a person steals the identity of a specific dead person, the ghost, who is not known to be deceased. The use of counterfeit identification falsely documenting a completely fictional identity is different from ghosting. A fictitious identification is useless in obtaining social services or interacting with government agencies. Ghosting allows the ghoster to claim an existing identity already listed in government records for his or her own use as that identity is dormant because its original possessor is dead."

"You've done your homework, I see," she replied. "I can, but it's risky. There's a lot of red tape involved. You've got to have a mortuary owner in your pocket."

"I do."

* * * *

Gant's visit to Doughty had been precipitated by the death of Leonard Schenk. Gant had met the man on a few occasions when flying in and out of J.F.K. Schenk had held a high ranking post with the United States Customs Service, the predecessor of Customs and Border Patrol (CBP). The U.S. Customs Service had three major missions: collecting tariff revenue, protecting the U.S. economy from smuggling and illegal goods, and processing people and goods at ports of entry. Schenk was the senior supervisor at JFK for over twenty years. As such he had access to information regarding all U.S. airports both large and small, the old man had access to a lot of information and Gant wanted it. Gant sought access to the inner workings of the Customs Service, it would enable him to infiltrate inspection schedules, airport security, and personnel lists.

While still in the Navy, Gant had access to an F.A.A. database which provided him with general information regarding public airport personnel. A veritable *Who's Who* of the civilian aeronautical infrastructure, it was really a directory of pilots, air traffic controllers, ground crew chiefs, and security officials within the federally operated airports. It provided biographical information and timely updates on the lives of those in the industry, it was really a fluff database. Updated on a daily basis, it allowed him to keep tabs on Leonard Schenk. Upon his discharge Gant had requested continued access to the database as he sought to keep up with friends in the field as he said. Gant's request was granted as he was, after all, a decorated combat pilot. He continued to track the life of the old man, patiently waiting for him to die. When the obituary appeared on the directory just after his discharge Gant flew down to New York.

To complete a death certificate, a funeral director must correctly provide the decedent's personal information, including the name, sex, date of death, social security number, age at last birthday, birth date, birthplace, race, current address, usual occupation, educational history, service in the U.S. armed forces, site and address of death, marital status, name of any surviving spouse, parents' names, and informant's name and address. They must also include the method and location of body disposition whether it be cremation, donation, or burial. Lastly they must sign the form. A physician must then complete, with or without use of an autopsy, his or her sections of the certificate. Included here are the immediate cause or causes of death; other significant conditions contributing to the death; the manner of death; the date, time, place, and mechanism of any injury; the time of death; the date the death was pronounced; whether the medical examiner was notified. The physician must then sign it.

The death certificate then goes to the responsible local and state government offices where a burial permit is issued. The death certificate information then goes to the state's bureau of vital statistics and finally on to the United States Center for Health Statistics. It's a long drawn out process during which a lot can go wrong and many mistakes can be made. It's not common, but certainly not unheard of for death certificates to get lost or disappear.

Entering the funeral home of P Walker & Sons at 22473 Jamaica Avenue in Queens Village, Gant surveyed the parlor and was hesitant to go through with his plan. It was the fifth funeral home he'd been in over the last hour. With twenty-seven still remaining on his list he hoped that this was the one. At seven-thirty in the evening it was packed with mourners. He walked on and read the names on each of the six doors and was at once relieved and disappointed to see that Schenk was not one of them. A crowd for the dead man's wake would have precluded any negotiations with the owner of the funeral home. Gant's plan called for discretion, he was wishing to find Schenk's name upon the door of an empty room.

Could this be the wrong place again? It's closest to his home? Maybe he's somewhere else. Gant approached an usher dressed in an ill fitting black suit and asked if he was in the right place. The usher nodded and directed him toward the funeral director's office.

At his desk, the funeral director—a man by the name of Milton Pearl—beckoned Gant to take a seat. After rather formal pleasantries, Gant asked to see the body. Pearl informed him that no next of kin, nobody for that matter, had inquired of Schenk and that he had already been cremated. Gant asked to see the ashes and when Pearl balked Gant knew he had him on the hook. When Gant threatened to call the police Pearl urged him not to, he explained that the ashes were temporarily misplaced and he would have them within two days. Gant called his bluff. He offered Pearl ten thousand dollars for the uncompleted death certificate and his promise to never fulfill his obligation to complete the document. Realizing Gant knew he had illegally disposed of Schenk's remains, Pearl took the deal, the two men even shook hands on it as the cash was exchanged for the incomplete death certificate.

* * * *

"Hmm, impressive, I haven't made a ghost in some time, six months at least," Doughty said.

"So, you can do it then?"

"Why not, I can make anything, but it will be more money for a ghost. There's a lot more work involved when stealing the dead's identity."

William chuckled, with phlegm gurgling deep down in his thick throat, apparently he got a kick out of that one.

"What's the cost then?"

"An additional three grand, make it eighteen total," she replied.

"So, you'd make me a fake for fifteen, but the real one costs eighteen," Gant asked, a little put off.

"Counterfeits are cheaper because there's no real identity involved. They'll get you across the border and through security, hell you can go anywhere you want, but they won't provide you with any income, credit, or access to anything, they're fake. Ghosts are simply more valuable. On the other hand, they're also much more dangerous for both of us. Ghosts can be tracked down more easily because there's a history attached to each one. If you get caught it's jail time for you, and if you flip me it's jail time for me, hence the extra money. Three grand isn't really all that much to ask for such a rick."

"Okay," Gant relented. "Eighteen it is for Schenk."

"Anything else I can help you with?"

"I'd like two fakes as well."

"Who are you hiding from? What did you do?"

"It's best to keep our business to ourselves, don't you think?"

"Sure," she replied rubbing a grubby finger over her double chin. "Complete sets for the fakes too?"

"Complete."

After some contemplation she informed him, "So you want a ghost and two fakes—that will be forty-eight thousand dollars."

"Make it forty-two for the bulk rate discount and you've got a deal."

Doughty considered Gant for a few moments tapping her spoon on the rim of the tea cup. "All right, what the hell, you seem like a nice guy."

"When can you be done?" he asked.

"When will you have the money," she returned.

"I'll give you twenty tonight, the remaining twenty-two upon completion."

William, who had merely shrugged and grunted to this point spoke up suddenly mumbling, "Cash up front."

Gant looked to Doughty without responding to the bull next to him. "This is between us. I don't know what his cut is and I really don't care. I'm prepared to give you twenty tonight, that's the deal. You can walk away with that money and

I'll never see you again or you can honor the deal and see it through, but I won't give you any more up front."

"And if I say 'no'?" Doughty asked, a sheen of sweat shining on her acne scarred forehead.

"I'll find someone else. Do you think you're the only I.D. forger in the world? I bet there are fifty just like you within Queens alone."

Doughty's eyebrows furrowed, she seemed insulted. Finding it difficult to pass up a large chunk of money for just a few days work, she replied, "None are as good as me, but you've got a deal."

"So then, when do you start?"

"Let's take a walk," she replied.

Gant and Doughty silently made their way down Hempstead Avenue with William trailing behind them when she said, "Hand William the cash and your documentation. I'll work on this now, tonight, I should be done within two to three days."

"I've only got the cash. I didn't bring any I.D. with me, I came to buy some," Gant replied.

"You should come back then, with your legitimate docs. I'll use your real docs to create the new ones. It's pretty simple, I use your existing photograph and simply change all of the information on the license and the passport. They are flawless and fast to produce that way. Besides, I don't like anyone to see my studio, it's bad policy."

"No way. Even if I had my I.D.'s I wouldn't give them to you. No offense, but why would I want you to know my real name?"

"You're really up to no good, huh," she said with a smirk.

"The opposite. I'm doing a world of good, but still have to be discrete about it," he responded.

"Uh huh; right."

"Listen, I don't care what you do or don't believe. I want you to make some docs for me. The offer stands as is, but I'm going to your shop. These need to be made from scratch. And for my own protection I need to know where you operate out of."

Doughty turned toward William for some guidance, he shrugged and grunted, "Nah, let's go."

"Yeah, you're right. Let's get out of here, we've got other work to do," she replied.

Without any further discussion, Gant began walking toward the train station. He was disappointed and angry at the same time. If William hadn't outweighed him by a hundred pounds, he would have taken a swing at him. Doughty trusted her body-guard, still forty-two grand was a lot to pass up. Gant was nearly a block away when he heard a shrill whistle behind him. He turned around to see the fat, ugly forger and the beastly bodyguard trudging their way toward him.

"I've had a change of heart," Doughty said, panting as she walked up to him.

"So, let's get started then. Where to?" Gant asked.

"It's only a few blocks this way, but let's have the cash first," she said.

"Don't fuck with me. Play this straight and we're both happy. If you screw around it won't be nice," Gant warned.

Both Doughty and William were taken back. Compared to William, Gant was slight of stature. They were amazed at the audacity of the little man. That he would make such a bold threat was unthinkable. Nonetheless, the two took him seriously.

Both sensed that Gant was able to back up his warning, something about him screamed danger.

"There won't be any tricks, I promise," Doughty offered her hand.

Gant seized her hand and gave it a brisk shake beneath the glare of the streetlights. He shook William's big paw as well and then handed him an envelope full of crisp bills.

"I never bring anyone back to my place. I don't expect to ever see you there again," Doughty said.

"Only if the documents are unsatisfactory, of course."

"They won't be. We'll get everything done right the first time. I don't like wasting my time."

"Agreed."

"I'll shoot you tonight, right now. I'll take down your height, weight, hair color..." she paused briefly, "eye color, etc. I'll get your physical appearance information down. Let's go."

"Good, that shouldn't take long. Painless for both of us," Gant replied waiting for one of them to lead the way.

There was a moment of awkward uncertainty and then Doughty turned around and headed down Hempstead Avenue in the opposite direction toward Belmont Race Track, William took up the lead and Gant followed. Five blocks later they stood before a beautifully restored brick Tudor on One Hundred and Fourth Avenue. An eight foot tall cyclone fence topped with razor wire marked the perimeter of the narrow side yard and the backyard. Doughty disengaged a series of locks and the three of them stepped inside.

The forged document business was good indeed, Gant thought to himself as he walked into the formal living room which boasted a flagstone fireplace. With three bedrooms, two and a half baths, a gourmet kitchen with Viking appliances, a full finished basement with an additional fire place, and both formal living and dining rooms, Doughty's Tudor was the crown jewel of the neighborhood, it was considered palatial by cramped Queens standards. While her house waned in comparison to Gant's mini estate, its price tag was not that far behind.

Doughty led Gant through the house to the kitchen and then to the door leading out onto the back patio. Gant followed her to the detached two car garage in the far corner of the property, William lurked at a distance behind. Gant was careful to keep the big man within sight, he was very leery of him despite the reassurances issued from Doughty.

As Doughty unlocked the garage door, William appeared by her side seemingly out of nowhere, Gant was impressed with the big man's speed and grace, he grew ever more ill at ease with him. William seized the handle of the garage door with one hand and hefted it upward with the flick of his wrist. Doughty flipped a switch on the wall just inside the door and the interior was bathed in soft light from recessed lights overhead. Doughty had converted the garage into a graphic production studio.

Doughty's garage had been modified, a wall was constructed down the middle effectively dividing it into two rooms. Gant stared into the room on the left and marveled at the equipment he saw before him. Atop a compact tripod, a Fuji IP10 digital passport camera sat facing a free standing photo id backdrop toward the far wall. On the rectangular table beside the tripod lay a Fuji IP10 printer, boxes of passport film, a photo cutter, and boxes of print media. The passport workstation was orderly and well stocked, it contained everything needed to manufacture a genuine looking passport.

William pulled the door down and quietly brought it to a rest on the floor. He took a cursory glance around and then his eyes fell on Gant. He yawned, stretched and then leaned against the wall and waited for the shooting to begin.

"What's with the backdrop, I thought you never bring anybody here?" Gant asked, watching William all the while.

"I was bluffing, you called me on it. Most people don't. Really though, the difference in quality between using an existing photo and shooting a new one is negligible. You can barely tell the difference."

"But you can," Gant said, squinting his eyes. "If it was you who was buying the document, which way would you go?"

Doughty blushed at that. "Oh, I'd go brand new. It's completely flawless. There's a slight bit of degeneration involved when using an old photo, but I can dress it up to look almost new. It's really not a big deal, but you did the right thing."

"I'm paying enough for these documents, I want the best."

Doughty shook her head like a chastised child.

"I hope I can count on you from now on to be honest with me. Can I?"

"Absolutely, yes. Now, the sooner we get started the sooner we can wrap things up for the night."

"Where's the computer?" Gant asked.

"Don't need one with this setup. I just compose, shoot and print directly from the camera. No computer, no software to install, just the camera."

"Cool."

"Very," Doughty agreed. After scribbling down Gant's vital information she said, "Take a seat over there," she directed him to the adjustable stool before the photo id backdrop. "Are you smiling or going the straight, somber route?"

"I'll smile."

"Sit up straight," she advised looking through the camera's viewfinder. "There's a lever under your ass. Pull it up, we need a little altitude. I have to get the angle exactly right or it won't look good. I shoot with the same equipment, use the same film, media and printers as the Feds do, otherwise, we're just fooling ourselves. It's got to be perfect or you shouldn't bother."

Before Gant smiled the flash bulb blew white light in his face.

"I was going to smile," he said.

"I always like the first one candid, it gives me something to work from. All right, go ahead and smile."

Gant smiled as Doughty shot him six times, he had kept track. "I think that'll do it. You can pick the one you like the most later, I'll erase the rest."

"I'll have to trust you on that, thanks."

"Of course, let's move on to the driver's license."

Gant remained seated. "I'll want dual citizenship for one of the passports, American and Canadian."

"Not a problem, piece of cake. Now let's do the shot for the licenses."

Gant remained seated, waiting for instruction.

"Well, get up will you?"

Gant rose from the stool. "Aren't you going to shoot me for the driver's license now?"

"That's next door," William kind of put a sentence together while nodding to Gant's left.

"Come," said Doughy. "We don't use the same equipment for the license, it's a slightly different angle, different hues and other variants. It's got to look legit, I don't cut corners."

Gant made his way into the other room in which a similar tripod held a Canon EOS-1Ds Mark III digital camera which was aimed at a free standing photo id backdrop identical to the one in the previous room. The square table next to the tripod held a MacBook Pro, Doughty liked the freedom it afforded her. She very seldom worked outside the comforts of her studio, but when she did she was well prepared to shoot and charge commensurate emergency rates.

The backdrop was unnecessary, of course, as the computer was loaded with Adobe Photoshop CS5. With that program Doughty was able to manufacture pretty much anything she wanted. Beside the MacBook Pro rested a Epson Artisan 837 inkjet printer and a half-used package of Teslin paper. Beside the package of paper was another printer, an HP- LaserJet Pro CP1525NW wireless color laser printer. In the corner of the room stood a sturdy looking little table with an Akiles ID-Lam 100 Heavy ID Laminator.

Beside the laminator were several sheets of very fine sandpaper. On the far side of the laminator there was a stack of heavy, cream colored parchment paper that Gant assumed was for forging the birth certificates he would most probably never need, but would nonetheless take. There was a bundle of banknote paper next to the parchment paper.

"How, exactly, do you do this," Gant asked.

"I can't tell you exactly or I'll be out of a job," Doughty answered. "In a nutshell, I take your photo and then use Photoshop to create any driver's license I want. I've got templates of every state."

"Have you done every state?"

"About half of them, mostly in the northeast as you would imagine."

"A little more detail, please?"

"I edit the texts fields as necessary, you know hair color, eye color, etc. I'll use MUL for your eyes, you know multicolor."

Gant nodded, and then said, "One of the fakes must have brown eyes and brown hair."

"No problem, with Photoshop I can do anything, green hair if you want."

"I'll pass, thanks."

"Then I scan in your photo and signature image files and the front is done. After I'm happy with the front of the I.D., I make the back. I create a barcode and a magnetic strip that both contain the exact information that appears on the front of the card. To do this I use an online barcode generator to produce PDF417 barcodes. I use an encoder to make a scannable magnetic strip which matches all of the information. I have an associate who can hack into the Department of Motor Vehicles database of any state. He downloads whatever new identities I've made and uploads those records into the corresponding DMV database. This is what you're really paying for. If you're pulled over the cop will take your license back to his patrol car. He'll scan the barcode I've created and you, rather your new identity, will appear. The best part is that you start with a fresh license, no points, past or present. So drive safe and don't screw it up and you're a model citizen, at least on the road."

"Beautiful," Gant replied.

"So 'Leonard Schenk' will be a New York license?"

"Yes."

"What about the other two?"

"Carl Heydrich should have a New York license as well as a Canadian license, can you do that?"

"Again, no problem. The Canadian DMV operates a similar database to that of the U.S., it's simple if you know what you're doing."

"I'd like Paul Previt to have a Texas license."

"Going south?"

"You never know," Gant replied.

"Yee-haw, consider it done."

"So, you make the backs, then what?"

"I print the front and back onto the Teslin paper and then glue them together, back to back."

"What is Teslin paper?"

"It's a synthetic, microporous material. It's waterproof and tear resistant, really tough stuff."

"So, that's it."

"I set the laminator for two hundred and fifty degrees and run it on through. If the state's license features a hologram, it gets the hologram. I prefer to use a transparent rainbow hologram. If you need a custom hologram I can do that too, for a little more money. I delicately sand the edges of the hologram to remove any jagged edges on the Teslin paper, and then give the whole card a light sanding with a fine grit sandpaper to give it a worn look. Ta-da, you've got a finished product."

"The social security cards must be quite simple for you then," Gant assumed.

"Yes, and no," Doughty replied.

"From a creative standpoint they're child's play. I merely input your information into the template I've designed in Photoshop and then print it out with the laser printer. I use banknote paper, as it's identical to the paper the Feds use." Doughty walked over to the little table and retrieved a sheet of the banknote paper. She handed it to Gant for him to see. "Look at it, it's perfect."

Gant immediately noticed the banknote paper was significantly heavier in weight and rougher in texture than ordinary printing paper. He observed small multicolored disc shapes in pink, yellow, and blue all over the paper.

"What are the specks called?" he asked.

"They're called planchettes. They're scattered on the entire Social Security card. That's the same stock as was used at the time of your actual birth. See how it's got a blue tint and contains a random, marbleized pattern?"

"I do."

"It's the real deal."

"So, creating a usable number is the hard part," he said.

"Uh, huh," William grunted.

"Well, it'll be easy in Leonard Schenk's case. You assume his number which is already on file," Doughty answered. "For the fictitious I.D.'s we have to be creative. Again my hacker friend has that covered using means he doesn't share, not even with me. But, rest assured the numbers he creates are unique to the alternate you. They are not, and never have been in use. The Social Security Administration is as easily hacked as the DMV, my friend tells me. All of your aliases will be fully documented, one of them in both countries."

"Thank you for the overview."

"We would be here all night if I went into any real depth about how I produce the documents, that's a very concise version. Now go have a seat."

Gant did as he was told while William stood steady behind Doughty, ever watchful with his bloodshot hound dog eyes. Gant looked at the camera and then toward the laminating machine to his left. He looked over at the blank sheets of banknote paper and the parchment, and then felt the need to ask about the birth certificates. "So, I'll be getting three birth certificates for free?"

"It's what I offered, if you want. It still stands. Look at the red dot, please." The camera's flash blared, illuminating the little room like a lightening strike. Before Gant could react, Doughty shot twice more. "Now, how about a smile for me?"

Gant smiled and the flash radiated again and again and again.

"That should do it."

"Supposing an official notices I'm wearing the same jacket in the passport and driver's license photos?"

"You won't be. Photoshop will give you a new wardrobe, don't worry about a thing. I've done this thousands of times before, I've perfected it."

Satisfied Gant rose from the stool. "About the birth certificates, how—"

"You are a curious one indeed, aren't you? I use a different template, of course and enter in all of your birth information including the social security number we created. I've got files of existing birth certificates from most of the hospitals in the northeast region. I can get a copy of a Texas birth certificate if necessary, it's easy enough. I simply download the certificate and then scan the attending physicians name and signature onto our blank. My advice is to go with New York State birth certificates, the parchment I have is genuine, the same stuff the Department of Health uses. Because you were born in New York, it doesn't mean you can't have a Texas driver's license, right?"

"Right."

"I print the document on the parchment using the laser printer, it comes out beautifully every time. Lastly, I emboss the certificate with, in your case, the New York State Department of Health seal. The seal is impressed in the parchment leaving a raised image without any ink at all."

"Outstanding, when will everything be ready?"

Doughty hesitated briefly and then asked, "I don't suppose you'll be giving me a phone number?"

"No, I can't do that."

"I didn't think so. I want to be sure everything is done at once, a single exchange." She paused in consideration and said, "It will all be ready within a week, that will give me a few day's cushion in case my tech geek associate is busy or runs into something unforeseen."

"Very well then. I'll see you next week," Gant replied.

"No offense, but despite William here, you scare me a little. Whoever you really are, I think it's best we never see one another again. William will meet you exactly where we met tonight, same time, in one week. You owe us twenty-two K, right?"

"That's what we shook on. As long as the documents are in order, that is."

"They will be, I assure you," Doughty replied. "William, will you show our guest out now?"

"It's a very nice studio you have here, you must know how to close a deal fair and square," Gant said giving Doughty one last look.

She nodded and turned back to her work. Wordlessly the big goon led Gant toward the side of the house where a narrow gate led to an alley which opened up onto the street. William reached into his trouser pockets and retrieved the key to the oversized Master Lock which drooped down from a thick chain on the inside of the gate. The big man opened the lock and pulled the chain through, unlocking the gate. He then waved Gant out. As William worked the heavy chain back into place Gant walked out onto One Hundred and Fourth Avenue and into the glittering lights and buzz of traffic that was Queens at night.

* * * *

A week later, Gant arrived fifteen minutes early at the little greasy spoon where he'd met Doughty previously. He waited for William in a corner booth toward the back, a letter carrier's bag on the bench beside him. The big brute walked in right on time and sat down opposite Gant. William pulled an oversized brown envelope from somewhere inside of his great coat and placed it on the table, he nodded wordlessly. Gant opened the envelope and examined all of the documents within it. Everything was there as promised. He had birth certificates, social security cards, passports, and driver's licenses in the names of Leonard Schenk, Carl Heydrich and Paul Previt.

Satisfied by their seeming authenticity, he replaced the documents and carefully slid the envelope into the letter carrier's bag. Gant flipped open his jacket giving William an eyeful of the Glock he was carrying, and then reached inside for the cash. He placed it on the table and slid it across to William. The big man opened the envelope and took a cursory glance inside. Having done this before he knew what counterfeit bills looked like, the stack Gant gave him was legit. William knew approximately how much money the envelope held by feeling its thickness. Also satisfied, he stood and exited the café and headed back down Hempstead Avenue from the direction he'd come from. The exchange took less than three minutes, the two men had parted ways without ever uttering a word to one another.

Gant boarded the Long Island Railroad east bound on his way to MacArthur Airport. He felt a freedom, a euphoria, which he hadn't felt since flying missions during the war. He was $42,000.00 lighter in the pocket, but that didn't matter in the least. He now had three complete sets of identification to employ as needed. Having prepared to begin his life's work, he was set to fulfill his destiny.

Chapter Twenty-Two

Dan Wilder found himself orphaned at age ten. His mother, a free spirit, had skipped out on him and his father in 1958—when he was only two. Eight years later, his father—Daniel Senior—died of kidney failure at the ripe old age of thirty. While the first successful kidney transplant was conducted in 1954, Daniel Wilder Senior's body rejected the kidney he received; another one never came. With a deep personal interest in the organ trafficking industry, it was Detective Wilder who spearheaded the research into the macabre black market.

After consulting representatives from the American Public Health Association (APHA), as well as the United States Department of Health and Human Services (HHS), Wilder contacted the World Health Organization (WHO). Between the three entities he gained a pretty clear grasp of how the black market for organ trafficking functioned. After a day and a half of research, he found himself aghast at his findings. While there was very little information on the trade within the United States because of its clandestine nature, there was a seemingly endless amount of data compiled regarding the industry as practiced overseas.

Wilder learned that internationally, like any other commodity, there were organ importing countries and organ exporting countries. China, India, Pakistan, Egypt, Brazil, the Philippines, Moldova, and Romania were among the world's leading providers of trafficked organs. China was well known for harvesting and selling the organs of executed prisoners. The other exporting countries had been using living donors, many voluntary, some not. Sometimes the organs were sold domestically, but more often they crossed borders to where they garnered a higher price. The major importing nations were the United States, the United Arab Emirates, Saudi Arabia, and the countries of Europe. Wilder found it odd that, per capita, Israel imported a tremendous amount of illegal organs.

He discovered that, unlike standard commodities such as sugar, wheat or oil, an organ importer was able to purchase their goods in two ways. Adhering to the traditional concept of importing, meaning remaining in one's own country and receiving an organ over the border, there was a second, more highly utilized method to purchase illegal organs. More commonly, organs were traded over borders using what had come to be known as transplant tourism. Using this method of procurement, potential recipients travelled abroad to undergo organ transplantation. Transplant tourism included the purchase of organs as well as other factors related to the broad, mainstream commercialization of organ transplantation.

The international influx of recipients was facilitated by intermediaries as well as health care providers who arranged the travel and engaged donors. The major advertising tool was the Internet. Using the World Wide Web, intermediaries were able to attract scores of foreign patients. Many of the middle men offered all inclusive transplant packages on their web sites. The term "organ-importing countries" in this context referred to the country of origin of the patients, travelling overseas to purchase organs for transplantation. A report by *Organs Watch*, an organization based at the University of California, named Australia, Canada, Israel, Japan,

Oman, Saudi Arabia and the USA as major organ-importing countries which took advantage of transplant tourism.

It didn't surprise the detective that poverty was the driving force behind the illegal organ trafficking industry. The donor nations hosted large populations of poor. Citizens of indigent nations or regions were often compelled to sell one of their kidneys on the black market. In some cases, these donors were recruited and flown overseas, where their organs were harvested in unsanitary, improvised operating rooms. In 2003, an illegal kidney-procurement network was discovered in South Africa. Its donors were recruited from the slums of Brazil and flown to South Africa where the operations were performed. These donors were paid and returned home with no after care, many would become sick from post operative infections, many died.

He was shocked at the markup on the organs though. While illegal goods were usually expensive and unstable on the black market, it seemed to Wilder the organ market was particularly steep and rife with danger. The amount a donor could expect to be paid for selling their organs depended upon the location and available supply. In 2007, the average price around the world a donor received for a kidney was five thousand dollars, while the average price paid on the black market to receive a kidney was one hundred and fifty thousand dollars.

Liver donors saw similar returns. In February of 2007, an investigation by *The Observer* into India's illegal organ trade found that intermediaries and brokers were getting very rich preying on desperate victims of the tsunami who were selling their kidneys on the black market. Wilder was saddened to see, there were few real winners in the organ trade besides the intermediaries, it was the street thugs and the immoral surgeons that always benefitted from each transaction. Both donors and recipients very often suffered as a result of their illegal activity. Newspaper articles had reported the deaths of patients who went overseas for illegal commercial transplants. The abuse, neglect, fraud and coercion of kidney donors were also frequently reported. These reports had raised serious concerns about the consequences of the international organ trade for recipients and donors.

Many studies reported a heightened frequency of medical complications, including the transmission of HIV and the hepatitis B and C viruses. Additionally, one study from the United Kingdom reported, patients who had been suspended from the local transplant list for medical reasons were operated on overseas, which would be indicative of the use of substandard medical practices.

While Wilder was busy researching the black market organ industry, Hamilton had been out speaking to the families of Tabitha Small and Alona Ricketts, the women whose remains had been found by the hunter's dogs. Over the previous two days she had scoured the case files for each of the missing women and spoken to the detectives who were originally assigned to the cases. She had re-interviewed any family and friends she was able to track down as well. She returned to the station before six in the evening, she was bone tired and none the wiser. Wordlessly, she flopped down into her chair across from Wilder and blew out a loud exasperated sigh.

"You look like hell," Wilder said. "Have you even eaten today?"

"I met my cousin for pizza outside of Kenilworth."

"Good pizza?"

"It was all right. Meeting her was more annoying than anything else," Hamilton replied.

"You don't get along?"

"No, we do, but she's always been a bit theatrical—a big exaggerator. Now she has what she called 'boy trouble'. She thinks her boyfriend's cheating on her."

"Is he?"

"How would I know, I've never met the guy, and who cares anyway," Hamilton replied, irritated once more.

Wilder went back to the sheaf of papers on his desk. After a minute he looked up from the printouts and asked, "Nothing new, huh?"

"*Nada*," Hamilton replied dejectedly.

"Nothing in the files?" Wilder asked.

"Not much to them, really," she responded. "It's like they both disappeared into thin air. Nobody could tell the detectives what either woman was wearing at the time of their disappearances. No evidence of foul play, zip for crime scenes. Neither was married or had a serious significant other. We don't actually know where these women went missing from. According to the file on Ricketts, she was a jogger and that definitely checks out with what her neighbor told me. The detectives who worked her case set up a perimeter with a ten mile radius from her house. There were lots of volunteers, but it was too much territory to cover, even if it were a desert."

"A shot in the dark," Wilder said.

"Exactly. After weeks of combing the fields, woods, ponds and streams, they came up empty. Within a month the volunteers became discouraged, they stopped coming out for line searches."

"After a month any trace of evidence would have been gone, either washed away by the rain or covered with snow. With the spring thaw, the mud would render anything useless."

Hamilton nodded her agreement before continuing, "There seems to be no clue of any kind. The Small woman is the same story. She'd been disowned by her parents and cut off from her allowance."

"She had her own money, though," Wilder said.

"She did, but she was still collecting a nominal amount from her parents on a monthly basis, it's probably the house she was to get upon their deaths that would have upset her. Back then nobody knew what caused the schism, but her mother informed me, Tabitha was sleeping around a lot and embarrassing the family name."

"Maybe mom and dad had her taken out of the picture," Wilder responded.

"Nah, no way. You should have seen all the pictures of her in the parent's house, it's like a shrine. They still had a hundred thousand dollar reward posted for anyone who knew about her whereabouts up until the remains were found. Mister and Mrs. Small were in Europe at the time anyway. That's a dead end, fortunately."

"So that leaves us where?"

"It was rumored Small's neighbor from three doors down stopped by occasionally late at night, presumably for some hanky panky. He's got a solid alibi for the night in question though, he was at the Sabre's game with three of his buddies, it all checks out. No priors on him either. She seems to have become very reclusive after getting estranged from her family. Her mother informed the detectives, her daughter was fond of going on long, solitary walks, even when she was a teen."

"Same problem, people can walk anywhere," Wilder stated.

"If they were out jogging or walking the city or even a densely populated suburb chances are somebody would have seen something," Hamilton said.

"They weren't on Main Street, that's for sure. That and a dollar…"

"I know. They're both like perfect crimes."

"Perfectly awful," Wilder said and then added, "I'd bet that neither of these women knew her murderer."

"Probably a complete stranger out prowling desolate roads for kicks," Hamilton agreed. "Could be a drifter, too. That only further complicates things. At least if the killer maintained a permanent base from which to work…"

"He does, I think. I'd bet he hangs his hat not too far from Marilla."

"What makes you think that?" Hamilton asked him. "And you shouldn't be saying 'he', remember?"

"These women were both single, athletic, and alone. They both suffered the same trauma as far as Herzlich can tell, they were carved up the same exact way. They were buried within sight of one another. The killer knows the area. He knows which deserted roads to drive, he knows where to dump a body and get away with it. Most importantly, they were local girls. I can't see anybody, no matter how crazy they are, driving to our neck of the woods, killing two locals, dumping them in the same place, and then driving any sort of distance. The killer has to know his territory like the back of his hand. Call it a wild hunch if you want, but I think this guy's a local."

"That's only speculation, and dangerous, Dan."

"That's half of this job," Wilder replied.

"Let's not argue on points," Hamilton said. "What have you got? Hopefully, more than me."

"Well I'm well versed in the illegal organ trafficking biz, that's for sure. How much it will help us, I really don't know."

"Tell me what you know."

"Let's get comfortable then," Wilder said. "I'll get some coffee."

Hamilton leaned back in her chair and kicked off her shoes. She got out of her chair and reached across Wilder's desk and grabbed a handful of the printouts he'd been reading. Halfway though the second page Wilder walked back in with two steaming mugs of coffee.

"I see you couldn't wait," he said to Hamilton.

She tossed the papers back onto his desk and fell back into her chair. "I'm too tired to read, let's have it."

"I'm not sure where to begin," Wilder replied. "There are two main forms of illegal organ trafficking. First, there are the organs taken from executed prisoners. China is notorious for doing this on a fairly grand scale, they're probably not the only country either. The second, and far more common form, involves poor people selling their organs for profit. The black market trade of human organs is sustained by wealthy individuals, sometimes on long waiting lists for transplants, traveling to foreign countries for the procedure. Poverty and corruption are the underlying motivators behind donors selling their organs as most of them see it as the only option to make money. For most buyers, who have been waiting on transplant lists for months or years, desperation and frustration force them to commit the crime. Often, the recipients are lied to, they are told the organ donors are healthy and in good shape which is very often not the case. Lots of prostitutes donate organs thinking they can make enough cash to get off the streets."

"Traveling overseas for implants? I've heard of it, but never really given it much thought," Hamilton said.

"It's called transplant tourism and it's pretty prevalent."

"It's an old story, the rich man lives while the poor one doesn't," Hamilton said.

"This takes it to a whole different level. I'll take you on a world tour. Here, listen to this," Wilder said, while putting on his reading glasses. Holding one of the printouts out before him he read, "In places like Egypt, which the WHO has declared an organ-trafficking hot spot, the destitute have been selling a kidney, sometimes for as little as two grand, to get out of debt. At seedy cafes, they are chased by middlemen that match donors and recipients, many of whom are foreigners drawn to Egypt's flourishing, underground organ trade."

He paused and went on, "In many parts of India, the poor use their kidneys as collateral for money lenders. Lawrence Cohen, UC Berkeley professor of anthropology, has documented that the kidneys in the region are often sold to the wealthy in Sri Lanka, Bangladesh, the Gulf States, the United Kingdom and the United States. Cohen went on to say, while most people sold their kidneys to get out of debt, they were back in debt very shortly."

Wilder paused once more before continuing, "According to an *Al Jazeera* report, the Iraqi capital of Baghdad is a central hub for the trade. Last year hundreds of Iraqis sold organs such as their kidneys to dealers who then sold them for massive profits to desperately ill people willing to pay."

"Big in the Middle East and Asia, huh?" Hamilton asked.

Wilder nodded in agreement. "Let's get back to China for a minute. China is the world's second largest performer of organ transplants. As we already know, the Chinese government is big on using the organs of executed criminals so they know exactly where those organs came from, right?"

"Right."

"So, listen to this then. During the years between two-thousand and two-thousand-and-five, the Chinese government has been unable to account for the source of over forty-one thousand five hundred transplanted organs."

"What about the rest of the world?"

"Brazil, Israel, South Africa, Indonesia, they're doing it everywhere, it's hip, it's cool," Wilder mused and then added, "Anywhere there are poor, the trade is strong."

"Israel? Israel doesn't strike me as being a particularly poor country," Hamilton said.

"No, it's not, but it has plenty of poverty around it, right? In April of twenty-ten, six Israelis were charged with suspicion of running an international organ trafficking ring and refusing to pay donors for the kidneys that been harvested. According to police, one of the arrested suspects was a retired Israeli army general. In November of twenty-ten, Israelis and South Africans were arrested for organ trafficking through Netcare."

"What's Netcare?" Hamilton asked.

"It's a South African health care company, the largest provider of private healthcare in both South Africa and the UK. They were buying and selling over the Internet. In December twenty-ten, Israelis and a Turkish national were reported to be involved in organ trafficking in Kosovo. It's happening right here in the states as well. Remember that corruption probe in New Jersey?"

"That was in two-thousand-and-nine, I remember."

"Forty-four people were arrested including state legislators, government officials and several rabbis. They were running an international money laundering racket that trafficked human organs. It put Israel into center stage of the illegal transplant industry, as much of the money was heading back there."

"Wow! I never would have thought it."

"There is good and bad everywhere," Wilder said. "The Israelis have also taken a different approach."

"How so?"

"The Israeli military has been routinely taking the organs of Palestinians they capture or kill."

"You're shitting me!"

"No shit. According to a major Swedish newspaper it's been going on for over twenty years, since the start of the first intifada in 1987. Israel banned all Swedish journalists shortly after the report. The journalist, who has received numerous death threats by the way, states that one victim, Bilal Achmed a Ghanaian, was shot and taken away by Israeli soldiers. According to villagers who witnessed the incident the nineteen-year-old was shot in both legs and the stomach.

When he was returned to his village five days later, he had been sewn together from his belly to his throat. The affected Palestinian families questioned the need for an autopsy as the cause of death was so obvious. The Israeli army responded by saying that any Palestinians killed are subject to an autopsy. The Palestinians countered it was always young men who were dissected. They are certain their young men, the strongest and healthiest, are being used as forced organ donors. I'm sure this happens in any modern day war zone."

"I'm not seeing it though. I mean, the Israelis hate the Palestinians. Many Israelis consider Palestinians sub-human. Would they really use their organs?"

"Regardless of their beliefs, if a baboon heart would save your life would you turn your nose up at it?" Wilder asked.

"I see your point."

"Besides, it sounds as if a lot of those forced donor organs end up elsewhere in the world."

"Over here?"

"Maybe. Without a doubt there are wealthy Americans taking advantage of the trade, particularly the market in Brazil. Western Europeans though, utilize the Middle Eastern and Asian markets to a higher degree. It's really citizens of neighboring countries that purchase most of the organs. Despite air travel, the organs do have a shelf life, after all.

"To throw some figures at you, according to the Sindhi Institute of Urology, approximately two thousand renal transplants were performed in Pakistan during two-thousand-and-five. Over two-thirds of them were performed on foreigners. The number of foreign recipients in China is hard to estimate, but a media report offers evidence, over half of the kidney and liver transplants were performed in one major transplant center which caters to foreigners. In two-thousand-and-four, non-Chinese citizens from nineteen different countries received organs at the center. Recipients can live around the corner or on the other side of the world. As long as they have the green it doesn't matter."

"How much money are we talking about here?" Hamilton asked.

"The donors earn remarkably little considering what they give up, the recipients pay through the nose, and the middle men take the lion's share. It's more clandestine than any other illegal trades, it's more difficult to tag on numbers, so the figures that are reported are very conservative, most of the experts think. They believe that, on the world market, monies in at least the mid to upper hundreds of millions range change hands each year."

"So, it's nowhere near the cocaine, meth, or marijuana trades?"

"I don't know, but I doubt it. I figure it this way. How many people light up a joint on a daily basis, or snort a line or two every weekend."

"Too many. Worldwide, tens of millions, probably like fifty million."

"Right, and how many of those people would be willing to be sliced open to make some money?"

"I see."

"The sheer volume of the drug trades has to put them well ahead of the organ trade. Still though, proportionately the money that exchanges hands during a single organ deal is staggering."

"Cut to the chase, give me the numbers," Hamilton said.

"For the sake of clarity we'll use the kidney as the example as it is the most trafficked organ and there is more data on it than any other."

"Why's that?" Hamilton wanted to know.

"According to the World Health Organization the search for organs has increased substantially around the world because of a higher rate of kidney diseases and a lack of available kidneys. Only ten percent of the estimated need was met in two-thousand-and-five. With the vacuum comes the black market. It's widely believed that organ trafficking accounts for over twenty percent of the almost eighty thousand kidney transplants performed worldwide each year." Wilder paused to adjust his glasses and then continued, "Nancy Scheper-Hughes, founding director of *Organs Watch*, an academic research project that deals with organ transplants at the University of California, Berkeley, says that fifteen thousand kidneys a year is conservative." Wilder put his papers down. "Kidneys are the safest to transplant as well. They dominate the illegal trade because they are in greatest demand and they are the only major organs that can be wholly transplanted with relatively few risks for a living donor."

"You've done your homework on this, huh?" Hamilton asked sensing some kind of personal concern in Wilder's tone. He seemed consumed by his research.

"I'm interested in it, yes," Wilder replied curtly, avoiding mention of his father.

Hamilton was quick to take the hint. "So, you were giving me the numbers then," she said.

"Like any market, legal or illegal, it fluctuates with the supply and demand. Now is the highest it's ever been. A seller generally earns between two thousand and six thousand dollars for a kidney, which to some people is a lot of money, to us its peanuts. Post operative care is nearly non-existent and not included. Very often the donors are ignorant of all the risks involved, they end up even worse off than before the operation, and with little or no money left to help them survive. Now on the other end a recipient can expect to pay between seventy and one hundred and sixty thousand dollars for a kidney package. Again, they are on their own for after care."

"What? That's a ninety thousand dollar difference!" Hamilton gasped.

"Supply and demand, and to take one from the real estate profession, 'it's location, location, location'. The further you are from your transplant the more costly it becomes. When the middle men know you're willing to travel an absurdly long distance for the organ they hike the price up some more. Recipients are not viewed as repeat customers, the middle men milk them for every last cent they can."

"So these middle men are making anywhere from say sixty to a hundred and fifty grand on each sale."

"Well, the doctor takes a cut, nurses get paid, and other "staff" as it were, but from what I've read the intermediaries take close to seventy percent of the profit."

"And some of the donors are coerced?"

"I'd say most of them are. I mean, let's face it, who would subject themselves to a life threatening procedure unless they were desperate for the money. Worse than coercion though, is the outright theft that goes on."

"Theft?" Hamilton asked.

"It happens," Wilder replied. "Listen to this one," he said, selecting a print out from the back of his sheaf of papers. "Horrific stories about victims waking up in a bathtub full of blood and ice cubes have often been discounted as urban legend. The fact is though, organ theft does occur. A day laborer, Mohammad Iqbal Khan, who resided outside of Delhi, India, was merely seeking a day's employment when he agreed to work as a laborer at a construction site for four dollars a day. The man was then held at gunpoint for several days, along with two other day laborers. After some unknown amount of days, the middle men were probably matching recipients, the three men were taken to a hidden operating room and knocked unconscious by chloroform. Each awoke in terrible pain and were informed one of their kidneys had been removed. A medical examination of Khan corroborated that his kidney had, in fact, been removed."

"It gives a whole new meaning to 'The Grim Reaper', huh? What about these doctors? Do they have no morals whatsoever?" Hamilton wondered aloud.

"Apparently not, lots of doctors don't. Look at all the unnecessary plastic surgery that goes on right here in the U.S. Here's another one," Wilder continued. "This time it's Egypt. The long scars slitting the sides of many Egyptians in impoverished Cairo neighborhoods testifies to illegal kidney sales to a rich fellow countryman or Gulf Arabs who are unable to find a donor. Dire poverty, legal indifference and religious conservatism have created a new mafia which is prospering in Egypt and turning the country into the regional hub for the human organs trade. In a country where social inequality is high and a quarter of the population lives below the poverty line, an increasing number of Egyptians are falling prey to the phenomenon. Most donors are poor and hoping to escape debt, but not all are volunteers.

Grisly accounts of forced organ 'donations' have earned Egypt the sinister reputation of being the 'Brazil of the Middle East'. Like millions of Egyptians, Abdul Hamid, Achmed Ebraheem and Mustaf Zakaria were seeking better paid jobs in the Gulf, but their quest cost them a kidney. The independent Al-Masry Al-Youm Daily reported the three men were promised jobs but were required to take a medical examination before they could begin work. The doctor," Wilder paused to glance at Hamilton, "suddenly 'discovered' all three men had kidney infections, which required immediate emergency surgery. They woke up later in the hospital each of them minus a kidney. Their employer contact disappeared and the men were left to make it home on their own."

"Doctors are supposed to help people, not butcher them."

"Some of these doctors may feel they are helping the more worthy people, a higher class. Sort of like a reverse Robin Hood deal, steal from the poor to give to the rich, and of course they get rich while they're at it. It all comes down to greed. Professor Zhai Zhu, a bioethicist from the Chinese Academy of Medical Science, states the organ brokers are well connected to doctors who care only about money. Doctors with any sense of social responsibility would be able to tell if a transplant package looked illegitimate, but often they turn a blind eye."

"I suppose you've found evidence of doctors here who've been on the wrong side of this, too?"

"I was getting to Doctor Barry Green of Brooklyn. Doctor Green had a desperately ill forty-eight-year-old female patient who he advised to get hold of a kidney any way she could. When she asked the doctor what her options were, he put her in contact with an intermediary named Gedalya Taber, a former Israeli police officer. Taber had a contact in Brazil, one Ivan Bonifacio da Silva, a retired Brazilian military police officer. The retired military policeman knew of a man named Davi da Silva, no relation, who lived in the slums outside of the Rio de Janeiro airport.

Age thirty-eight, Davi da Silva, was one of twenty-three children of a prostitute. He agreed to donate his kidney to the New York woman in return for six thousand dollars. With the minimum wage about eighty bucks a month and work hard to come by, it seemed a fortune. Doctor Green's patient paid eighty thousand dollars for the kidney, while he, Taber, the surgeon, and da Silva, the retired military policeman, split up seventy-four thousand amongst themselves, the good doctor taking ten grand as his referral fee.

The international organ trafficking ring exploited two very different sets of needs, the need for cash and the need for life, at the far ends of a knotted chain thousands of miles long. The journey of Mister da Silva's kidney across four continents and into a one-bedroom apartment in Brooklyn, revealed the inner workings of a network that is by no means unique. Rather, it represents a global black market for organs, including livers, kidneys and lungs, which reaches dozens of countries and generates hundreds of millions of dollars a year."

"It seems too easy."

"In much of the world it is," Wilder agreed. "Middle men clearly advertise on the Internet. One Chinese kidney trading website is packed with organ brokers 'advertisements where contact numbers are openly on display. The ads ask potential sellers to contact them, promising a safe surgery and a quick cash payment.

In April twenty-eleven, unbeknownst to his parents, a high school student in China's Anhui province, sold his kidney for three thousand dollars so he could buy an iPad two. The broker contacted him over the internet. In 2007, a man in Wales became the first person convicted under the Human Tissue Act for selling his kidney online for twenty-four thousand pounds in order to pay off his gambling debts. I could give you seemingly crazy accounts like these all night. The truth really is stranger than fiction."

"It's more difficult here in the states, though."

"It's not all over the Internet like it is elsewhere. Also, the ghoulish association it carries has stigmatized it in the West. In the United States most of the trade lies with corrupt morgue operators and funeral home directors who sell organs from cadavers. The families of the victims most often never find out. If a body is delivered to the mortuary quickly enough after expiration there are organs suitable for harvesting."

"So, what do you think, Dan? Is our perp involved in the organ trade?"

"I think so. The murder weapon, the precision cuts, the similarities of the victims in terms of health and fitness, the close proximity of their residences, it's all too much to be coincidental. I think the killer is selling the organs."

"Well, that gives us some focus."

"I can't figure out the faces though, I mean the hair I can understand. The hair can be sold for profit, but there's no market for face transplants. There are a few people here and there like that guy who got mauled by the chimpanzee."

"That cop on Long Island who took the shotgun blast in the face," Hamilton added.

"Right," Wilder agreed. "Poor bastard was three years from retiring and 'pow', a twelve gauge point blank. I don't know how he lived."

"I heard his wife left him. What a bitch," Hamilton lamented.

Wilder nodded solemnly.

Hamilton took a moment and then asked, "Do you think doctors and hospitals around here participate?"

"Up here, I kind of doubt it. I'd think that someone selling organs would need to go to a major city, New York, Detroit, Boston, Pittsburgh, Philly, maybe even Baltimore or D.C." After a moment he added, "If it's trafficking that's going on the person we're looking for can move organs quickly."

"What about Montreal or Toronto?" Hamilton posed.

Wilder's eyebrows went up. "That would be very difficult time wise, but just about perfect, wouldn't it?"

"The Canada Border Services Agency is somewhat lenient and the U.S. Border Patrol isn't nearly as active up there as it is down south. It could be relatively easy to smuggle organs across the border into Canada."

"There aren't any cadaver dogs working the borders as far as I know."

"Tens of thousands of people cross the border every day. Too many to find the one we need," she said.

Wilder shook his head in agreement.

"Back to the time element for a minute. If the dealer had an accident or got stuck in traffic, the organs could perish and the sale would literally expire," Hamilton said. She then leaned back in her chair, stared at the ceiling, and exhaled in frustration. "Too risky to drive."

"That might be it," Wilder said, looking at her, his eyes steady.

"What?" she asked.

"Maybe we should be looking for someone who has access to a plane," he suggested.

Chapter Twenty-Three

After his disagreement with Bergstrom, Gant spent the next two days away. She had called his cell phone often without any success. He felt a pang of guilt, but was able to minimize his feelings as he rationalized he had a lot of work to do. He planned on leaving for Orchard Park the following morning anyway to dispose of Geignetter's remains.

Gant drove less than a half an hour from home to put the boy to rest. He pulled over on a deserted stretch between Chestnut Ridge Road and Scherff Road east of Hamburg, New York. In the shallow waters of a small pond hidden within the wooded area James Geignetter's remains Sunk to the bottom, bubbles from his digestive tract rippling up to the surface. Gant trudged off toward the Econoline in search of salvation.

* * * *

The taxidermy work on Geignetter's face went smoothly, Gant was nearly an expert now. He found it therapeutic to work on the skin after the sordid conversation he had been forced to absorb with the woman he loved. The slicing and peeling had a certain calming, even balancing, effect on his mind. Geignetter's mask was nearly finished, it was still wet and maintained a good bit of elasticity, qualities mostly associated with living tissue, it was the optimum time to try it on. Gant held it up to the light to admire it and then slipped it over his head. He looked out through the eyeholes of James Geignetter in an attempt to commune with the spirit of the departed boy. Gant did not wear the masks of all of his victims, only those he had a certain respect or admiration for.

Geignetter had been a good boy who'd stumbled into an unfortunate situation. Gant stared at himself in the little mirror overhanging the slop sink in the basement trying to imagine what it was like to be James Geignetter. He felt a strong kinship with the boy, so much so tears of sorrow sprang from his eyes and rolled down his cheeks wetting his shirt. Gant believed this ritual provided him with insight into the life of the person whose face he was wearing. In a semi-delusional state, he imagined living vicariously through the dead boy's soul and the boy living physically within him for all of eternity. Assuming another's identity, even for twenty minutes, gave him inspiration for the future, enriching his own soul while paying homage to the person who made the ultimate sacrifice. When he was satisfied he very gingerly slid the mask up off of his face and then fit it snugly over a mannequin head, he would later fit with the creamy brown replica eyes. With a clean white rag he wiped preservative solution and conditioning oil from his face and then went upstairs to shower.

Gant left the mask to dry while he attended to legitimate business affairs with several large air carriers and dozens of small time operations. The generous incoming stream of revenue justified maintaining the business, even to a man like Gant. In the meantime, he counted the days until his latest masterpiece would be ready.

* * * *

Two weeks later, he had spoken only sparingly to Bergstrom, so much did her crude interpretation of his being bother him. They had agreed he would return home the following day to talk things out. He had one more night to himself for awhile and looked forward to it with baited breath.

The exterior of Gant's farm house was run down and badly weathered, he sought to keep up appearances. As all of the surrounding neighbor's houses and farms were in poor repair, he had no desire to draw attention to himself by having the nicest place within ten miles. Inside though, the house was immaculate with oak floors, cherry wood cabinetry, marble counter tops and all of the modern amenities on both floors. The basement, a small sterile operating room, was better equipped than many hospitals in poor rural areas of the country. The attic was rustic, but well appointed. It resembled a hunter's lodge.

The airtight glass canister measured twelve inches in diameter and eighteen inches in height, it held three gallons. James Geignetter's face and hair were stretched over the mannequin head inside of it, his coffee colored eyes stared off into oblivion. Gant hugged the canister to his chest as he ascended the spiral staircase into the attic of the old farmhouse. At the top of the staircase he carefully placed the boy's mask on the pine plank floor amid the fading light of the early evening Sun. He reached over to his right and flipped on the light switch; the attic was suddenly bathed in soft light. He picked a remote off of a nearby table and hit the play button. As the string section ramped up, and Wagner's *The Ride of the Valkyries* soared from the ceiling mounted Bose speakers, Gant stepped up onto the unfinished planks and surveyed his shrine. He was instantly filled with bliss.

Staring back at him were the glass-enclosed faces of thirty-seven of his closest confidantes. He told them everything. He took pride in the fact that he attained such a large following without having been suspected of anything. He was confident he would never be found out.

The masks were carefully stretched over form fitting mannequin heads. Each mask occupied its own four foot tall black walnut stool. While the trombones rolled forth he made a triumphant circuit, meandering in and out of the carefully placed stools, soaking up the admiration of his followers. Gant wove around amongst his gathered flock as the percussion section thundered its way into the forefront. Only when the fat German woman began to sing of Valhalla did he settle down to gaze back at his audience, while in the recesses of his mind the great composer's horses leapt from cloud to cloud.

The attic was wide and spacious, Gant positioned his disciples in a geometric progression so he was able to make eye contact with all of them at once. Directly beneath the peak of the roof a walkway four feet in width stretched from the stairs to the lone window on the east side of the old farm house. To the left of the window a gold framed picture hung all alone. The photo was an old black and white of Gant as a child, no more than four years old. He was sitting in the bucket seat of the International Harvester tractor, his grandparents stood off to the side beaming with delight.

On either side of the walkway, which Gant sometimes envisioned as a tarmac, were four rows of five stools each neatly placed at forty-five degree angles to the staircase. From his vantage point at the top of the stairs Gant gazed into the sightless eyes of his friends as if he were a professor lecturing to a class. Propped up in front of each mask's canister was a typed index card which provided vital information about the donor. Gant would never forget who these people were, how they'd lived, or how they died. He arranged the masks in chronological order, with his early kills located at the far end of the attic near the single window. Nearing the staircase, the masks of the deceased grew more and more recent. The face of James Geignetter would occupy the furthest of the three remaining empty stools toward the very front, it being the newest acquisition for the time being. Gant planned on filling the empty stools shortly thereafter. He had dozens of stools waiting in the barn and the entire other side of the attic to fill up.

Gant placed Geignetter's mask upon the stool and then stepped back to see how he would fit in with the rest of the crowd. Much to his satisfaction, the teens face blended in very nicely with the assembled group of worshippers. Of varying races and sexes, they were all attractive people, Gant wouldn't have it any other way, he considered them to be his extended family after all. His anticipation mounted as the string section spiraled down, and when the final cymbal crashed he turned off the sound system. He then took a seat in the sole remaining rocking chair from his grandparent's house. Swaying back and forth in the old rocker, he was at eye level with his entourage of admirers, he was most comfortable.

Surveying the attic, moving from face to blind face, Gant absorbed what he interpreted to be love, adoration, and awe in the visages of the dead. He envisioned his victims as heroes and heroines for all of mankind, almost as heroic as he was himself. Gant realized that taking the life of anything was inherently wrong, but not evil, not at all. On the contrary he saw himself in a benevolent light. He justified his actions as being for the greater good of humanity.

Providing needy, sick people with life saving organs is truly a noble act, is it not?, he thought. *Small sacrifices are acceptable if they serve the greater good* echoed in his mind. *One dies so that so many others may live.* According to his accounting ledger he'd already saved, or at least touched, the lives of well over three hundred people.

"What is thirty-eight when compared to over three hundred?" he asked the mute gallery before him. Envisioning himself as a kind of messiah with godlike attributes, he reasoned that he was indeed a creator as he provided salvation and life to so many. While Gant was well off partially to his proclivity to harvesting, he easily absolved himself of that as well. Seventy percent of his wealth came from his legal air parts business; he donated the overwhelming majority of the profits from his organ trade to various cancer research institutes. *Small sacrifices are acceptable if they serve the greater good.*

He vindicated himself for skinning and scalping his chosen people as well. For his benevolent efforts he rewarded himself with a prize each time, the mask of the donor. For his countless hours of tiresome work and dedication he deserved the masks, they fed his inner hunger for recognition and adoration he would never be able to realize in society. In his mind Gant's aiding mankind now with the organs and in the future with his generous donations to find a cure for cancer, what he viewed to be the scourge of humanity, was all the justification he needed.

He saw himself as a superhero of sorts, without the cape. Nobody knew the true identity of any super hero, so too he reasoned, he must remain anonymous, working on the outskirts of accepted norms. He performed his benevolent deeds in the shadows, so he would never be recognized for his acts. The shrine served to boost his self image. In his complex psychology which he realized most people would consider warped, as his girlfriend would no doubt say, he was a deeply conflicted man to say the least.

As nobody knew of his good deeds and never would, he craved attention and praise. The shrine of masks filled this void for him. The glass-eyed masks served as surrogates, providing him with a sense of admiration he'd sought his entire life. They validated his own self-worth. The shrine of masks provided him with a captive audience of adoring fans. He'd known his victims for a short time before ending their lives and now they were his admirers forever.

They worshipped him for all eternity, and likewise he worshipped them. Gant treated the masks with deep reverence and the utmost respect when visiting the shrine to view and handle them. In his shrine he maintained a relationship of mutual respect. Seeking a balance of give and take, Gant reaped what he perceived to be his disciples love, admiration, and gratitude while he engaged severe reverence, often breaking down in tears while he passionately prayed for the souls of his donors.

While many serial killers begin as animal abusers, Gant was very different. He'd learned to clean fish and butcher animals for consumption only—never leaving anything to waste. Graduating to humans, he also killed as mercifully as possible, there was absolutely never any torture involved. It was his grandfather's death that pushed him over the edge, causing him to murder other human beings. As an adult reflecting on his grandfather's needless death, he became angry and bitter. He felt impotent about his inability to save the old man he loved so much. He pledged to never again feel that way, he swore to help mankind for the greater good. He vowed to be proactive in the fight against death by becoming a killer himself.

After an hour in which Gant was lost in a delusional state of grandeur he suddenly stood and strode toward the lonely window back beyond the collection of masks. He stopped beside the masks of Tabitha Small and Alona Ricketts which were side by side as his first ever donors. As they were recently of national interest Gant intended to tender them with the reverence and respect they so richly deserved.

He went to his knees and peered into the eyes of Small, her mask stared back blindly, but not for Gant. In Small's replica hazel irises he saw the small woman's strength and selflessness, her willingness to give of herself to better others.

Touched, he lifted the top off of the glass canister, carefully reached inside and took her death mask out for closer inspection. He laid the mannequin bust beside the canister atop the stool. He brushed the delicate features of her face with the back of his right hand, he was particularly fond of her high cheekbones. From her cheekbones his hand ascended up to her forehead and then back down the bridge of her button nose, over her lips, which he had painted with a rich, ruby red and finally to the cleft of her chin.

After a brief hesitation, he brought up his left hand and ran his index and middle fingers downward from her chin toward the base of her throat to where the mask ended in a clean, straight line.

Gant then turned his attention to Ricketts, whose red-rimmed brown eyes would forever be a disappointment to him. Early in his taxidermy career, he was unable to reproduce the woman's bloodshot eyes to his liking. Although his early work was better than most seasoned taxidermists, Gant was the consummate perfectionist, always finding fault with his work. As time went by and he practiced more and more, even he was hard pressed to find flaws. To him, Ricketts looked soulful and sad, it was probably his own psychological response to the immense guilt he felt for taking her life. He ran his fingers over her pudgy cheeks, her broad nose, and her full, brown lips. He then gently stroked the corn rows of hair which he was able to keep entirely intact which was no easy feat.

With one hand upon Small's stool and the other on Ricketts', Gant bowed his head, and still kneeling, began to pray for the lost women's souls. Gant was not a particularly religious man, but sought to do the best he could for his flock. After reciting *"The Lord's Prayer"* he spoke directly to what he considered the "Ultimate Being" for nearly an hour. He never asked forgiveness for his sins as he considered himself to exist outside the bounds of redemption.

He asked for forgiveness for the sins committed by Small and Ricketts though he had no idea what wrongs either woman had committed during their relatively brief lifetimes. He asked for help to provide, provision and protection for the souls of both women. After Gant was finished praying he talked to the masks of his first donors. He begged forgiveness of the deceased women before him as he thumbed their information cards with either hand. He apologized to them for what he had done to them, but justified his acts and explained his reasoning to them while tears ran down his cheeks. Gant sobbed, his head hanging low, between the stools until his throat dried up. His head splitting and his eyes bleary, he stood and kissed both masks upon the forehead. He then gingerly placed them back into their canisters and sealed the lids. He turned his back on his first donors and walked toward the staircase.

Gant walked past a work table which housed cleaning solutions and preservative oils and gels. He made it a habit to maintain the integrity of the masks to the best of his ability. Each mask was dutifully cleaned and oiled every six months. Cleaning the masks was meticulous, time-consuming work. With a clean hand towel and the cleansing solution it took him close to an hour to thoroughly cleanse each one. A few light spritzes of the preservative oil from a squeeze bottle kept the masks and hair soft and pliable.

Hanging from the ceiling of the opposite side of the attic was a fifty-two inch Sony television. Gant dragged the rocking chair before the wide screen and inserted a DVD which he'd converted from a video cassette recording. For the next half an hour he watched the interviews of Small and Ricketts which he'd recorded, moments before he killed them.

Gant believed watching the videos provided him with an insight into the fragile innocence of life, it served to keep him focused and respectful. Tonight as a tribute to his first donors he watched as they cried and begged for mercy reliving the experiences, keeping them fresh in his mind. In his logic if he remembered them, they were not forgotten and therefore he revered them in his way.

While the shrine was certainly Gant's euphoric reward as he reveled in his engrossed audience's glorification of him, it was as much a torture chamber for him. While watching the videos, he cried violently—sometimes shielding his eyes with his hands. He breathed a deep sigh of relief, when the videos were over and he could turn off the television. Gant had a tremendous masochistic streak. He embraced self-torture, it made him feel better about his deeds later. Gant viewed tormenting himself as an act of penance. Although he associated himself with no particular religion or any definable god, he did believe in right and wrong and felt strongly that his wrongful acts, no matter that they were, had to be atoned for.

The praying, begging for forgiveness, and watching the videos was a sobering experience after the elation he'd felt during his initial triumphant return to the shrine. Feeling somber and heavy of heart, he took one last glance at his shrine before turning off the light. The Sun had set, it was now pitch black in the attic. He crept down the stairs into the amber light of the upstairs hallway feeling purged and oddly refreshed.

Chapter Twenty-Four

Nicole Lutz taught third grade at Windom Elementary, a nondescript one story brick building on Sheldon Road a mile south as the crow flies from Gant's farmhouse on Milestrip Road. It was after four o'clock when she exited the school and walked into the nearly empty parking lot. She pulled the door of her 2005 Subaru Forester shut and keyed the ignition. As the slate-colored SUV rolled out of the parking lot she tuned into Star 102.5 FM and heard Kid Rock babbling some nonsensical gibberish. She hurriedly tuned to Country 106.5 FM, and was relieved to hear Shania Twain singing *Home Ain't Where His Heart Is Anymore*. It had been a long day, many of the kids were sick, runny noses and the like, one had vomited on his desk. She looked forward to getting home to see Mush, her four-year-old Alaskan Husky, he'd be climbing the walls to get out. After a long walk she planned on slowly sipping a glass of merlot by the fire before preparing dinner. Or maybe she'd meet a friend for a drink and a bite to eat.

It was Thursday afternoon, one more day to go until the weekend, and then three more days until Thanksgiving break, she needed the time off more this year than she could ever remember. At age twenty-nine, it was her sixth year teaching and she had plenty of enthusiasm and energy, it was the class size that was killing her. She truly loved her job, but it was ever more demanding. Keeping twenty-seven boisterous eight-year-olds on task and engaged was no small feat no matter what the naysayers said.

Making the right turn onto Abbott Road she felt the stress drain out of her body as she drove further away from the school and contemplated the upcoming days off. At fifty miles per hour she was approaching Southwestern Boulevard and was about to take her foot off of the gas when the Subaru hit a deep pothole beneath the remnant crust of ice and snow on the street and her right front tire blew out. The SUV pulled sharply to the right, the wheel spinning in her hands before she knew what was happening.

Level-headed, and a veteran snow driver, she seized the wheel and jerked it to the left bringing the Subaru away from the six foot high wall of snow which the plows had piled up just beyond the breakdown lane. With the vehicle under control she let it coast to a stop a quarter of a mile short of the intersection. Breathing a sigh of relief as well as frustration, she flipped on her hazard lights and stepped out into the fading light of the cold late afternoon.

* * * *

Slowly cruising east on Southwestern Boulevard, Gant planned to turn left at Abbott Road and head north, back toward home. He'd been out driving for fifteen minutes to clear his head. Detective Wilder would say he'd been out prowling the roads for victims.

In actuality Gant had been thinking he did some of his best thinking behind the wheel. He stayed home in Amherst for several months attempting to mend his fractured relationship with Bergstrom and it seemed as though things might work out for them. He was happy and feeling good about himself. He hadn't seriously thought about recruiting another donor during that time and felt that maybe he had done enough, maybe he was finished.

He wondered if his contribution to mankind was complete. He pondered that possibly it was time for a change, time to retire from his trade and settle down and live like everybody else.

Feeling he may have turned a corner in his life, Gant switched on his left turn signal and slowed the car to ten miles per hour before gliding onto Abbott Road. Banking left he immediately caught sight of the Subaru's flashing hazards in the failing light. Drifting to within a hundred and fifty feet of the Subaru, Gant saw a figure crouched along the right side of the jacked up vehicle.

Flat, he thought to himself. *It'll be dark soon. I better see if I can help.*

Gant veered over the yellow line, there was no oncoming traffic, and crept into the breakdown lane, the Volvo facing against traffic. He wasn't concerned about a ticket, any trooper would be happy he'd stopped to help. He rolled closer and came to a stop twenty feet before the immobilized Subaru before he saw the stranded driver was a woman. Her straight blonde hair in a pony tail, she wore a yellow cardigan sweater over a white turtle neck, and a knee length brown plaid skirt. Her legs were stockinged, and she wore brown leather flats. He cut the ignition.

She'll freeze to death, he thought. Gant threw his hazards on, pulled a red wool cap onto his head and slid a pair of black leather gloves on. Dusk was at hand, he leaned over to the glove compartment to retrieve a flashlight and then got out. The woman glanced up to take a peek at him only briefly before getting back to the job at hand.

Stepping up to the Subaru, Gant asked, "You're a little underdressed, don't you think?"

"I work so close to home I usually don't take much with me or dress right. It's a real short walk from the parking lot to the school." She didn't even look at him.

"May I help you?" he asked, shining the flashlight down onto the flattened tire.

Nicole Lutz peered up into Gant's face as he stared down at her. They took one another in for a moment before she replied, "Well, the light's great, but no that's all right, I've almost got the nuts off." Daddy's little girl was quite the tomboy growing up. She'd gone hunting and fishing with her father and uncles when she was only eleven, changing a tire was no big deal to her.

Gant was about to insist that he help when he stopped to admire her dexterity with the tire iron. Working on the second to last lug nut, she was spinning the iron effortlessly as if it were a cheerleader's baton. "Well, at least let me get the spare out for you, then."

"Thanks, that's very nice of you," she said matter-of-factly.

Gant walked to the trunk and freed the doughnut wheel from beneath the storage bed and carried it back up front. He rested the spare against the snow bank while she twisted away on the tire iron. She had three of the lug nuts off and was zipping through the last when she suddenly withdrew her hand.

"Ouch," Lutz uttered shaking her right hand in the air.

"Are you okay? What happened?" Gant asked.

"My hand slid off, I scraped my knuckles on a stud," she said.

She even knows the correct terminology, he thought thoroughly impressed.

He focused the beam of his flashlight on the woman's hand and saw the gouge across her knuckles, a thick rivulet of blood began to pool and run down toward her wrist. "That's enough for me, move over," he said, reaching for the tire iron.

Against her better judgement, she gave the iron up. "Thank you," she relented with a sigh. "I've changed many flats and that's never happened to me before."

Ever the gentleman, Gant offered, "Why don't you go wait in my car, you must be freezing. Besides it's dangerous out here. You never know when some drunk will swerve wide and really mess things up." He would have made the same offer to anyone as he really was the caring sort.

Lutz seemed reluctant to take Gant up on his generous offer. It was common sense never to get into a stranger's car. Still, it was so cold, she looked down and saw her nipples poking through her sweater. She crossed her arms over her breasts, doing her best not to drip blood on the sweater. The ghastly media coverage surrounding the Marilla findings of the previous summer flashed through her mind. "I'll stay out here, thanks."

"At least take my coat," Gant said removing his heavy winter parka.

"No, I couldn't."

"Please," he insisted, draping the coat over her shoulders. "I'll be fine, this won't take long."

"You're so kind," she said, her voice softening, now warmer more trusting.

"First though," he said, "let me get you something for your hand." Gant trotted back to his car and quickly returned with a roll of gauze and a roll of surgical tape.

"Look at us, total opposites. I've got nothing and you're prepared like a boy scout," she said.

"You've got to be. You never know what might happen."

The wound was largely superficial and, as the temperature was hovering just above freezing, the blood had ceased to flow and had nearly coagulated already. It didn't take Gant long to wrap and tape her hand. When he was done, he handed her the flashlight and went to work on the last lug nut.

"So, you're a teacher?," Gant asked as he slid the ruptured tire off of its studs.

"I am," Lutz replied. "I teach third grade."

"Do you like it?"

"I love it, most of the time. It's been getting more difficult though."

"Why's that?" he asked laying the flat on its side.

"Well you know, with the economy the way it is, there have been big budget cuts to education. They jam more kids into less classrooms, it really doesn't work so well. I guess I should just be happy that I have a job."

"So, you teach third graders. That must be fun, and you're close to home."

"I'm at Windom Elementary. It's right over on Sheldon Road. Do you know it?" That was enough.

"I've passed by it, sure," he replied sliding the spare onto the studs.

"What do you do, besides show up like a superhero?" she asked.

Attempting to be as vague as possible, Gant replied, "I'm a salesman." Quickly turning it back to her he asked, "So you live close by?"

"Yes, I do, just a couple of miles from here."

Gant hoped she would tell him what street she lived on, but she didn't. *Wise girl*, he thought to himself. He began to hand screw the first of the lug nuts back on when he probed, "You grew up around here, you have family?"

"No, I'm from Arlington. It's just outside of Poughkeepsie. So, what's your name?"

"Len," he said, twisting the third nut on.

"I'm Nicole, my friends just call me Nic."

"Nice to meet you, Nic. I'll be done here in just a few minutes," Gant replied, picking up the tire iron. He noticed she moved back a few steps when he reached for it.

"I'm so lucky you stopped, there are a lot of weirdos around."

"That's for sure," he replied while pumping the tire iron clockwise on the first nut. "You can never be too careful."

There was an uncomfortable lull in the conversation then. Gant felt as if the woman was sizing him up, like she intuited he was not at all what he seemed. Glancing out of the corner of his eye as he tightened the second nut, he noticed she clutched her cell phone in her right hand, no doubt it was on. She moved completely behind him as she made her call.

"Hey Jenny!" she said. "I wanted to let you know I'll be a little late, I got a flat tire."

She paused to listen.

"No, I'm fine. A really nice guy stopped and he's changing it for me."

She paused again.

"I'm on Abbott Road, north of Southwestern Boulevard."

Was she talking to somebody or just bluffing? Gant asked himself as he began to twirl the third nut tight.

"His name is Len, stop it," she laughed with embarrassment.

Another pause.

"A Volvo, yeah, it's black. No, don't bother coming out. He's almost done."

There was a long pause.

"I know. Don't worry. He's nice. I will. Bye."

The time had passed, probably.

After a moment's hesitation, she stepped back into Gant's periphery and said, "That was my friend Jenny. We're supposed to be meeting for happy hour and a burger at Webb's. I wanted to let her know I'd be a little late."

"I've never heard of it," Gant replied finishing with the third nut. Without pause, he began spinning on the last one.

"It's new. The burgers are great. I don't know about the rest of the food, though."

"I'll have to check it out some time."

"Why don't you join us? Happy hour is packed, it'll be fun. The least I could do is buy you a drink. I'm stopping at home first and then going right there, probably a half hour, forty-five minutes, tops."

Gant couldn't make her out. *Is she afraid of me or does she want me?* In his experience most women were attracted to him, they found him charming as well as handsome. He had almost expected to get a date out of this tire changing ordeal, but Lutz was difficult to pinpoint.

Despite her obviously bleached blonde hair, she was gorgeous. With a high forehead, beautifully rounded cheekbones, a slender Greek nose, full lips, and a triangular chin, she should have been a model. Before offering her his coat Gant had noticed the lithe, muscular legs beneath her stockings. He imagined her rear end was just as well shaped. He took note of her trim waist and firm breasts under the sweater. He didn't get a look at her arms, but knew in order to spin a tire iron the way she did, she had to work out regularly. She was striking to say the least, she could have most any man she wanted.

Why the hell is she teaching? he asked himself. *Must really love the kids.* Reigning in his hormones, he replied, "Thanks, but I've got to get home. My girlfriend's waiting."

"Oh, I'm sorry.".

There it is, she's interested, he thought. "Don't be."

"Well, thanks a bunch"

"No thanks needed. You would have done the same for someone else," Gant said yanking the tire iron for the last time.

"You're right, I would," she replied.

Gant lowered the jack, leaving the Forester to set on four tires once again. He hefted the flat tire into his arms and dumped it into the rear of the Forester and then returned for the jack and tire iron. The jack was there, but the iron had disappeared. He didn't question it. He placed the jack beside the blown out tire and pulled down the hatch. He turned to walk back to Lutz, when he heard the door shut, she was already inside. He walked purposely along the passenger side and knocked on the window. The window came down at once.

"Thank you so much. I really have to go. It was great to meet you," Lutz said starting the ignition.

"Can I have my flashlight?" he asked.

"Oh, I'm sorry," she replied, reaching over toward the passenger seat.

Gant looked at her exposed back, his eyes hardened. *I'm not prepared, no chloroform, I don't want a mess.* "I'll see you around," he said.

"I hope so," she offered.

"I'm sure," he replied.

As Lutz's Forester lurched off into the darkness, Gant committed her license plate to memory, BBG1156. He knew her car and where she worked—the rest was elementary. He would go online to get the school's time of dismissal and then give it another half an hour. He imagined her to be a most dedicated teacher.

* * * *

Before Gant was able to stalk the teacher, he needed to resolve a problematic ethical dilemma gnawing at the edge of his consciousness. He had been contemplating retirement from the organ business moments before turning on to Abbott Road and spotting Lutz. Yet, it seemed like destiny that this spectacular specimen seemingly fell right into his lap. Upon speaking with her those thoughts of retirement evaporated as if they'd never existed. His desires flooded back, he'd forgotten all about Lydia Bergstrom and a seemingly normal life. Nicole Lutz was the embodiment of health. There was no doubt she would be Gant's most beautiful disciple, his most magnificent specimen, a highly prized addition to the shrine. She would be his finest reward, her skin was smooth and supple, unblemished by alcohol or nicotine.

On the other hand, he felt a twinge of remorse at the consideration of her demise. It would surely be a serious offense to take someone so completely beautiful, so wholly fit and seemingly healthy, and in the prime of life. *Small sacrifices are acceptable if they serve the greater good.* Gant found himself wanting to get to know the woman, hopefully dating her. He quickly repulsed these primitive urges, knowing it could never be so. There was something in her eyes—cool deliberation, he recognized it as. She had stared him straight in the eyes when they had been face to face, it was something women rarely did with Gant, probably because of his different colored irises. Possibly it was because she couldn't really get a good look in the failing light. There was something about her demeanor too. She was friendly enough, but also sagely suspicious as if she knew he was something other than he appeared. She seemed eager to get away from him, which he naturally resented.

Maybe she's been attacked, or even raped. Or maybe she has that sense that some people have, she knows danger when it's near. Either way, Gant figured that a relationship was entirely out of the question.

Gant found himself at a crossroads, he either made a fresh start, pledging to never harvest again, or he continued on his current path. He felt that he would be happy either way. Gant stood on the precipice of forsaking his cherished hobby and surrendering his ideals for what he considered an ordinary pedestrian life. After a few minutes of deliberation, he selfishly decided to watch Lutz and see how things played out. There was no guarantee he would take her, there were times when he ended up not making a move on his targets.

Quite often, even after spending weeks or even months conducting surveillance, he decided against taking action. Circumstances and routines changed all the time. Sometimes targets suddenly moved away, or sometimes other people moved in with them causing changes in their ordinary activities. Everything was dynamic and subject to change. Even the weather and time of year could play important roles in his pursuit. The ever-changing nature of humanity is what most excited Gant, at heart he was a hunter.

* * * *

The following afternoon at three-fifty Gant's Econoline rolled to a stop on Lynn Drive which ran west of the parking lot beside the Windom Elementary School. As the students were dismissed at three-fifteen, he figured Lutz would stay at work until four o'clock. The widely spaced houses on Lynn Drive afforded him an unobstructed view of the parking lot which was less than two hundred yards away. Bringing his compact hunting binoculars, a pair of Steiner 12x40 Predator Pros, up to his face, he scanned the lot for the Forester and was happy to see that it was still there, one of only seven cars left in the lot. He confirmed the license plate and then turned off his engine to settle in to wait. A minute or so later an old lady wearing an old fur coat, with a matching fur hat and stole, opened the front door of the house directly to his left. She sat down on the porch with the newspaper and a mug of coffee.

Christ! It's freezing out here! What's wrong with her? Gant wondered aloud. As if hearing him, the old woman glanced at the van and dug into her jacket pocket to retrieve what Gant presumed to be her glasses. Keying the ignition he didn't wait around to find out. He quickly put the van in gear and headed for the far end of the street. He cursed himself for failing to remember that Lynn Drive was a dead end, he'd have to pass by the old biddy again. He gave it a few minutes hopeful she would get cold and return inside. As the Econoline passed by the house, the old woman was still on the porch, but to Gant's relief a copy of *The Buffalo Criterion* shielded her eyes from the street, he crept by unnoticed.

Gant pulled back on to Sheldon Road and noticed there were two contractor's vans parked on the south side of the road. He passed both vans and then looked for a space to park.

With most of the road's shoulder caked with snow, he squeezed the van in as tight as he could and came to a stop about a hundred and fifty yards beyond the vans, he had a clear view, there were no trees in front of the school. He was less than a hundred yards from the parking lot and when he held the binoculars to his eyes he found that Lutz' Forester was still there. There were no cars in the two driveways before or aft of him, he felt relatively comfortable staking out the school from there.

Carefully monitoring the front door, Gant was impressed with her work ethic as a man and two women left the building while he watched. Gant reasoned she must be one of two or three faculty members left inside. At least one of the cars had to belong to a custodian. It wasn't until four-twenty-five that Lutz burst through the door and marched toward her car.

Gant started the Econoline and waited for Lutz to pull out of the parking lot. As her Forester rolled out onto Sheldon Road heading east, he paused while a black '68 Chevy Camaro barreled past, and then eased out onto the road to follow her. He was comfortable having the muscle car between them, he had great experience tailing people and found that lying back and keeping some distance was advantageous, it allowed for cover at lights and stop signs.

As he made the right going south on Abbott Road, Gant was nonetheless surprised to see how far out in front Lutz had pulled. She was nearly at the intersection of Southwestern Boulevard already.

She's got to get home for something, hopefully a pet, he thought to himself as he stepped on the accelerator and the van lurched forward.

Lutz had picked up more cushion after she turned onto Abbott Road; an old, rusted out Ford F-150 lazily followed in the wake of the Camaro. Gant came to within thirty feet of the pickup before easing off the pedal. Far ahead of the pickup was the Camaro, it was burning up the road right behind the Forester. If she made the light and he got stuck behind the pickup he would have to call it a day and try again on Monday afternoon. The light at the intersection turned yellow as the Forester drew to within a hundred feet.

Ever responsible, Lutz pumped her breaks until she came to a stop, first in line. Gant smiled to himself as he pulled up three cars back. As Lutz, the two interlopers, and Gant passed over Southwestern Boulevard, Abbott Road took on the additional name of Jim Kelly Boulevard.

Travelling south on the local legend's road, the Forester and Camaro once again raced out in front, Gant patiently trailed after the pickup a third of a mile back. As the two frontrunner's raced by the west side of Ralph Wilson Stadium Gant felt her slipping away. He was resigned to calling it off when the pickup signaled right and turned onto Campus Drive heading toward the southern campus of Erie Community College.

With renewed vigor, Gant stomped down on the accelerator until he tailed the Camaro by no more than fifty feet. With the Forester in the lead the three cars motored south with the football stadium's parking lots on either side of them. Passing

Bills Drive, Abbott Road became just Abbott Road once more as the cars drove further south toward a more rural section of town.

Passing vast tracts of wooded, undeveloped land, about a mile later the Forester signaled left and headed east onto Elmtree Road, the Camaro continued racing south. Gant eased up on the gas and crept onto Elmtree Road some two hundred feet behind the Forester, he slowed to a crawl to let Lutz gain a little distance again. Tailing her from an eighth of a mile Gant recalled that all of the houses on the street's north side backed up onto a nature preserve. The backyards opened up onto a virtual forest stretching over a half a mile northward. Though he had no intention of using the woods behind the house the isolation comforted him. Less than fifteen seconds later, her break lights gleamed in the fleeting light of dusk as she turned into the driveway of a modest ranch house.

Lutz was quickly out of the car and running for the door. Gant slowly coasted by, glancing at her as she stepped up to the front door to unlock it. He then drove a few hundred feet further down the street before executing a three point turn and driving back toward what he presumed was Lutz's home.

What he saw on his second pass made his heart soar and the hair on the back of his neck stand up. Rushing right back outside was Lutz being dragged by a large Alaskan Husky. Gant was ecstatic, there were so many times when a stake out like this ended up a dead end, his time frittered away.

Ah, the routine that pets provide, it's perfect, he thought. He watched as the big dog led Lutz east, away from Abbott Road. He gave the van some gas and passed them by without a glance. In less than an hour he'd gotten what he wanted.

Driving home, Gant wondered why Lutz walked her dog on the street instead of the wooded preserve behind her house. She probably walked the preserve during the day, he thought. It must be too dark already at this time of year though, and much too dark at night, he concluded. Whatever the reason it could be advantageous to him that she walked on the street, it was less of a distance to carry her. He had to pick the right spot to intercept her, wait for darkness, and then hope the street was devoid of traffic of any kind. He had to be patient, but that was not a problem at all.

Gant knew Lutz would have to walk the dog again before bed and planned to return later that night.

He spoke to Bergstrom, she was in Detroit, and then had dinner, seared salmon, mushroom risotto, and asparagus. After dinner he read for awhile before getting ready for his return trip to Elmtree Road.

At ten-fifteen the Econoline was parked five houses west of Lutz's on the opposite side of the street in front of what appeared to be an abandoned house. Ten minutes later the big Husky padded down the front steps followed by the beautiful young teacher.

He reached across to the passenger seat and grabbed a pair of Bushnell night vision binoculars and raised them to his eyes. The infrared illuminators worked spectacularly, Gant had her in clear sight despite the meager light thrown off by the widely spaced arc sodium lights overhead. He watched Lutz and the dog march down the street for nearly five minutes when their silhouettes grew too small to follow.

He started the van and slowly crept east after them. When he came within a hundred yards he scanned for a house with no lights on and found one some two hundred feet behind Lutz who was still walking east.

Gant killed the engine and lights and settled back in with the binoculars. From his new location he could see there was a vast expanse of darkness toward the end of Elmtree Road. He'd not driven to the end of the street earlier in the evening, but now remembered there was a wide cut of undeveloped land, probably at least five hundred feet wide, on both sides of the street.

The green alley, as he thought of it, was thick with oaks, maples and sassafras trees. There was only a solitary street light in the dark corridor, it was a virtual black hole until houses sprouted up on its far side. Lutz and the dog walked right through the dark corridor and kept going into the dim light afforded by the homes. Gant looked at his watch, it was ten-thirty-five, Lutz had been walking the dog for ten minutes now.

He realized Huskies needed a great deal of exercise, but it was cold out, below freezing. He was impressed with Lutz's vigilance and obvious dedication to her dog. Again, pangs of guilt flooded his mind. He pushed them away, thinking of her adoring face within the shrine. By ten-forty Lutz reached Dorchester Road. She and the dog turned around and headed for home. Gant placed the binoculars on the passenger seat and started the van. Turning around long before Lutz got close enough to make out the shape of his van, he sped down the street toward Abbott Road and home.

* * * *

Gant spent the next six weeks monitoring the night time activities of Nicole Lutz. Ever wary, he had to make certain she lived alone and stuck to her routine. Gant visited Elmtree Road twice a week over the six week period which spanned Thanksgiving, Christmas, and the New Year. Though not religious himself, he'd never taken anyone over the holiday season, he considered it to be cold and heartless. Regardless of his personal feelings, the surveillance work was most important to conduct anyway. There was nothing worse than when, during the course of an abduction, an unwanted somebody showed up to spoil the plans.

Gant randomly chose different week nights, he never ventured there over the weekend when there were more cars on the road at all times. He drove the short distance to her home, spied on her for a half an hour or so, and was back home in Amherst all within an hour. Sleeping in Orchard Park when Bergstrom was gone cut his trip down to the degree that he could have walked or easily jogged the distance if he'd wanted. It was getting cold though, and he sought to avoid drawing any unwanted attention to himself. Gant snooped on her on random weeknights never appearing on Elmtree Road the same night, two weeks in a row. He alternately drove the Econoline and the Volvo in order to avoid anyone noticing a strange vehicle on the street. While Bergstrom was out of town working the Ohio Valley hospitals, clinics, and doctor's offices he used her car, a 2009 Chevy Volt. Bergstrom made a fine living selling pharmaceuticals, but she was green at heart, preferring to drive the little electric car rather than a sleek, shiny German import or a gas-guzzling SUV from Detroit.

Lutz stuck to the script perfectly. She was away on Christmas Eve, Christmas Day and the day after visiting her family in Arlington. She also spent the four day Thanksgiving holiday with her parents back home, down state. Gant wouldn't have known of her absence as he himself was with his mother on Long Island through the holidays. Lutz stayed home with her best friend Mush on New Year's Eve, she had the flu. After the month and a half of surveillance had turned up no surprises, Gant was satisfied his plan was sound, he was ready to execute.

* * * *

On a Thursday night in early January Nicole Lutz patiently waited for Mush to finish with his business before heading home. It was after ten-thirty, it was dark and cold, the temperature had dropped to twenty-one degrees and the wind began howling out of the east. Orchard Park had two feet of fresh snow on the ground from a storm that morning. The snow plows and salt spreaders had cleared the streets, it was routine winter living in western New York. Despite the timely clean up, the roads had a thin layer of ice on them, there were very few cars out. With no traffic on Elmtree Road, Lutz unleashed Mush, the Husky lumbered over the icy street and bounded over and around the drifts on either side of the road, he was truly in his element.

Gant gave himself additional time for travel because of the snow. Besides needing the van for his intended use, the Econoline was far heavier than the Volvo and therefore performed better in the snow. He followed a plow south on Abbott Road and then took the left onto Elmtree Road, it took him twice as long as usual, but he was within striking distance. Driving slowly down Elmtree Road Gant carefully maneuvered the van between two cars which had been parked on the street across from one another and were now snowed in.

He considered postponing the evening's plans, but couldn't bring himself to do so. Bergstrom was in Pittsburgh, but was expected home by Saturday night. If he didn't act now he would have to wait another month at least. He couldn't bear the thought. Anything could happen in a month. Lutz could move, acquire a live-in lover or get hit by a bus, the possibilities were endless. More importantly though, timing was everything to Gant. His organ deliveries had to coincide with legitimate business to be safe. Besides Bergstrom being out of town, he had actual business to attend to in Montreal on Saturday morning. Gant was scheduled to make a parts delivery to the Gaskill Corporation, it was his ticket to fly. With his flight manifest indicating his point of departure, flight path, destination, and purpose for flying, he was free to do as he wished. With the signature of a Gaskill representative as the purchaser of the parts, Gant's manifest was rock solid, he was conducting business as always. He would have the freedom to move around the city unencumbered, if necessary, to meet Monseaux. The pressure to take her now was overwhelming. He had to have her now and that meant seizing the moment.

With the swirling snow blinding his vision Gant killed his lights halfway down Elmtree Road. He drove the remaining quarter of a mile to the green alley, which now resembled a ski run between a gorge, at less than five miles per hour. He edged over to the side of the road and parked the van. With his night vision binoculars he was able to make out a lone figure at the end of the street, he hoped it was Lutz, but wondered where the dog was. He was sure whoever was at the end of the street could not hear his engine with the wind blowing at their backs, nonetheless he cut it and slid out from behind the wheel. Gant scurried to the other side of the street and took up position behind a mammoth snow drift. He peeked out from behind it to take a look at the figure at the end of the street.

Mush barked as Lutz playfully underhand tossed a snowball in his direction. He jumped up to catch it in his mouth, it broke into a cloud of fine powder. Lutz laughed and called the dog to her. Obediently he trotted toward her and sat down at her feet. She bent down to pet him, he laid down on the icy street and rolled over onto his back.

Gant heard the bark and the feminine laughter before he saw the dog appear next to the figure which he now knew to be Lutz. He breathed a deep sigh of relief, he would have hated to take the wrong person. He hadn't counted on the dog being off the leash, but this didn't bother him too much. He slipped the binoculars into one of the inside pockets of his heavy, black parka.

Lutz and her Husky continued their walk home, they were within fifty feet of Gant, in the very middle of the houseless green belt. The Husky had been walking in step with its master taking off now and again to ramble over a drift, but always coming back, a rarity for the half wild breed. At thirty feet she leashed the Husky and then walked on.

Gant watched the woman leash the big dog and relaxed. It would be that much easier with the dog leashed. At twenty feet Gant took off his leather gloves and slipped out from behind the corner of the drift to get a better angle. His right boot caught a ragged chunk of ice, he fell forward and while trying to right himself, slipped and went down backwards onto the ice. He smashed his elbow on the ice, it felt as if it were hit with a hammer. Still behind the drift, Gant did his best to stifle the cry of pain roaring up from his throat. He covered his mouth with his bare hand, but a little wince escaped.

The Husky's ears went up immediately. Downwind or not, the dog's keen hearing picked up Gant's muffled cry. Mush began to growl, Lutz pulled up and stopped twenty feet short of the drift concealing Gant. Lutz stood there in the dark for a few seconds peering into the black and white world before her, scanning it for anything threatening, while the dog growled. Had she walked straight on things may have worked out differently, the dog might have gotten to Gant before he had time to recover.

Gant needed five more feet, but was fairly certain that Lutz and the Husky weren't coming his way soon enough, he had to end this as quickly as possible before anyone happened by. It was time to show himself. Like a phantom, Gant appeared beside the drift, both hands shoved deep into either of his parka's pockets. Before Lutz could react he took three steps toward her, and that was all he needed. Striding toward the woman and the snarling dog, Gant withdrew his hands and began raising them up toward dog and master, Lutz instinctively let the Husky loose. Like a gun fighter in the Old West, Gant leveled the Taser C-2's, one at the dog, the other at Lutz. The Husky made it to within ten feet of Gant before he squeezed the trigger. Flashes of blue white light streaked through the dark air, the Husky momentarily went stiff and then collapsed in a pile of steaming fur. At near maximum range, Lutz threw out her arms and turned to run when Gant unloaded the other taser. The fierce bolts slammed into her right hip sending fifty thousand volts through her body. She stood rigid for a half a second before dropping.

Gant moved quickly. With zip ties he bound her hands behind her back and then secured her ankles together. He stuffed a clean, white shirt into her mouth and then hoisted her up onto his shoulder. He nudged the dog with the toe of his boot. The Husky looked dead, but it would be fine. Gant was confident it would come to on its own within a few minutes. If it took a while longer for it to rouse itself, its coat would protect it from the cold. Grimacing, Gant gingerly walked the thirty or so feet to the van. He held on to the incapacitated Lutz with one arm while he opened the rear cargo door with his free hand, his elbow was throbbing, he hoped he hadn't broken anything. With one great heave he hefted the groggy woman up over the bumper and into the rear of the van.

As it was a short trip home he didn't fuss with her comfort, she'd be in a state of semi-consciousness anyway. Gant slammed the doors shut and started the Econoline. Flipping on his lights he saw the Husky began to recover already, the dog was attempting to gain its feet. Gant was careful to avoid the dog as he made a U-turn. He then headed west on Elmtree Road toward home.

Chapter Twenty-Five

Martin Glick, a specialist in logistical analysis with the F.B.I, had already contacted the Federal Aviation Administration as well as U.S. Customs and Border Protection in regards to examining the flight manifests of small planes operating in the northeast. The good news was that both agencies informed Glick they would be happy to assist the F.B.I. in providing any manifests which were of interest. The bad news was according to the F.A.A. there were nearly six hundred thousand certified pilots actively operating within or from the United States. Glick sank back into his chair upon hearing this number.

Glick realized this was coming, therefore with his next inquiry he appealed to each agency for manpower to assist in the examinations. As expected both immediately dismissed the idea, they were short-staffed and overworked as it was. It sounded as if both agencies had been through this before and had collaborated to come up with a unified front of defense. He hung up the phone to make some quick calculations.

Conservatively, he assumed each pilot flew once a week, he knew for sure there were many who flew two to three times a week, and there were those who flew only once or twice a year. If every pilot were to fly once a week there would be over thirty-three million manifests to check. In reality it was probably more like double, or triple. "Impossible," Glick said aloud. "We'd have a better chance of finding the proverbial needle in a haystack." He felt defeated before he'd gotten started.

His next inquiry was to the National Transportation Safety Board. With such an overwhelmingly daunting task, he sought to involve the N.T.S.B. as well, hoping to garner some additional manpower. An N.T.S.B. official immediately declined any help explaining it was the N.T.S.B.'s duty to report on accidents only, not passenger or cargo lists. He said he was very sorry he couldn't help.

Glick immediately went back to the F.A.A. and asked them to tell him how many of the almost six hundred thousand pilots lived or operated near the greater Buffalo, New York area. He was patched through to a senior member on Independence Avenue.

"Agent Glick, my name is Martin Clark. I understand you've asked for some assistance in identifying an individual you think to be smuggling illegal goods. How can I help?"

"I'm looking for an individual who may be smuggling human organs."

"Okay, we've seen it before. It's rare, but not unheard of."

"I need to find someone, a man I imagine, who I believe operates out of the Buffalo area. Can you provide me with a list of pilots flying from the greater Buffalo area?"

"Well, that's a tough one. Pilots are transient creatures by nature, their work demands that they be. Buffalo sees hundreds of flights come in and go out every day."

"How many flights a day?"

"Give me a minute."

"Of course," Glick replied, listening as Clark tapped away at his keyboard nearly four hundred miles away.

"There are ten airports in the region. Buffalo Niagara International Airport averages one hundred and ten flights a day. Niagara Falls International averages eighty-five. Right there you have one hundred and ninety-five pilots on any given day, and that doesn't account for copilots and navigators. Many of these pilots fly in and out of airports all over the world pretty randomly. I'd feel safe saying if you were to begin looking into each pilot who works the Buffalo region you'd be looking for a very long time. If I had to put a number on it I'd say there are easily over a thousand, and that's very conservative."

"It's a start though," Glick replied.

"In the wrong direction I'd say."

"What do you mean?"

"The person you're after would never use a major airport, there's far too much security. We use X-ray machines for passengers and their luggage, we pat down many passengers, conduct shoe inspections, the whole nine yards. Another nine-eleven is not an option we're open to. The small airports, on the other hand, are very lax. Most often there are no gates to walk through, no luggage inspections and no real security at all. It's more like park your car and walk right on up to the plane. If there is someone doing what you think, the person would be working out of one of the small airports."

"How many small airports are there in the Buffalo area?"

"Hold on a second. Grab a pen, I'll give you a list."

"Ready whenever you are," Glick responded, tapping his pen on the desk.

"There are eight small airports in the region. They are Mesmer Airport, Flying F Airport, Evans Airways Airport, Smith Airport, Clarence Aerodrome Airport, Potoczak Airport, Taylor Johnson Airport, and Donnelly's Airport."

"How many flights for each of them?"

"One minute."

"Sure."

Two minutes later Clark replied, "We estimate between two-hundred and fifty and three hundred planes go in and out of those airports on a daily basis."

"Estimate? Don't you have an exact number?"

"No, we don't. The F.A.A. controls the major airports, the big planes can be, well, flying bombs, for a lack of better words. These small airports are often privately owned and as such are free to make their own ground rules, as it were."

"What about the flight manifests? Doesn't every flight get filed with you guys?"

"No, they don't. It's embarrassing to admit, but it's easier and more efficient to file privately," Clark replied dryly. "Technically speaking, every flight manifest should include the plane's point of departure, its destination and its flight plan. Passenger planes should include a passenger list which is closely guarded to protect the rights of those individuals. Cargo planes should include each parcel aboard the plane. A manifest can be completely legitimate, but it doesn't mean there are not persons or items which have been purposely omitted."

"Sounds as if the F.A.A. is being fazed out?"

"We are in the small arena. More and more of the small airfields are privatizing. Soon we'll oversee only the major airports."

"Is there a manifest database I could search?"

"You can search ours, but again, it's only inclusive of the major airports. I think that's a dead end," Martin replied and then added, "Oh, sorry."

"Don't be, I get that all the time," Glick said.

"The privatized airfields maintain their own databases," Clark said.

"Of course the private airports won't willingly give up their manifests."

"Not good for business, but I wouldn't even bother until you've narrowed this down a great deal. Then get a subpoena if necessary."

"So the F.A.A. really has no control over the manifests of the small airports, then."

"No, we don't. We never see the manifests from the private airports. There are simply too many of them to keep track of. Even with a massive database we'd need multitudes in manpower to monitor it. The cost in salaries would be enormous. The public would never stand for it, taxes would go further through the roof."

"So planes from these small airports can fly wherever they want as long as their manifests dictate it?"

"As far as their little gas tanks will take them."

"Across borders?"

"Land borders are easy as long as the countries are on friendly terms. Traveling over international waters is a bit more tricky, but not all that difficult to do. It's really only a matter of the applicable paperwork."

"I would never have thought, in this day and age, in this political climate, that pilots would enjoy so much freedom," Glick said.

"The sky's the limit, so they say," Clark responded.

"How about plane inspections before and after take off. I'm assuming Customs and Border Protection handles that."

"C.B.P. handles that and a lot more. They secure the borders by preventing the illegal entry of goods and people. They regulate and facilitate international trade, collect import duties, enforce U.S. regulations, including trade, customs and immigration. C.B.P. has over forty thousand officers and agents."

"So are their officers stationed at every airport?"

"Sorry to sound like a broken record, but again, only at the major airports. It's the money problem as always. There are too many small airports to staff with F.A.A. or C.B.P personnel, it's not possible. When the C.B.P. agents show up at small airports it's normally for a random spot check, it's hardly routine. Unless they're acting on a tip, they visit the small airports once a year, twice at most."

"When they do come, what are the inspections like?"

"Pretty low key unless prior suspicion is in play. A cursory search of a small plane can be done in minutes."

"That's because they do every plane?"

"No, the searches are quite random. I'd say one in five gets searched. It's because the officers have to get to another airport later that day."

"The C.B.P. has canine units I take it?" Glick asked.

"Sure, but those dogs are trained to sniff out drugs and other illegal substances, explosives and the like. You would need cadaver dogs, and they don't use them. So, your would be smuggler is a most curious case indeed."

"How about the Canadians? Are they more stringent up there?"

"They're the opposite. Canada Border Services Agency is loose by the standards of our C.B.P. They have one-third of the agents we employ. They are responsible for border enforcement, immigration and customs services. Let's face it, they haven't had a nine-eleven. The Canadians consider it to be an American problem. Their security measures have changed little in the past ten years.

"It seems that pilots, actually people in general, have too much freedom in the sky. Why doesn't our government compel the small airports to consolidate and conform to F.A.A. standards?"

"It would destroy small business which this country needs. Small businesses are the backbone of the nation. Besides, it works fairly well with a few strange exceptions, like the one you think you have. We make small sacrifices for the greater good every day, don't we?"

"I suppose so," Glick replied.

Clark remained silent to let Glick compose his thoughts for a moment.

"Could you cross reference the flight manifests for the Buffalo region with the pilot registry focusing on males between the ages of eighteen and fifty? That would pare down the possibilities a good bit."

Clark smiled at that. "I think the vast majority of pilots are men between those ages."

"I suppose you're right."

"I've got a better idea, I thought about it earlier, but was hoping we would come up with something else," Clark replied.

"I'm all ears."

"According to the FAA, every airplane is required to undergo an annual inspection. Federal law dictates no person may operate an aircraft unless, within the preceding twelve calendar months, it has had an annual inspection and has been approved for return to service by an authorized inspector."

"The F.A.A. does the inspections?"

"About half of them," Clark replied.

"Let me guess, the ones on the big planes," Glick said hollowly.

"Of course, but it doesn't matter, we have all the inspections on file. Private or not, every plane has to be inspected and we receive the reports."

"Obviously the owner's identity appears on the report, right?"

"Absolutely."

"That's a home run. Why'd you hold out?"

"It's not that simple really, it'd be nice if it was. Beside the fact that many planes are owned by corporations, many more are used as rentals. Corporations can have many different individuals tied to a single plane. If a plane is rented the situation is far more complex. It's like renting a car, the list of renters can be long and storied," Clark explained.

"How many people rent airplanes?"

"Over two-thirds of the pilots flying in this country rent planes."

"That's got to be a hell of a lot of money."

"On the contrary, it's cheap, that's why it's so popular. In some places, pilots can rent a single-engine airplane for twenty-five dollars an hour. Plane rental is so easy and inexpensive, less than a third of the active pilots actually purchase their own planes. Think of it this way. Last summer I spent over eight hundred dollars for four tickets to the Paul McCartney concert, me and my wife and kids love him. The show lasted a little under three hours and it was a great show, I'd do it again. For about a hundred and fifty though, we can rent a four-seat aircraft and soar through the air until the kids get bored. Also, you pay only for the time you're actually in the air. If you have a three hour flight to drop your son off at college and decide to spend the night there and return the following day you pay for six hours of air time, the total trip time there and back."

"I'm confused, are we back to square one now?" Glick asked.

"Not exactly. What I can do is search the inspection database for small planes in the Buffalo region which are registered to individual owner/operators. You can look through them and see if you like anyone. This is problematic because it cuts out two-thirds of the pilots that you may want to look at, but the alternative is impossible unless your agency decides to dedicate much more manpower to this."

"I guess that's where we'll have to start until I can pick up some help."

"If you burn through the owner/operators with no luck then you should look at the corporations. The rentals will be a real headache, but your guy may very well be there."

"When can you have the inspection registry of owner/operators sent to me?"

"I'll email it to you within half an hour, how's that?"

"That's great, I really appreciate your help," Glick said.

"Not a problem. If you need anything else my direct line will be in the email."

"Thanks."

"Good luck with this. I hope you get your man."

"Me too, take care," Glick replied ending the call.

As promised, the email came in twenty-five minutes later. Clark had sent a list of four hundred and eighty-seven men who flew their own planes, and were registered as having inspections within the Buffalo region.

Glick divided the list as evenly as possible and gave four of his subordinates the task of checking each man's social security number to find his date of birth.

Early that evening, after all of the men outside of the eighteen to fifty age group were excluded, the list of names was down to four hundred and twelve, still a big number with no guarantee of success. Feeling as though he were driving down a dead end, he picked up the phone and punched in Dan Wilder's cell phone number.

Chapter Twenty-Six

Phillip Gant turned thirty-four when he walked into Mercy Hospital prepared to donate a kidney. After being dropped off by a car service Gant sat in the pre-surgical waiting room in one of western New York's largest hospitals, he was told he would be admitted as soon as possible, his tests checked out and the recipient was quite grateful for his donation. Wherever he looked he saw members of the scrub attired staff staring at him. It wasn't often that someone donated an organ to a complete stranger after all, he was a bit of a novelty. He found his copy of *The Hellfire Club* by Peter Straub at the bottom of his carry on bag and began reading about halfway through.

Ten minutes later an admitting nurse sat down rather close to him and almost whispered, "You know you could make a lot of money off of your kidney."

Gant coolly turned his eyes toward the woman not wanting to appear affected. He'd been waiting for this opportunity for what seemed like a very long time to him, but had no viable contacts to make it happen. Surprised and relieved at once, he sat with one leg over the other, book in hand.

"What do you mean," he asked, knowing full well what the nurse was offering.

"You're giving up a kidney for nothing, you're a damn fool. You could be making big bucks."

"How?" he asked.

"Sell it. I could get you ten grand for it today."

Gant laughed and turned away from the nurse bringing the book back up toward his eyes.

"I'm not kidding. I've given you your chance, I'll deny anything you say, ever." She rose from her chair and stormed toward the doors leading into the surgical suites.

It was another forty-five minutes before Gant saw the nurse again. This time she approached him and in a business-like tone said, "Mister Heydrich, we're ready for you now."

"Oh, thank you," he replied getting up from his chair.

The nurse, a middle aged white woman with a plump bottom and bony legs, escorted Gant through a long hallway toward a prep room in which he would be put on a gurney, anesthetized and then shaved prior to the procedure. He realized this was his last chance with her. Momentarily they would be surrounded by a team of surgical staff. Midway through the hallway he reached out and gently tugged on the left elbow of her scrub top. She stopped and turned toward him, scrutinizing him with wonder.

"About before, I didn't know if you were serious," he said.

"I don't know what you're talking about, sir," she replied.

"Yes you do."

"It's too late to pull out now, don't you think?" she asked him. "Your recipient is being prepped too."

"For the future, I'm saying," he replied.

"You'll be spent after this, nothing more to give."

"Not me, I'm going through with this, but I know others," he responded pressing a wad of cash into her hand.

She looked at the roll of crisp bills. "Do you know this person you're donating your kidney to."

"I'm told she's sixteen, diabetic and the dialysis isn't working any more."

"That's all?"

"Her name is Jennifer Mott, that's all."

The nurse eyed him suspiciously. "I'll check your story and get back to you after the procedure," she said pocketing the cash.

"Good enough, that's all I can ask for."

* * * *

When Gant came to after the operation, he was one kidney light but optimistic of mind. It didn't take long for the pre-op nurse to visit. He was still groggy when she walked into his room. It was dim inside; the room lights were off and dark clouds sailed across the mid-morning autumn sky.

"I talked to my friend," she whispered low beside his bed. "He says he'd like to speak with you. He was impressed with your story, he'd like to see if you really have anything to offer."

It took most of Gant's strength to concentrate on the nurse's face. She wavered in and out of focus as if he were dreaming. She appeared to be speaking from very far away.

"I do," he mumbled.

"I believe you do," she responded squeezing his hand. "You rest up now. You'll see me again before you're released."

* * * *

The following morning, Gant sat in a chair in the corner of his room fully dressed waiting to be released. He watched the maple and oak leafs floating down through the air as the wind gusted outside. With a cup of orange juice in his hand, he felt remarkably good. Beside the dull ache in his right flank, Gant felt better than he'd anticipated, the prescribed hydrocodone eased the sharp pain from beneath. He had rehearsed what he would say to the nurse at least a dozen times if she were to pay him a visit. Expecting to be released at any time he had almost given up hope when she walked into his room.

"How are you feeling Mister Heydrich?" the nurse asked stepping up toward the bed.

Gant sat there, his legs swinging back and forth to an internal beat only he could hear. "I've felt better, but much worse, thanks."

"I wanted to stop in to say good-bye," she said, palming a small piece of paper, no larger than a post-it note, into his right hand. She squeezed his hand shut around the note and then stepped back.

"That's very nice of you," he responded, folding the paper. He then tucked it into the pocket of his jeans.

"Good luck," she said as she went for the door. He never saw her again.

* * * *

It was a week later that Gant dialed the number on the sheet of paper, it was a five one four area code, he recognized it as being from Canada. He waited and after three rings a female robotic voice invited him to leave a message if he wished. He did so, leaving his home, work and cell numbers. He hung up hoping to hear back.

Three days went by before Gant's cell phone chimed Aaron Copland's *Fanfare for the Common Man* and his caller identification showed a number of Canadian origin.

"Hello," Gant answered the phone.

"Mister Heydrich?" came a stiff, French accented voice.

"Yes."

"I'm told you wish to speak to me."

"Who am I speaking to?" Gant asked.

"My name is Mont Blanc, but that is unimportant."

"Okay."

"Your passport is in order?"

"It is."

"Good. If you are serious, you will meet me at Fouquet's, in Montreal, at seven tomorrow evening."

"I'll be there," Gant replied not having the slightest idea where he was going.

"Bring references."

"I will," he replied having none.

"I will be seated at the bar alone reading *La Voix Populaire*. Pin-striped suit, green tie, I will be drinking scotch, neat."

"I'll find you, I'm sure."

"*Bon jour*," the man said.

"*Et vous*," Gant replied.

The line went dead. Mont Blanc's articulation was not what Gant had imagined an organ dealer would speak like. He had expected to be speaking to someone a little rough around the edges, but the man on the phone seemed cultured, almost regal. He shrugged and clicked the phone off.

Gant had researched the black market organ trade extensively and had an educated idea about the worth of organs, nonetheless he spent the next few hours online surfing the net to confirm his assumptions, watching to see if there was a recent flux in the worldwide supply and demand. Through dark, clandestine blogs he navigated, taking mental notes as he went. Before he turned in for the night he had a good idea about how he would proceed with Mont Blanc, or whatever his real name was. The following afternoon he would dispatch and harvest the young man down in the basement and then fly to Montreal.

* * * *

Touching down at Montreal's Dorval International Airport at five the following evening, Gant felt confident in his ability to strike a working relationship. After splashing some water onto his face, and changing from jeans into a charcoal gray Dolce & Gabbana suit, he was ready. Black bag in hand, he took a taxi from the airport downtown toward the restaurant. Within fifteen minutes he found himself stepping out of the cab on Rue de la Montagne, it was just before six. With an hour to kill he entered Fouquet's and walked to the back of the bar where he found an empty stool. He placed his bag atop the bar, ordered a coffee and settled in to watch the door.

Half an hour and another cup of coffee later, Mont Blanc, or a man fitting his description, strode through the door alone as he had said he would. In a finely tailored pin-striped suit, the man was tall and broad, but not fat. In his late fifties, he looked very much like Robert Goulet, the pencil thin mustache and all. Gant's eyes followed the man to the bar where he sat at the stool closest to the front door. Gant watched the exchange between the man and the bartender and when the bartender poured a rock glass of Glenfiddich he knew he was the one. Gant waited for Mont Blanc to open his newspaper, his elegant white hands wrapped around the edges, before walking over to him.

"Mister Mont Blanc. My name is Carl Heydrich," Gant said, offering his hand.

Mont Blanc appraised him with cool indifferent eyes before taking his hand and giving it a brief, powerful shake. A waft of Hermes cologne drifted off of him.

"Thank you for meeting with me," Gant said.

"If you're willing to give a nurse a thousand dollars on trust, you must have something to offer," Mont Blanc replied.

"I do, I do."

"Well then, let's get to a table then," Mont Blanc replied, snapping his fingers for the maitre d'. "I'll take that table early, Claude."

"Very well, sir. Right this way," the maitre d' replied.

Mont Blanc rose from the bar stool and followed the maitre d' to the table in the far corner of the restaurant. It was an alcove, isolated from the rest of the dining room, there was not another table within earshot of it as long as the baroque music continued to drift down from the ceiling mounted speakers. Gant followed a few feet behind.

Mont Blanc stopped short of the table and wheeled around, he was face to face with Gant. Shielded from view by the alcove he instructed, "Hold your arms away from your body, Mister Heydrich."

Gant did as he was told. Mont Blanc ran his hands over Gant's torso, his arms, legs and crotch, searching for a surveillance device. Gant found the man's seemingly elegant hands to be iron taut, most capable. It caused Gant to view the man in an entirely different light. Behind the air of cultured civility, the man was a thug, or at least had been at one time and still maintained the instincts and wherewithal to revert to once again if need be.

Finding nothing he said, "Sorry, Mister Heydrich, I've got to be careful. Wires are bad for business." Mont Blanc took a seat, his back to the wall.

Gant rested his bag on the chair beside Mont Blanc and sat down opposite of him.

The maitre d' left menus and shuffled back toward the front of the restaurant.

After perusing the menu for a minute, Mont Blanc snapped his shut and stared at Gant. "If you like fish, I'd suggest the merlan colbert, it's always very fresh."

"I'm in the mood for beef, what would you recommend?" Gant asked.

"The filet is wonderful paired with the a good Bordeaux. Let's do that. Phillipe!" Mont Blanc shouted.

Gant's eyes widened at the call of his name, French pronunciation or not.

Attempting to recover he rubbed his eyes feigning fatigue. Mont Blanc picked up on it, but made no comment for the moment.

"Phillipe, the waiter, appeared table side out of nowhere. "Phillipe, we'll both be having the filet, rare, right Mister Heydrich," he said lifting his head in Gant's direction.

"Rare, of course, it's the only way to have beef," Gant offered.

"Open a bottle of the 2004 Chateau Pichon-Longueville and bring it to me."

"Very well," the waiter said gathering up the menus. He turned and scurried off toward the bar.

"So, Mister...Heydrich?" Mont Blanc began with an obvious air of distrust. "Am I to believe that is your real name?"

"Names are not important as you yourself earlier said, deals are. Besides, am I to believe your real name is Mont Blanc?"

"Indeed. At least we both know what we're dealing with going in, right?"

"Indeed."

"So, you met up with my Millie in Buffalo and she steered you to me, yes?"

"That's the way it went."

"Millicent's a good woman, solid recruiter, she's never sent me anyone I couldn't use."

Gants eyebrows furrowed at the term "use", thinking he was well above being used.

"How do I know you're not with a branch of your strong-armed country's law enforcement agencies?"

"You really have to trust me. You have to ask yourself, why would I come up here to another country to chase down a man like you, it's a long way, I'd have no jurisdiction whatsoever."

"Stranger things have happened, I've seen them."

"I don't doubt that for a second," Gant replied as the wine was poured. "What would be in it for me, I mean really?"

After the waiter left, Mont Blanc said, "Millie said that you seemed most eager to make a contact. Can I assume you've never done this before?"

"You are correct, I've never worked in the field before."

"I told you to bring references. You have no references?"

"I have something better than a silly piece of paper with a name on it."

"What would that be Mister Heydrich, your word, I suppose?"

Gant picked the black bag up off of the chair between them and carefully laid it on the middle of the table. He pushed it over the table until it rested directly before Mont Blanc. He said, "Open the bag, have a look inside."

After a brief hesitation Mont Blanc seized the bag, it was cold in his manicured hands. He unzipped the bag, a cooler bag he now knew, wisps of smoky vapor drifted up from within. He looked at Gant, his eyes cold, but still somehow smiling. He pushed aside the package of dry ice and gazed at the healthy reddish brown liver inside. "This is most unexpected at the dinner table Mister Heydrich."

"There are two kidneys, a heart, a set of lungs, a pancreas and a pair of eyes in there as well. I'm sorry if I offended you, but I had to make sure you know I mean business."

"Apparently so," Mont Blanc replied, zipping the bag shut and placing it back on the chair.

"You don't want it?" Gant asked, clearly puzzled.

"We haven't yet agreed upon terms and prices."

"That is free. Consider it a gift from me, a gesture of good faith."

"That's most generous of you Mister Heydrich. Thank you, thank you very much."

"From here on out though, we have to come to agreeable terms."

"Of course, one minute," Mont Blanc said retrieving a cell phone from his interior jacket pocket. He punched a single button sending a call to a saved contact. The call was answered at the other end almost immediately. "Come to Fouquet's, right now. Call Osborne on your way and tell him you have a full load, he should contact buyers and have them ready to go. He should call in Collins and Dimancescu to assist. Tell him to get prepped and have the buyers, with cash in hand, in his office within the hour." He ended the call and placed the phone back into his jacket pocket. "Those are not getting any fresher, they must be used now or perhaps never," he said to Gant while pointing at the black bag.

Gant nodded his agreement.

Neither man took a sip of his wine as their entrees were set down before them. Mont Blanc dropped his head over the plate of beef, pearl onions, steamed spinach and garlic mashed potatoes and took a deep breath inhaling the tantalizing commingled aromas. He picked up his glass of Bordeaux by the stem and held it up to the dim light afforded by the alcove's small chandelier. He brought the glass to his nose and again breathed from within. He exhaled with pure satisfaction. He lowered the glass, swirled the ruby wine around a few times and then tilted the glass back to his lips. Placing the glass back on the table he rolled the wine over his tongue before swallowing. "That is fantastic! Do you enjoy wine, Mister Heydrich?"

Gant took a sip of his wine, making no great show of it. "I do, very much, in fact. I actually make my own," he responded.

Mont Blanc's eyebrows rose, "You make your own? You own a vineyard?"

"No, it's for personal consumption. There are a few vines in my back yard, I harvest the grapes in late September, sometimes early October depending on the weather."

Mont Blanc thoughtfully chewed a slice of beef and swallowed it before asking, "Red or white?"

"It's red," Gant responded taking a forkful of mashed potatoes.

"What kind of grapes do you grow? Are they cultured?"

"The vines grow wild, I'm not sure what type of grapes they are. They might be Concord."

Mont Blanc cringed. "More suitable for jelly I'd think. Is it any good?"

Gant laughed a bit at that. It was the first light-hearted moment of the encounter. "I think so, but I'm probably biased. It's certainly very different from this, this is spectacular, perfect with the beef."

"Thank you," Mont Blanc replied as if he had vinted the wine himself. "So, you make wine using wild grapes…"

"Often I don't get enough juice from my grapes so I supplement it with raw juice I order."

"What type of juice do you purchase?"

"Merlot or cabernet, sometimes both."

"Ah, so you combine three juices to make a meritage," Mont Blanc rightly assumed.

"Exactly, and it's actually fairly palatable," Gant said, savoring a particularly tender piece of meat.

"How many bottles do you get?"

"About thirty," Gant replied.

"That's' not a bad number, perhaps I'll get a chance to try it some time."

"If we end up doing business together I'll bring a couple of bottles with me next time."

"That would be nice. Do you have a name for your wine?'

"I call it R.I.P. Reserve," Gant said with a hint of pride.

"As in Rest in Peace," Mont Blanc said taking a sip of his wine.

"Yes."

"A bit preoccupied with death, Mister Heydrich?"

"It's inevitable, it's all around us."

As Mont Blanc was about to add his thoughts on the subject of death, a large man entered the alcove and stood beside the table. Looking up at him from his seated position Gant estimated the man to be at least six foot five and well over two hundred and eighty pounds, he seemed to engulf the little eating area. The big man looked from Gant to Mont Blanc and awaited instruction.

"Ah, Jerome. Take this," Mont Blanc said handing Gant's black bag to the giant, "and get it to Osborne immediately. He should have the rest taken care of. Be sure to get paid up front for all of it or the deals are off, understand? The prices are current if Osborne has any reservations. Good?"

"Yes," was all the big man said, and then he was gone.

"Jerome's one of my trusted workers. He's strong as an ox and actually a good bit smarter than he looks."

The wine conversation abandoned, Mont Blanc focused on business as it was a business dinner the two men were sharing. "Let's talk terms and agreements then. What can you do for me?"

"Quite a bit, I think. I'm aware of what the going rates are and am willing to accept the going rates initially," Gant said.

"That's very big of you considering you're unproven," Mont Blanc scoffed.

Gant lowered his voice to a whisper. "I can supply you with all of the materials you need to conduct your business. I'll provide you with the full complement that can be harvested, kidneys, eyes, heart, pancreas, liver and lungs, you get it all for one hundred and fifty thousand dollars cash upon delivery."

Mont Blanc mentally calculated Gant's request, comparing it with his own bottom line, he stood to profit upward of four hundred thousand dollars if this arrangement were agreed to, it was more than satisfactory. Still, he replied, "That's very steep for a first time supplier. I can't agree to that, I don't know how reliable you are, how fresh the delivery will be. You have to prove yourself."

"You saw that liver, it's been outside of its previous owner for two hours. The same is true for the rest of the bag's contents. I know what that's worth on the open market. What I'm offering you is more than fair and you know it."

Mont Blanc was hesitant, "It sounds appealing, I must be honest, but I need guarantees of quality."

"I assure you that my donors are young, fit, non-smokers, no drugs, very little alcohol. I screen them myself."

Mont Blanc nodded his acknowledgement.

"What I'm telling you is I can provide you with a steady supply. Once we've been doing business for a while you'll see how generous my offer is."

Mont Blanc rested his knife and fork upon the near empty plate and asked, "How often are we talking about?"

"Twice a year at the least, probably more often though, it's the only variable. Otherwise everything is set in stone."

"You would give me advanced notice?"

"I will provide you with three day's notice. The products will be less than two hours outside, well refrigerated and carefully transported. I'll know the blood types and provide any relevant donor information. All you have to do is match the recipients, have them paid for, prepped, and have the doctors ready to go. If we do this right these organs could be outside of a body for no longer than three hours. It's genius."

Intrigued, Mont Blanc agreed, the logistics were the best he'd ever heard. "Where will we meet?"

"To save time, we'll meet at the small carrier area at Dorval, there's practically no security in place. It's almost too easy."

"At one hundred and fifty thousand?" Mont Blanc verified the number.

"U.S.," Gant stipulated.

Mont Blanc nodded agreement.

"We work this way for a year and then renegotiate. I think you know you're getting a hell of a deal. Add in today's gift and you should be smiling."

Mont Blanc was smiling, but then said, "I don't want to know where you get them. In the event I'm called in to testify, the less I know, the better."

"Of course. So do we have a deal?" Gant asked.

"We have a deal," Mont Blanc said, reaching across the table to offer his hand to Gant. Gant seized the organ trafficker's hand and marveled at his hard, vise-like grip.

"A toast then," Gant said. "To saving many lives together."

"While making lots of money in the process," Mont Blanc added winking his right eye.

"To that too," Gant responded clinking his glass against Mont Blanc's.

Mont Blanc took a hearty gulp of wine which surprised Gant, the man had delicately sipped it up until this point. In a celebratory mood he ordered another bottle. Gant had only a single glass from the second bottle as he would be flying back to Buffalo shortly. The two parted ways with the understanding that Gant would contact Mont Blanc as soon as he recruited enough donors to make the trip monetarily viable.

* * * *

For the next year Gant worked in concert with Mont Blanc as agreed upon, he'd made three deliveries in that time, all of which were quite satisfactory to Mont Blanc as well as being financial boons. At the beginning of their second year together Gant renegotiated their agreement to pay him an additional twenty-five thousand dollars for each delivery with the understanding that the contract would be restructured each year.

Two deliveries into his second year, Mont Blanc introduced Gant to Luc Monseaux, his silent partner, who Gant would later find out to be a French diplomat living in Montreal. Monseaux was in his early forties then, but looked a good deal younger. Gant couldn't help but feel the younger Monseaux was biding his time, waiting for Mont Blanc to retire and hand the reigns of their criminal enterprise over to him. There was something in the man's eyes which Gant recognized at once as avarice and deceit.

Later that year, as luck would have it for Monseaux at any rate, Mont Blanc died in an auto accident. Officially, it was thought that Mont Blanc's driver, Edouard Fils-Aime, a Haitian immigrant, had been drunk when he crashed the Mercedes-Benz E Three-Fifty into the side of a gas truck at five o'clock on a Sunday morning. The gas truck was parked in the middle of a side street which Mont Blanc favored when returning home. The truck was empty, no driver was ever found. The car was torched, most of it had disintegrated in the blast, what was left was largely melted and misshapen steel. The bodies of both Mont Blanc and Fils-Aime were charred beyond recognition, an autopsy on the driver found nothing indicative of alcohol consumption. Gant was certain Monseaux had something to do with Mont Blanc's death, but would never say anything about it. Perhaps Monseaux sensed Gant's suspicions as he offered him an additional twenty thousand dollars for each of his continued deliveries. Gant agreed and the two men worked together for the next eleven years.

Chapter Twenty-Seven

The list was daunting to put it mildly, four hundred and twelve people of interest, Wilder had never heard of anything so ludicrous. Nonetheless, at two o'clock on Friday afternoon, he'd assured Agent Glick, he and Hamilton would assist in any way they could, they had no other real leads anyway. The list of suspects was divided alphabetically between Glick and the four agents assigned to him as well as Wilder and Hamilton. As most surnames begin with letters toward the beginning of the alphabet, it was front loaded. As the last to receive a copy of the list, the two Buffalo cops pulled the names beginning S through Z. There were the names, addresses, and phone numbers of over a hundred subjects to look at.

"Wow, the S's, T's, and W's make up over seventy percent of these names," Hamilton stated, holding the emailed printout up to her eyes.

"They're all men," Wilder stated.

"I guess the Feds have ruled out a woman."

"Fantastic detective work they do," Wilder replied. "Do you want to begin with the U, V, X, Y, and Z's so we can at least think we're making some sort of headway?" he asked half joking.

"Nah, let's start at the beginning. It's gonna suck either way."

"This isn't why you became a cop and then a detective, Marguerite? I thought you liked a challenge," he said facetiously.

"Put a sock in it, Dan. I'm not in the mood."

"You've got more problems with your cousin's overactive imagination?"

"I sure do. Now she thinks her boyfriend is cheating on her, she wants me to visit and snoop around a bit. She's nuts, I tell you. I'm supposed to go see her tonight if I ever get out of here. Some of the things she says scare me."

"Sounds like it's safer to be hunting for our guy than visiting your cousin," Wilder mused.

"Whatever, let's get this started. You take the s's and I'll take the T's, they're about even."

"Fine with me," Wilder said, kicking back in his chair to examine the list in his hand. He began by reading the names aloud, "Sacca, Santini, Santos, Sapp, Scarsdale, Schadt, Schenk, Schmid, Schmidt, Schubert, Sensabaugh..."

"Please, Dan, keep it to yourself. I've got a booming headache, and I'm having a hard enough time concentrating."

"Right, sorry, I'll shut up," he responded, his eyes falling back to the paper.

Counting down the list of 's' men Wilder found he had thirty-three individuals to look at. He started with background checks looking for prior records, particularly violent offenses. He sat down at his computer, resting his coffee beside the mouse. For an older officer Wilder was fairly computer savvy. He began his search by accessing the National Data Exchange, known in law enforcement circles as N-DEx.

It was a tremendous database which allowed federal, state and local law enforcement officials in the United States, access to vast volumes of records within the U.S. Justice Department system. It provided millions of criminal investigative records from thousands of law enforcement agencies stored in data warehouses, giving investigators and analysts a powerful weapon to counteract crime.

The database permitted two hundred thousand state and local investigators and federal counter-terrorism investigators to search millions of police reports in over fifteen thousand state and local agencies, with just a few mouse clicks. A one-stop shop for criminal justice information, the mega database brought together data from law enforcement agencies throughout the United States, including incident and case reports, booking and incarceration data, and parole and probation information. N-DEx recognized relationships between people, vehicles, properties, locations, and crime characteristics. It effectively linked data that was seemingly unrelated. It supported multi-jurisdictional task forces, improved national information sharing, linked regional and state systems, and streamlined regional information sharing.

Within minutes, he had made it through the list finding only three violent offenders, Juan Santos, Leonard Schenk, and Aldon Stanhope. Wilder's eyebrows rose at finally having a few men he considered to be people of interest. He drained his coffee and began to read each man's file.

According to the police reports, Juan Santos had been arrested in Florida numerous times for domestic abuse. *He's worth a look*, Wilder thought to himself. Reading the man's file a bit further he learned that Santos had moved to the Buffalo area three years ago to make a fresh start. Santos turned out to be a dead end though, he was doing five years in Sing Sing for narcotics trafficking and assaulting a police officer.

Leonard Schenk was arrested for spousal abuse in a Queens, New York suburb in late 1989, there was a temporary restraining order put in place, but the charges were later dropped. *Sounds good so far.* He was sixty-two at the time of the incident. *Ah, shit, not again.* Besides that incident Schenk had no criminal history. Wilder looked closely at Schenk's mug shot. He wore coke bottle glasses, his hair was gone and his face was gaunt and splotched with liver spots. According to the file the man would be eighty-three years old now. *Forget that one.*

Aldon Stanhope was a blue blood banker with a short fuse. He was arrested in 1998 for felony assault. While tailgating at a New York Jet's game he had been harassing women when a good Samaritan stepped in to stop his aggressive actions. Stanhope waited for the good Samaritan to turn away before hitting him from behind with a full bottle of beer. Stanhope then kicked the man unconscious. He retained a high priced lawyer and plead guilty to battery. He received three hundred hours of community service.

"Hey, I've got one guy to look at," Wilder stated more to himself than to Hamilton.

"That's one more than me," she said. "I'm through the T's with not a single subject I'd seriously consider questioning. What's up with your guy?"

"Well, he cold-cocked some poor bastard and then kicked him to sleep."

"Not really the profile we're looking for," she pointed out.

"I know, but there are only two other guys with violent criminal records. One of them is ancient and the other's been in the joint for the last four and a half years."

"I know, these pilot types tend to be squeaky clean."

"I may try a different approach, I think," Wilder said, only half joking.

"Pin the list on the wall and throw a dart at it?"

"I'm looking at the squeakiest, cleanest of them right after I rule out the violent offenders."

"It can't hurt, tell me how it works out."

To rule out the three men he'd found a bit of interest in, Wilder compared the information provided by N-DEx with the pilot's registry sent over by Agent Glick. Almost immediately he knew something was wrong with Leonard Schenk. Besides the fact the man was eighty-three, he wore very thick glasses, his vision must be exceedingly poor. *He certainly doesn't look like any pilot I'd feel safe flying with,* Wilder thought.

He's no pilot, Wilder realized. *There must be another Leonard Schenk, that's all. Or...the old wife beater is dead and some crazy bastard assumed his identity.*

* * * *

Assuming the identity of a dead person had long been popular among criminals. "Dead" people applied for credit cards, attempted to purchase firearms, and committed other fraudulent, illegal activities every day. Every year "dead" people filed for tax refunds.

One of the federal government's most useful tools to combat financial fraud, as well as other criminal activities was a massive database of deceased individuals called the "Death Master" file. Maintained by the Social Security Administration (SSA), the Death Master file stored information on over sixty-five million deceased individuals, most of whom were issued a social security number during their lifetimes. The Death Master file most often included each decedent's name, social security number, date of birth, date of death, state or country of residence, zip code of last residence, and zip code of lump sum death payment.

Government agencies as well as financial institutions, investigative consortium, credit reporting organizations, and medical research conglomerates accessed the Death Master file in an effort to prevent fraud. By comparing financial, credit, payment and other applications against the Death Master File, the financial community, insurance companies, security firms and state and local governments were better prepared to identify and prevent identity fraud. Medical researchers, hospitals and continued care programs used the database to track former patients and study subjects. Investigative firms used the data to identify persons, or the death of persons, in the course of their investigations. Pension funds, insurance organizations, Federal, State and Local governments and others responsible for payments to recipients and retirees used the file so they didn't send checks to deceased individuals.

Unfortunately, because it lacked the death records of all persons, the absence of a particular person from the Death Master file was not absolute proof the person was still alive.

* * * *

Wilder logged on to the Death Master File and keyed in Schenk's name. Sure enough the man died in 1998, at the age of seventy-one. Wilder matched Schenk's social security number to the one provided on the pilot registry and felt for sure he was on to something. He learned that Schenk, the deceased Schenk, was born in Kingston, New York in 1927. He last resided in Queens Village, New York.

"I've got something here," Wilder said to Hamilton spinning around in his chair. He was surprised to see she was gone. So engrossed in his research, he hadn't noticed her slip out of the room. *Must be in the john*, he thought.

Having confirmed Leonard Schenk was dead, and someone else had an airplane registered under the dead man's name and social security number, Wilder pushed on. He typed his password into an online obituary registry and went to work. A common German surname, there were hundreds of deceased Schenk's in the New York area, but only seven Leonard Schenks.

When Hamilton returned, Wilder was again lost in cyberspace scrolling down through the obituaries of the seven men of like name. He merely nodded and said, "Take care," when Hamilton told him she'd had enough and was leaving. She said she'd speak to him in the morning. Wilder was so enthralled in his research he hadn't paid her any attention, he hadn't really even heard her at all.

After a few minutes during which he ran into dead ends he found the Leonard Schenk he was looking for, the fourth dead Leonard Schenk in New York. The full text obituary informed Wilder, Schenk had retired at the age of sixty-five. He had been a regional supervisor with the United States Customs Service. He was living alone when he died of heart failure six years later. There was no next of kin listed.

Truly excited now, Wilder went back to the pilot registry and wrote down the address of the residence provided by the F.A.A. inspection. In sloppy chicken scratch he scrawled "Two Hundred Lebrun Road, Amherst" and then reached for his phone.

Wilder was on fire, sweat dripped from his brow as he dialed the accounts payable department for National Grid to confirm the property at Two Hundred Lebrun Road was an active account. He was told it was indeed active and the account was in the name of Leonard Schenk. According to the company records, they had been receiving checks from Mister Schenk's checking account for the past five years. Schenk was paid up to date, always was, without fail.

At least he pays his bills, Wilder thought as he hefted himself out of his chair and grabbed his keys.

Chapter Twenty-Eight

Nicole Lutz woke on the same cold autopsy table so many before her had. She moaned, her head ached, she was still fuzzy from the shock of the taser.

She began to nod off again, then snapped her head back laboring to keep her eyes focused. The cold actually helped her to maintain her concentration. Teeth chattering and body covered in goose bumps, she willed herself back into consciousness. She peered around in the dim light provided by the lone, low watt bulb hanging from the ceiling over her head to find herself in a basement.

Clean swept, it was nonetheless bleak and drafty. She had no misconceptions that she was dreaming, she knew she was in real danger. Lutz took a deep breath and attempted to sit up, she felt something bite into the flesh of her neck, her head fell back onto a pillow.

Straining to see what was holding her back, she was unable to see the plastic harness strapped across her throat, but certainly felt its presence. She tried moving her arms and again found them to be immobilized, the same went for her legs. Her heart began to pound within her chest, she willed herself to relax, she had to keep it together if she was to figure out what had happened to her and escape her predicament.

With deep, slow inhalations she turned back the growing sense of panic. *I can get through this, I really can.* To occupy her time more than anything else, she contemplated her options which were admittedly slim. Yelling for help didn't seem to be the answer, the walls of the basement were cinderblock, much to thick for any noticeable sound short of a shotgun blast to penetrate. She was able to flex her leg enough to raise it slightly and bring down the back of her knee with enough force to make a dull thud upon the stainless steel table. The metallic thud was low and muffled, it sounded much like a slight wind blowing through an old, battered buoy. Realizing she could only attract the attention of her abductor, she stopped after five bongs. She decided to conserve her strength and wait for whoever it was who'd grabbed her.

She began to slowly piece together what had happened, and how she'd ended up in the dim, dank basement. *I was playing with Mush, there was a lot of snow on the ground. We were walking home, almost out of the undeveloped property and then Mush went down. God, I hope he's not dead. I saw a man, he looked familiar...*All at once it rushed back to her. *It was that bastard who'd changed my tire, he shot me with something. He shot Mush, that fucker. I knew there was something wrong with him. Even in the darkness I could feel him looking at me, sizing me up. I could feel something wrong, something bad, coming off of him in waves. If I get the chance I'll scratch his eyes out and run for it.*

Lutz prepared herself for what she would do given the opportunity. A free arm or an unbound leg would suffice, she just needed a chance. If she was unable to get to his eyes, she'd already made up her mind to go for his testicles.

I'll grab and squeeze and squeeze and squeeze, she thought. If he came close enough she would head butt him, anything to give herself a shot at escape. Lutz was a virile, independent woman, but as time ticked by she started to question her own inner strength. After over an hour of stewing, her bitter resolve evaporated and fear crept in.

Raped by her older brother's friend when she was fifteen, Lutz spent much of her high school years in a psychologist's office, miserable and feeling alone, abandoned. The boy was sixteen, and as a minor was sentenced to a year in a juvenile detention center. He continued with the state curriculum while serving his time and was released within nine months for good behavior. He was readmitted to his high school, albeit with a restraining order against him, and graduated later that year as if nothing at all had happened.

Although she had a compassionate and caring family that provided her with overwhelming support, she remained despondent throughout her middle teens. It wasn't until her attacker had graduated and went away to college, she began to emerge into the land of the living. Promising herself she would never again be a victim, she'd enrolled in a tae kwon do class with her father and within a few months had become adept at self-defense. An avid student, what she lacked in size she made up for in sound technique.

By the time the boy, now a young man, had returned from his first year of college, Lutz knew how to handle herself and walked with a quiet confidence. Nonetheless, the first time she saw her attacker outside of a movie theater on a rainy night in mid-June, she was overcome by fear. The brutal act he'd inflicted upon her came back with a swell of force, smothering her new-found confidence. She felt the same fear now waiting in Gant's basement unable to free herself.

As more time dragged by she wished he would show himself, the waiting was the hardest part. Agonizing over her situation past and present, she imagined the worst and closed her eyes to reality. Turning inward, she once again relived the horrid rape in all its terrifying detail, her torn underwear, the blood between her legs, the shameful feeling. She was degenerating into an emotional wreck. She knew she couldn't afford to obsess on the past, it might get her killed. She had to snap out of this downward spiral, she had to keep positive, keep her head straight. She realized she had to help herself, but found she was helpless to do so. It seemed she was at her weakest when she heard light footfalls descending the basement stairs. Mustering her courage she vowed to wear a brave face. Prepared to die, she swallowed hard and hoped for a break.

Gant peered into the dim light to find Lutz, not whimpering and crying like most of his victims, but staring right back at him with cool detachment. He was at a loss as to what he had on his hands, he wondered if he'd made a mistake. He edged toward the table, clipboard in hand, not knowing exactly how to approach the situation.

He was about to open his mouth when Lutz beat him to it. "Where's my dog?" she asked. "Did you kill Mush?"

Gant's mouth drooped into a frown at that. "No, I didn't kill him. I'm sure he's fine. He was struggling to his feet as we left, a little groggy, that's all. He's probably waiting at your front door right now. Maybe one of the neighbors already took him in. I wouldn't worry about him, he's made for this weather."

"If you're lying, I'll kill you," she responded.

Gant was blown away. *Who does this woman think she is? Who does she think is running the show?* He stopped then to take a better look at her. She was shaking as they all did, but it could merely be the cold. Surprised by her candor and disregard for his power and authority over her, Gant frowned before advancing on the table. He liked this woman, she wasn't groveling, not even shedding a tear as far as he could see.

"I respect your loyalty to your dog. I like your temperament, too. You're a little fiery, but that's refreshing, really. But please, don't threaten me, it's illogical and unseemly. I hold all the cards, you and I both know that."

"Why?" she simply asked.

"We'll get to that shortly," he replied, glancing at his watch. "A few questions now, I'm rather short on time," he added, bringing a pen up to the clipboard.

She waited silently.

"Any history of heart disease?"

"You're not a doctor. Are you a doctor?"

"No, I'm not. Answer the questions and we can move on."

"Move on to what," she persisted.

"Have patience, please. Answer the questions."

"My heart is fine."

Gant recorded her response onto the clipboard before saying, "I thought as much. Any kidney problems, are you diabetic?"

"No. What's this all about?"

He held up his hand to quiet her. "Non-smoker, right? Your lungs are healthy?"

"I don't smoke."

"Are you a big drinker?"

"Socially, I like to have a few drinks."

He nodded and scribbled onto the clipboard. "Do you wear glasses or contact lenses?"

"Reading glasses when I can find them," she replied.

Gant grimaced as he wrote it down. "Any history of any sexually transmitted diseases? You don't have anything now, I hope."

"Fuck you," Lutz shouted, her face blooming crimson. This question hit on a particularly delicate subject. When she was raped, her attacker had infected her with gonorrhea. It was painful and embarrassing, simply adding insult to the savage injury inflicted upon her. She'd never let go of her inner shame.

"I'm sorry, I have to know, it's important."

"Important to who?" she blurted out.

"To me, to a lot of people actually," came his response.

"I'm not answering another question until you tell me what's going on here."

"I need you, rather, we need you."

"Who are 'we'?"

"People, sick people from all over, but mostly across the border in Canada," Gant responded.

"I don't even know anyone from Canada, I've only been there a few times."

"They don't know you either. They never will, but you'll always be close to them. You'll always be a part of them," he said, smiling slightly.

"I'm not understanding you. What do I have to possibly offer to complete strangers?"

"You have an extremely healthy body."

She dreaded where this was going. Visions of a creepy bordello filled her head.

He's selling me into the sex trade, she thought. "I won't do it, you'll have to kill me. I'll never fuck to live," she said. "Go ahead and kill me right now."

Calmly Gant responded, "I'm not selling you to be a sex slave, it would be reprehensible."

"What then?"

"I don't normally tell this to people in your position, but you're strong enough to know the truth. You're making the ultimate sacrifice, but you'll be revered forever, considered a martyr for the betterment of humanity."

"What are you talking about?"

"Your body will die today, but you will live on in others for many years to come. Your spirit will endure and grow stronger with each breath that each one of your recipients takes. To a woman with cataracts you will give sight, to a man not responding to dialysis you'll provide new found freedom, to a child with liver disease you'll offer hope, a child with debilitating asthma will receive breath from you, and a man with a weak heart will have your strong one. You are a savior, you will be revered. In death you will provide life for six, seven, possibly eight others."

Awestruck, Lutz was rendered mute. *This man is insane. He's talking about me playing savior to people I don't know. I don't want to be anybody's savior. I don't want to make the ultimate sacrifice, I want to go home. I want my dog and my comfy bed. More than anything though, I want to kill him.*

Gant expected Lutz to whimper and plead for her life, but she did neither. He again wondered if he'd made a mistake taking her. With such a strong spirit, perhaps she deserved to live. More so than with any other donor, he felt regret for abducting her. It was of no use to concern himself with it now though, it was already too late. The woman may remember his name, he'd told her after all when he'd changed her tire. She had to know he lived, or at least worked locally. Having met him face to face twice, she surely knew exactly what he looked like as well as the sound of his voice. She knew too much, way too much to live. Heavy-hearted, he turned and headed back up the stairs to the kitchen, he needed to eat before beginning work.

"Wait!" Lutz croaked, willing back the tears.

Halfway to the top of the stairs Gant turned to look back down upon her. She stared silently at him, her mouth pursed down at the corners, her pulse was visible as the veins on either side of her throat throbbed. *It wasn't immediate, but now the begging begins*, Gant thought as he gracefully stepped to the bottom of the stairs.

"Come closer," Lutz whispered.

"You have something to say to me?" Gant asked, making his way to the cruel table.

Breathing heavily, Lutz merely nodded.

As Gant closed to within three feet of her, Lutz snorted a great mass of mucous down from her nasal passages into her mouth and spat it into Gant's face. Wide-eyed with surprise, Gant was temporarily blinded by her spittle, he instinctively took a step backward. A gray-green glob of snot clung to his cheek, small strings of slime dripped from his nose and chin. He reached down and pulled his shirt out from the waist of his jeans and pulled it off over his head. With the shirt, he swabbed the snot from his eyes and face and took a deep breath. He deserved that, he knew, but nonetheless, he gave her a steely gaze. Undeterred, she smiled at him. He knew it was a false smile, a show of bravado, on her part. Otherwise, she would not only be very brave, but also quite insane, in his opinion.

"That's fine. I understand your frustration and fear, and I'm sorry for that."

"You understand?" Lutz screamed. "How can you say that? Let's trade places and then see if you really understand."

Gant shook his head in disapproval. "We both know it's not going to happen. I wish this could be done a different way, but it's impossible. I hope in time you'll forgive me." He turned back to the stairs.

"You won't kill me; you can't," Lutz shouted, hoping her saying this would make it so. She watched as Gant's Doc Martens disappeared from the last step into the kitchen above her. She listened as the refrigerator and cabinets opened and closed. Ten minutes later the microwave dinged.

Come and get it while it's hot! I hope the fucker burns the hell out of himself. Lying there naked in the dank basement the walls of fear once more closed in. Lutz had done her best to put on a brave front. It was dreadfully short of what she needed, but did give her a hint of satisfaction. She closed her eyes and began to pray.

* * * *

While Nicole Lutz woke up bound to the sinister heap of steel that was the autopsy table, Lydia Bergstrom pulled into the driveway of Two Hundred Lebrun Road in Amherst. Home a day early from Pittsburgh, it was past three on Friday afternoon. She wasn't in the least surprised to find Schenk's car was nowhere to be seen. He wasn't home—he never seemed to be of late. She unlocked the door, entered and dropped her bags inside the doorway. She leaned back outside to pick up the mail, which was falling out of the overstuffed mailbox. She trudged into the kitchen and dropped the pile of mail onto an existing stack which Schenk had started on the counter beside the sink. She turned toward the phone to check the messages.

The red light pulsing, she found there were twenty-three messages, this only heightened her suspicions regarding her boyfriend having an affair. She began to review all twenty-three of the messages hoping for one which would clue her in to what he was up to. Keeping a keen eye on the caller I.D., she listened for what she anticipated would be a female voice calling for a rendezvous. Credit card companies, the gas company, the cable and Internet provider, general contractors, electricians, three different cancer research foundations, the VFW, and the New York Blood Center. There were various charities canvassing for donations. Having listened to all of them she found no call from a mystery lady. She found it odd there were no personal calls at all. It seemed all the callers wanted something from him, not him. She dialed his cell phone.

"Hey, Lyd," he picked it up on the first ring, his voice was strong, she noticed, almost as if he were in the next room.

"I'm home, Lenny. Where are you?" she asked impatiently.

"I'm on my way soon," he answered evading her question. "You're home early! You grew tired of Pittsburgh? How was the trip?" he quickly changed the topic.

She went with it, "It was fine, the usual. I picked up some new accounts. I miss you, when will you be home?"

"Tomorrow morning, eleven the latest. I've got an early morning delivery to make."

"You're spending the night on the plane?" she assumed he was at some airport or another.

"I've got some loose ends to tie up, some paperwork to do. I'm kind of tired, yeah, I'll sleep here."

"When was the last time you looked at the answering machine, there were over twenty messages?"

"I could ask the same of you, I've been busy, like you."

"It's your house, Lenny. It's not my business, or job, to check your messages. What about the mail? When was the last time you were home?"

"It's been awhile. Okay, you're right. I'll be better about that," he failed to actually answer her question. There was an awkward silence. "Well, then, I've really got an awful lot to do so I'm going to say goodbye, alright."

"Are there any bills due? Do I have to pay any of these?"

"No, no, leave the bills for me," Gant replied curtly.

"Lenny?"

"Yes?"

"Do you still love me?"

Gant hesitated before answering. "I do, but there are things we have to talk about."

"I agree," she replied, and then added, "but I still love you, too."

"We'll talk," he responded and ended the call.

Bergstrom rested the phone in its cradle and walked up to the bedroom they shared. She'd snooped through Schenk's belongings before, but now she had an entire evening to find anything which would point to his infidelity. She began with his walk-in closet. She rifled through his suits, button down shirts, and ties looking for a smudge of makeup, a smear of lipstick, a hint of glitter. She sniffed at his clothes seeking to find a feminine scent, organic or from a perfume bottle that would give her the evidence she needed to confront him. Finding nothing she went onto his jeans, sweaters, and sweatshirts. There was no point in ransacking his boxers or undershirts as they were already run through the washer and dryer. She checked beneath them anyway looking for a memento, perhaps an alien pair of panties taken in conquest. She didn't know Schenk to have any type of fetish for women's undergarments, but her imagination was on the loose, she was desperate for an answer.

When the contents of the bedroom turned up nothing, Bergstrom returned downstairs to search Schenk's study, he spent a lot of time there. In the center of the room was a handsome mahogany desk with a brass letter "G" in Olde English font in the center of the top. Bergstrom had asked him about the significance of the "G" and he had explained how he'd found the beautiful old desk at a garage sale some ten years before. The desk had one central drawer and three others on each side. Bergstrom felt sure inside of this desk lay the clues to unlocking the enigma that was Lenny Schenk. She was flooded by a strong feeling of guilt then. *Do I pry into his business, his private life? This would be like him reading my diary without me knowing.*

For a moment she hesitated to even try one of the drawers, then on blind impulse, she pulled the center draw open. Inside she found flight manuals, parts catalogs, old copies of Naval History Magazine as well as Proceedings Magazine, another Navy publication. Desperate to find something of use she unwisely pulled the entire draw out and dumped it onto the desk top. A pair of Rosary beads, many cards from wakes, letters from his mother, and numerous scraps of paper with the names and numbers of men scribbled on them fell out.

All men? Is he gay? No, definitely not, that's for sure. Probably old Navy buddies. That was it, nothing of any use to her. *I'll never get this shit back in the way he had it, he'll know I went through his things. Why did I dump it all out?*

For the next ten minutes Bergstrom placed the items back into the drawer as best as she could remember. Satisfied that she had gotten everything sorted out she went on to the side draws. The topmost right hand draw was filled with neatly arranged wine magazines, Wine Spectator, Wine Enthusiast, Food and Wine Magazine and on and on. The second draw contained a stapler, tape dispenser, letter opener and other ordinary office supplies. The third draw held, nothing but an old catalog for International Harvester farm equipment. Bergstrom blinked in wonder at the folded and yellowed catalog from 1968. *Why does he have this?* She pivoted in the leather swivel chair and pulled open the top left hand side draw, and found nothing, not even a dirty magazine. The two below it were empty as well.

Frustrated she stood up from the desk and eyed the Rolodex sitting by the phone. She knew it was a futile exercise, but she nonetheless began flipping through the Rolodex searching for any unfamiliar names. Having gone through over a hundred and fifty names some twenty minutes later, she got to the Z's, there were no contacts there.

She then went for the file cabinet in the corner by the window. She pulled open the top draw to find it stuffed with neatly hanging files; surely over fifty of them. The second and third draws looked much the same, the last just a bit lighter in volume. She pulled the swivel chair out from behind the desk and went to work searching the files. It didn't take her long to determine all of the files were legitimate customers, but she went through every last one anyway, hoping there was something within one of them which would help her out. It took nearly three hours for Bergstrom to scan over each document and then return it to its proper place. *Good Lord, he's got a lot of customers. Maybe he is working all the time. I've had enough.*

Bergstrom returned to the kitchen. Exasperated by her failed search, she sat down at the kitchen table. She considered scouring the formal living room, the den and the rest of the house, maybe even the garage and guest house, but then thought better of it. *This is all in my mind. Lenny's a good guy. He's not cheating on me. He'd never do anything to hurt me. He'd never hurt anyone unless he had a really good reason.* Guilt overcame her, she felt foolish for her behavior. She decided to open a bottle of merlot and wait for her cousin's call. She could trust her cousin for advice. It was possible the two of them would be turning the house upside down later that night, she'd wait and see.

Halfway through the glass of wine her cell phone rang, it was on the kitchen counter next to the big stack of mail she'd left there earlier. She walked to the counter and picked up the phone, "Hi Marguerite."

"Lydia, are we still on for tonight?" Hamilton asked at the other end.

"Yes, please. I really need to talk to you. I feel like I'm going crazy," she replied, resting her wine glass between the sink and the pile of mail.

"You still think he's...what's his name again?"

"Lenny," Bergstrom told her cousin for the third time.

"I'm sorry. I don't know why I have so much trouble remembering his name. Lenny, right. You still think he's cheating?"

"I don't know what to think. I've spent the last four hours snooping around through his stuff and have come up with nothing, maybe he's really busy. I looked in his file cabinet, he's got a lot of customers."

"Could be business is good."

"Come anyway, please?"

"Of course. Where and when?"

"I thought we'd meet out for a bite to eat, but Lenny's not coming home so why don't you come here. I'll show you the house, it's gorgeous. It may be the first and last time you ever see it."

Hamilton didn't know how to respond so she simply didn't. In the background she could hear water running.

"Marg, are you there?" Bergstrom asked, the phone cradled between her shoulder and chin, while she washed a small plate. She'd left some dishes in the sink over a week ago, before her trip to sell to the doctors throughout the Ohio Valley region. She planned to wash and rinse the coffee cup, knife, fork and spoon next and then leave them beside the sink to dry.

"I'm here."

"Come as soon as you can."

"I'll walk Chauncey and be there in forty-five minutes if not sooner."

"Thanks Marg, see you then," Bergstrom said ending the call.

Trying to keep the phone dry, she eased it down from her shoulder with her thumb and index finger. Attempting to rest it back once more atop the counter, the phone slipped from her slick grasp and bounced once before sliding half a foot across the counter directly into the base of her wine glass. Bergstrom held her breath as she watched the glass topple, she helplessly clutched for it, but was too late. The glass tipped over and shattered, bathing the pile of mail in the rich, ruby merlot.

"Shit," Bergstrom uttered as she gazed at the shards of broken glass atop and around the mess of crimson envelopes. She quickly reached for a roll of paper towels and tore off a wad to soak up the wine before it began to drip off of the countertop and onto the cherry wood cabinets. After mopping up the wine she began to wipe down the counter, taking caution to avoid slicing herself on any of the tiny slivers of glass. Much to her surprise and satisfaction she got the glass and excess wine into the waste basket without any incidence.

Frowning, she stared over at the ruined mail. She felt like tossing it all into the garbage, it looked mostly like junk mail anyway. Holding the pile over the sink, she rifled through the pile of mail, discarding the junk into the waste basket beneath the sink as she went. Envelopes containing bills or anything she was uncertain about went back on the side of the sink. She planned to wipe them down and hoped that they dried without too much smudging. She was almost done, had only three envelopes left when she got to the one from the Erie County Water Authority. It was addressed to Seven Milestrip Road.

There must be some mistake, she thought and took a closer look. It was addressed to L. Schenk, there was no mistake. There was no question about who owned this bill. The question was, why he hadn't told her he owned another property. *Is it a house? A farm? Lots of undeveloped land out there. A bill from the water department means it has running water, so it has to be an existing structure.*

Bergstrom was furious, she grabbed her cell phone and keys. She pulled her warmest parka on and stormed out of the house slamming the door behind her. With the water department bill clutched in her hand she slid behind the wheel of her little Chevy and took off toward Milestrip Road.

Racing south on the Buffalo Skyway, Bergstrom found herself within minutes of confronting Schenk face to face when she remembered she'd made plans to meet her cousin in half an hour. She dialed Hamilton's cell phone, it went straight to voice mail as she was out walking the dog.

"Listen Marg. I'm sorry, but I've got to reschedule. It looks like I'll have plenty of time on my hands though. Lenny, the asshole, has another house I didn't know about. I found a utility bill for Seven Milestrip Road addressed to him. It's only twenty minutes away, maybe a half an hour at most. The bastard's probably there right now, screwing some whore. I'm going there now, hoping to catch him in the act. I'll call you later."

* * * *

Hamilton got Chauncey in the door and washed her hands. She gave the dog a snack and patted him on his head. She took a quick shower and slipped into a pair of jeans and an Irish knit sweater. She grabbed a bottle of wine from the refrigerator and pulled her shoulder holster over her head. She looked at her cell and saw she had a message from her cousin. She retrieved the message.

Good, she cancelled, I'm off the hook for tonight, she thought. She looked out the window, snow began to fall in the early evening darkness. She was falling in love with the idea of staying home by the fire with Chauncey, but something nagged at her conscience.

She dialed Lydia Bergstrom's cell number. It went straight to voice mail. Hamilton frowned in frustration. Mother hen to her younger cousin, she pulled on her coat and went out into the frigid, unforgiving night. She put her Honda Pilot into gear and headed out to Milestrip Road.

Chapter Twenty-Nine

Lutz heard a muffled conversation emanating from the ceiling above her. She clung to the hope she might be able to get out of this alive, but deep down she doubted it. Alone again, fear and despair slithered once more into the forefront of her mind. As the conversation from the first floor died, she felt she was soon to follow.

It was then she caught sight of a spider out of the corner of her eye. A small wolf spider, it was creeping over the thin sheet which covered her nakedness. Immobilized, she was helpless to brush the spider away, she strained to follow its path. Willing the spider to go away, it steadily advanced until it rested upon her chest, less than a foot from her face. She wanted to scream, but held her tongue.

I won't give the pycho upstairs the satisfaction. The spider is the least of my troubles anyway. It's winter? I guess it's warm enough down here for it, but what is it eating?

The wolf spider inched forward, its hairy legs delicately feeling its way along when Lutz inhaled as deeply as she was able and blew at it like she was blowing out birthday candles. The fuzzy little beast scurried backward toward the foot of the table. Her courage bolstered, she looked on her predicament in a new light.

Gant shuffled down the stairs a few minutes after Lutz had chased away the spider. She stared into his eyes with cold defiance. Without a word he disappeared into the back room. Lutz strained to listen for any telltale signs of impending doom. She heard a cabinet shut. A few seconds later she heard a sharp clack and wondered what it could be. Then she noticed a low rhythmic humming, like the sound a refrigerator made when its motor kicked on if you left the door open too long. Then there was a violent smack, almost like the report of a pellet gun, she shuddered.

Gant reappeared moments later, donned in surgical scrubs. He quickly made his way to the table with two snow white rags in one hand and a small, vial-like bottle in the other. He looked at Lutz, his eyes turned down in apparent remorse.

"I am truly sorry, but it's too late to go back," he said unscrewing the lid of the bottle. He covered the mouth of the bottle with the rag and turned it upside down for just a second. "Thank you for your generous gift, you'll be saving many people."

Before Lutz could utter a word Gant had covered her nose with the chloroform rag. Struggling to breathe through her mouth, she snapped at Gant's hand almost catching his thumb before he stuffed the other rag into her mouth. With her last line of defense rendered useless, Lutz let out a deep breath and then tried to hold out, but it was hopeless. Within a minute she began her hazy descent into unconsciousness.

Gant wheeled in his instrument tray and the then the surgical lamp. Less than a minute and a half after putting her out, he hovered over Lutz with the cordless nail gun in his hands. He gingerly pulled the rag from her mouth and replaced it with the muzzle of the gun. Lutz had a smaller than average mouth, he noticed, the gun would not fit without some help. He'd run into this problem many times before.

    Not wanting to tear the flesh of the woman's lips, he had two options. He could either lubricate her mouth or remove her teeth. He went for the tube of edible lubricant on his instrument tray, it was strawberry flavored. Gant liberally applied the lube to Lutz's lips and teeth as well as the walls of her mouth. It took just a minute and he wanted a perfect mask after all. With Lutz's mouth lubricated, Gant began to work the business end of the nail gun between her strained lips. He patiently wiggled the gun up and down and from side to side to get the firing mechanism at the end of the muzzle securely wedged into the roof of her mouth. After three minutes of cautious maneuvering he was finally there. He put pressure on the gun's firing mechanism jamming it into the soft, pink roof of her mouth, the nail gun's motor revved, his index finger flexed on the trigger, and then the doorbell rang.

    "Shit," Gant sighed under his breath, taking his finger off of the trigger. It was quite rare for anybody to call on him. Nobody he knew had any idea he owned the house. It was much too far off the beaten track for any solicitors to bother with.

    I have to see who it is, she can wait a few minutes. I'll get rid of whoever it is and then begin the harvest. Reluctantly, he slowly eased the gun out of Lutz's mouth and rested it on the lower level of the instrument table. He walked toward the north end of the basement where a window looked out onto the front driveway. He pulled the shades slightly apart and peeked through to see his girlfriend's Chevy Volt.

    "Christ help me," Gant murmured as he fled to the back room and stripped out of his scrubs. He was pulling up his jeans when Bergstrom pounded on the front door. His shirt was on and he ran up the stairs when the pounding stopped and she began to scream.

    "Open the fucking door, Lenny," Bergstrom shouted. "I know you're in there, you lying prick. You left your goddamned car right here. Whose van is that? Does the whore you're fucking drive that thing?"

    Gant opened the door prepared to bear the brunt of Bergstrom's rage, but saw no way out of this. She stood there for a half a second, her fiery eyes drilling holes in him. Then she barged inside knocking him back a few steps.

    "Where is she, Lenny? Where is she? I want to meet the bitch who broke us up!" she screamed.

    Thank God, I don't have any neighbors for miles, Gant thought before saying, "I'm not sleeping with anybody else. There's no one, what are you talking about?"

    "This is what I'm talking about, you lying, cheating bastard," she cried, waving the crimson-stained utility bill in his face. The bill looked as if it had been used to clean up a murder scene. She threw it in his face, it floated to the oak floor at his feet.

    Gant bent over to pick up the bill and Bergstrom backhanded him on the back of the head. He grabbed the bill and slowly rose up to face her with a steady gaze.

    "Don't hit me. Mindless violence solves nothing," he said while glancing at the bill.

    Shit! I shouldn't have brought that home. Should have left it here like I usually do. So, what's the big deal? I have another house."

    "Where you take your sluts, Lenny?"

    "I told you that there's nobody else. It's not like that, honestly. Have I ever lied to you?"

Bergstrom paused and took a breath. "No," she conceded.

"And I'm not now. Yes, it's true I didn't tell you about this place. Is that a crime? Are we married?"

"No," Bergstrom began to calm down a bit.

"Sometimes I need to get away—to be by myself with my thoughts."

"So, you're really not cheating then?"

"No, I'm really not cheating."

"Whose van is that outside?"

"It's mine. Do you want to see the registration?" Gant was beginning to think he might get rid of Bergstrom without killing her.

"No. Show me around," she said.

Gant paused, he knew Lutz would be unconscious for at least another hour, but was hesitant to let Bergstrom snoop around. "Sure, I'll give you the tour," he replied.

* * * *

Hamilton was halfway to the farmhouse out on Milestrip Road when her cell phone chimed. She fumbled her Bluetooth headset on as she drove.

"Hi Dan, what's up?"

"I'm doing a little surveillance, but nobody's home. How about you?" Wilder replied.

"I'm on my way to Orchard Park."

"What's going on down there? A date?"

"I should be so lucky. I was supposed to meet my cousin tonight, but then she cancelled on me. She said she had to go see her boyfriend in Orchard Park. She said he's hiding stuff from her."

"And you're getting in the middle of it? Good luck with that."

"I know, I know. There's something that's bothering me, but I can't put my finger on it. They live together in Amherst, and now she's found out he has another house in Orchard Park," Hamilton said.

"Amherst, huh? That's where I am right now."

"No kidding, whereabouts?" she asked.

"I'm sitting outside Two Hundred Lebrun Road."

Two Hundred Lebrun Road?, Hamilton's memory wavered and then her eyes grew wide.

"This is the first lead I really like. I came here over half an hour ago. Nobody was here so I've been in the car across the street waiting..."

"Two Hundred Lebrun Road? Did you say Two Hundred Lebrun Road, Dan?" Hamilton interrupted him.

"That's what I said. Does it mean anything to you?"

"That's where my cousin lives. I was supposed to meet her there tonight before she cancelled."

"Small world, isn't it? The house is owned by one Leonard Schenk, does it ring a bell?"

"That's Lenny—her boyfriend."

There was a dead pause.

"Dan, are you there?"

"I'm here. I'll bet Leonard Schenk looks real good for his age. Does your cousin like older men, like men in their eighties?"

"What are you talking about, Dan?"

"The 'Death Master' file indicates your cousin's boyfriend is dead, yet somebody has a plane registered under the deceased's name and a social security number."

"Oh, my God, Dan. That means..."

"It means your cousin may be dating our guy," Wilder finished her sentence. "At the very least he has some explaining to do, identity theft and all."

"Lydia, my cousin, that's her name, is with him right now. I've got to call her. I've got to warn her, maybe she stopped to pick something up and hasn't gotten there yet."

"What's the address?" Wilder asked.

"It's Seven Milestrip Road, I'll be there in ten, maybe fifteen minutes."

"I'll be there at about the same time."

"I have to go now. Bye."

"Marguerite?"

"Yes?"

"Don't go in there alone. This guy could be our killer," Wilder warned.

"Bye, Dan," Hamilton said ending the call. She quickly dialed Bergstrom's cell number and was informed by a robotic voice that her cousin's phone was not in service.

Wilder called into the station and requested two patrol cars meet him at Seven Milestrip Road. He turned the Crowne Vic's flashers on and sped off into the strengthening snowstorm. Pushing the limits on the icing road, he was determined to get there before his partner.

* * * *

After touring the two main floors Bergstrom stood outside of Gant's bedroom. She looked at the spiral staircase in the center of the hallway. "It's kind of rustic, but I like it. It has an attic I see."

"It does," was all Gant offered. *Good Lord, not the shrine!*

"Let's take a look," she pressed.

"There's really nothing up there you'd be interested in, Lyd."

"No randy women?"

"Absolutely not," he replied.

"I love attics, my parents let me live in ours when I was in high school. Come on."

"I'd really rather not," he replied, the tension building behind his eyes.

Bergstrom turned for the staircase and stepped toward it. From behind Gant seized her by the wrist and spun her around to face him, "Let's go downstairs, have a glass of wine," he said holding on to her. It was the first time he'd ever touched her in anger. It was the first time he'd ever touched any woman in anger.

"Ow, Lenny stop it! That hurts," Bergstrom replied pulling away from him and tearing free from his grip. "What are you doing?"

Gant stood there with his hands at his sides, unsure of what to do or say. "I'm sorry, I've got a workshop up there. I'm making something for you. It's a surprise," he lied. Gant could count the number of times he'd actively lied as an adult on one hand. His was a world of deception, not overt lies. This was an emergency though, so he overlooked his transgression.

"You're full of surprises, aren't you?"

"It's for your birthday."

"That's two months away."

"It takes time when it's really important. I hope you'll like it."

"I'm sure I will. Alright, let's go down. It has a basement, right?"

When Gant failed to reply Bergstrom again grew suspicious of him. *He won't show me the attic or the basement. He's hiding something from me, I know it.*

Anxious to have Bergstrom away from the attic staircase, Gant backed away from her and then turned toward the staircase leading down to the main floor foyer. That's when she bolted to the open topped staircase.

He was about to take his first step down when he heard her boots clanging against the steps of the wrought iron staircase behind him. He whirled around to find her halfway up the circular stairway, he was surprised at her quickness. Gant lunged toward the staircase stretching out to grab at her ankles. Bergstrom's head was about to break the plain of the attic ceiling giving her a clear view of the shrine and its ghastly collection of human masks when his right hand and then his left wrapped around her left ankle.

Using all of his weight, he savagely pulled her leg down toward his chest while he climbed up the first few steps. Clawing at the floor above her, Bergstrom struggled to pull herself up onto the attic landing with no success. She pumped her knees in an effort to free her feet, but was unable to overcome his strength. He reached up with his right hand and grabbed the leather belt in her jeans. With a jolting yank, he tore her from the staircase and dragged her down, her face bouncing off of the steel steps as she went.

"I told you I didn't want you up there," Gant said as he glared at her.

A dazed heap of confusion, she blubbered, "Wha...wha...what's wong wit you?". Her lips and chin were split, running a bright, glossy red. Her nose was flattened, ruining her once beautiful face, it gushed crimson. Her eyes swam in her head, gliding back and forth as she looked up at him.

"Nothing," he shouted. "There's nothing wrong with me. You shouldn't have stuck your nose in where it didn't belong. Now you've given me no choice, my hands are tied. Get up."

He offered his hand. Bergstrom took his hand and staggered to her feet. She swayed unsteadily as if she'd been drinking way too much.

"Turn around," Gant told her.

"Wenny..." she began.

"Shut up, Lydia!" he snapped. "I can't stand the sound of your voice. Don't say another word, I've got to think."

When she turned around he seized her roughly by the wrists drawing them together, rubbing bone on bone. She winced in pain, but kept her mouth shut. Gant pushed her toward the staircase to the first floor. Holding her hands behind her back he followed her down the stairs into the foyer.

"You wanted to see the basement, huh Lyd?" Gant asked her gruffly. "Well, guess what? You've earned a look at it. Soak it in, enjoy." *I'll call Monseaux and let him know I've got a double delivery. It's short notice, but he'll be able to match up some more buyers. Maybe this is for the best.* He shoved her into the kitchen and guided her to the corner door which led down into the basement. He momentarily gripped both of her wrists with one hand as he snagged a wet dish towel with the free hand. In less time than Bergstrom needed to react, his other hand clamped back down, the towel tightly lodged between her wrists and his throttling hands.

Down the steps they descended, Bergstrom quivering in fear and pain. In the dim light she was able to make out cobwebs and dust bunnies she associated with most unfinished basements. It didn't bother her, but then she smelled an alcohol smell. It was an antiseptic odor that surprised her nose. *It smells like a hospital down here.* She became completely unnerved when she got to the bottom of the stairs and saw Lutz, shrouded and seemingly dead upon the autopsy table. She opened her bloody mouth to scream, but Gant stuffed the dish towel into it cutting off her cry.

Gant steered her toward the rear room where he bound her hands together with a zip tie. He then directed her back into the operating room and over into the far corner of the basement. "On the floor, Lyd," he directed her.

She flopped down onto the cold, concrete block, confused by what she saw on the table, by everything actually. Gant quickly zip tied her ankles together. Breathing through her pancaked nose she sniffed up blood and began to cough violently, her eyes bulged from their sockets.

Not wanting her to asphyxiate on her own blood, Gant held up his hand and said, "Alright, Lyd. I'll make a deal with you, okay?"

She nodded, blood pouring out of her nose, running over her mangled lips, and dripping off of her chin onto the floor. She had been sitting in the corner no more than ten seconds and already the steady splatter had pooled into a small puddle between her thighs. Her eyes were clear and pleading.

Good God! The upstairs must be a mess, like something out of a horror movie. I hope the bleeding stops soon or I'll have to stanch it myself, Gant thought, looming over her. He knelt down and yanked the towel from her mouth, it was drenched, sticky with blood and mucous. "Now, breathe, but don't talk. It'll waste your breath."

She glanced from him to Lutz, a shiver of fear coursed down her spine. *Is that what he'll do with me? I made a big mistake coming here.* Unable to hold her tongue, she spit out, "Dead?" nodding toward the shrouded table.

"Sleeping."

"Don ill me, pease," Bergstrom uttered through her bludgeoned mouth.

"I might have to," he answered. "You've seen too much already." He dug into the front pocket of her jeans and withdrew her cell phone. He dropped it onto the concrete slab and stomped down crunching it beneath the heel of his boot.

Desperate to save herself and hoping it was true, she murmured, "Wemme wiv. Cops on way. Cusin knows address. Jus weeve," the words slithered out of her ruined mouth.

Gant believed Bergstrom, he remembered her mentioning her cousin was a cop, a detective with the Buffalo PD. "You told her about this house?"

Bergstrom nodded. "I'm elping you. Go, now. Wemme wiv, Wenny, I was goot do you."

Gant cursed himself for smashing her cell phone. He should have checked it first to see who she'd been communicating with for the last couple of days. Frustrated he stormed into the back room.

He was back within thirty seconds, he held the little twenty-five caliber Beretta Bobcat in his right hand. He squatted down face to face with Bergstrom and leveled it at her forehead. "Are you telling me the truth, Lydia?"

Bergstrom nodded and began to open her mouth, but he covered it with his hand. Not exactly sure what he would do with her yet, Gant knew he needed to silence her. With a short extension cord, he gagged the wheezing woman rendering her speechless while leaving enough space for her to breathe through her mouth. He sprang upstairs and turned out all of the lights in the living room.

* * * *

Wilder was creeping along the New York State Thruway when he heard the report of an accident involving a tractor trailer. According to the report a minivan slid into the truck's lane, the trucker was helpless to avoid the collision. The big rig had swerved out of control on the icy highway before jackknifing, at which point three other vehicles had slammed into it. With the Crowne Vic's flashers gleaming, Wilder shook his head but drove onto the shoulder and passed the building traffic, he was sure he'd be able to pass.

As he edged closer to the accident scene it was worse than he'd imagined. The trailer had completely blocked both lanes and two of the cars which had crashed into it were crumpled hulks obstructing the shoulder. Wilder pulled closer to the cars when he saw firefighters began to cut the passengers out with saws, it was going to be a while before those cars were moved. Cursing his luck, he turned and drove against traffic in the direction he'd come from. He'd also lost fifteen minutes, he stepped down on the accelerator.

* * * *

Hamilton's Pilot pulled into the driveway of Seven Milestrip Road, fresh snow and gravel crunching beneath the Pilot's wheels. She recognized her cousin's Volt and saw two other cars, a Volvo sedan and a Ford van. She parked and looked up at the dilapidated farmhouse. She checked her Glock nine millimeter before opening the car door.

Gant watched from a living room window as Hamilton came to a stop in his driveway. He fingered the Beretta in his back pocket. Loaded and ready to shoot, he took it out and carefully wedged it into his waistband at the small of his back. He waited in the shadows of the living room.

* * * *

The doorbell rang, Bergstrom's heart soared. She straightened up, cocking her ear to the basement ceiling in an effort to hear what was going on upstairs. There was a long silence—too long for her liking. She rotated her head in the opposite direction and caught a glint of light toward the front of the basement, it was the reflection of the dull bulb hanging over the autopsy table.

It's a window! It's gotta be a window! If I can make it over there and break it whoever's up there might hear. She pumped her thighs until her rear end butted up against the wall and then sat there gasping through the slit Gant had allotted for breathing.

She backpedaled furiously, digging her boots into the concrete floor while simultaneously thrusting upwards with her thighs. Her boots inched closer to her crotch as the small of her back edged up the wall until her feet were under her. Her breath came in deep heaves.

With her remaining strength she hopped toward the glinting light reflecting off of what she hoped was a window. She was halfway there when she stumbled on a raised cracked in the concrete and went down with a crash. The wind knocked out of her already straining lungs, she lay on the dusty floor despondent, nearly beaten. She gazed up toward the reflected light and gained new strength and hope.

It is a window! It is! But it's so high. Without hands, I'd have to jump up and try to break it with my head. It'll hurt like hell, she thought. In the next instant she realized, *He's gonna kill me.* Bergstrom rolled over to the wall with the window and began kick shimmying her way up toward the glimmering reflection.

*****

Gant peered out at Hamilton from behind the depths of the sheer curtains hanging in the living room window. Illuminated by the dull glow of the front porch light, the fine features of her face struck him. He instantly recognized the strong resemblance between this woman and his girlfriend, it was indeed her cousin, she could have been her sister. Bergstrom had been telling the truth, the police were here. Gant knew Bergstrom's cousin wasn't going away, he flipped on the lights. Time, as always, was of the essence to him.

Hamilton was surprised when the lights went on almost immediately upon her ringing the bell, she'd expected to be pounding on the door. Her head tilted slightly upward, she saw a face, quite handsome, peering out from the little entry door window. The face smiled and then retreated to the side. There was a brief pause, she listened intently and heard a dead bolt clack open behind the door.

The heavy oak door swung open and Gant gazed at her from within the doorway, she was somewhat blinded by the light emanating from the living room and the porch light. "Can I help you?" he asked, his eyes glistening with life behind the falling snowflakes.

"I'm looking for my cousin, Lydia Bergstrom, you know her?"

"Sure, she's with Lenny."

"You're not Lenny?"

"No, my name's Carl. I work with Lenny though. He's my boss, I guess you'd say."

"Where are they now?" Hamilton asked.

"They've gone for a walk, left a note on the kitchen table. I just got here a few minutes ago. I was hoping to talk to Lenny about an extra parts shipment."

"A walk? In a snowstorm?" she asked suspiciously.

"You got me. I guess they thought it would be romantic."

"Can I see some identification, please?"

"What for?"

"Because I said so," Hamilton replied pulling out her detective shield and waving it in Gant's face.

"Sure, I didn't know you were a cop, give me a second," he replied. "Why are you looking for Lenny? Is he in trouble," he asked, as his right hand went toward the back of his jeans.

Hamilton dropped her shield and instinctively went for her service pistol. She pulled the Glock out of her shoulder rig and leveled it at Gant.

"Easy, nice and slow," she directed him.

"Whoa, hold on. I'm getting my wallet. You asked for my I.D., right?"

"Let's see it, then."

Mockingly slow, Gant pulled his wallet from the pocket of the jeans. He opened it up and fished out a New York state driver's license and gingerly handed it to Hamilton.

With her gun still drawn upon him, she scanned the license. "Carl Heydrich?"

"That's me," Gant said.

She holstered the nine millimeter and handed the license back to him. Suddenly he didn't seem the least bit dangerous. On the other hand, Hamilton found him disarming, even wholesome looking in his jeans and thermal pullover.

"I'm sorry. I need to find your...your boss and Lydia Bergstrom. Do you have any idea in which direction they may have headed off in?"

"Lenny's got a lot of property, over thirty acres, I think."

"Crap, I'll be looking all night. It's a good thing my partner's on his way with some uniform..."

Glass shattered to Hamilton's right. She glanced in that direction, but saw only darkness shrouded by falling snow. She reflexively went for her gun.

Turning back to face Gant, she found a little Beretta in her face. Hamilton's eyes went wide as she screamed, Gant pulled the trigger and her world exploded in a flash of red which quickly faded to black.

Gant knelt down to take a closer look at the fallen cop. His bullet had torn through her open mouth disintegrating many of the upper molars on the right side. He turned her head to the left and found the hair on the back of her head to be slick with blood.

It's a justified homicide, I had no choice. It was self-preservation, damn it. I can't be taken, it will cost hundreds, if not thousands, of people their lives. My life's work is yet to be realized. Go, go, go, Gant thought.

He kicked Hamilton's pistol off of the porch and ran back into the house leaving her for dead at the foot of the steps. Down into the basement he went with a feverish intensity. Bergstrom lay in the corner blood pouring from the gash on her scalp suffered from head butting the window, shards of broken glass littered the floor. Gant strode to her and wordlessly pumped two rounds into her upturned face. *You ruined everything!* It was the first time he had ever killed in anger, it felt good to him.

Back upstairs, Gant pulled the door to the coat closet open. He grabbed a woolen overcoat and a heavy, insulated parka and ran back down into the basement with them. He tore the thin sheet off of the naked body of the still unconscious Nicole Lutz and tossed it to the floor. He leaned over her to unclamp the restraints which had pinned her to the monstrous table for the last day, her head lolled to the right, she was completely oblivious to anything that was happening. *They'll be here any minute, there's no time to harvest. Why waste her, she's such a fine specimen. There's no use killing her if she won't help anybody. She is, after all,* innocent. She's never caused me any trouble. I owe it to her. It would be fruitless bloodshed at this point.

Gant pulled Lutz up to a sitting position and wrapped the overcoat around her. He hoisted her over his shoulder and tramped toward the door leading to the side driveway. He threw open the door and trudged up the steps into the near white out conditions. He marched away from the house and laid Lutz down in a clearing between a stand of oak trees. The cold began its work on her already, she murmured softly in her waking sleep. He left her and headed back to the basement.

Gant pulled open the big Viking refrigerator and tossed out everything within it, jars and vials shattered as they hit the floor. He ripped open the freezer and likewise dumped the lone package it housed. He was running again then, this time to the barn.

Gant returned from the barn with two five gallon gas cans, one in each hand. He left one in the basement and plodded up to the first floor with the other. Up to the second floor he went and then up the spiral staircase to the shrine in the attic. With great remorse he liberally splashed the gasoline along the perimeter of the attic. He was bitter that he had no time to say goodbye to his loyal disciples, the clock was ticking. He walked down the aisle between the rows of masks heaving the can back and forth, dousing them with fuel.

After finishing with the attic, Gant spilled the rest of the can throughout the second and first floors as he descended toward the basement, there was nothing incriminating on either floor, they weren't priorities. Again in the basement, he unscrewed the other can and poured it out around the perimeter. He drenched the autopsy table, the chemicals and preservatives, and all of the medical equipment. Then he lit the match.

* * * *

When Wilder pulled up to the farmhouse, the two patrol cars were already there. Flames shot up from the roof licking the sky, fire poured out of every doorway and window. The blazing house burned so intensely that the falling snow turned to rain high above the hissing conflagration, glittering sparks flew heavenward against the will of the near blizzard storm.

Wilder frantically ran toward Hamilton's car before one of the uniformed officers called him over to his patrol car.

Hamilton was stretched out in the back seat, bloody, but alive. The round from Gant's small caliber Beretta had rebounded off of her jaw bone and exited out of her left ear, it never came near her brain. She would be deaf in that ear, but she would make a full recovery otherwise and be back at work within three months. He sat in the back seat with his partner until an ambulance arrived to take her away.

Wilder was walking back to his car when he saw a dark silhouette stumble forth from the wooded area to the west of the house. Approaching the figure, he realized that it was a woman, and she appeared intoxicated. Lutz was understandably shaken and very cold, but otherwise fine. Not yet reported missing, she told her story as succinctly as was possible in the shelter of Wilder's car.

* * * *

The following morning, the last of the embers had finally cooled off. Fire and police personnel combed through the wreckage. There was not much left of the big old house. It had burned down to the foundation and concrete slab in the basement. With nearly everything incinerated, the fire marshal believed that the fire had exceeded at least two thousand five hundred degrees.

Inspectors were surprised to find the charred remains of two individuals down in the basement. The scorched skeletons were found to be that of a woman and a man. The female skeletal remains were later identified as being that of Lydia Bergstrom. The remains of the male were never positively identified, but it was strongly presumed that they were that of the deceased woman's boyfriend, the individual impersonating Leonard Schenk. In all the excitement of the inferno nobody responding to the scene had thought to establish a perimeter around the property. The ensuing blizzard all but covered any tracks in the area.

Epilogue

Drifting down through the clouds toward the canopy of the rain forest, a Cessna Corvalis TTX came into view, its three hundred and ten horsepower engine humming in the still, mid morning air.

The little airplane had travelled over six thousand miles in the previous five days. Stopping to refuel in small airports outside of Shreveport, Louisiana, Villahermosa, Mexico, Panama City, Panama, and Cusco, Peru, it was finally near a thin landing strip carved into the rain forest some thirty miles north of Buenos Aires, Argentina. The plane skirted the lush Sun-drenched trees, sending the inhabitant monkeys howling and screaming as the pilot approached the runway still over a mile distant.

Sailing through a man-made canyon among the towering palo rosa trees, the pilot eased the Corvalis down onto the asphalt. Tires squealing, the plane touched down as a silver Range Rover drove out onto the tarmac to greet the new arrival.

The plane's engine died and the pilot door swung open. Wearing coffee colored contact lenses to conceal his mismatched eyes, Paul Previt surveyed the suffocating beauty afforded by the thick tangle of jacaranda, tipa, and lapacho trees.

With his right hand, he swept his newly dyed sandy brown hair away from his face and drew in a deep breath of the heavy, moist air. In his left hand he held all of his documentation—it had always been onboard. Pocketing the identifications, he exhaled and smiled with anticipation. Leonard Schenk was now truly dead, Carl Heydrich had never existed. Phillip Gant was a non-entity having transferred all of his assets, with the exception of his home, far south.

He was nowhere to be found. It was as if he vanished from the face of the Earth. Previt walked toward the vehicle, toward a new life on the other side of the world, and got in. The most cosmopolitan of all South American cities, Buenos Aires had enough European influence to suit his tastes and needs.

As the Range Rover rumbled over the narrow dirt road which zigzagged through the jungle leading to his villa, the International Harvester realized a fresh start, he eagerly looked forward to beginning his new practice.

About the Author:

A native of Long Island, New York, Matt Erickson was born in 1970. The youngest of nine children, he grew up on the beach in Point Lookout where he learned to swim and fish at an early age.

Graduating from Fordham University, Matt holds a Masters degree in Library Science from Queens College. Married fifteen years, he's the proud father of eleven-year-old twins.

Crafting novels and short stories, Matt's works examine the human psyche in all its strength and frailty. Writing broadly across the science fiction, suspense, mystery, and horror genres, he is unafraid to delve into any area of fiction.

His works are the products of everyday occurrences as he sees wondrous stories within his own life and those around him. Favoring a swift pace, fully developed characters, profound description and thrilling action, his long and short works often end with a twist. Matt writes because he loves the process as it provides a certain release for him that nothing else can. In his writing he is able to transgress the limits of time and space to intermingle fact and fantasy.

Visit him online at http://www.mattpen.com

Also from Damnation Books:

Portal to Murder
by Michele Acker

eBook ISBN: 9781615725342
Print ISBN: 9781615725359

Thriller Speculative Fiction
Novel of 112,002 words

In the middle of the 21st century, felon Michael Spinner is given the chance of a lifetime—he can redeem his future by traveling back in time to kill the man who ruined his life. Meanwhile, at the start of the 21st century, homicide detective Jennifer Castle is stymied by an impossible case. Several people—including a pregnant woman and her unborn child—have been killed by a weapon that just doesn't exist.

It doesn't take Michael long to realize that Jennifer is the one woman who can thwart his plans. She seems to be at the nexus of time travel itself—unwittingly connected to him by the unspoken circumstances of her birth. As the bodies pile up around her, Jennifer finds herself caught in a battle of wits against an elusive killer from the future who seems determined to destroy her career, her love life, and her family. If Jennifer keeps getting in his way, can Michael kill her without causing his own destruction?

Also from Damnation Books:

Intricate Entanglement
by Su Halfwerk

eBook ISBN: 9781615723393
Print ISBN: 9781615723409

Horror Thriller
Novella of 48,538 words

Trapped in a lunatic asylum and compelled to listen to the stories of the deranged patients, Doug Pinkham becomes entangled in the twisted mind of a cold-blooded killer. As the reporter tries to get to the bottom of a mysterious murder case, he gets more than he bargained for. He must separate truth from fiction as he realizes he no longer controls his own world. Will Doug manage to escape the asylum, or will the killer's stories lure him into an enigmatic world full of mazes, each so fascinating that he can't stop listening?

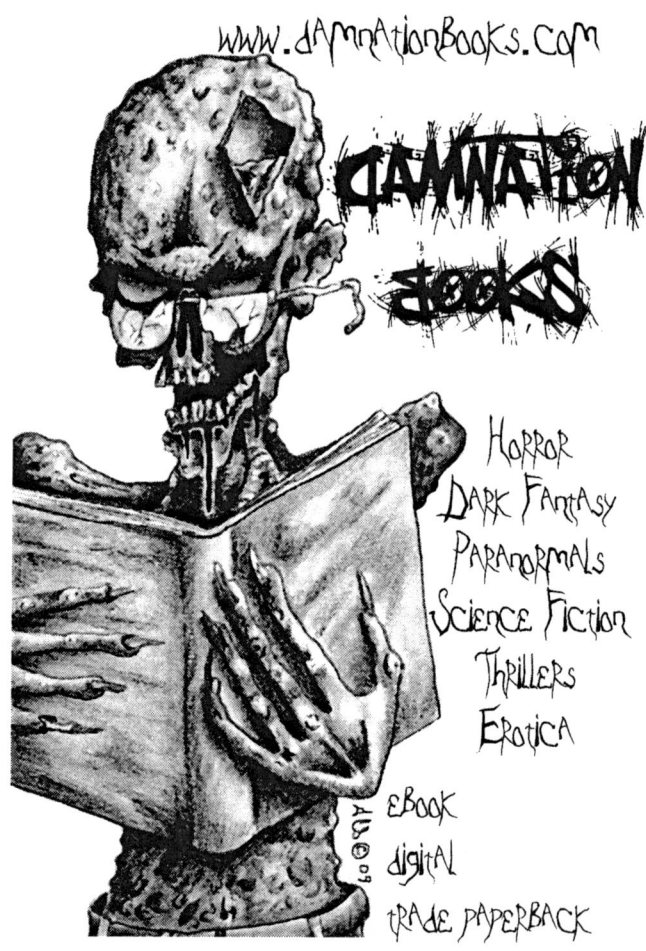

Visit us online at:

Our Blog—http://damnationbooks.wordpress.com/
Twitter http://twitter.com/DamnationBooks
Facebook—https://www.facebook.com/pages/Damnation-Books/80339241586
Goodreads—http://www.goodreads.com/DamnationBooks

CPSIA information can be obtained at www.ICGtesting.com
Printed in the USA
BVOW081845101012